Unfulfilled Passion

Cady went all soft inside whenever he said her name. She had the strangest urge to run her fingers through his dark hair. She gave a short laugh. "Seems funny—you know my first name, but I don't know yours."

He flicked his cigarette into the grass. She watched it smolder while she waited for him to speak. "It's Jesse."

"What?" He'd whispered—she wasn't sure she had heard right.

"Name's Jesse. You can call me that. I'd like it if you did."

"All right." A slow smile bloomed on her face.

"You sure are pretty when you smile."

"Oh . . ." Cady knew she was blushing. "Mr. Gault, you're flattering me." Her cheeks got even hotter. He leaned closer. He dropped his gaze from her eyes to her mouth. They were going to kiss. She wondered how it would feel. He had a beautiful mouth. They inched toward each other. She shut her eyes.

"Miz Cady?"

It was Levi calling through the closed door of her office.

Jesse didn't move, just smiled a slow, sexy smile while Cady jolted up straight, plucking at the closed throat of her robe. . . .

Outlaw in Paradise

Patricia Gaffney

A TOPAZ BOOK

TOPAZ
Published by the Penguin Group
Penguin Books USA Inc., 375 Hudson Street,
New York, New York 10014, U.S.A.
Penguin Books Ltd, 27 Wrights Lane,
London W8 5TZ, England
Penguin Books Australia Ltd, Ringwood,
Victoria, Australia
Penguin Books Canada Ltd, 10 Alcorn Avenue,
Toronto, Ontario, Canada M4V 3B2
Penguin Books (N.Z.) Ltd, 182–190 Wairau Road,
Auckland 10, New Zealand

Penguin Books Ltd, Registered Offices:
Harmondsworth, Middlesex, England

First published by Topaz, an imprint of Dutton Signet,
a division of Penguin Books USA Inc.

First Printing, August, 1997
10 9 8 7 6 5 4 3 2 1

 REGISTERED TRADEMARK—MARCA REGISTRADA

Printed in the United States of America

For Grace Pearson,
with love, affection, and gratitude.
You give mothers-in-law a good name.

One

Some folks said it was a coincidence that the church clock got stuck at three o'clock on the day the gunfighter rode into Paradise. Maybe so, but what about the leak that sprung in the water tower the same afternoon? And what about the grease fire at Swensen's Good Eats & Drinks? Not to mention the fact that Walter Rideout keeled over and died in his own outhouse that very day. Walter was pushing ninety, but still. It made you wonder.

Most people could tell you where they were and what they were doing the first time they laid eyes on the gunfighter. Nestor Yeakes was sitting out in front of the new livery stable, eating a green apple and reading the Paradise *Reverberator*. "I see a shadow, I look up, and there he is, dressed in black and covered with guns. Two Colts in his belt, a Winchester in his saddle, another pistol in his boot, and I swear I saw a derringer's butt sticking out of his vest pocket." Later on it turned out the gunfighter was only carrying two six-shooters and the rifle, but no one blamed Nestor for overestimating, and nobody disagreed with him that it "Looked like a damn army'd rode into town."

"Stable your horse?" he inquired, and according to Nestor the gunfighter curled his lips under his long black mustache and sneered.

"I didn't come here for a haircut," he answered in that low, whispery voice you had to lean close to hear. Gave you gooseflesh, that whispery voice, and he talked slow, too, Nestor said, like he wanted you to understand every word, and if you didn't he'd just as soon shoot you as repeat himself.

"This is Pegasus," Nestor said he said, introducing his big black stallion like they were all at a barn dance or a box supper. "What he gets is whole oats in the morning and ground oats at night. Cottonseed meal and clover in the afternoon. Two ounces of salt. No timothy. You feed him timothy, I'm afraid I'll have to kill you."

Nestor opened and closed his mouth a few times before he got out, "No timothy. No, siree."

"Pegasus better look good when I come around to check on him tomorrow. He better feel good. He better be singin'."

"S-singin'?"

"Some real happy tune. Like 'Little Ol' Sod Shanty on the Claim.' "

Nestor kind of grinned at that. But then he saw the shine in the gunfighter's eye, the one that wasn't covered up with a black patch, and the icy cold in that steel-gray eyeball froze the blood in Nestor's veins.

Floyd Schmidt and his brother Oscar were playing checkers outside the grange hall when they first saw the gunfighter. For once Floyd, who's been known to stretch the truth to make a story tell better, didn't exaggerate when he said, "Feller didn't have on one stitch that weren't black. Black britches, black shirt, black vest, black coat. Black boots, black hat. Black cigarette. Looked like a one-man funeral walking down Main Street."

"Friend," Oscar said the gunfighter whispered to him, making what little bit of hair Oscar's got stand on end. "What's the best saloon in this town?"

Floyd, who was drunk at the time and had more courage, answered when Oscar couldn't get his tongue to work. "Well, we got Wylie's Saloon, which you done passed comin' in. Then there's Rogue's Tavern up here at the other end. That's about it, saloon-wise."

The gunfighter squinted his eye on the Rogue, which you can just barely see from the grange hall. "Red balcony on the second story? Rocking chairs settin' around?"

"Yep. You can rent a room there, too." Floyd could never explain afterward what possessed him to say that.

The gunfighter thumbed the brim of his Stetson up a notch and sort of smiled. "I got a hankering to set down in a rocking chair and watch the world go by." Floyd and Oscar both shivered when he whispered, "Never can tell who you might see passing down below. Ain't that right?"

They said that sure was right, and watched him stroll on down the street real slow, spurs jingling, saddlebag over one shoulder and his rifle on the other.

Levi Washington, the colored bartender at the Rogue, almost dropped the whiskey glass he was drying when the gunfighter came through the swinging doors, quiet as a puff of smoke. "You could hear the head fizz on a beer," Levi claimed, "when he thunk that rifle butt down and say he'd take a double shot of bourbon, best I got. Not many customers that time o' day, and what we did have cleared off quick, shot out the door like they pants was on fire. I was glad Miz Cady wasn't here in case trouble started, but kinda wishin' she was here, too, 'cause she prob'ly coulda headed it off. You know what she's like.

" 'House brand all right?' I say, and he cocked his head and whispered, 'Talk into my good ear, friend,' just like that, like his voice comin' outa the grave or a coffin or something. I begun to suspicion who he was, but I don't know for sure till he say he want a room upstairs lookin' out on the street. Corner room, he say in particular. He give me four silver dollars, and say if anybody want to see him, I should send 'em right up. Somehow I get enough spit in my mouth to ask his name.

"I swear the wind died down and some dog quit barking just before he say 'Gault' in that turrible whisper that make your insides freeze. 'The name's Gault.'

"Well," said Levi, "I knowed we was in for it then, because I seen it happen before. Nothin' the same once a killer come to town."

Cady McGill always took Friday afternoons off. Lately, now that spring was here and the weather had finally dried out some, she'd taken to renting a buggy and driving out to the old Russell place by herself.

She'd unhitch the horse and let it graze while she wandered around the old going-to-seed orchard, running her hand over the scaly bark of the wild-blooming apples or down-at-the-heels pear trees. Butterflies fluttered through knee-high wildflowers, and the smell was so sweet she could feel it purifying her lungs, making her forget all the smoke she'd inhaled for a week at the Rogue. She'd stroll over to the big house and press her nose to the wavy front-door window, imagining what she'd be doing right now if she owned the place. She might be sitting in the parlor, which she could see about a quarter of from the door, drinking a cup of afternoon tea, maybe paging through a seed catalog and planning her summer garden. Or maybe she'd be reading a book, a novel, nothing serious, while she sipped a cold glass of lemonade. No, on second thought, not on a gorgeous day like today. If she wasn't planting flowers, she'd be working in the orchard alongside her men. Two men—three if she could afford it. This might be a daydream, but she was practical enough to put at least two sturdy day laborers in it.

Le Coeur au Coquin. The Heart of the Rogue. Thirty years ago, after the Rogue Indian wars ended, that's what the Russell family had named their three hundred acres of orchard and pastureland on the cliff edge of the river. Nowadays people just called it River Farm, all that French being too big a mouthful for honest Oregon tongues. But Cady liked both names, and some nights she even fell asleep whispering them to herself, pretending she was standing on the high cliff and watching the blue-green Rogue rage from side to side in its half-mile-wide canyon. Her bit of the river. Her orchard. Her dark hills and pretty green pastures.

Well, someday, maybe. If everything worked out just right.

Time to go home now, though. It looked like rain in the west, and besides, she had work to do.

She hitched up the buggy, climbed in, and gave the gray mare a switch, thinking about Merle Wylie's latest offer for her saloon. If she combined it with her nest egg, it might be enough to buy River Farm, but not enough to do anything with it afterward. Like put it in working order. Anyway, Wylie could kneel down, fold his hands, and kiss her butt before she sold him so much as a shot glass. Why did the one man who could've helped her buy her dream place have to be her worst enemy? Life sure was funny sometimes. Ha ha. Life had been funny to Cady a few times too many. She wished it would hurry and sober the hell up.

Not that she had much to complain about nowadays. Nothing like in the old days. Some might say she had it made—a few good friends, her own place to live, a business she owned free and clear. Why, she even had a gold mine. She had to smile as the buggy passed by the muddy, poky, weed-infested turnoff to the Seven Dollar Mine, the second thing any man had ever given her. (Third if you counted the tattoo.) *If it weren't for Mr. Shlegel, you wouldn't have anything at all, Cady McGill.* She reminded herself of that whenever she was feeling down on men. Which was pretty often. Being in the saloon business, she figured it came with the territory.

Riding past the entrance to the Rainbow Mine a few minutes later wiped the smile off her face. Merle Wylie's turnoff wasn't scraggly and overgrown, and his mine wasn't placered out like hers. Which just went to show, there wasn't any justice in this world. If there was, a no-account rodent like Wylie wouldn't still be digging gold out of the ground, and a saint like Gus Shlegel wouldn't be moldering in his grave. He'd still be running Rogue's Tavern and hauling gold out by the bucket from the Seven Dollar. And Cady would be . . . his mistress? Wife by now? She couldn't quite picture herself in those roles, although she'd wished for either one of them often enough when Mr. Shlegel was alive.

But all that was water under the bridge. You couldn't get anywhere by ruminating on the past, which wasn't going to change no matter how much you wished it would. You couldn't count on the future either, but sometimes you were allowed to dream about it. Paint yourself a picture of what you thought it would look like. For Cady, it always looked like an orchard farm in the Rogue River Valley.

Jesse almost set himself on fire lighting one of his damn black cigarettes. He was sitting in a rocker on the red balcony outside his room, doing his badass sonofabitch outlaw routine, when half an inch of red-hot ash fell in his lap. It's hard to look menacing when you're jumping up and down and slapping at your privates. Nobody was ogling him just then, though—which was a miracle, since about the only thing the good folks of Paradise had done since he hit town was stare.

He liked Paradise. It didn't look like much, but with gold towns, looks could be deceiving. He was sure there was money under the wheel ruts in the dusty, unpaved streets; big money in the pockets of the rough-looking customers stumping up and down the wooden sidewalks; buckets of money behind the yellow brick facade of the First Mercantile Bank & Trust Company. All an enterprising fellow had to do was be patient and wait for it.

Knock knock knock.

Well, shoot.

He got up, moving cool and slow in case anybody was watching. But he had to look down to hide a grin. This trick was getting so easy, it wasn't hardly even any fun anymore.

"Gault?" somebody mumbled through the door to the hallway. "Speak to you, Mr. Gault?"

Strapping on the gunbelt he'd hung on the bedpost, Jesse said, "It's open," in his creepy whisper.

"Mr. Gault?" *Knock knock knock.*

Which was so often the trouble with creepy whispering. He cleared his throat and yelled, "The door's open!"

The knob turned and the door cracked an inch, two inches. Three, four. Tired of waiting, Jesse yanked it all the way open, and a bowlegged, ginger-haired man with a smell on him like dead buffalo half fell, half jumped into the room.

"Don't shoot, I ain't packin'!" he shouted with both hands in the air. He was built like a cob horse, short and stocky, and if he'd changed his clothes in the last year or so it didn't show. He didn't look like much, but Jesse had learned opportunity came in many different shapes and sizes.

"State your name," he hissed, flexing his fingers over one of the Colts, like a nervous habit.

"Shrimp Malone. Name's Shrimp Malone."

He looked like a shrimp, little and orange-headed. Then, too, he could've been *Chicken* Malone because of the blond eyebrows and eyelashes. That and the fact that he didn't have any lips to speak of.

"I've been expecting you, Mr. Malone," Jesse said, and Shrimp's red face turned pasty under the dirt and grime and gingery whiskers. "Close the door."

"You wouldn't shoot me here, would you?"

"Depends. Close the door and sit down."

Shrimp pretty much fell into a spindly ladderback chair by the door, while Jesse moved back as far as he could and still be heard in the creepy whisper, because the stink coming off his visitor was strong enough to wither trees. Under the reek of booze and sweat lay the sour odor of clay dirt, though, and that told him Mr. Malone was a prospector. Which made him as welcome as if he'd smelled like a perfumed hankie.

The fastest way to make a man with a guilty conscience talk is to keep quiet. Shrimp Malone stood the silence for about twenty seconds before blurting out, "Well, hell's bells, did you *see* 'er? God *damn*, that was the sorriest-lookin' female I ever clapped eyes on! I only poked her in the first place on accounta I was shit-faced drunk. Which she knowed, and so did her whole idiot family. They *tricked* me. Any man woulda ran off if he'd saw the chance— you'd'a done it, too! God Almighty, she looked like a goddamn possum, breath like a shut-up cave, and them two black teeth stickin' out like dominoes. Whuh!"

Jesse shuddered in sympathy, picturing the kind of woman Shrimp would scorn because of her personal hygiene. "That ain't worth two cents to me," he said, figuring it was time to bring money into the conversation.

It worked. "How much are those halfwits payin' you? Whadda they want you to do, drag me back to marry 'er, or just plug me right here and put me outa my misery? It don't hardly make a difference to me—I'd as soon be dead as shackled to that horse-face hyena the rest o' my days." He looked cocky and resolute for half a minute. Then he caved.

"Okay, okay, here's the deal." Jumping up, he dragged a filthy cloth bag out of the deep pocket of his brown, baggy, dirt-crusted dungarees. "Here's sixty-four ounces of dust, all's I got in the wide world. Took me four months to sift and pick and scrounge it outa the river. You take it and tell the Weaver boys you done killed me. Pocket what they give you an' this, too, and ride on. They'll never know, 'cause I don't aim to set foot in Coos County for the rest o' my days, and that's the God's truth."

Jesse caught the bag one-handed. It hefted like about four pounds. Gold was bringing twelve dollars an ounce these days. Twelve times sixteen, two sixes are twelve, carry your one is seven . . . Seven hundred and fifty bucks. He didn't bother opening the bag to make sure it wasn't full of sand. In his short but profitable career, nobody had ever stiffed Gault yet, and Shrimp Malone didn't look like the man to start.

Jesse sent him his fiendish, one-eyed glare. "You wouldn't be trying to bribe me, would you, Mr. Malone?"

"What? No, sir! I'd never do nothin' like that."

"I hope not. Because I've got a reputation to uphold."

"Yes, sir. No, this 'ud be like . . . like a gift. This little bit o' gold for my life. A trade, like."

He looked thoughtful. "How'll I prove to them you're dead?"

"Huh?"

"The Weavers. They'll want proof. What'll I use to convince them?"

Shrimp looked baffled for a second, then crushed. "Aw, shit," he mumbled, digging down in the other pocket and pulling out something gray and nasty-looking. "This here's the onliest thing that'd do it. My lucky pig's ear."

Jesse, who'd been hoping for a watch, took the bristly, petrified ear between two fingers. It appeared to be a hundred years old, so it must be his imagination that it still stank. "If you're trying to birdlime me, Malone—"

"I ain't, I swear I ain't! Anybody who knows me'll tell you, I'd ruther die than part with my lucky pig's ear."

Jesse lifted the eyebrow over his good eye.

"Heh heh," Shrimp said nervously. "Leastways, that's what I always use t' say. Ask anybody."

He pretended to think it over while the miner shifted from foot to foot. After a long time he whispered, "I'm in a good mood today. Reckon I'll take you up on your offer, Mr. Malone."

Shrimp's knees almost buckled. "Oh, thank you, Mr. Gault. You won't regret it, I swear."

"I better not."

"You won't."

"Because if I do, that'll put me in a bad mood."

"Yessir. No, sir, you can rest easy." He started backing toward the door, smiling hopefully, tipping his chewed-up hat. "Well, I'll say adios—"

"I aim to stay in Paradise for a while. I'd sure hate to hear any rumors about our little business deal."

Shrimp made an X over his chest with a black thumb. "Cross my heart, nobody'll ever hear about it from me."

"Because if they did, you know what would happen?"

Shrimp was smarter than he looked. "It'd put you in a bad mood."

"That's right. Folks say I get irrational when I'm in a bad mood."

"Yessir." This time he twisted two fingers in front of his mouth, and vowed, "My lips're sealed."

Jesse could've pointed out that he didn't have any

lips, but that would've been unkind. Besides, the smell was getting too bad. When Shrimp scrabbled for the knob behind him and finally got the door open, Jesse sent him one last steely-eyed glare and let him go.

Then he felt like letting out a rebel yell, or tossing his hat in the air. But the walls were too thin and the ceiling was too low. He settled for throwing himself on the bed and crooning, "Yee-ha," in a soft, celebratory tone.

PARADISE—YOU'LL LIKE IT HERE, a sign said at the top of Main Street. Yes, sir, Paradise was an all right town. Gault liked it here just fine. So did Jesse.

Cady had passed that sign so many times, she didn't even see it anymore. Today, driving by it, something else caught her eye anyway: Ham Washington, Levi's boy, flying straight at her down the middle of the street like rabid dogs were chasing him. If she didn't know Ham so well, she'd've thought the saloon was on fire.

"Miz Cady, Miz Cady!"

The calm, slow-footed mare shied a little, halting just short of a collision with Ham. "Abraham, how many times have I told you not to run at a horse like that?"

He was too excited to apologize. "Miz Cady, a man—a man—" And too winded to make sense. "Guns, guns, a black horse—stayin' at your—place, and Poppy say—"

She reached her hand down, he grabbed it, and she hauled him up beside her on the seat. Ham was tall for seven, but skinny as a weed, all elbows and shoulder blades. "Slow down and catch your breath," she advised, handing the reins to him out of habit.

Handling the mare calmed him down—Ham was crazy for horses. "A man done rode in, Miz Cady," he managed all in one breath. "Bad man, Poppy say. He at the Rogue—done took a room. He have guns an' rifles all over, an' Poppy say he look like death walkin'. Just like death walkin'," he repeated with relish.

"What are you talking about? Why is he a bad man?"

"He a *gunslinger*. Look at him cross-eyed, he shoot you, Mr. Yeakes say. I ain't seen him yet—he up in his room, got the door shut. He named Gault."

They were almost in front of the Rogue. "Stop right here," Cady commanded, and Ham reined the mare in at the corner. "Take the buggy to the livery for me," she told him, jumping down, "and tell Mr. Yeakes I'll pay him later. You come straight back afterward and stay with your daddy, you understand?"

"Yes'm." If anything, he looked more agitated than before—her urgency had confirmed his worst, most exciting fears.

Watching him drive off, she noticed a knot of men across the street in front of the French restaurant. She recognized Stony Dern and Sam Blankenship; Gunther Dewhurt tipped his hat to her, but didn't come over. On the opposite corner, Livvie Dunne and Ardelle Sheets were talking to a third lady; Cady could only see her hat and the back of her gray dress. Like the men, all three were staring across at the small, red-painted balcony that ran across two sides of her saloon. Nobody was up there, though. Nothing stirred except the rocking chairs in the wind, and one blackbird flapping its wings on the railing.

She looked back at Livvie and Ardelle—who saw her and immediately turned their backs on her, the way they always did. If they'd had their children with them, they'd've gathered them up and herded them down the sidewalk, as if they were sheep and Cady was a big drooling wolf. She made her snooty, careless face, wishing they'd turn around so they could see how little their scorn mattered to her. Just then Levi poked his head out the swinging door. She picked up her skirts and hurried across the street toward her tavern.

"Cady," Levi greeted her, holding the door open. Over his shoulder, she noticed the saloon was almost empty, nobody but Jersey Stan Morrissey playing poker by himself, and Leonard Berg and Jim Tannenbaum, drunk and squabbling as usual. This time of day on a Friday, the place ought to be half full at least, and getting livelier by the minute.

"I just saw Ham," said Cady.

"Yep, I seen 'im fly by in the buggy."

"What's he saying about a gunfighter, Levi?"

The bartender smoothed one long-fingered hand back over his ear, feeling for bristles. Levi shaved his head every morning, shiny and smooth as an eight ball. "Sho' look like it to me. He say his name's Gault. *Bad*-lookin' white man. Scared off all but these here," he said, nodding toward the three stragglers at the bar.

"You gave him a *room*?"

He ducked his head. "Didn't see no way not to. He look jus' like I heard he did, one eye an' one good ear. Look like a killer to me. But he ain't *did* nothin' yet, an' plus . . . tell you the truth, I was scared not to do what he say."

"It's all right," she said quickly, "I'd have done the same thing." Following his nervous gaze to the stair landing at the back of the saloon, she half expected to see Gault standing there, guns drawn. "Think Wylie hired him?"

"I don't know. I hope not."

She hoped not, too, but what else would a gunfighter be doing in Paradise? "Where's Tommy?"

Levi shrugged, and added a roll of his eyes. Which meant, *What difference does it make?* She had to agree. Sheriff Tom Leaver (Lily Leaver, some people called him for a joke) was either dutifully shuffling papers in his office or else mooning around Glendoline Shavers, Cady's best bar girl. Either way, if the man upstairs really was a hired killer, the sheriff wasn't going to be running him out of town anytime soon.

She looked back at the empty staircase. Looked around her mostly empty saloon. "I don't need this, Levi."

"No, ma'am."

She bit her lip for a while longer, scowling into space. "Well, I guess I'll go up there."

Levi sighed, as if he'd known that was coming. "Guess I'll go with you."

She looked at him doubtfully. Levi was tall as a telegraph pole, but he weighed about as much as she did. He never touched guns, and there wasn't a violent bone in his body. He kept the peace by talking men to death, reasoning with them in a calm, practically hypnotic voice that soothed the meanness out of the surliest customers. And if it didn't, Cady threw them out herself, with help from the little Remington five-shot she kept in her garter.

"No need for that, Levi. I can handle myself," she said.

"Prob'ly can, but I'm still comin'."

If she kept refusing, it would embarrass him. "Okay, but partway. Just see me into his room. After that, if you hear shooting, run for the sheriff." She said it with a smile, but she wasn't sure if she was kidding or not.

Jesse was dreaming about women. Two women, a blonde and a brunette. The brunette was taking his boots off and the blonde was sitting on his lap, wetting the end of a cigar, fixing to light it for him. She wet it by running her tongue around and around the tip, making little humming noises. Somebody said, "Bet's to you," and all of a sudden he had three kings and a pair of aces in the hand that wasn't resting on the blonde's little round behind. "See that and raise you a hundred," Jesse said, and everybody laid down their cards. Slop everywhere—he won. The blonde kissed him on the ear. He reached for the pot—

Knock knock knock.

He opened his eyes, smiling, disoriented, unable to remember where he was. Big room, soft bed, yellow wallpaper—he sat up fast, going for his guns while he called out, "Who's there?" in a sleep-rough voice.

"Cady McGill."

A woman. No need for a weapon, then. In the mirror over the bureau, he noticed his eyepatch had slid over to his temple. Righting it, raking his hair back with his fingers, he padded over to the door and jerked it open.

And broke into a big, tickled grin—all wrong, not Gault at all, but he was just so glad to see her. She was a little thing, no more than about chin height, but she was real shapely. Real shapely. Shiny dark hair tied back in a ribbon, and eyes the same color as her hair. Plain brown skirt, no bustle, and a faded blue blouse with a piece of white lace at the front to draw your eye, in case it wasn't there already. She had on a man's felt hat, hanging down in back by a leather strap, dark against the smooth white of her neck. He liked the thin, friendly line of freckles across the bridge of her nose. Most of all he liked her wide, sexy mouth, currently set in a nervous straight line.

"Mr. Gault?"

Gault, right, right. He changed his smile into a leer. Pretty girls had guilty consciences, too, he knew for a fact, so he didn't say a word, just widened the door and stepped back. It was a fine line, though; he wanted her to come in, so he didn't want to look *too* dangerous.

She hesitated. After a glance down the hall to her right, she lifted her chin, like a stud player bluffing a flush when she's holding a pair of deuces, and stepped over the threshold.

Before he closed the door, he checked to see who was out there. Aha—the tall Negro bartender, on guard at the top of the stairs. He looked petrified, but he was standing his ground. Jesse liked that in a man.

Cady halted in front of the unmade feather bed. A black, bullet-studded gunbelt with twin holsters was slung over one of the posts, and a black Stetson hat hung at a rakish tilt on the other. Something, maybe the contrast between the friendly, rumpled sheets and the dangerous-looking gunbelt, threw her off her stride. *So,* some frivolous part of her mind noted, *even outlaw gunfighters take naps. Under the covers, just like the rest of us. Maybe they even snore.*

Which was a stupid thing to be thinking right at this moment. With a mental shake, she pivoted to face the outlaw.

He was even meaner-looking than Levi had warned her he'd be. He was taller than she was—who wasn't?—but not exactly a giant, maybe six feet or so. He wore his wavy hair long, and it was the same shade of dark brown as hers, only his was streaked with silver. Prematurely silver, though—he looked young, not even thirty. While she watched, he did up one button on his black shirt. But he didn't bother with the top button of his black denim trousers.

He folded his arms and leaned against the door, crossing his bare feet at the ankles. It was hard not to stare at the patch over his right eye. Was he terribly scarred under it? Maybe he had no eye there at

all. The notion horrified and fascinated her about
equally.

She knew his name, but only vaguely, mostly from
unreliable barroom gossip. She remembered something about him being wounded at Gettysburg before
his gunfighter career started—but how could that be?
In 1863 he couldn't have been much more than
twelve or thirteen years old. She also remembered
something about him being killed in a gunfight a
few months ago in California. Apparently that story
was exaggerated.

"What can I do for you, Miss Katie McGill?"

"Cady," she corrected automatically.

"K. D.?"

"No, Cady. It's short for Cadence." *Oh, this is how
you talk to hired gunslingers: you make sure they know
what your name is short for.* "What about you?" she
said aggressively. "Don't you have a first name?"

He narrowed his one eye, which was an eerie
shade of silver-gray, and didn't say anything for so
long, she began to perspire. "I don't need one," he
finally sneered, but by then she'd forgotten the
question.

She resented it that he was scaring her. She put
her hands on her hips and said combatively, "I own
this place."

"That so?" He nodded, glanced around. "Nice
view. I'm real partial to a rocking chair."

"Yeah, I thought they'd be a nice touch." She
waved her hand toward the low door that led out to
the porch roof. "Airy and all."

"Real nice touch."

Well, this was a pleasant conversation they were having. She caught sight of a Winchester .44-.40 leaning against the wall, and it brought her back to the point.

"What are you doing here, Mr. Gault? Who hired you?" He just stared at her until her palms began to itch. "Wylie," she answered for herself, because it was so obvious. "Right? It was Wylie, wasn't it?"

"Why would Wylie hire me?"

"Maybe to burn me out, the same way he did Logan's livery stable. How much is he paying you?"

Instead of answering, he started to walk toward her, naked feet slow and quiet on the thin carpet. She couldn't stop herself from stepping back, then sideways. Without even pausing, he passed her by and sat down at the foot of the bed.

It took a whole minute for her heart to slow down.

"You listen here," she said when it did. "I'm not paying you anything, and I'm not leaving. Rogue's Tavern is mine, and Merle Wylie's never getting his dirty paws on it. He can't have the Rogue, he can't have the Seven Dollar, and he can't have me. And you can tell him I said so." Her anger got hotter with every word; by the time she finished her little speech, her hands were shaking.

Gault stroked his mustache thoughtfully, looking at her with more interest than menace. "I'll tell him if you want me to. What's he look like?"

She blinked. "What?"

"Fellow Wylie. I don't know him, but I'll be glad to deliver your message."

"You're saying he didn't send for you?"

"Never heard the name till this afternoon. I stabled my horse at his livery."

"*His* livery. Hah. That's because two weeks ago he burned Logan's down to the ground," she shot back, mad all over again.

"Now, why would he do a mean thing like that?"

Was he playing with her? "Because he wants the whole town to himself, that's why."

He stood up and started walking toward her again, but this time she didn't give way. "Greed'll do funny things to a man," he said in a low, rough, whispery voice that sent a little thrill across the tops of her shoulders. He was standing so close, she could smell him. Tobacco, bay rum, and leather. And danger.

"How long were you planning to stay in Paradise?" she asked, sticking her chin out at him, glad when her voice didn't quiver.

He turned his head to the right, and she remembered he was deaf in one ear. "Long as it takes to get my business done, Miss McGill."

No need to ask what his business was. Professional gunfighter—he might as well have a sign across his chest. Who had hired him, though? And who could he be gunning for in Paradise? "Well, you're welcome to stay here as long as you don't cause any trouble," she said firmly as she backed toward the door. "I won't stand for any trouble in my place."

"Sometimes trouble has a way of following a man, and there's nothing he can do about it."

So, the frivolous part of her brain piped up again. *It's not just in corny dime novels—gunfighters really do talk like that.* She hunted for the proper response, and finally settled for, "I expect that depends on the man, Mr. Gault."

"Yes, ma'am, I expect it does."

They stared at each other somewhat blankly until she said, "Well," and searched behind her for the doorknob.

"You know what I want?"

The question made her nervous. Rather than ask what, which would've betrayed too much interest, she just lifted her eyebrows.

"I want a hot bath, a steak dinner, and a poker game."

For some reason—relief, probably—she smiled at him. "Sorry, there's no plumbing on the second floor—which Levi should've told you. But you can get a bath at the barbershop for a dollar. We don't serve meals, either, but Jacques' is right across the street. He says the food's French, but it's really Creole. Then there's Swensen's on Main Street, but I don't recommend it. Not unless your stomach's made out of cast iron."

That made *him* smile, the same infectious, almost sweet smile he'd greeted her with at the door. It hadn't lasted long, but she hadn't forgotten it. Now it struck her the same way as the rumpled bed and the six-guns—a funny contrast to the scary-looking rest of him.

"And the poker game?" he reminded her.

"Ah, now, there I can help you."

"Square game?"

"Absolutely. The fairest in town." Which definitely wasn't saying much. Gault smiled again, as if he'd read her mind. They shared a look, and just for a second she thought it was a companionable look, almost . . . conspiratorial. "Well," she said again. "See you."

He touched his index finger to his forehead in a cocky salute. When he took it away, the smile and the look, whatever it had meant, were both gone. He didn't say "See you" back; in fact, he didn't say anything. Oddly disappointed, Cady slipped out the door and closed it softly behind her.

Levi was still waiting for her on the stairs. Walking toward him, she had the strangest sensation: that she'd just had a conversation with two men, not one, and she had no idea which was real. Or which one interested her more.

Two

Everything in Rogue's Tavern went dead quiet when Jesse walked in—from carnival noisy to church still, just like that, as soon as he pushed open the swinging doors and sauntered over to the bar. On the way, he came within two inches of smacking into a post on his blind side. Which took some of the cockiness out of him. But he got it back when the fellows around the bar fell over themselves trying to get out of his way. "Bourbon," he whispered into the reverent hush, "and don't water it down this time."

The tall, spindly bartender bobbed his bald head and slid a bottle and a glass in front of him. While he was at it, he started to pour what looked like sarsaparilla into the glass that belonged to a pale, thin, cadaverous-looking gent on Jesse's left. The man stuck one bony hand over the glass and threw a half dollar on the bar with the other, backing away as if a scorpion had stung him. "Doc?" called the bartender, frowning. Mumbling something, hunching his scrawny shoulders, the corpselike fellow turned and headed for the door.

Jesse poured two fingers of bourbon and took a thoughtful sip.

"Are we playing cards here or not?" a woman's voice cut through the uneasy silence. "Chico, finish that song, I liked it."

He didn't have to turn to know it was Miss Cady "Short for Cadence" McGill, saloon proprietor and dream interrupter. He'd been thinking about her all evening, even hurried through his pretty good dinner at Jacques' so he could see her again. He had a weakness for pretty girls, but that didn't explain why he'd passed up a golden opportunity by admitting to her he didn't work for Wylie. That wasn't like him. Not like him at all. He hated to think he was getting soft, not this early in the game.

A short, handsome Mexican in a derby hat went back to playing "The Drunkard's Hiccup" on the piano. A roulette wheel spun; dice dropped; conversations started up again. Jesse poured another inch of booze and turned around real cool and slow, resting his elbows on the bar, hitching up one boot on the brass rail. And squeezed his eyes shut tight so they wouldn't fall out of his head.

Miss McGill had changed her clothes. His memory of her brown skirt and blue blouse getup, vivid until just now, faded into nothing. Red exploded, temporarily blinding him. He recovered by making out bits and pieces of her slowly, gently, working up to the whole picture in stages so he wouldn't hurt himself.

She was perched on a stool with her legs crossed, dealing blackjack to four lovestruck cowboys. Understandably lovestruck, because her dress . . . it was like she'd melted red candle wax all over her sweet little body, that's how tight it fit her. The cowboys who weren't staring at her high, white bosom were staring at the bare foot and six inches of bare calf swinging under her ruffled red skirt, and the sexy high-heeled red shoe hanging off the end of her toes. "Hit me," they begged her, going bust on purpose so she'd lean over and deal them another card.

Jesse looked away in self-defense, scanning the spacious, high-ceilinged room, trying to work up an interest in what kind of a saloon he was in. He liked saloons, liked to think he was an expert on them. A saloon gourmet, you could say. This one had the usual equipment—stag's heads and spittoons, mirrors and hanging lanterns, the requisite naked lady at ease over the bar. A stone fireplace took up half the back wall; dark wood paneling covered the other three to chest height, then ivory-painted plaster up to the tall beamed ceiling. Handsome. Cheerful. And something else he couldn't put his finger on that set the Rogue apart from the ten thousand or so other bars he'd been in.

Then it hit him: the place was clean. No smudges on the mirrors, no oily head prints. The waxed bar glowed like Chinese lacquer. He could see his reflection in the crystal-clean plate-glass windows. Strangest of all, the smoky air smelled pretty much like air, not the inside of a wet coal stove.

Well, wasn't that just like a woman? He wanted to sneer and call the place prissy, dismiss it as a dandified bar no self-respecting man would drink beer in, but he couldn't. The Rogue was a great bar. And it *was* just like a woman to run a clean saloon, but it turned out—who'd've thought?—a clean saloon was nice for a change. It probably made you feel a lot better while you were defiling your lungs and pickling your liver and squandering your wife's egg money on simpleminded games of chance.

Natural caution told him to stay away, but Miss McGill's red dress was calling to him like a siren. First, he poured a little more liquor, though, and stuck a thin black cigarette, prerolled, in the corner of his mouth—for that *look at me wrong and I'll blow your brains out* effect so vital to a man in his line of work. Nobody stared openly, but he felt the cautious, veiled looks as he moseyed around the tables of drinkers and poker players, heading for the blackjack table.

A man saw him and started to scramble up off his stool, but Jesse put a friendly hand on his shoulder—which still made him freeze like a bird dog—and whispered, "Just watching." He was pretty sure McGill knew he was there, but was making a point not to look at him. So he looked at her.

She sure had good posture. And she wasn't barefooted after all; she had on flesh-colored stockings. This afternoon she'd worn her curly dark hair down, but tonight it was up in a big, top-heavy pompadour that took some getting used to. In fact, he couldn't get over how completely different she looked from a couple of hours ago. Not that he was complaining. But even the freckles were gone. She had rouge on her lips, and perfume he could smell from here. Which was fine, great, he liked perfume and red lips on a woman, but . . . But nothing. She was gorgeous, and as soon as he got over the shock he'd start to appreciate it.

That dangling shoe looked in danger of falling off as the swinging foot bobbed faster and faster. He liked the idea that he was making her nervous, but except for the foot you'd never have known it. She kept her face poker straight, as the saying went, and she handled the cards with the crisp, quick, slightly bored snappiness of a true professional.

"You're busted, Gunther," she told a plaid-shirted, lumberjack-looking fellow, and leaned over to scoop up his cards. Jesse's eyes went where every other man's went, and that's when he saw it.

Or thought he saw it—it only flashed for a second, and afterward he wondered if it had been a trick of the light. So he waited until the game was over— dealer won—and she swept up everybody's cards with one long, leaning-over pass. There it was, no mirage, no bourbon-induced hallucination: a genuine tattoo on the shadowy inside curve of her left breast. Some kind of a bird, an eagle or something, flying out of the cleft and nose-diving toward the nipple. His cigarette fell out of his mouth.

He stepped on it, pretending he'd meant to drop it, hoping nobody noticed it wasn't even lit. Hell, no danger of that: who'd be looking at his cigarette when they could look at Cady's tattoo? She dealt another round, and he was so fixated on catching another glimpse of the elusive bird he forgot all about trying to catch her at card-palming or double-dealing. Which might, now that he thought of it, be the whole point. Hm.

He was thinking about other uses for the tattoo, less practical but more interesting ones, when a tall, willowy blonde trapped his arm between her powdered breasts and breathed, "Hi," on a gust of gin and bitters.

He was glad to see her. It was good that he struck fear in the hearts of men, but the down side was that hardly anybody talked to him. He got lonely. "Hi," he returned, then wished he'd said something meaner, more menacing. But what? *Those real?* Not very gentlemanly. And say what you would about Gault, he always tried to be a gentleman.

"I'm Glendoline," the blonde confided in a childlike whisper, blinking dreamy blue eyes and pursing her lips as if she wanted to kiss him. "And you're Gault. I heard all about you."

Ah, now he had her number. He'd never known about this species of woman before, the kind who liked dangerous men and would go to amazing lengths to get them. After the money, they were the second-best thing about being a gunfighter. Or at least they had been in the beginning, when he hadn't wasted a minute taking advantage of their breathless interest in him. Lately, though, it was starting to wear thin. It wasn't that flattering anymore. It was like getting a compliment on your hair when you were wearing a wig.

"Want to sit down and have a drink with me?" Glendoline purred, pointing to an empty table for two. "You could show me your gun." Her china-blue eyes were innocent as a doll's, so he decided she meant the suggestion literally.

"Why not?" he said in the gravelly whisper, which made her roll her eyes in ecstasy, and turned to follow her. Her skinny, sashaying butt was a cute distraction, but he glanced away from it to see if Cady was watching.

She was. But she looked away quickly, slapping cards down hard in front of her customers, pretending she couldn't care less. Everybody was playing a game, Jesse philosophized pleasantly. He was just playing a bigger one than most people.

He made a big deal of taking the chair facing the door so he could sit with his back to the wall, which almost sent Glendoline into a swoon. Another girl, a plump, buxom redhead named Willagail, was serving drinks to the customers at the next table. What kind of a place was this, it occurred to Jesse to wonder. If his new friend wasn't a whore, he'd eat his hat. So . . . did that mean McGill was, too? Well, God *damn*. No, she couldn't be.

Why not? Just because a girl had freckles didn't mean she couldn't turn tricks. He sat down slowly, peering at her across two tables of poker players, trying to picture her in the role of madam. It was hard, but not impossible. What did he think of that? He had, as they said, mixed feelings. He'd been thinking about her and him together in his big feather bed since approximately the moment they met. Now, for some reason, it needled him to think that all he might have to do to get her there was pay her.

He bought Glendoline—"Call me Glen, honey"— a drink, then another drink, then another. It went without saying that the bartender was watering them down, but still, for a skinny girl she sure could put away the booze. She asked him the usual questions, how he'd become a gunfighter, how many men he'd killed, what it felt like to shoot somebody, and he avoided them with the usual sinister stares and enigmatic grunts. Glendoline wasn't too bright, but under the bloodthirsty curiosity she seemed sweet. He missed her when she went off to "see about something." After all those drinks, he was pretty sure what she was seeing about was the privy behind the saloon.

Something bumped his leg. Looking down, he saw a little black boy, a miniature version of the bartender but with hair, squatting at his feet, halfway under the table. He had a whisk broom in one hand and a cigarette-filled dustpan in the other.

"Howdy," said Jesse. The boy jumped, never taking his scared, white-rimmed eyes off him. "How's it going? You like that job? How much they pay you? I had a job cleaning out horse stalls once. I was about your age, twenty, twenty-one," he teased—the kid looked about seven. "Paid diddly squat, a quarter a week. Which is worse, you think, raking up horse manure or cigar butts and spit? Hm? Who's dirtier, horses or cowboys?"

"Horses," the boy ventured, scuttling out a few inches.

"I don't know," Jesse said thoughtfully, rubbing his jaw. "Some old boys are mighty damn messy."

"Yeah, but they don't do they business on the flo'."

"Well, that's true, that's surely true. That is a very

good point. Cigarette? So tell me, what's a smart fella like you doing in a god-awful place like this?"

"This a *good* place." His huge black eyes went wider still. "Why you think this a god-awful place?" He came all the way out from under the table, and when Jesse casually pulled Glendoline's chair out for him, he perched on the edge, curiosity getting the better of his nerves.

"You *like* it here? This place?" He looked around in mock disbelief. "What's good about it?"

"Well, Miz Cady the best thing, and I like it when Chico play the piano, and Miz Glen and Miz Willagail, they nice, plus sometimes I get tips or candy or a piece o' licorice. And my daddy, he the bartender and everybody like him, so that make 'em like *me*."

"Uh-huh. So why's Miss Cady the best thing? By the way, what's your name?"

"Abraham."

"Pleased to meet you. You married?"

"Naw." He giggled, then instantly sobered. " 'Cause. She just is. She let me do anything, drive her buggy, come in her room and play with stuff. And she always give me things, like a book or a apple or something. She funny, too, and she always smell good."

"I noticed that myself."

Abraham banged his heel against the chair leg, more at ease now but still devouring Jesse with his eyes. "Poppy say you a gunfighter," he said shyly.

"Yep."

"Why?"

"Why what?"

"Why you wanna go and shoot people?"

"Well, it isn't that I *wanna* go and shoot people. Anyway, I only shoot people who really need it."

"Who? Who you shoot?"

"Bad guys. People who'd shoot other people if I didn't shoot 'em first."

Abraham's mouth made an O. "So you one o' the *good* guys."

"That's it." Jesse smacked the table with his hand. "I'm one o' the good guys. But listen." He leaned close; Abraham blinked in alarm but didn't flinch. "Don't tell anybody, hear? Because I don't want this getting out. Me being a good guy—this is a secret between us and nobody else, okay?"

"Okay. Why?"

"Why." He was mulling over reasons when Glendoline came back.

"Ham Washington, your daddy said get your skinny ass off that chair and back to work right this minute or you're gonna be good and sorry."

"Uh-oh." He scrambled up, grabbing for his pan and broom, darting a worried look toward the bar. His father scowled back at him. Jesse sighed, feeling dispirited when his new little pal scampered away and Glendoline took his vacated chair.

"So, honey, you gonna show me your gun or not?"

He was wearing two guns—maybe she *was* driving at something else. Luckily a new interruption came along before he had to answer.

He didn't even have to look up to know why the room quieted down all of a sudden, or whose shoes were marching dutifully toward him from the swinging doors. He had experience at these things. He'd lay twenty to one it was the law.

Glendoline, who had sidled closer so she could press her knee against his thigh, sat back guiltily. "Oh, hi, Tommy," she said in a careless tone, patting the corkscrew curls at the back of her head. "Fancy meeting you here."

You could tell it was the sheriff because he had a badge on his starched white shirt, but otherwise you'd have guessed some other line of work. Bank teller, maybe, or telegraph clerk. "Good evening," he said, nervous but polite. "It's Mr. Gault, isn't it? I'm Sheriff Leaver."

Ordinarily Jesse, being a polite kind of fellow himself, would've taken the slender, uncallused hand Sheriff Leaver held out to him. But Gault wouldn't, and besides, half the customers in the saloon were eavesdropping on this conversation, and the other half were trying to. So he ignored the hand and gave the sheriff his dead-eye stare, until the poor guy blushed and Glendoline giggled uneasily.

"Glen," said the sheriff, "would you excuse us, please?"

"Why, what'd you do?" She laughed at her witless joke, but nobody else did.

He coughed behind his hand. "I mean, would you mind leaving me and Mr. Gault alone?"

"Oh, you can talk in front of me."

Sheriff Leaver had red hair and a skimpy goatee and the kind of fair, delicate skin women wished they had. The kind of skin that's like a thermostat under a clock in the middle of town where everybody can see it. White, terrified; pink, scarified; red, mortified. Currently it was a sort of rusty salmon shade, moving toward lobster.

Jesse couldn't stand it. "Take a walk," he suggested pleasantly. "What the sheriff and me got to say might not be fit for a lady's ears."

Glendoline, who had started to sulk, turned almost as red as the sheriff when she heard the word "lady." Falling over herself getting up, simpering and cooing, she couldn't move fast enough. " 'Scuse me, then, I'm sure. I'll come back when you *gentlemen* finish talking your business." She gave Jesse a smitten look, trailing her hand across his shoulder as she sidled away.

The sheriff looked pained watching her go, like he'd banged his thumb with a hammer and was trying not to cry. "Have a seat," Jesse said to distract him. "Drink?"

"No, thank you." He wouldn't sit, either. He cleared his throat, knowing as well as Jesse did that this conversation wasn't private, and that anybody not hearing it direct would be getting it secondhand soon enough. Clawing at his goatee, he stated his business. "Mr. Gault, would you mind telling me what you're doing here in Paradise?"

Shiny badge and shiny shoes, pants hitched up to his ribs. Squeaky-clean and smelling like cologne. White hat and no gun. Jesse sized the sheriff up fast: heavy on earnestness, light on balls.

Which was surely no sin, and not even a half-bad thing in the average run of men. Just maybe not what you'd want in the man keeping order in your town.

Jesse had no stomach for embarrassing him, but they were like two dogs sniffing at each other's butt. The sooner one dog rolled over and gave up, the sooner they could both get on about their business.

"Yeah, I'd mind," he said with a wiseguy snarl, leaning back in his chair, sticking his boot heels up on the table, and crossing his arms over his chest. Had he missed anything? Were there any more ways he could look insolent? He could spit on the floor. But then Ham would have to clean it up. "You ask everybody that when they come to your town? Not very neighborly, Sheriff. In fact, I'd call that downright unfriendly."

Leaver swallowed audibly. "I was just wondering how long you're fixing to stay."

"Haven't decided. Nice little town, nice folks. Maybe I'll settle down. Retire, get me a place with one of them white fences all around. Raise posies."

Somebody snickered; across the way, somebody actually guffawed. Sheriff Leaver turned a nice mulberry color. "Could I"—he coughed behind his hand again—"could I ask why you're here?"

"Business."

"What, ah, kind of business?"

Time to demonstrate a short fuse. He picked up one boot and let it hit the floor with a *stomp*, and everybody jumped, nobody higher than the sheriff. "Private business," he said menacingly. "You got a problem with that, friend, we can take this conversation outside." He cracked his knuckles one by one, to make sure everybody knew what he was talking about.

It took the sheriff two tries before he could say, "I don't have a problem with that."

"Good. Then you can sit down and have a drink with me. Bartender."

"No, thank you." The sheriff flared his nostrils a little, offended. His squared shoulders got squarer and he poked his chest out beneath his incorruptible white shirt. "I only wanted to say, I hope there won't be any trouble, Mr. Gault."

Jesse guessed that was as assertive as he was going to get. "I don't plan on starting any," he said in the creepy whisper. "But when it comes my way, I always finish it."

They stared at each other for about an hour and a half, until the sheriff's Adam's apple started bobbing up and down behind his string tie and his eyes started to water. He touched the brim of his hat with an upright forefinger. "I'll say good evening to you." Jesse kept quiet. Sheriff Leaver turned around and walked out of Rogue's Tavern with as much dignity, under the circumstances, as a man could hope for.

As first meetings with the law went, Jesse figured that one had gone all right.

Gradually people started to mutter and then to talk, and pretty soon the noise level in the saloon was back to normal. Jesse took a deck of cards out of his pocket and laid out a four-card game of solitaire he'd invented, wishing Ham would come back and talk to him. He pretended he'd known Glendoline was there all along, but really he didn't notice her until she ran her fingers inside the back of his collar. "Hey, honey," she breathed boozily in his ear.

He grunted, debating whether to ask her to sit down. In truth, he was a little disappointed in Glendoline. The sheriff appeared to have a case on her, but she wasn't giving him the time of day. Jesse wouldn't be surprised if she laughed at the upright lawman behind his back—men like Leaver invited that reaction from some women. Well, it was none of his business. He swung his boots off the table and muttered, "You might as well—"

"Glen, would it be too much to ask you to take care of those men at the back table? The ones with their tongues hanging out because nobody's brought them a drink in the last forty minutes?"

Glendoline blinked dimly across the way. "Those guys? Oh, sure, Cady. Be right back," she told Jesse with a flirtatious wave and strolled away, swinging her skinny behind.

Cady rolled her eyes slightly, subtly; you wouldn't have noticed it if you weren't staring at her closely. Which was how Jesse was staring at her. He'd seen better-looking women before, but not too many. Anyway, it wasn't only how she looked right now that made it hard to take his eyes off her. It was this dolled-up Cady *in combination* with the one he'd met this afternoon, the freckle-faced girl in a faded blouse and an old felt hat. How did women do that? Some women, not all; Glen, for instance, in bib overalls and a kerchief wouldn't have gotten a rise out of him. Ah, but McGill, she was another story. He wanted to see her in other getups, other styles. What did she look like in church, for instance, or the general store? First thing in the morning?

"Mr. Gault, you're scaring off my customers."

He glanced behind her and saw it was true: half the saloon had emptied out when the sheriff left. The scrawny, cadaverous fellow he'd seen earlier was back at the bar, though. Jesse accidentally caught his eye. The man stopped with a glass halfway to his mouth, set it down with a clatter, threw a coin on the bar, and hightailed it out the swinging doors like dogs were gnawing on his ass.

Interesting.

Jesse stood up and waved his hand at the other chair. "Have a seat, Miss Cady?" She looked back and forth between the chair and him. *No, thanks* was on the tip of her tongue, he could tell. "To prove to 'em I don't bite," he threw in, jerking his chin at the handful of customers she had left.

She thought about that, nodded, and sat.

"Drink?"

"No."

Reaching for the bottle to pour one for himself, he missed and knocked it over with the backs of his knuckles. McGill caught and righted it before too much bourbon spilled on the table. *Goddamn eyepatch*, he cursed for the thousandth time; damn thing threw off his perspective. He felt like an ass, but the blunder did have one side benefit: he got to see her tattoo again. Not for long, just a flash of bluish bird against white skin, but it was worth it.

"Mr. Gault, I have to ask you a favor."

'Name it."

"Don't take this the wrong way," she cautioned, plucking nervously at the links of a silver bracelet on her wrist. "Nothing personal, but would you mind moving to another hotel?" He lifted an eyebrow, and she started talking faster. "The Dobb House is right up the street—you probably passed it on your way in. It's a lot quieter, plus it's got a restaurant, you'd—"

"I like noise. A saloon makes me feel right at home."

She looked at him speculatively. "Then you'd probably like Wylie's. In fact, you'd love Wylie's. It's bigger. Much noisier. Yeah, I think Wylie's is definitely the saloon for you."

He grinned. "Then I could scare away *his* customers."

She gave him a half smile, not denying it. "You really don't work for him?"

"Never met the man."

"Then who did hire you?"

Time to clam up, get evil. She was getting too bold, too free with her questions, she wasn't nearly scared enough of him. But he just said, "How do you know anybody hired me? Maybe you shouldn't jump to conclusions."

She raised an eyebrow of her own and didn't answer.

He reached for one of his thin black cigarettes. He'd taken to rolling them ahead of time, without witnesses, because he was still all thumbs at it; it took him five minutes to do one, concentrating hard and using both eyes. Sticking it in the corner of his mouth, he got a wooden match from another pocket. This move he was good at: with great nonchalance,

he flicked his thumbnail across the head, and it fired
up in one try. Staring into McGill's direct, dark-eyed
gaze, he held the match to the cigarette tip and inhaled. Nothing. He inhaled some more. Still nothing.
Turning his head a fraction, so he could see with his
working eye what the hell he was doing, he realized
he had the match a good inch down and to the left
of the cigarette.

Ow. "Shit."

He dropped the match and shook his stinging fingers. When he blew on the still-flaming match, he
spit the cigarette out on the table. He picked the
glowing match up—*ow*—and dropped it in the ash-
tray, brushing ash off the table with the side of his
hand. Retrieving his unlit cigarette, he thought about
throwing it across the room.

He finally got up the heart to look at Cady. She
stared at him without blinking, almost without expression. Almost. Was she smiling? No, but she
looked like she was trying hard not to.

He stuck the goddamn cigarette back in his pocket
and pulled his hat down over his eyes, his absolutely
meanest look according to the mirror he occasionally
practiced in front of. He ought to say something vicious now, put the fear of Gault back into her. Too
bad he couldn't think of anything.

"How did you hurt your eye?" she asked interestedly.

She'd never have dared ask him that before. He'd
lost a lot of ground, bad guy-wise, but somehow he
didn't really regret it. "The war."

"You must've been very young. *Very* young."

Yeah, about nine. "War makes you grow up fast," he whispered. "Sure I can't interest you in a drink?"

"No, thanks, I don't drink. Maybe a beer on a hot day," she elaborated, "but that's it."

Since they were being so chatty, he said, "Mind if I ask how you got in your current line of work, Miss McGill?"

"What's wrong with it?" she said, bristling.

"Nothing. Not a damn thing."

"I inherited the place."

"Your father?"

"No, a friend."

"Ah. A friend."

She smiled at him cynically. "Maybe you shouldn't jump to conclusions, either, Mr. Gault."

Immediately he was sorry for using that slick, knowing tone. He didn't want McGill smiling at him cynically.

The little boy, Ham, came over at just the right moment. "Hey," he said shyly, leaning against Cady's chair. Jesse winked at him. He looked pretty brave with Cady's hand resting on the back of his neck, but his eyes on Jesse were still wide as half dollars.

"Hey," Jesse returned. "Look what I found on the floor just now. I don't know how you missed it when you were sweeping."

"Whose is it?" Ham asked, staring at the quarter Jesse laid on his palm.

"Well, I reckon it's yours now."

"Golly! Thanks, Mr. Gault."

"Don't thank me. Finders keepers."

Cady, he noticed, was looking at him with soft eyes, which was a first. And what eyes they were, when they weren't guarded and suspicious. Dark warm brown, true brown, the color of polished saddle leather. You could fall right in those eyes and make yourself real comfortable.

"Did you get your meal and your bath, Mr. Gault?"

He roused himself to say yes and tell her about the steak dinner he'd enjoyed at Jacques'. Ham hung on his every word, and Jesse thought of himself at his age, when his sister had whispered to him in Sunday school once that Sister Mary Aloysius was just like a regular person—she ate food, slept in a bed, went to the privy, *everything*. Gault the gunfighter was a legend to Ham, a myth right up there with Johnny Appleseed or Wild Bill Hickok. And yet the legend ate rib-eye in the restaurant across the street, and got naked to take a bath in the back room of Cuomo's barbershop. Jesse sympathized with his amazement.

"If you're still looking for a poker game," Cady said, "those boys over there play for pretty fair stakes. They start every night around ten or so. They're not high rollers, but the play's square. I don't put up with any brace games in my place."

"That's good to know." She looked like she didn't believe him, but it was true. He was a pretty good poker player, but a lousy cheat.

"Then of course, there's always blackjack." She smiled, daring him.

"I don't think so," he said, smiling back.

"No?"

"Don't think I'd care for the odds."

"Never know till you try."

"I make it a point never to play against the house."

"It's riskier," she conceded. "But if you win, the payoff's a lot bigger."

They just looked at each other for a while. Something fun was going on under this conversation, and it wasn't blackjack. Even Ham could tell.

"Well," said McGill, and pushed back her chair. He could swear she looked reluctant. He'd made headway, considering she'd sat down in the first place to ask him to leave. He wished she'd stay longer; except for Ham, he hadn't talked to anybody for this long in weeks.

"Don't suppose you'd care to show me around the town tomorrow, would you, Miss McGill?"

What a boneheaded move. The expression on her face brought him back to earth with a thud. She got up fast, remembering all of a sudden who she was dealing with. "No, sorry," she muttered, not looking sorry at all, "I'm busy tomorrow."

"Tomorrow's Saturday," Ham pointed out. "What you busy doing, Miz Cady?"

"Things."

"What things?"

She took in an exasperated breath. "Important things."

Jesse stuck his feet up on the chair she'd just left. "Never mind," he said carelessly. "I just remembered, I got important things to do, too."

Now she looked uncomfortable. Regretful? "Well,"

she repeated. He didn't help her out, just glared at her with his evil eye. " 'Scuse me," she finally said, and went away.

Soon after that, Ham deserted him, too. Jesse thought about getting drunk, just for the hell of it, then decided it wasn't worth it. In a foul mood, he threw money on the table and walked outside for some fresh air.

This was the quiet end of town. Down the street to his right, a few faint drunken shouts sounded from time to time—Wylie's customers, probably—but for the most part Paradise had gone to bed at a decent, law-abiding hour. A sliver of new moon hung over the church steeple like a platinum comma, still too thin to shed much light. He strolled to the railing at the edge of the board sidewalk in the black shadow the porch roof cast. He didn't notice the man leaning against the upright post until the tip of his cigar glowed in the dark, and by then they were almost side by side. "Evening," Jesse muttered absently, resting his hands on top of his guns and taking in a deep breath of the clean night air.

The man didn't answer. His slowness in turning drew attention more than any quick move would have. Unwillingness showed in every line of his body, every deliberate inch he turned. He moved as if he was greeting the devil, or his own certain death. In a spill of light from the saloon, Jesse finally recognized him: the gaunt-faced man at the bar. The one who kept trying to avoid him.

"Doc," he whispered cautiously, remembering the

bartender calling him that. He slipped a cigarette out of his pocket. ''Got a match?''

It took forever, but the doctor, if that's what he was, finally fumbled a match out of his pocket and lit it on the porch railing. His right hand shook so badly, he had to use his left to steady it. He was clean-shaven and pale as death, with black hair growing straight back from a high forehead. In the brief flare of the match, his eyes gleamed eerily from the shadows of his sharp-boned, corpselike face.

Jesse took a deep drag on his cigarette and waited.

It didn't take long. ''I haven't had a drink in eight months,'' Doc announced in a low voice, staring up at the moon instead of at Jesse. ''Since that night. Not one drop.''

A long silence.

''Did he tell you she might've died anyway?''

Jesse kept quiet.

''No, I reckon not. It's true, though. Even if I'd gotten there on time, even if I'd been sober through the whole labor, she probably wouldn't have made it. The child . . .'' He hunched his shoulders, holding on to the rail with both hands. ''The cord was around its neck, it might've been dead already. That happens sometimes. Jeffers knew that, knows that, but he . . . well, no sense telling you what he's like.'' He straightened up with slow arthritic movements. ''How'd you find me?''

Jesse said nothing.

Doc's long, thin upper lip lifted in a sneer of pure contempt. ''Proud of yourself, Mr. Gault? Like the way you make your living? I made a bad mistake once, but at least I was trying to save a life. You . . ." He turned his head and spat in the street.

Jesse didn't move and he didn't speak. He couldn't think of anything to say.

Doc backed up against the rail again. The fight went out of him; he wilted, folded up on himself. "How do you do it?" he asked disinterestedly. "Shoot me in the back? Challenge me to a duel?" He laughed, a rough, ugly sound. "I could've made it easy for you a couple of times. Not that long ago. Done it myself, I mean," he explained with a sick grin. "Now . . . tell you the truth, I don't want to die. That make it harder for you? Or better? Not that I give a good goddamn."

Jesse said, "Listen."

"No, you listen, you son of a bitch. Look here— this is what I've got. A hundred and seventy dollars. Took it out of the bank today when I heard you were here. Every cent I own. I was going to send it—well, never mind what I was going to do with it. It's not much, but I figure it's more than what my life's worth. If you'll take it, I'll be gone by morning." When Jesse didn't move, the doctor slammed the wad of bills down on the rail in front of him. "What's it to you? Jeffers won't know. Maybe you just *want* to kill me. Or you want to hear me beg first, that it? Well, you can—"

"I'm not here for you."

"What?"

"You've made a mistake. I don't know any Jeffers."

He had to look away when the older man started

to tremble. Holding on to the railing, Doc stumbled over to the steps and dropped down on the bottom one, thin legs seeming to give out under him. With his elbows on his knees, he stared at the ground between his feet. His shoulders shook as if he was laughing, but he didn't make any sound.

Jesse took the money and set it down beside him. For a long time neither of them said anything. Then Jesse spoke quietly, not looking at the doc but straight ahead, at the shadowy storefronts across the street. "I guess you made a mistake once. None of my business, but it sounds like you haven't finished paying for it. Inside, I mean. I don't know anything about you, but if you came here to . . . work it off or something, maybe start over, I'm saying that's fine by me. None of my business. And what you just told me—it never happened. We never talked. We never even met."

Very slowly the doc raised his head and looked at him. There was color in his face for the first time, and his dark, sunken eyes glittered. With tears? "I—"

"Well, g'night," Jesse muttered, backing up, panicky. Embarrassment flooding through him felt like scalding water. "Gonna take a walk, stretch my legs. See you around." He felt like running, but forced himself to stride off at a reasonable pace. But he had to get away before the doc said the two words that would've just about killed him: *Thank you.*

Three

"Yup, Peg's just fine, Mr. Gault, fine and dandy. Gave him oats and clover like you said, and no timothy. He—"

"What did you call my horse?"

The liveryman, who went by the name of Nestor Yeakes, stopped dead with a plug of tobacco halfway to his open mouth. "Peg? I thought you—"

"He didn't hear you call him that, did he?"

"Why—why—yeah, he did, 'cause I was brushin' 'im, talkin' soft, you know, tryin'—"

"And he didn't *kill* you?"

"What? What? No, he—"

"Mister, you are one lucky son of a bitch."

"I am?"

Jesse ducked through the dark doorway and moved down the dusty corridor to Pegasus' stall, while behind him Nestor hurried to keep up. "Last man to call my horse P-e-g only called him that once. After that, he didn't call anybody anything." Poor Peg, he thought; it'd hurt his feelings to hear Jesse slander him like that.

"Hey, fella," he crooned, and the stallion bobbed

his handsome black head three times over the stall door before setting his chin on Jesse's shoulder and snuffling in his ear. *Beautiful boy*, he'd have called him, and *big black baby*, if he'd been alone. Baby talk would spoil his image, though. Not to mention Peg's.

"No timothy?" he said in a warning tone, running his hands down the sides of the horse's sleek, muscular neck.

"No timothy!" Nestor swore, spitting on the floor for emphasis.

"Well, he looks good," he finally begrudged. "Looks real good. I think he's happy here. Think that's a happy look in his eye? Right there, see that gleam?"

"Yessir, I did notice that! Fact, I caught him smilin' right after his ground oats yestiddy."

Jesse checked the liveryman's round, beard-stubbled face, wondering whose leg was getting pulled now. "Take him out for a run for me today. In the afternoon, after it cools down."

"You want me to ride this horse?" he asked, pointing, as if Jesse might be talking about some other horse.

"You ride, don't you?"

"Yeah, sure, but—"

"Just remember what I said, and you'll be okay."

"Don't call him P-e-g?" Nestor whispered, wary.

"Right. Not if you value your life. He's smart as hell and he's got a lot of heart, but that's the one thing . . ." He trailed off, squinting in the dimness at the stall next to Peg's. "What the hell is that?"

Nestor shuffled his feet, stared at the ground, and

spat again. "Horse," he mumbled. "Name's Bell
Flower or something like that. She—" He jerked his
head up when Jesse made a fast movement in his
direction. "I didn't do it! I was startin' to put some
salve on her when you come in!"

Jesse shouldered him out of the way, swearing
softly in a steady, wondering stream. Without thinking, he lifted his hand toward the big chestnut horse
in the next stall, and the animal threw up her head
and screamed, half rearing until the rope on her hal-
ter caught and held, jerking her back to the ground.
"Easy, easy," Jesse soothed her, "you're all right
now, big girl, easy there, nobody's gonna hurt you,"
and so on in a low murmur, until the chestnut's ears
went up and her breathing slowed. "Who did it?"
Jesse asked Nestor, grazing with his fingertips the
bloody, foam-flecked corners of the mare's mouth.
Then he saw the raw, blood-crusted gouges on her
flanks, and started in swearing again.

Nestor hesitated, but only for a second. "It's Lyndon Cherney's horse. He got 'er in San Francisco
back around Easter time. Paid a thousand dollars for
'er, I heard. She's a blood horse, s'pose to have Arab
in her."

"Who's Lyndon Cherney?"

Nestor flinched at his tone, but answered promptly.
"Vice president of the Mercantile Bank. Important
fella. Town father."

"He did this?" The mare's gory sides and the
blood around her tender mouth had been caused by
a vicious rider, not an incompetent one. He smoothed
his hand down the animal's fluttering shoulder, try-

ing to soothe the nervousness out of her, get rid of the wild look in her white-rimmed eyes.

"He ain't much of a horseman," Nestor hedged. He bit off a new chaw, fixing Jesse with a doubtful eye. "Thing is," he said, standing up straighter, as if he'd come to a decision. "Thing is, he's mean. Broke the horse he had before this one. White and gray gelding, a real beauty. Claimed he didn't run right for him and broke 'im down. Ended up selling him for nothing to the meat man. Damn shame, but he weren't any good by then. Peckerhead done broke 'im down. And if this one ain't headed that way, I don't know horseflesh."

"Where is he?"

"Cherney?" Nestor backed up a step. He gave Jesse a quick up-and-down, and came to another decision. This one brought a glitter to his faded blue eyes. "He'd be up at the bank by now. Done had his morning ride and changed into his banker clothes. Reckon he's up there countin' his money."

"Not for much longer," Jesse said, and his dead man's voice not only didn't scare Nestor this time, it made him downright gleeful.

"Give 'im hell," he called as Jesse strode off down the dusty length of the stable toward the doorway. "Give 'im one for me! Shoot 'is balls off, one at a time! Tell 'im to—"

"You take care of that horse," Jesse cut him off, glancing back over his shoulder.

"Yes, *sir*!" It was hard to be sure in the half-light, but it looked like Nestor saluted.

The sun had shone all morning, but clouds from

the west were blowing in and fat drops of water
had begun to thud in the street, setting off little dust
explosions. Women put up their parasols and men
jammed on their hats; people who had been strolling
before started to run. Jesse knew where the bank was
because he'd passed it riding in yesterday. A yellow
brick building with a stone portico, it occupied one
of the four corners in the middle of town, where
Noble Fir Street crossed Main. The rain started in
earnest, so he jogged toward the sidewalk, heading
for shelter under the awning of Baker's Canvas &
Tents, Hunting & Trail Outfitters. He barely noticed
the three men loitering in front of the store until one
of them pushed off the clapboard wall and slouched
to the middle of the boardwalk. Jesse took one look
at him, and knew. Shit. It had to happen—it always
did—but he'd been hoping it wouldn't happen for a
while yet.

"Hey, Mr. Gault, how you doing?"

Jesse called them jokers, these punks who had to
make an impression on him, one way or the other,
or die trying. This one was slight and bandy-legged,
sandy-haired and mean-faced. He tongued a toothpick from one corner of his mouth to the other, and
Jesse thought, *A toothpick—now, why didn't I think of
that*? He could see that it gave a man that mean,
careless look he was always after, plus you didn't
have to roll it, light it, or smoke it. Well, too late
now. Gault smoked thin black cigarettes, and everybody knew it.

"Come on, Warren," one of the joker's sidekicks

muttered, backing up, flashing a weak, apologetic grin.

"Shut up, Clyde." The one called Warren never took his eyes off Jesse. "So, Mr. Gault, you like our little town? Nice quiet place, real peaceable. That's how we like it."

Jesse whispered, "I didn't catch your name, friend."

"Maybe that's because I didn't throw it."

The third man snickered, and Jesse slowly swiveled his head in his direction. Their eyes locked. The man's face, swarthy before, lost all color.

"Warren, let's go," the second man, Clyde, said again.

Warren ignored him. "I hear you're pretty fast with a gun, Mr. Gault."

Jesse said nothing. He was thinking how sick he was of that opening line—"I heard you're pretty fast with a gun," or some blockheaded variation of it. Behind and in front of him, people were either scurrying away or gathering in fascination.

"Some say I'm pretty fast, too," Warren pressed on, undaunted. "Real fast."

Jesse unfurled his evilest smile, like he'd just been handed some nasty, disgusting present he'd wanted all his life. "That's good," he whispered. "I'm mighty glad to hear that. Because I haven't met a man with a fast gun in eleven days, *Warren*. That much time goes by, I get to feeling itchy. Off kilter, you know what I mean?"

Warren slowly lifted his right hand to pull his jacket away and uncover his gun. From the butt, it looked like a double-action .41. Small—built for little hands—but fast and deadly accurate. People who hadn't gotten out of the way by now dove for cover.

Jesse showed his teeth. "That's a pretty little pop-gun you got there. You want to step out in the street and show me how it works?" His heart was racing; all his energy, every cell, was concentrated on keeping his good eye focused and unblinking on Warren the joker's sharp, ratty features. Sweat trickled down between his shoulder blades; he was glad for the mustache that hid the sweat on his upper lip.

Then Warren swallowed—Jesse saw his throat contract, his jaw muscles clamp. The mean smile faltered and the beady eyes darted away.

This was when he always let them off, gave them some graceful out, while his own insides quaked with relief. But this two-bit joker irritated him. He wasn't only a punk, he was a coward to boot.

"I asked you a question," Jesse whispered, taking a deliberate step toward him, then another. "You want to show me how that little bitty .41 works? Or are you gonna shut your mouth and stay out of my way for the rest of your stinking life? What's it gonna be, *Warren*?"

Again the third man snickered, but this time it was a mistake. Fast as a snake, Warren whirled and cold-cocked the bastard, catching him on the point of the chin and sending him crashing back against the wall.

Watching him slide to the ground, Jesse suppressed a sympathetic groan but didn't move, except to flex his fingers over his gun handles. Facing him again, Warren's cheeks turned apple-red from frustration. Jesse braced, his mind going blank in sudden panic. The son of a bitch was going to draw!

But then—he didn't. His ready stance stayed the same, but the light went out of his eyes. Just like that, like a vicious dog that turns tail when you run at it, Warren went from killer back to coward.

This time Jesse didn't give him a chance to change his mind. He walked straight toward him, feinted left at the last second, and deliberately smacked him on the right shoulder as he passed. He could hear him suck in an outraged breath, but he didn't stop, didn't look back. He kept walking, moving at that slow, infuriatingly casual pace that drove men like Warren crazy, while inside his heart felt like it might punch through his chest and flip out on the sidewalk.

He'd won again. One of these days, though, sure as shooting, Gault's luck was going to run out.

It was cool inside the First Mercantile Bank & Trust Company. Cool and dim because of the rain, and quiet, like a high-class library. Two of the tellers were busy with customers, but the third gave Jesse a brisk nod, telling him to come forward.

"Lyndon Cherney—is he here? I want to see him." He said it straight out, no whispering. The encounter with Warren had jolted him; he wasn't all the way back to being Gault yet.

The teller's face paled as recognition dawned. "And your name, sir?" he inquired, fatalistic—the way you'd ask, "Is he dead?" about a man who's been hanging from a gallows for a day and a half.

Jesse said his name.

The teller pivoted and skulked off, to a closed door behind a low railing that stretched across the back of the bank. A full minute later he reappeared, looking ill.

"I'm very sorry, sir, very sorry, but Mr. Cherney is not able to see you just now. He, ah, he's in conference."

In conference? If it was true, all the better—there could be a witness to the conversation Jesse had in mind. "Thanks," he told the teller, who smiled with relief until Jesse stepped over the little railing and strode across the marble floor, spurs jingling, to Cherney's closed door.

"Oh! Sir? Please, Mr. Gault—"

Jesse shoved the door open just as a man on the other side reached out to lock it. Couldn't be anyone but Cherney—he was alone in the room. Guess he'd lied about the conference.

"Morning," Jesse said pleasantly, simultaneously backing Cherney toward his big oak desk and giving the door a savage kick that nearly shattered the frosted glass window. *Slam!* Cherney jumped like he'd been shot. Jesse gave him a little tap on the chest and he fell back against the desk, plump buttocks sitting on it. "You irritate me, Lyndon. I don't like slimy little bugs like you." A memory of the bloodied mare made his anger genuine, no act this time. "What I like to do is squash 'em. Step on 'em and watch 'em bleed." He grinned ghoulishly.

Fear made the banker's light blue eyes pop behind rimless spectacles. He uttered gasping noises, mouth opening and closing, guppylike, while he shook his manicured hands in the air, as if erasing some huge, invisible mistake. "It wasn't my fault," he finally got out. "I'm telling you, it wasn't my fault."

Jeez, thought Jesse, *news travels fast in Paradise*. "Not your fault? So you were just having a bad day? Decided to take it out on—"

"I didn't have any choice!"

Jesse swore at him, on the verge of losing his temper. This dandified little twerp was as bad as Warren. No, worse—Warren only beat up on people, not defenseless animals.

Cherney cringed and flung up his hands again. "He started it," he said in a crying whine. "What I took was peanuts compared to him."

"Compared to—" Who? he almost said. He bit his tongue in the nick of time. "Him? Compared to him? You really think so?"

"I'm telling you!"

"What are you telling me?" He eased back a little so the banker could sit up straight. He should've recognized the signs—God knew he'd seen them often enough—but in his anger he'd missed them. A lot more was going on here than met the eye.

"I'm telling you, I didn't do anything he didn't do."

"So what's that to me?"

Cherney straightened his tie with a shaky hand, straightened his diamond stickpin. He had dark yellow hair the shade of a sepia photograph; whatever he put on it made it lie flat on either side of a sharp white center part. "You think I'm the only one who's been skimming? Ha! Wylie's got fake accounts all over the place. Anyway, I only stole from him," he added, shooting his cuffs with dignity. "*He* stole from everybody."

Wylie. Well, well, well.

"My God! Are you going to shoot me?"

Jesse had absentmindedly rested his hand on one of his Colts. He fingered the butt suggestively. "I'm thinking about it."

"I won't draw against you," Cherney blurted, stiff-lipped, starting the hand-waving thing again. "Please, I'm a banker, not a gunfighter. If you draw on me, it'll be murder."

Jesse sneered.

"I'll pay you. How much is Wylie giving you to kill me? I'll double it. I'll *triple* it. Please—what do you care? I'll open an account for you, put money in it, whatever you want."

"And then what?"

"Then—I'll go away!"

"What do I tell Wylie?" He kept sneering, but added a thoughtful look.

"Who cares? You aren't afraid of him! Tell him to go to hell."

"Hmm." He stroked his mustache and squinted his eye, exaggerating the thoughtfulness. He kept Cherney in suspense for a minute or two longer, then growled, "What kind of money are we talking about?"

Cherney was so relieved he collapsed, went all boneless and saggy; it was like watching a suit of clothes fall off a hanger. "Anything," he mumbled weakly; even his lips were flabby. "Twenty, twenty-five thousand. Just name it."

"That's what you stole from the bank?"

He nodded miserably.

"Where'd you stash it?"

"Accounts. It's still here, just in different names, places. Nobody's missed it."

"I'll take a list of all those names and places."

He hung his head. "Right."

"So how much did you swipe from Wylie?"

"What?"

"Him personally, not the bank."

He started to deny it, then gave up, shrugging. "Not much. Four or five."

"Four or five thousand dollars?"

"Yes."

Payday. "Okay, here's the deal. You got a family, Lyndon?"

"I beg your pardon?"

Jesse hated exiling a family man. "Wife? Kids?"

"No. I'm divorced."

Figured. "All right. Soon as I walk out of here, you put four thousand dollars in an account in my name. Got that?"

"Yes, yes," he said eagerly, "it's not a problem, I can do it in ten minutes."

"Good, because that's all the time you've got. That gives you about nine hours of daylight to go home and pack your things. By ten o'clock tonight, you're gone."

"I'm gone. You won't regret this, Mr.—"

"And pack light, because you'll be on foot."

"I'll be—what?"

"That's the last part of the deal. Your horse stays here—I'm liberating it."

"My *horse*?"

"I want her sale papers and pedigree. Put 'em in an envelope and leave it with the bartender at Rogue's Tavern on your way out of town. And you never ride a horse again."

He started to sputter. "But—I—but you can't—"

"From now on you're a carriage-riding man, Lyndon. I hear of you sitting on top of anything four-legged, I come after you. Understand me? And we won't be making any deals—I'll just kill you. You getting this? Tell me you understand."

"I—I—I—understand."

"Good. Now let's go open an account."

Next time, Jesse swore, burning his bottom lip on a sip of the black acid Swensen called coffee, he was going to pay attention to Cady McGill's restaurant recommendations. He belched in between fiery sips, not sure if the "sheepherder's pie" he'd just consumed was going to come back up or stay down there and poison him. "Bleh," he said for the second time to Ham, his new best friend, who rolled his eyes and giggled at him.

"C'mon, Mr. Gault, show 'em to me, please?"

"No."

"Please?"

"No."

"Please?"

"No."

"Jus' one? C'mon, jus' show me one. I won't even touch it, I won't do nothin' but look. Okay? Show me one?"

Jesse swore a long, soft stream of mild expletives while Ham grinned at him, tickled. Not only had he lost all fear of Gault, now he liked to tease Gault, play little verbal jokes on him, cornball riddles and puns that Jesse pretended to walk into blindly. They always sent the kid into gales of laughter.

"All right, but only so you'll shut up."

"Hot damn!"

"And if you tell anybody—"

"I won't." He squirmed closer on the bench they were sitting on, half hidden from the other diners at Swensen's Good Eats & Drinks by the tall back of the booth. His handsome pixie face screwed up in thought. "How come?"

"How come what?"

"How come I cain't tell anybody?"

"Because it's a secret."

"Oh." That made it even better. By the time Jesse reluctantly reached for one of his Colts, Ham was squirming with anticipation.

"This is the Peacemaker," he told him, placing the gun, butt first, on his two small, flat palms. "That's the Mexican eagle emblem on the grip. Real ivory. Pretty, isn't it? Single-action .45. The best gun Colt ever made."

"Wow." Awe wasn't a strong enough word for the look on his face; the kid was dumbstruck. "Oh, oh, wow," he kept saying, holding the heavy gun like a priest holding a chalice. "Wow."

"Open it up. Flick that little latch with your thumb."

The cartridge cylinder swung out, and Ham spun it around, carefully checking all six empty chambers. "I like that noise," he said, and Jesse grunted in agreement. That clipped, metallic *chink* of revolving chambers was a satisfying sound. "Khhew, khhew!" Ham pointed the Colt at the empty wall across the way and pretended to sight and shoot. "Khhew!"

"Get him?"

"Right between the eyes."

"Good shootin'."

"Wish I could draw. You teach me to draw, Mr. Gault?" He laid the side of the revolver against his thigh, jerked it up, and blasted at the wall. The gun, which was longer than his forearm, made him look even punier. When he blew imaginary smoke across the top of the muzzle, Jesse laughed out loud.

"Who would you draw on?" he asked, slouching down in the booth, folding his arms.

"Bad guys."

"Like who?"

"Bank robbers and cattle rustlers. And men who call my daddy a name. Men who give Miss Cady lip."

Jesse nodded thoughtfully. "So you'd just kill 'em?"

"After we done fought fair an' square. Or . . ." He sighted at the wall again. "Maybe I just wound 'em. Khhew! Shoot at they hand or they leg."

"That might be better."

" 'Cause then they be scared o' me an' quit doin' bad things.''

"There you go. And that way you'd never have . . ."

A whirl of powder-blue skirts, fluttering hands, and flashing dark eyes diverted him. Cady came at him like a small, compact tornado, taking a bead on the object in the path of her concentrated fury. Jesse was the object.

"What the hell are you doing? What is wrong with you? Are you out of your mind?" The questions were rhetorical, because each time he tried to answer she cut him off after half a syllable. 'Give me that," she snapped at Ham, snatching the Colt out of his hand. Her anger doubled, tripled, kept multiplying as she stared in disbelief at the revolver—which began to look wicked and deadly, practically obscene on top of her soft pink palm. Jesse reached for it, but she jerked away and clapped it down on the tabletop instead, as if the possibility of actual physical contact with him was too disgusting to risk. *What the hell were you thinking of?"*

"I—"

"He's seven years old!"

"He—"

"What kind of man gives a gun to a child?"

"It's not—"

"Shame on you. *Shame!"*

Jesse hung his head. "It's not loaded," he muttered in defense.

"Not loaded?" She stopped short of screeching, but he flinched anyway. "Come on, Ham."

"But, Miz Cady—"

"Miss Cady, nothing." She took hold of his elbow and yanked. She had parting words for Jesse. "You give this child a gun again, Mr. Gault, and you'll have me to deal with. *I will not tolerate it.*" With a furious twirl of skirts, she was gone.

He stared down the smattering of diners who dared look back and forth between him and the door she'd just flounced through. Damn her and the horse she rode in on. How was he ever going to live this down? He reached automatically for a black cigarette and stuck it in the side of his mouth. Lit it in one try. Blew badass smoke at the ceiling. Hoped nobody noticed his hands were shaking.

Four

"Evenin', Cady. Say, ain't you best hurry up? Gettin' on for five, y'know."

Cady shook the hair out of her face and nodded to Levi in the bar mirror she was polishing. "I know, I'm hurrying." Right now the saloon was sparsely populated, only Jersey Stan and a couple of hands from the Sullivan ranch. But in half an hour the Saturday night crowd would start trickling in, and Cady tried never to let those relatively big spenders see her in occupations like mirror polishing. Or table cleaning or window washing. It would spoil the illusion. In public, at least, she tried to live up to her customers' fantasies, and as far as she could tell, their fantasies of her ranged all over from mother to sweetheart to priest, not to mention madam and cardsharp. But not domestic servant.

She gave a few swipes to the bottles of booze lined up on tiers in front of the mirror, then started on the bar.

"Here, I'll do that," Levi protested, trying to tie on his apron with one hand and snatch the rag from her with his other.

"No, it's okay. See that box behind the door? Came in the mail today. I think it's the new glasses, so you be unpacking them while I finish here."

She waited until he dragged the box behind the bar, slit it open, and began to unwrap the glasses inside before saying, "Levi, I don't want to worry you, and I'm sure there really isn't anything to worry about, but I think you should know. I saw Ham today with that gunfighter. In Swensen's. They were sitting in a back booth together like trail buddies, having a high old time."

Crouched down behind the box, Levi glanced back at her and said, "Hmpf."

"And, Levi?"

"Ma'am?"

"Mr. Gault was showing Ham his gun. His *gun*," she repeated when he only hmpfed again.

"Mm mm mm. That boy," he said, shaking his head. "I'll swan."

Cady put her hands on her hips, nonplussed. "I thought you'd be mad as hell. Goodness, Levi, don't you even care that Ham's hanging around with a hired killer?"

"Well, if that's what he be."

"What?"

He stood up, six feet three inches of lanky bones and beautiful brown skin. "And I spec' that's what he be, 'cause that's what everybody say. I saw him with Ham last night, though, and I couldn't see no meanness in him. Maybe he a killer, but I b'lieve he got a sof' spot for chirn."

"Well, but—even so, even if he does—is that the point?"

"What the point?"

"Maybe he *dotes* on children, but still— Maybe Jesse James was the world's best father, but would you have wanted him raising Ham?"

Levi chuckled.

She shook her head, bewildered. "I'm telling you, Levi, there was Ham at Swensen's restaurant, taking pot shots at the wall!"

"*What?*"

"Pretending, I mean."

"Oh, pretending."

"Playing with that man's six-shooter like it was a toy."

"I don't like that."

"No. I grabbed him and got him right out of there. And I'd've smacked his skinny behind, but I figured you'd want to do that yourself."

Levi said, "Well," noncommittally, and went back to stacking glasses.

Cady shook her head some more. She couldn't get over his attitude. Levi was the kindest, most loving father she'd ever known, but he was strict, too. Strict and principled and upright: Ham might sweep up and do chores in a saloon, but if Levi ever caught him saying curse words or spitting or acting like a ruffian in any way, his punishments were quick and predictable. So why wasn't he more irate about his son's friendship with an out-and-out gunman? It didn't make any sense to her.

"*The Five K-Khan*— What is this, Levi? *The Five*

Khandha of Bud—Budd—" Glendoline gave up and put the book back on the bar. "What is that, Greek?"

"You're late," Cady said automatically, as she did every day when Glen decided to mosey in to work. She picked up Levi's book, but had no better luck than Glen at pronouncing the title. *The Five Khandha of Buddha.* She looked up at him questioningly.

"No, it ain't Greek," he said with dignity. "It's about Buddha."

"What's Buddha? Ohhh," Glendoline said wisely, wriggling her blond eyebrows. "Oh, *I* know. Buddha's a religion, and it just *happens* to be the religion of a certain Chinese lady who lives on Noble Fir Street. Over her daddy's laundry," she threw in, in case anybody wasn't sure which Chinese lady she was referring to.

Levi plucked the book out of Cady's hand and stuck it under the bar, not looking at either woman. He didn't like to be teased, especially about Lia Chang, so Cady quit grinning at him, at the same time she slipped Glen a good-natured wink.

But then she remembered she was mad at Glen. "I noticed you had a pretty good time last night," she said sourly. "What with one thing and another."

"I did," Glen assured her, patting her ringlets, "why, I surely did. Last night was just plain fun. I swear—"

"Glendoline."

"What? Oh." Comprehension dawned. "You're mad because I sat on Sam Blankenship's lap."

"I didn't even see that." Although it didn't surprise her.

"No?" She put her finger on her cheek, which meant she was thinking hard. "What else did I do?"

Cady could've ticked them off on her fingers: you came in late, you got drunk on the job again, and you left early and went home with Gunther Dewhurt. "I'm talking about you and that gunfighter."

"Mr. Gault? Mmmm," Glen hummed, like a cat purring. "He's dreamy, isn't he?"

"Dreamy? Well, I guess so, if you like hired killers. Glen, when are you going to get some sense? Why in the world . . . oh, hell. Never mind, it's none of my business."

"That's right," Glen agreed tartly. "I know what you're thinking," she mumbled after a snippy little pause, facing the bar mirror to stuff cotton down the bust of her yellow satin dress. "You think I do it on purpose. Go after rotten men and let 'em treat me bad. Well, don't you?"

Cady shrugged. But she thought of the day, eight months ago, when Glendoline first showed up at the Rogue looking for work. She had a split lip and a black eye, and that was only what showed. People were shocked, but not really surprised; most had a suspicion about how Merle Wylie treated women, and Glendoline had worked in his saloon for almost a year—long enough to become a lot more than one of his bar girls. What had surprised everyone was that she'd finally gotten up the gumption to leave him.

"We've had this conversation before," Cady said. "You do what you want on your own time, I won't say a word. But here in my saloon, you go by my rules."

"But I do!" Nobody could do wide-eyed innocence like blond-haired, blue-eyed Glen. No wonder the sheriff was in love with her.

Which reminded Cady. "You weren't very nice to Tom last night, either."

"I don't know what you're talking about." She finished padding her bodice and looked around for something to drink. "Anyway, I'm as nice to old Lily Leaver as he deserves."

"Why do you call him that when you know he hates it?"

"Huh? I think it's cute."

"Cute. You—" She sighed. They'd gotten off the track. Cady and Glendoline were about the same age, but as far as men went, Glen had eons more experience. So what was it about her that always made Cady feel old, practically grandmotherly? Once she'd put that question to Levi, and he'd answered in two words: "She's stupid." Cady didn't believe she was, though, not really; Glen just didn't *think*.

"We were talking about Gault," she reminded them both. "It's looking like he might stick around for a while."

"You think so?" She pinched her cheeks, studying her face in the mirror.

"Yeah, and I don't think you should be cozying up to him. You know what I'm talking about," she said when Glen opened her mouth to utter some wounded protest. "He's dangerous—you only have to look at him to see that. So leave him be, Glen."

Don't take him home with you, she meant, but she didn't say. It wasn't necessary; they really *had* had this conversation before.

"I saw *you* talking to him, too."

"That's beside the point. Shoot, here comes Curly Boggs and all those Witter ranch boys. You take care of them while I get dressed." She untied her apron and threw it on a shelf under the bar.

"I saw you smile at him," Glen called after her. "You even laughed at something he said. I heard you!"

Cady flapped her hand and kept going. "Owner's prerogative," she threw back. It would've made a better exit line if she'd thought Glen had the slightest idea what "prerogative" meant.

In her room, she took a long time deciding what to wear. That wasn't like her; she had eight or nine "saloon dresses," as she thought of them, all in different colors, and normally she just pulled out the one she hadn't worn in the longest time. Now she stared and stared, plucking at a gaudy feathered shoulder or a jet-beaded bodice, dissatisfied. Why all this girlish indecision? She knew, but she didn't care to think about it. She reminded herself too much of Glen.

Finally she yanked out her dark green taffeta and threw it across the bed. She found the green high-heeled shoes she wore with it, and the little fake-emerald tiara thing she sometimes stuck in her hair—men were crazy for jewelry, the flashier the better. She hadn't had time to wash her black fishnet stockings, so she'd have to wear a pair of flesh-colored ones, she guessed, even though they wouldn't be as good with the green dress, which had black lacings across the bosom. The green bracelet that looked like jade, the jet earbobs, her little onyx pinkie ring . . . Was that enough? What about the pale green cameo on a black ribbon around her neck? No, she decided; no. Even if you did deal blackjack in a small-town saloon, it didn't mean you had to decorate every appendage you had with jewelry. Enough was eventually enough.

She undressed behind her screen and put her robe on over her underwear. She had a little time left; she'd bathed earlier, and she'd gotten dressing down to ten minutes flat—which was pretty darn good considering she had no maid. "You move your big fat butt," she said to Boo, who hadn't opened his eyes or even twitched his tail since she'd come into the room. She put her hand on the back of his head—and the cat jumped and squalled as if she'd electrocuted him. "Excuse me," she said to his arched, resentful back. "Terribly sorry, no offense. But it is my chair." He let her pick him up, all fifteen pounds of him, and settle him on her lap, whereupon he yawned, purred, and fell back into a coma.

"Some pet you turned out to be." She ran a finger around his ear, halfheartedly trying to tickle him into wakefulness. He'd appeared on her doorstep last winter, scrawny and scabby, fresh from a fight he'd obviously lost. She'd liked nursing him back to health, and especially his heavy, earnest devotion afterward, when he'd lumbered after her everywhere, a black, constant, overweight shadow. But she'd succeeded too well, because now all he did was sleep in her chair, or in her lap on the rare occasions when he relinquished the chair. "Boo, you are a deep disappointment," she murmured, coaxing a soft purr out of him before he went back to snoring.

She let her head fall against the high back of the padded rocker, closing her eyes, smiling a little. This was nice. In an hour the noise from the saloon would be deafening, but this time of the day it was still nice. Sundays were the best, though. The Rogue closed down for the Sabbath (unlike Wylie's bar, which stayed open all day every day, even Christmas). Sunday mornings she took care of any leftover bookkeeping matters and saw to any emergencies from the night before—broken chairs, shattered mirrors, and the like—and usually by three or so in the afternoon she was free. She didn't go out, didn't ride over to the old River Farm and wander around the orchard—that was strictly a Friday afternoon pleasure. On Sundays she stayed in her room and listened to the quiet. Sat in this chair, propped her feet on her crocheted footrest, lit the tasseled lamp on her piecrust table. Put on her mail-order spectacles and opened a book. Or wrote a letter to the only friend she still kept up with from Portland. Or read the Paradise *Reverberator* she'd saved from Friday, for the local gossip and the smattering of "world news." "Ahhh," she would say from time to time to Boo. "This is the life."

Every great once in a while she'd wonder if she was happy or not, considering that the finest hours in her week were the ones she spent alone in a rocking chair with a cat on her lap. But usually the question didn't trouble her; she was either too busy or too tired, or enjoying too much the respite from business and tiredness, to think about it. And whenever she was seriously blue, which luckily wasn't often, she had a saying that always put whatever was getting her down in the right perspective: *It beats canning salmon.*

Sometimes on her Sunday afternoons she didn't do anything at all, just sat here and gazed around the room. Even after two years, the fact that she owned it and everything in it still amazed her. That was her brass bed and blue-flowered quilt, for example; her two pillows with embroidered sayings on the pillow slips. She owned this old wooden rocker. She owned that Wellington phonograph and the four opera discs she'd played so often they barely sounded like music anymore. This was her window, overlooking the live oak in her postage stamp-size backyard, and her very own cedar-shingled outhouse.

Not that she'd done much to earn them. (She certainly hadn't done what most people *thought* she'd done to earn them.) She'd been nice to a dying old man, that was all. As a result, she now owned everything he'd owned. Last week she'd passed by two ladies staring in the window of Jurgen's Retail-Wholesale Furniture Co., and overheard one of them say to the other, "That sofa's all right, but it's not really to my taste." She'd thought about that all day, and on and off since then, fascinated by the brand-new idea of "taste." Imagine picking out something like a sofa—or a bed, or a rocking chair—according to whether or not it suited your *taste*. How did you know what your taste was? She'd been studying her room, or rather Gus Shlegel's room, in a different light ever since, realizing how masculine it was, and the little ways in which it didn't really suit her. The lady's remark hadn't ruined her pleasure in the room, not at all. But it had set her to thinking.

She jumped when a hard knock sounded at the back door. "Ow." Boo, startled too, dug his claws into her thigh before jumping out of her lap. "*Ow.* Damn it, Boo." She retied her dressing-gown sash and went to the door. "Who is it?" No answer. "Ham, is that you?" She opened the door a crack to peer out. "Ham? Are you—"

"Why, if it ain't Miz Cady." Warren Turley leered at her, at the same time he shoved the door open before she could get her foot in front of it.

"Hey!"

"Hey? That how you greet old friends? Me and Clyde just came by to pay our respects." She stood in his way, but he muscled past her, jostling her aside, grinning the whole time, and sure enough, Clyde Gates was right behind him.

"You two can just march yourselves right out of here. What do you think you're doing? You want a drink, you go around to the front like everybody else. Listen here, Turley—"

"Now, now, Cady, simmer down, we just wanna talk to you. Ain't she looking pretty today, Clyde? And looky here—this what you're wearing tonight? That is one fine—"

"Get your paws off that." She shoved him away

from the bed with her hip, slapping at his hands on her taffeta dress. "Wylie sent you, didn't he?" She kept trying to herd him back toward the open door. It wasn't easy without touching him. She was more mad than scared, but something told her it would be dangerous to touch him.

"Mr. Wylie gave us a message for you, yeah," Clyde said. He was a big, tall, dumb-looking cowboy from someplace like Texas or Oklahoma; she liked him a little better than Warren Turley, which was to say she didn't hate him like the bubonic plague. He worked for Wylie, though, same as Turley, so in no way was he welcome in her bedroom.

"I'm telling you both to clear out right now."

"Or you'll what? Plug us with your peashooter? Where's it at, anyway?" A light came into Turley's squinty little eyes. He had a mean smile to begin with; it got downright diabolical when he started walking toward her. How had Clyde gotten around behind her? "You wearing that peashooter now, Miz Cady?" said Turley, pointy nose twitching. "Let's see if you got it on now."

Cady knew a lot of curse words. She only got a few out before Clyde clapped his hand over her mouth and Turley grabbed her, grinning like the very devil.

"Keep your shirt on," the black-skinned bartender, whose name was Levi, muttered under his breath to the cowboy at the end of the bar, who kept yelling at him to hurry it up, step on it, get a move on. "Impatience," Jesse could have sworn he added while he poured out a glass of beer, "shows up the ego. Patience counteracts egocentricity, because everything is impermanent and substanceless."

"Huh?" said Jesse when Levi moved back over to his side of the bar. "Say what?"

Levi folded his big, bony-knuckled hands on the edge of the bar and looked at him. Jesse stared back, a little unnerved by the bland, half-smiling peacefulness in his face. He looked like he had a secret, something really good, and he might tell you about it or he might not. "Everybody suffers," he said slowly, his voice soft and deep, rumbling. "Suffering doubles when we resist it. You push against something hard enough, your hand hurt. Put your hand *gentle* on a wall or a door, you got no pain. Resisting and wanting—that's where all our suffering come from." He smiled with his whole face, all the straight lines and sharp angles turning up, and Jesse couldn't help smiling back.

"Is that right?"

"Yup."

"Where'd you learn that?"

"From the buddha."

"Bartender!" some drunk called out across the way. "Gimme a whiskey! Move your sorry ass!"

Levi lifted his calm, dark gaze. His smile stayed on, but it looked a little pained. "And sometime," he said even softer, "you want to push your hand real hard on somebody *head*, and fuck suffering."

Jesse chuckled. "Wait," he called, and Levi stopped partway to the drunk, bottle in hand, looking at him questioningly. "Is Miss McGill here tonight?"

"She here. She gettin' ready."

"Where is she? She have an office here or something? I'd like to have a word with her."

"Bartender!"

Levi served the drunk, then came back over. "Why you want to see her for?" No smiling now, no bland good humor; he looked like a suspicious father, interrogating some questionable suitor for his daughter's hand. Jesse thought about the time he'd seen Levi standing guard on the stairs while Cady knocked on Gault's door. He'd been scared, but he hadn't budged from his spot.

"It's personal. I just want to tell her one thing." That she was right and he was wrong, he should never have let Ham play with his gun. Just then it occurred to him that he probably owed Ham's father an apology, too. Things were getting too damn complicated. Anyway, gunfighters didn't apologize. Not in public, anyway.

Levi studied him, then came to a decision. "She in her room. Through that do' over there, keep going. Knock on the office do' first—that's the little room before you get to her room. She hear you, she might decide you can come in."

"Thanks."

Levi nodded once, narrowing his eyes in a serious warning. *I'd hate to come after you, because you'd surely kill me,* the look said. *But I will if I have to.* You had to respect a man for that.

Edging through the gradually thickening crowd of drinkers and gamblers, Jesse accidentally bumped into a man on his blind side. "Sorry, didn't see you."

God *damn* this eyepatch. The man threw up his hands and said, "It's okay," about twenty times, backing out of his way.

A dark doorway he hadn't noticed before opened in the corner behind the bar. He went through, noting an open door to his left, full of boxes and furniture and miscellaneous junk, and a closed one to his right, probably full of booze. The hallway ended at another door, closed. Miss Cady's office.

Jesse knocked. Nobody answered. He opened it and stuck his head in.

Office? This hidey-hole was more of a closet, and a pretty small one at that. As far as he could see in the windowless dark, she had a desk, a chair, a half-assed file cabinet, and that was it. Somebody's picture in a frame sat on the desk. He picked it up, held it toward the trickle of light from the hallway. Nice old guy, chubby-cheeked, with a full beard. Her father? If so, he didn't look a thing like her.

A voice sounded from the only other door, the one that must lead to her room. A man's voice.

"Shit," Jesse swore out loud, softly, taken unawares by a sinking feeling in his stomach. A *man*. In broad daylight, too. If she was going to carry on like that, the least she could do was wait till dark.

He was silently pivoting when the man's voice suddenly barked out something loud and angry. Jesse halted. Cady's voice next, saying something he couldn't hear. She gave a yelp. "You goddamn polecat," he distinctly heard her say. "Quit it!"

Racing across the small room, Jesse shoved the

door open so hard, it sounded like a gunshot when it hit the wall.

Bedroom. Striped wallpaper, red rug, big, sexy brass bed—he registered the details in the instant before his eyes locked on Cady and two men.

He knew them. Clyde, the reasonable one, he'd thought, had her arms hooked through his behind her back. He was holding her still so Warren, the little sawed-off peckerhead who'd wanted to shoot him this morning, could reach inside her paisley dressing gown and touch her—gingerly, his hips cocked back to avoid a kick in the groin from one of her bare, flashing legs.

Everybody froze. Jesse said, "Well, now, look at this," in an unsmiling whisper, and the eerie, pitiless sound made his own blood run a little cooler. "You know what I hate to see, Warren? Grown men picking on a woman."

Clyde let go and stepped back. Cady jerked away, twitching her shoulders furiously, yanking the robe closed over her underwear. Her hair was down and wild, dark, long, almost to her elbows. Around the edges of the anger in her face, Jesse saw fear.

He was afraid, too, but he didn't have time to feel it. "That and whipping on a horse—those are two things that make me feel mean. You know what I do when I feel mean?"

"This ain't none o' your business," Warren, the bandy-legged needle dick, rallied to point out. "Ow! Shit!" He bent over to grab his knee—which Cady had just kicked as hard as she could with her bare foot.

"Get out of here, Turley, and don't ever come back!" She looked ready to murder him, her fists clenched, eyes flashing. "You don't have to shoot him," she told Jesse. "Not that I care, but he's not worth it. Clyde either."

"I'll take your hardware," Jesse told them softly. "Both of you."

"You ain't getting my gun." Turley—Warren—pulled his coat away from his .41, the same way he'd done this morning in the street. "Now you're really asking for it."

"Wrong. I'm not asking. I'll shoot you through the heart. You're alive now—in five seconds you'll be dead. That's a promise."

He never got over how words like that could pour out of his mouth at the absolute scariest moments. Jesus God, he was born for this life.

Holding out his hand, he whispered, "Butt first." Turley's ugly face reddened, but he obliged, cursing a blue streak. "Shhhh," Jesse warned, and he shut up. "Now you." Clyde handed over his shooter without a peep.

Cady had a goldfish bowl on top of her bureau. Turley almost jumped him when he saw what Jesse meant to do; his knees flexed and his hands started to reach out. But Jesse smiled the egging-on smile at him, like he wanted him to do it, *hoped* he'd make a wrong move, and Turley chickened out.

Splash. Splash. Three little orange fishies spurted out of the way just in time. Bubbles floated out of the barrels of the two six-guns, swam to the top, and popped.

"Now, get out. Come around bothering this lady again, I'll kill you both. And I'll do it slow."

Turley bared his teeth, impotent. If looks could kill, Jesse would be lying on the floor dead as a doornail, with Cady right beside him. Turley was too beaten down to swear again, though; he walked out the back door in a sullen, furious silence, and Clyde scurried after him.

Cady couldn't get over it. *He never even drew his gun,* she kept marveling, clutching her dressing gown, staring at Gault like he was the Second Coming. But really—Warren Turley was a mean, rotten son of a bitch, but you had to give him credit for one thing: guts. And Gault had taken his gun away. Dumped it in the fish bowl. She looked at it now as one last bubble popped out of the barrel and floated to the surface; Maude, Gracie, and Cecil swam around it, nosing it with interest.

"Thank you," she started to say. Nothing came out but the consonants and a puff of air. At the same moment, she realized her legs were shaking. "Breath of air?" she managed; it would've sounded nonchalant if it hadn't come out an octave higher than her usual register. Mr. Gault put out his arm in the most gentlemanly way, like an usher helping an old lady to her pew. Cady gave a shaky smile and waved it away, and somehow she made it out to her back steps and dropped down on the top one without fainting first.

"Well!" she said, while Gault stepped around her and sat down on the stair below. He had long, long legs, hard-looking under the black denim of his trousers; he bent one and threw his forearm across it, and stretched the other one straight out. "Wasn't that interesting?" Her robe touched his hip; she made a business of gathering it around her legs, tucking it in just so, going all ladylike on him while she tried to get her wits back. Her heart was still hammering. Today wasn't the first time Turley had tried to strong-arm her on Wylie's orders, but before now he'd never gone further than words. This new tactic scared her more than she wanted to admit.

"This kind of thing happen often?" Gault had taken his hat off and set it on the step beside her. The setting sun through the live oak lit up the silver in his dark brown hair.

"No." She shook her head vehemently. "Definitely not."

"They, um . . . they didn't hurt you, did they?"

It came to her what he was thinking, what it must've looked like when he smashed the door in. "Oh, no. Not at all. They were just looking for my gun." Mainly; Turley had snuck a feel in the process, but she wasn't going to dwell on that.

"Looking for your gun?"

He looked so surprised, she smiled. "Yeah. And if I'd had it on me, I'd've plugged 'em both," she boasted. It was probably a lie, but just saying it made her feel calmer. "I keep a .22 in my . . . on my person," she said delicately.

"What kind?"

"Remington Elliot. Five-shot."

"With the ring trigger?" She nodded, and he

pursed his lips in an approving whistle. "Guess things can get a little rough in your line of work."

Not as much as in yours. "Once in a while. But I can handle it. Anyway, Turley and Clyde were just trying to scare me."

"Why?"

She lifted her eyebrows. How strange to be explaining to him who her enemies were. Until now, she'd been pretty sure he was one of them. "Because Merle Wylie told them to," she said.

"Why?"

"Because." She rested her chin in her hands and contemplated him. His one gray eye looked harmless for a change, not evil. Interested. "He wants the Rogue," she said with a sigh. "Wants me to sell out, sell him the Rogue and the Seven Dollar. He just wants everything."

"What's the Seven Dollar?"

"A mine. It's placered out, not worth anything."

"Why does he want it, then?"

"I just told you—because he wants everything. That's what he's like, that's the kind of man he is."

He looked thoughtful. "I've been hearing a few things about Wylie," he allowed after a pause.

"I'll bet. I told you he burned down the livery."

"What?"

She touched his shoulder when he started to jump up. "The old one—Wylie's is the new one. Nestor Yeakes runs it for him."

"Oh." He relaxed, sank back against the step. "Yeah, you told me that yesterday. What the hell did he do that for?"

"Bob Logan wouldn't sell out to him. He couldn't foreclose because Logan owned it free and clear, so he burned him out."

Gault swore, as if that shocked him. "So Wylie's a banker?"

"No, but he's got one in his pocket."

"Cherney."

She blinked. "Yeah. You know him?"

"We met." For some reason, he smiled.

"Well, Cherney's his hatchet man, you could say. He's making him foreclose on Forrest Sullivan's sheep farm, pretty much just for the hell of it. The Sullivans have four kids, and the oldest is seven. I don't know what they're going to do."

Gault took a cigarette out of his pocket and started to roll it between his fingers, play with it. Cady watched him out of the corner of her eye. The more time she spent with him, the less she could figure him out. He could barely line up a match and a cigarette, and yet he was so confident of his triggerman skills, he didn't even have to draw on his enemies. *Didn't even have to draw.* She still couldn't get over it, the way he'd cut Warren Turley down to size— cocky, black-hearted Warren, who wasn't scared of anybody. She'd been scared herself when Gault had banged that door open, even knowing he'd come to save her. (How *had* she known that?) There was just something about him. He only had to squint his eye to put the fear of God in you, or whisper something, or stretch his lips in his wicked smile. But then he could say charming, downright flirtatious things when he felt like it, and he had a different kind of smile, tickled and lighthearted, for Ham. And once or twice for her.

"Paradise is a nice little town," she said offhand-edly, leaning over to trace a line around her bare toes on the warm wood step. "Used to be even nicer. Since Wylie got this bug up his behind about owning everything, it's changed. People are scared now. When you rode in, most of 'em assumed he'd hired you. You say he didn't." She stole a glance. He was watching her, stroking his fingertips across his long, sexy upper lip, brushing the edges of his mustache. She looked back down at her feet.

"The thing is, people are starting to feel outnum-bered. Tommy—Sheriff Leaver—he's not very . . ." She hunted for the right word, gave up. "He could use some help. We could all use . . . somebody on our side."

She came to a stop, hoping he would fill in the silence, say, "Why, I'll help you! You should've asked sooner; I had no idea you were in such a pickle." But as the pause lengthened, she understood what a foolish hope that was. He fished a match out, struck it on the step, and this time lit his thin black cigarette in one try. Slouching down, legs crossed, he stuck his elbows on the stair behind him and blew unconcerned smoke at the sky.

"Why did you come to my room anyway?" she wondered testily. "Did you want to see me about something?"

"Oh, yeah." He turned on his elbow to face her. "I wanted to tell you." He fingered one of the green paisley curves in the dangling belt of her robe; he might've been doing it unconsciously, but she was aware of every move of his fingertip. "That I'm, you know, sorry."

"For what?"

"Today." Even with the sinister patch over his eye and the smoke curling up from his cigarette, there was something boyish in the angle of his head, the way he looked up at her through his thick eyelashes, then quickly away. "I'm talking about me and the kid," he explained, mumbling. "You were right. Had no business handing over a gun to a seven-year-old. Even though it wasn't loaded."

"Yes, but you can never—"

"You can't be sure and you can't take a chance, not with children. I know that. Don't know what got into me, Cady. I won't be doing that again."

She went all soft inside when he called her Cady. She had the strangest urge to run her fingers through the lock of black-and-silver hair that fell sideways across his forehead. Push it back, and cup his ear with her palm while she was at it. "It's okay. Gault. Mr. Gault." She gave a short laugh. "Seems funny— you know my first name but I don't know yours."

He flicked his cigarette into the grass. She watched it smolder while she waited for him to speak. It died before he did. "A man in my line of work," he finally said, and stopped.

"It's okay. I understand." But she didn't, not at all, and she was really disappointed. She couldn't get over how disappointed she was.

"It's Jesse."

"What?" He'd whispered—she wasn't sure she'd heard right.

"Name's Jesse. You can call me that. I'd like it if you did."

"All right." A slow smile bloomed on her face.

"But I'd appreciate it if you wouldn't tell anybody else."

"I won't. I promise." The thrill of conspiracy made her wind her arms around her knees and squeeze. Jesse Gault. It suited him. "Gault" was a hard word, but "Jesse" . . . "Jesse" could go either way.

"You sure are pretty when you smile."

"Oh . . ." She swatted a hank of hair over her shoulder, hoping she wasn't blushing. Thinking she could give him the exact compliment.

"You're pretty all the time, but especially when you smile. Your eyes get little and crinkly, and they twinkle. And the corners of your mouth turn up just so."

She *knew* she was blushing. He looked like he was telling the truth, although he was smiling, too. Men said things to her all the time, ridiculous things, she didn't pay any attention. But they usually didn't go into all this . . . detail.

"Mr. Gault, you're flattering me," she actually said. She'd heard a girl say that to her beau once, on the church steps one Sunday morning. It had stayed with her for some reason; she'd thought it was silly but also kind of dignified—and here she was spouting it out to Jesse Gault, like some antebellum miss in a crinoline. Her cheeks got even hotter.

"Where'd you get skin like that?" He was murmuring, almost whispering, but it was nothing like that dark, scary whisper he used on men. This was more like soothing, more like a caress. "And I don't even know words for that color you turn sometimes. Like now. Like a peach. No, lighter. Miss Cady McGill, you are just about the prettiest girl I ever saw."

She put her chin on her knee; he leaned closer. Their faces were about five inches apart. He dropped his gaze from her eyes to her mouth, and she imagined the corners were probably turning up "just so" right now. They were going to kiss. Right here on her back stoop. How would it feel? He had a beautiful mouth, full and manly under his black mustache, the ends of which looked soft, not bristly. His lips were closed. She closed hers. They inched toward each other. His breath blew out through his nose, fluttering softly on her cheek. She shut her eyes.

"Miz Cady?"

Levi. Calling through the closed door of her office.

Jesse didn't move, just smiled a slow, sexy smile while she jolted up straight, plucking at the closed throat of her robe. "Yes?"

"Miz Cady, you okay?"

"Fine!"

"Boys're askin' for you. They ready to play cards. Tol' 'em you'll be right out."

"I will be. Thanks, Levi."

"Ma'am."

She heard his soft footsteps fade. "Well," she said.

"Well," Jesse said, still smiling at her.

For some reason she felt like laughing. Nerves, she

guessed. She stood up. He stayed where he was, studying her bare feet for a second, then leaning back so he could see her face. She had never seen a man look so . . . *appreciative.* The heat of the day was fading, but she felt warm all over. "Well. Guess I'll get dressed."

"Right." He still didn't move, so she left him where he was and took her green dress and the rest of her things with her behind the screen.

It was a pretty screen, three-paneled, painted with a scene of a lady taking a bath in the woods surrounded by naked nymphs. Needless to say, it hadn't been in this room when Mr. Shlegel lived here; she had found it up in a third-floor room, and brought it down because she liked it, and because it gave her some privacy while she dressed if she had company. Ham or Levi, for instance, or one of the girls. She hoped Jesse was enjoying it.

She didn't feel like hurrying—some kind of lethargy was weighing her down very pleasantly, making her arms and legs feel heavy—but she could hear Chico playing "Buffalo Gals" on the piano, a sure sign that Saturday night was getting under way. "How do you like your room?" she asked, for something to say, while she pulled on her stockings and rolled garters up to the tops.

"Like it fine." The nearness of his voice surprised her. She peeked over the top of the screen, and saw that he'd moved. He was sitting on the foot of her bed.

"That's good," she said. "The balcony's nice."

"Real nice. I like to sit out in a rocking chair, watch the world go by."

"The world," she said with a laugh. The population of Paradise hovered around four hundred.

"Yeah, it's a real nice room. Gets kind of lonely, though."

Shimmying the tight green taffeta down over her hips, she heard the bed springs creak. She was turned away, facing the oval mirror nailed to the wall. She saw the reflection of four fingers and the top of a thumb on the screen edge, overlapping one of the naked nymphs. Her heart, which had finally slowed down since their almost-kiss, recommenced racing.

"Specially late at night. When I'm lying there in that big bed all by myself. I thought about you last night, Cady. Kept me awake. Couldn't get you out of my mind."

She started to turn, but he moved faster. She saw him behind her just before he put his hands on her bare shoulders, and for no reason she could think of she closed her eyes. Maybe it was so she could concentrate on the way it felt to be touched by him, undistracted by the sight of him. God knew the sight of him was a distraction. "Mr. Gault, I do believe . . ." She smiled with her eyes closed, thinking that leaning back against Jesse was like leaning back against a hard, strong wall. "I do believe you're toying with my affections."

His laugh was nice, a huff of breath followed by a soft, infectious chuckle. His hands slipped slowly down from her shoulders to her elbows, then her sides. "There's nothing I'd rather toy with, Miss

McGill," he said with his mouth against her hair, "than your affections." He was staring in the mirror at her breasts. She couldn't get over how much she liked this, this blatant . . . *thing* they were doing that she never allowed and always discouraged, wouldn't put up with past this point from almost any man. This man . . . this gunfighter she'd known for a day . . . she very much wanted to go to the next step with him. She dropped her head back on his shoulder and watched, heavy-lidded, as his big hands slid up and across her rib cage, a soft, slow, full-handed caress. Reckless, out of control, she felt like she was drunk.

"Miss Cady," he murmured, dipping his head to kiss her on the neck. "When you're through tonight?"

"Mmm?"

"If you don't have any other customers . . ."

She felt his lips, then his teeth on the bony-soft side of her ear. "Customers," she breathed, pressing her palms against the tops of his hands to keep them still.

"If you'd save tonight for me, I surely would appreciate it." She stole a glance at him in the mirror. He had his eyes closed, his smiling lips pressed to her temple. "I don't know what you charge for toying with your affections," he whispered. "But whatever it is, it's not enough. Luckily, I can cover it."

Her eyes flew wide open. Everything changed. A second ago she'd liked the feel and the look of him, black-clad, hatless and long-haired, a sturdy wall of warm muscle and bone at her back. He looked predatory now, his roving hands ready to take what she no longer wanted to give. She didn't even like his handsome profile anymore. *Don't be angry*, she commanded herself. After all, it wasn't as if this had never happened before.

"You've made a mistake," she said calmly, mildly, turning in his arms to face him.

"I don't think so." He still looked drowsy, dreamy-eyed.

"Oh, yes. I'm afraid so." Slipping past him, she walked to the open back door and stood by it. "Would you excuse me, Mr. Gault? I've still got a few things to do."

He came toward her uncertainly. He didn't get it. "What's wrong?"

"Nothing's wrong, everything's fine. I told you, you made a mistake."

"What? What mistake?"

His total bewilderment was undermining her resolve not to lose her temper. "It's not for sale," she said through her teeth, smile hanging on by a thread. "What you can get here at the Rogue is beer, whiskey, pool, and poker. That's it. That's all I sell. Sorry if you were misled."

"Aha." He bent his head and rubbed the back of his neck, glancing up at her through his eyelashes. His lips quirked in a wry, one-sided smile. "Oops."

"Yeah, well." She waved her hand, indicating the open doorway. After a loaded second or two, while he seemed to be making up his mind about something, he walked out.

She started to close the door when he turned and said, "Sorry. Hope I didn't offend you."

"Not in the least. Not the least little bit."

"Good. That's good."

She wasn't angry, she wasn't offended. Why would she be? She was used to this; it or something like it happened about once a week.

"Cady—"

" 'Bye."

Nope, she wasn't angry. Slamming the door in his face was an accident.

Five

Two days went by, and two more people gave Jesse money so he wouldn't kill them. Paradise was turning into a flaming cesspool of guilty consciences. He'd never had luck like this before, not even in bigger towns like Medford or Crescent City. One of the sinners had stolen his mining buddy's poke two years ago in Silverado, and been more or less on the run ever since. The other, a woman, had emptied her husband's bank account and lit out with a piano tuner, who'd had his fun and then stranded her in Paradise last December. Ethel Payne, her name was. She'd landed on her feet, though, had a good job now in the insurance agent's office. But she was scared to death of her husband, and after she told him a few things about him, Jesse was scared, too. So he only took ten dollars, and told Ethel they were square.

Gault had his flaws, but bilking frightened runaway wives wasn't one of them.

Besides, now that he was filthy rich, he could afford to be generous. He could start a damn foundation. He could become a charitable trust. Instead, for the time being, he was redistributing the wealth by losing it at poker. Not on purpose—a run of bad luck. He didn't mind. He had so much of it, it felt like play money. And losing it widened his circle of acquaintances, which was a nice side benefit. At first the men he sat down to play stud with were scared to beat him, but they got over it as soon as they figured out he wasn't going to shoot them for it. Then they started to like him. He tried to tone down his own natural friendliness, act surly and dangerous and half-nuts, but his heart wasn't in it.

He was lonesome.

It was all Cady's fault. Every time she saw him she gave him the same polite, freezing-cold smile and moved on. If he managed to corner her, she said polite, freezing-cold things, and always turned down his offers to sit or have a drink with him. Politely. She was killing him with politeness. Last night he tried to get a rise out of her, maybe torture her a little, by sitting down at her blackjack table, but he only ended up torturing himself. She wouldn't even look at him. Slapped his cards down like she was trying to kill flies with them, and took him for two hundred thirty dollars before he knew what hit him. After that he stayed with the boys, his new poker pals, glowering one-eyed at her over the head of a beer or the lip of a whiskey glass.

Okay, so he'd made a mistake about her. So shoot him. What exactly was the big deal? If he'd phrased his suggestion to her just a little differently, left out that one tiny, unfortunate reference to commerce, she might have said yes. She sure had seemed to be heading in that direction. He remembered how she'd felt leaning back against him, all soft and blowsy with her pretty hair down, no corset, smiling and dreamy-eyed in the mirror. He thought about her bed a lot, too, how big and soft it was, how it didn't squeak. Cady McGill, saloon proprietor and blackjack dealer. Period. Not whore, and not madam. She didn't sell it, she gave it away. Just not to him.

Not yet, anyway. The sixth sense that never let him down was telling him he was finished here, Paradise had given up everything it was going to, and if he was smart he'd ride out today. But all the other senses, the ones McGill seemed to have pretty much taken over, told him he couldn't leave, because he had unfinished business.

Five to one.

"Uh, so, Mr. Gault, I see you read our little paper. That's, uh, very flattering. Sir."

Jesse, half dozing, daydreaming of Cady, lifted a corner of the hot towel Cuomo the barber had slapped over his face. He blinked up at a pair of horn-rimmed spectacles perched on a skinny nose over a wisp of a mustache. "Who're you?"

"Will Shorter, Mr. Gault. I'm with the Paradise *Reverberator*."

"Junior," Cuomo stuck in, stropping a straight razor behind Jesse's left shoulder. "Will Shorter, Junior."

Will Shorter, Jr., acknowledging that with a testy nod, stuck out his hand. Jesse ignored it, and the kid—he couldn't have been more than twenty or twenty-one—bobbed his head and blushed. "Sorry to bother you, Mr. Gault, but I was wondering if by any chance you'd mind posing for a photograph. For the *Reverberator*." He pointed to the newspaper lying open on Jesse's sheet-covered lap.

"Why?"

"Why? Um, because our readers would be very interested, you being a notor—a famous personage and everything. It would only take a minute or two. At your convenience. It's a nice sunny day—we could do it outside."

"Who'd take it?"

"Why, I would, sir. I'm the paper's junior reporter *and* official photographer."

"Hm." Jesse twitched his nostrils; Cuomo the barber was trimming his mustache, making his nose itch. "What's in it for me?"

The reporter looked flummoxed. "We're not allowed to pay you."

"Why not?"

"Um . . . ethics. Sir."

Jesse reared up and sneezed, blowing mustache hairs off his chest. "Then I'm not interested."

"What about lunch?" Cuomo suggested. "Buy him lunch at the Frenchman's."

Will Shorter, Jr., widened hopeful eyes behind his horn-rims. "The two-dollar lunch, Mr. Gault. Steak and potatoes, best in town."

Jesse fingered his smooth chin thoughtfully while Cuomo flicked at his shoulders with a brush. "Vinegar pie for dessert?"

"Absolutely."

"Let's go."

*   *   *

It took a lot longer than a minute or two to have his picture made. Will had to go get his camera at the *Reverberator* office, then set it up on the sunny corner of Main and Noble Fir. While he waited, Jesse idled in the shade, smoking cigarettes, staring back at people who stared at him. He could sense a change in the average Paradise resident's attitude, and knew it was still another reason why it was time for Gault to move on. People weren't as afraid of him as they used to be. He'd been here for days and hadn't shot a single person, so now they were more curious than scared. That was bad. He ought to do something to stir them up, but he just didn't feel like it.

In truth, he was getting a little tired of Gault. Sure it was fun to scare people, and sure it was nice to walk into a room and have it go all quiet and cautious, while everybody checked him out and decided not to mess with him. But then again, there were aspects of Gault that struck him at times as pretty damn silly. Face it: sometimes Gault was a real horse's ass.

A man on crutches came hobbling toward him in the street. He had his head down, concentrating on his good foot, swinging his splinted right leg through the beat-up crutches clumsily, jerkily, like a beginner. Jesse didn't recognize him till he'd passed all the way by, and then it was more the smell than the sight that tripped his memory.

"Shrimp Malone."

The red-haired prospector stopped, teetered,

hopped around in a half circle, squinting into the sun. "Gault?"

"What the hell happened to you?"

"Fell down a cliff, broke my damn leg. You ain't gonna shoot me, are you?"

Will Shorter was watching them with interest. Jesse said, "Be right back," and left him to join Shrimp in the street. They started walking together. "Where you headed?" Jesse asked, shortening his steps to match the miner's gimpy shuffle.

"Church."

"Church."

Shrimp slanted him a funny look from under the bushy ledge of his ginger eyebrows. "They give out stuff," he muttered.

"They what? Give out what?"

"Soup," he clarified shortly. "Once a day. They dole it out to the poor an' the infirm. Which I'm both of these days." He clamped his chicken lips together and concentrated on walking. He looked terrible, worse than the first time they'd met, and that was saying something. He smelled worse, too. Moving along on crutches in the hot sun made him sweat; his dirty undershirt was soaking wet.

"When did this happen to you?"

"Satiddy. Day after I give you all my money. Every dad-blamed cent." He turned his head to hawk and spit.

"Where've you been staying?"

No answer.

"Where do you live?"

Shrimp stopped short and faced him, swaying

slightly, splinted leg cocked back at the knee. "Listen here, Mr. Gault. No offense, but you can't git blood from a stone. Since I already done give you everything I own, I figger that makes us even. I don't got to tell you all about my private business anymore." He almost looked dignified when he straightened his shoulders, turned around, and stumped away.

Jesse caught up to him in three long strides. "Sleeping outside, huh?" Shrimp snorted and didn't look at him. "That's rough," he went on conversationally. "Only happened to me once. After a poker game in San Francisco. I didn't care much for it. Speaking of poker games—let's go over here for a second, you mind? Out of the sun. Yeah, this is better. Sit down, take a load off."

"I only got a minute," the miner grumped uneasily, lowering his backside to a shady section of sidewalk. "They don't give out soup all day long, y'know."

"In that case I won't keep you. Just wanted to mention—you know that seven hundred dollars' worth of dust you gave me?"

"It rings a bell."

"Well, would you believe it? Last night I tripled it with three jacks and a pair of queens."

"You don't say. Well, that brings tears o' joy to my eyes, Mr. Gault, it surely does. Now, if you don't mind—" Jesse put a hand on his arm when he tried to get up. Shrimp froze. "No offense," he blurted. "I'll sit here an' jaw all day if you want, no problem whatsoever. It ain't like I've got anything else to—"

"So the way I figure it, you're like my good-luck charm, Mr. Malone."

"I am?"

"Now, I'm the kind of fellow who pays people back. Know what I mean?"

"Uh . . ."

"Somebody does something bad, wrongs me in any way, I'm inclined to shoot him. Or wound him, leastways—sometimes a good maiming's better than an outright killing, you know?"

"Heh heh."

"Same thing if a man does me a good turn."

Shrimp started to scoot sideways. "You *shoot* him?"

"No, you idiot. I pay him back."

"Oh." His little pig eyes lit up. "You do?"

"Course, it'd have to be a secret between you and me."

"Sure, sure. Sure. How come?"

"How come! Because I got a reputation to think about. What would happen if it got around that I was donating to the poor and the infirm? Somebody might say I was soft, and pretty soon somebody else might decide to call me out. Then I'd have to shoot 'em both, and maybe it wouldn't be convenient right then. Maybe I wouldn't be in the mood."

"Yeah," Shrimp said thoughtfully. "Yeah, I can see how that'd be a problem."

Jesse glanced around. The coast was clear. "So— here," he said, pulling a wad of bills out of his pocket and stuffing it into the miner's outstretched paw. "Quick, put it away. Anybody asks where it came from, make up something good."

"I sure will." Stunned, dazed, Shrimp shoved the

money into his grubby dungarees. The sudden change in his fortunes hadn't sunk in yet. "Thanks, Mr. Gault, thanks a lot. You're a real—"

"Okay, but keep that quiet, too. Last thing I need is people hearing somebody *thank* me."

"Oh, right. Sure, sure."

When they stood up, Jesse had to stop himself from giving the miner a helping hand. Gault had been saintly enough for one day, and then some. "Well, so long."

"So long." He didn't move, though. "Uh, Mr. Gault?"

"What."

"You been a real trump about this, no mistake, and I'm much obliged—"

"Yeah, yeah. What?"

"Well, I was just wonderin' if by any chance you still got my ear. And if you do, if you'd consider givin' that back, too."

"Your what?"

"My ear. You know. My ear?" He scowled, incredulous. "My pig's ear! You done made me give it to you, and ever since then it's a fact I ain't had nothing but bad luck."

"Oh, your ear." What had he done with it? Thrown it out the window, he vaguely remembered. "Sorry, Shrimp, I sent it to the Wilsons."

"Sent it to who?"

Oops. "The, uh . . ."

"Weavers?"

"Weavers, Weavers. Sent it to them to prove I'd killed you. Remember? That was our deal? So then they paid me—which is another reason why I don't need your piddling seven hundred bucks." He was babbling, but Shrimp had a brand-new expression on his whiskery, pocked, pug-ugly face: intelligence. "So I haven't got it. The ear. Sent it to 'em, and they mailed back my pay right away. Real sweet deal, way I look at it. I don't even miss killing you. In your way, you're not a bad sombitch. Well, so, good luck, see you around—"

"What was 'er name?"

"Who?"

"Girl they wanted me to marry. You wouldn't recollect her name, would you, Mr. Gault?"

"You're joshing me, aren't you? That horse-faced hyena? She had a *name*?"

Shrimp looked at the ground, chuckling; the crafty look wavered. Then he cocked his head to the side. "What town in Coos County they from? The Weaver boys."

Jesse let go of his grin, let it fade slowly, slowly, like an unhurried black cloud covering up the sun. When it was all gone he narrowed his one eye on Shrimp Malone in a stare that could've frozen bathwater. "What did you say to me?"

"What? Nothin'. I didn't say nothin'."

"I think you asked me a question."

"No, I didn't."

"I think the question had a *tone* to it."

"No, it didn't."

Every slow step Jesse took toward him, Shrimp took a hop backward. "I think it had a tone of *disbelief*."

"No, it—"

"*Disbelief.* Which says to me you think I'm lying."

"No, I don't! No, I don't!" He threw up his hands. His crutches stood alone for a second before they toppled over. He looked down at them blankly, realized they weren't holding him up anymore, and pitched face first in the dirt.

"Oh, shit fire," Jesse swore, hurrying over and hauling the old fool up by the belt and the collar. "You okay?"

"Ow! Shit! I think I broke it again."

"No, you didn't." He scooped up the crutches and stuck them under Shrimp's armpits. "Quit that caterwauling, you're all right."

"No, I ain't."

"Yes, you are. Now, what was I saying?"

Suddenly Shrimp was fine, not a thing wrong with him. "I don't recollect. Nothin' important. Well, so long, Mr. Gault, nice talkin' to you."

"Maybe I'll see you around sometime."

Shrimp said sure, definitely, you never know, the whole time he was hobbling down the street as fast as his good leg could go.

Stinking, ungrateful old goat, thought Jesse. Seven hundred bucks were limping out of sight, and he'd bet Shrimp Malone wouldn't even buy him a drink if they met up again. Ingrate.

Will Shorter's camera was all set up. Jesse posed for pictures standing up, sitting down, smoking a cigarette, pointing his guns. Before he was finished he'd drawn a crowd, and a couple of people in it started making suggestions. "Take off your hat," somebody advised; an old lady called out, "Couldn't you try to smile just once?"

"That's it," Jesse decided, breaking a particularly badass pose. Will came out from under his black leather covering looking confused. "We're done here, Shorter. Where's my lunch?"

They went over to Jacques' restaurant and took a corner table. Maybe it was all the ice-cold beer he slugged down to quench the thirst he'd worked up standing in the hot sun. Or maybe Will Shorter, Jr., was a lot smarter than he looked. Either way, when the reporter casually drew a notebook out of his vest pocket and said, "So. How'd you get started in the gunfighter business, Mr. Gault?" Jesse told him.

> ### OUTLAW COMES TO PARADISE
> *Exclusive Interview—Secrets Revealed*
> *How Bad Luck Started Wounded War*
> *Vet Down Path of Violence*

"Listen to this part," Glendoline told Ham and Willagail. All three were lying on Cady's bed, while Cady sat at her dressing table, trying to fix her hair. "'A man doesn't set out to be a gunfighter. But sometimes circumstances don't leave him a choice,' Gault confided to this reporter. 'I fought for the Union, but after the war, sick and disabled, I came home to find carpetbaggers on my family's land, living in my father's house. It wasn't legal, but the law wasn't going to help us. Traitors and scalawags found a way to force us out and leave us with nothing, so I found a way to re-recip—'"

"Reciprocate," Cady supplied without thinking.

"Ha!" Glen pounced. "I thought you couldn't be bothered reading about him. You said we were wasting our time."

"You are. I can't believe that blowhard's life story is on the front page, and the news about Lyndon Cherney swindling thousands of dollars from the Mercantile and escaping in the middle of the night isn't even *mentioned* until page three."

"Go on, Glen," Willagail urged, dismissing Cady with a wave. "Get to the good part."

"Yeah," said Ham. "Get to the part 'bout how Mr. Gault have to kill somebody to get his house back."

"Fat lot of good it did him," Cady couldn't help throwing in. "He had to leave Kentucky to evade the law, and he *still* doesn't have a home."

Glendoline shushed her and went back to the story in the *Reverberator*. The paper was a weekly—it came out on Fridays—but this story was deemed so newsworthy, it merited a Wednesday Special Edition.

" 'I won't lie to you,' Mr. Gault said. 'For the sake of justice, I took the law into my own hands. I righted a wrong with the only weapon they left me: my gun. What I didn't count on was the government I'd fought and nearly died for siding with the very thieves who'd stolen everything from my family.' "

"It ain't right," declared Ham.

"What else could he do?" Willagail sighed, lying back, punching Cady's pillow, making herself more comfortable. "I don't blame him for doing what he had to do. I think it's admirable."

Cady snorted. "He shot a man and ran away. That's admirable?"

"But it was a fair fight—it says so right here—and they didn't leave him any choice. I think it was brave. And sad, because now he can never go home."

"And he loved his home," Glendoline said sadly. "The Kentucky bluegrass. Doesn't it sound beautiful? I love that word—bluegrass. And all those horses his daddy raised. What a life."

"All lost," Willagail murmured with her eyes closed. Cady thought she might cry.

"Well, I for one think Will Shorter's lost his mind." Cady pulled all the pins out of her pompadour and let it fall past her shoulders. She was tired of that style. Maybe a French roll? "Notice how he doesn't ask any tough questions. He just lets Gault go on and on, and it ends up sounding like the life of Robin Hood—some *hero* instead of a hired killer."

"I don't b'lieve he's a hired killer," Ham said sulkily, picking the stuffing out of a hole in her quilt. "What make you think he's a hired killer?"

"Because he kills people. He does admit *that*, at least."

"Yeah, but only the bad guys."

"And they always drew first. Look, it's right here somewhere . . ." Glen ran her finger down a column of newsprint, searching for the place where Gault said he was innocent.

"Oh, so because he says it, that means it's true? You three, I'll swan." They all smiled; "I'll swan" was one of Levi's sayings.

"Say the part about how he gets wounded in the eye," Ham said. "An' how he be okay now."

Even Cady quit fooling with her hair and turned around for that. This was the part in the article she'd read and reread numerous times, fascinated, wanting to believe it but finding it all but incredible.

"It was during the battle of Kenesaw Mountain, Georgia, that Mr. Gault suffered the devastating head wound that left him partially blind and deaf. 'I was just a kid. I lied about my age to enlist in the First Kentucky Volunteers, and they put me in the mortar and gun crew. Confederate shells hit the artillery wagon I was unloading, and a box of case shot blew up in my face. But I was lucky—our commander, General McCook, died that day in the battle. The war ended during the year I spent recuperating in a Union hospital. I went home scarred and crippled, only to find out I'd lost everything.' "

Glen paused to fish her handkerchief out of her pocket and dab at her eyes. "Keep going," Ham said impatiently, and Cady sympathized: they were just getting to the good part.

"It was at this point in the interview when Mr. Gault confided a secret to this reporter, a secret never before revealed in any recent press accounts, or even hinted at in the numerous rumors that constantly circulate around him. 'About a year ago, I started seeing something out of my right eye. At first it was just a gray smudge, like smoke, but lately it's been getting clearer and clearer. I went to a special eye doctor in San Francisco, and he told me I ought to start exercising it by taking the patch off a few hours every day.

I'm up to about half a day now. I don't see perfectly, and I don't expect I ever will, but I can see something, and that's a miracle to me. I attribute it to God and clean living."

That was the line that always got her. She'd be reading along, thinking, *Isn't that wonderful*, get to the "clean living" part, and burst out laughing.

"What's so funny?" said Willagail. "It *is* a miracle."

"I can't wait to see 'im without the patch." Ham jumped off the bed and ran over to Cady. "Bet he look *good.*" He threw his arms over her lap and hung on her, swaying. "Las' night he gave me another quarter, Cady. Say he found it on the flo', but I think he jus' like givin' out money. I like him a lot, don't you? He talk to me like he a old friend."

"An old friend, eh?" She rubbed his back, smiling.

" 'Don't miss Part Two of this exclusive story," Glendoline finished. " 'Coming Friday: A dramatic account of the gunfighting career of a living Western legend. Read how Gault killed his first man; read how he gunned down every challenger to his skill and deadly quickness; read how a jammed six-gun almost ended his career—and his life!' "

"No doubt about it," Cady marveled, swatting Ham on the behind to make him move so she could finish dressing. "Will Shorter has completely lost his mind."

"With or without?"

"With," Nestor Yeakes decided after a moment's thought.

Jesse put his eyepatch back on. Sticking his thumbs in his gunbelt, he glared at the camera. Beside him, Nestor, dressed in his Sunday clothes and a flower in his buttonhole, pressed his hat to his chest and grinned.

"All right, now, hold it . . . hold it . . . hold it . . . gotcha." Will came out from under the black camera hood, sweat running down behind his eyeglasses and dripping off the fuzzy ends of that pitiful little growth he called a mustache. "Okay, that's it for a while. I need to get out of this sun."

"Fine with me." Jesse wiped his forehead with his sleeve and walked over to a bench under the porch roof of Rogue's Tavern.

Nestor trailed after him "When you reckon the picture'll be done?" he asked, still grinning.

"Ask Will, he's the photographer." But Jesse was getting eighty percent—four dollars—on every five-dollar photo Will sold. Peanuts; not even worth his time. But old habits die hard. It wasn't so long ago that he'd had to scrounge for every dime, and some of the ways in which he'd made his precarious "living" he'd just as soon forget. Back then, five bucks a pop for standing next to some awestruck villager and having his picture made would've felt like a miracle.

"I took Bell Flower out for a run this morning, Mr. Gault."

"Bellefleur," Jesse corrected; he'd checked the name on Cherney's sale papers. "Yeah, I saw you ride out." From his rocking chair on the balcony. "How was she?"

"Better'n I thought she'd be. Nervous, o' course. Fact, she'll probably never get over being scared altogether. But she wants to do what you tell her, and that's a real good sign. Reckon Cherney didn't break her heart after all. Didn't have time."

Jesse grunted. Nestor didn't look like much, and when he talked he didn't sound like much. But he knew horses, Jesse was finding out, and for that alone he respected him more every day.

"Wanted to say . . . I like what you did, Mr. Gault."

"Yeah, all right." He started hunting in his pockets for a match.

"Dunno how you did it, but I surely do admire you for doin' it."

"Okay. Take Peg for a run this evening, hear? And comb him good afterward. And give him a bath tomorrow. He likes a bath about once a week. Like me."

Nestor cackled and spat tobacco juice. "Sure will. Sure will, Mr. Gault." Like a lot of other folks, Nestor wasn't scared of him anymore. Jesse knew he ought to care about that more, but he couldn't seem to work up a good goddamn. He'd had a nice time today posing with the likes of Sam Blankenship, the real estate and insurance man, and Floyd and Oscar Schmidt, a couple of coots who sat outside the grange hall all day every day, minding everybody else's business. Jersey Stan Morrissey, who owed Jesse some poker money, came out of the dark, cool Rogue long enough to get his picture made, then scuttled back inside like a mole, blinded by the light.

Even Shrimp Malone had limped over for a photograph. He'd moved back into his boardinghouse after Jesse gave him his money back, and he looked a little cleaner, and a lot healthier now that he was eating three squares again.

Will Shorter came over and flopped down beside Jesse on the bench. "This a good time to continue our interview, Mr. Gault?" he asked politely, mopping the back of his neck with a big handkerchief. "Folks say they're really looking forward to tomorrow's edition."

"Sure," Jesse said agreeably. "Shoot."

"Heh heh." Will always laughed before he made a little joke, to be sure you got it. "I sure wish you'd rephrase that, Mr. Gault. It makes me nervous when you say 'Shoot.' "

Jesse said, "Heh heh," back, to humor him. Will had been asking him questions on and off all afternoon, in between photographs. These weren't quite as easy to answer as the last time. Jesse figured somebody had told Will Shorter, Jr., to toughen up, quit being a sucker. Most likely Will Shorter, Sr.

The newspaperman whipped out his notebook, flipped pages. Uncapped his fountain pen, cleared his throat. Sent Nestor a meaningful look.

Nestor ignored it and lowered his backside to the curb, all ears.

"Ahem," Will said again, frowning, but Nestor stayed clueless. Finally he just shrugged and plunged in. "Mr. Gault, some people are interested in knowing how it is that you seem to be all healed up from your devastating wound. Uh, how it is that just three months ago, according to the Oakland *Courier*, you were shot so badly in the right hand that you said you were going to give up gunfighting. Hang up your Colts and retire."

Will had been doing his homework. "*Who's* interested in knowing it?" Jesse demanded, bluffing indignity. "You saying somebody thinks I'm lying?"

"No. No. No, no, no, no, no."

"Because I'd like to know who they are. I'd like to hear 'em say that to my face."

"No, no, no." Violent throat clearing. "Not at all." He unwrapped a folded-up piece of newspaper he found in the back of his notebook. "It's just that here in the *Courier* you say . . ." He ran his thumb down a column. " 'My hand's shot to . . .'—uh, they put 'h___.' Heh heh. Guess you said heck." Jesse didn't laugh back. "Uh, 'My hand's shot to hell. I'll never draw a six-gun again. Now some might call that lucky, but I don't. I never knew when or where, but I always knew how I'd die—by fire, taken out by the hand of some faster triggerman than me. Now I got to recalculate.' "

"Yeah, well, I had a lot more to recalculate than I thought. See this hand?" He flexed his fingers, turned his palm up and down. "Three months ago it was paralyzed. But the papers got it wrong—the bullet hit me in the arm, right here, between these two tendons." He pointed to a spot under his sleeve. "But it was *temporary* paralysis. After the wound healed, I started to practice and exercise. Did nothing but draw and target shoot for eight weeks. And you know what? I'm faster now than I was before. Anybody who doubts that is welcome to come and try me." He said that with a snarl, but Will missed it. He was too busy scribbling.

"What happened to the man who shot you?" he asked next.

"I'd give a lot to know the answer to that."

"He seems to have disappeared. Did you ever know his name? What do you think became of him?"

"I think he ran scared. Because he didn't beat me to the draw—I beat him. The only reason he plugged me is because my gun jammed." He whipped out his right-hand Colt, causing Will and Nestor to jump, and fanned the cylinder a few times. "She let me down," he said sadly. "Not her fault, o' course. I'm suing the Winchester Company—did I tell you that? No? There's a scoop for your paper. I buy my .45 cartridges straight from the factory in New Haven, Connecticut, and what happens?" He shook his head in disgust.

"Let's see your arm," Nestor said. "Scar must be pretty bad."

Will looked up at that.

"It's not pretty. I don't care to show it. A man's scars are private."

Will and Nestor continued to stare at him.

" 'Specially a man in my position. And I'm not just talking about my reputation." He looked down at his hand and made a slow and somehow dignified, even a tragic, fist. "This scar, it's not the only one I've got. But I don't show the others, either. I don't know how else to explain it. I'm a man. I've got . . . pride."

Nestor nodded solemnly, pressing his lips together

hard to show that he was touched, but in a manly way.

Will finished scribbling and looked up. Behind his glasses, his magnified blue eyes were positively fawnlike. He'd swallowed every word, and it was all hogwash. Jesse didn't even know what he was talking about.

"Hi, Mr. Gault!"

Good timing, he thought, watching little Ham, Levi's kid, barrel toward him on the boardwalk. He stood up when he saw who was strolling along behind him.

"I heard you was takin' pictures," Ham exclaimed, breathless, barely screeching to a stop before slamming into Jesse's hip. "Can I get a picture with you? Can I?"

Jesse rested one hand on Ham's head and whipped his hat off with the other. "Afternoon, Miss McGill." He flashed his winningest grin. "How're you today? A little warm this afternoon, though it looks like we might get a shower later. Been shopping?"

Finally she had to stop, all the words he'd flung at her making it impossible for her to keep walking without saying anything. Plus he was keeping Ham stationary, and she couldn't very well go on without him. "Good afternoon, Mr. Gault," she said coolly. "Yes, it's warm today." She had a big hatbox by the handle in one hand, a hankie in the other; she took the opportunity to dab at her temples and under her nose. She had on a blue dress with a kind of apron thing in front, very demure, and a starched white collar that had wilted in the heat. She looked about

eighteen with her hair like that, tied behind her neck
in a big white ribbon bow. He wished he could take
her for a ride. Right now. Scoop her up on Pegasus
and run along the river with her, fast as the wind.

"I tol' you he look good," Ham said to Cady, and
before his eyes, for no reason Jesse could think of,
she blushed. Bright pink, pretty as a rose. "Can I git
my picture took with Mr. Gault, Cady?" Ham begged,
big brown eyes wide and hopeful on her face.

She scowled at him, the blush fading. "I don't see
how. Not unless you've got five dollars. That's what
you're charging, isn't it, Will? You ought to be
ashamed of yourself. I bet your father doesn't know
about this."

"What's wrong with it?" Will lifted his chin, offended. "Nobody else is complaining. My father
would say it's free enterprise. Anyway, Mr. Gault's
getting most of—"

"Ham's a special friend of mine," Jesse butt in
hastily. "No charge for him. Okay, Will?"

"Well, sure," he agreed, "I don't care," while Ham
jumped up and down, crowing with excitement.

"How about you, Miss Cady?" Jesse wheedled.
"Want to be in the picture with us?"

"No, thanks." But she was smiling.

"Sure? You can put on your new hat."

"Yeah!" Ham could hardly contain himself. "It got
yellow feathers an' a nest an' ribbons all over, and it
the prettiest hat—put it on, Cady, okay?"

"No."

"Please?"

"No."

"Please?"

"Ham, don't *start*. I'm not putting on this hat and I'm not having my picture made." Now she wasn't just smiling, she was *laughing*. It tickled him so, Jesse threw back his head and laughed with her. When he stopped, he realized they were all staring at him with their mouths open, as if he'd just spouted out the Russian alphabet or all thirty-eight state capitals.

"Let's get this show on the road," he said with as surly a snarl as he could muster, whipping his own hat off and pulling on his eyepatch, slamming the hat back on his head. "You set up, Will? Ham, you ready? I ain't got all day."

That's about how long it took to get the picture right, though. "Right" according to Ham. First he wanted Jesse sitting down with him, Ham, standing between his knees. Then—no—that was too "baby-ish"; he wanted to sit on the bench beside the gun-fighter, mimicking his cross-legged posture. No, on second thought, they both ought to stand up and face the camera. Or—pretend to draw on each other! Yeah! Jesse could lend Ham one of his guns and he could stick it in his belt and—

"Ham, that is not going to happen," Cady declared, in a voice that for Jesse brought back memories of his mother, on those rare occasions when she'd put her foot down. But Cady must be in a good mood today, because she didn't leave—she stayed out in the hot sun smiling at Ham's antics and Jesse's pretend-exasperation. Once she did go in the saloon, but it was only to come back with an armful of vanilla pop bottles—five of them; she even remembered

Nestor. Jesse found himself trying to make her laugh again—making faces at the camera, tickling Ham a second before Will snapped off a shot. When he lay on the ground and told Ham to rest his foot on his chest and blow smoke from an imaginary gun, she lost it.

"Quit wriggling," Will commanded, but Jesse couldn't help it: the sight of Cady doubled up, giggling and snorting, hands on her knees, made him start to guffaw along with her. Which made his chest shake and Ham's knee bob up and down, which made everybody laugh harder, which made Ham lose his balance and pitch over on top of Jesse. Then, naturally, they had to have a wrestling match.

"Well, well, now ain't this cute."

Cady stopped laughing. Jesse let Ham out of a loose armlock and peered past him to see Warren Turley's beady eyes and nasty smile looming over them. Clyde, his shadow, stood half a step behind him.

Ham scrambled up and headed for Cady, who pulled him back against her and wound her arms around his shoulders. Jesse got up much, much slower. After he smacked his hat against his thigh for a while and slapped at his pants to get the dust off, he finally glanced at Turley. "Something you wanted? Like your gun back?" Cady drew a breath at that, and Turley's ugly face darkened.

"Mr. Wylie wants to talk to you, Gault," he said belligerently. "He's up at the saloon right now, waiting for you. *Wylie's* saloon," he clarified, throwing a sneering look at Cady.

"You don't say." Jesse turned his back on him and moseyed over to the bench. Slouching down, back against the wall, he stuck his feet up on the railing. "Tell him I'm busy."

Nestor snickered. Will Shorter started putting his camera equipment away, pretending he wasn't listening. Cady kept her arms around Ham and didn't move.

"He's waiting for you," Turley repeated, starting to turn purple. "It's important."

It was so easy to get his goat, it wasn't even any fun anymore. "Listen, Warren, here's what you do. You go back and tell your boss what I told you—I've got too much going on right now to go see him." To rub it in, he lit a cigarette and blew a slow, lazy smoke ring at the sky. "If he wants to talk, he can bring his important ass down here. I'll be here for as long as it takes to finish this." He took another drag, flicked ash on the wood floor. "Probably take five, six minutes. Maybe you better hurry along."

Poor Warren, he looked like his head was going to explode. Before he stomped off, he shot back a look of loathing scary enough to give Jesse a chill. But he caught sight of Cady's face—excited and pleased and downright admiring—and it warmed him clear through to his bones.

Six

Wylie hadn't shown up by the time Jesse took a last puff and flipped his cigarette butt over the railing. He stood up, stretching. Cady had taken Ham inside; Will was long gone; Nestor scratched under his armpit, said, "Guess he ain't comin'," tipped his hat, and strolled off toward the livery.

Jesse's stomach growled. The sun was sliding down behind the second-story roof of the Frenchman's restaurant. He decided to go have dinner.

He sat at a table by the window while he ate "trout almondine," which turned out to be not half-bad, although the trout was haddock and the almonds were only chopped-up peanuts. Jacques claimed vinegar pie was a Parisian specialty, which didn't seem likely. It was good, though; Jesse got it whenever he ate at Jacques'—once or twice a day. Merle Wylie passed by the restaurant while he was sipping his coffee. He assumed it was Wylie—he was with Turley and Clyde, and he walked between them and half a step ahead. While Turley and Clyde went inside the Rogue and Wylie leaned against the hitching post waiting for them, Jesse studied him.

He looked like a strong, well-fed bay horse, maybe a little too well fed, with a thick, gleaming mane of mahogany-colored hair. His expensive broadcloth coat fit tight across bullish shoulders and a barrel chest. He was around average height, Jesse's height, but he outweighed him by forty pounds, easy. His features were murky in the dusk, but from what Jesse could make out, they matched the man—fleshy, prominent, and powerful. He pulled a long-chained watch out of his vest pocket, glanced at it, shoved it back in with small, jerky movements. He was furious, but he was trying to hide it.

Clyde came out, said something to him. Wylie turned his back on him and paced away, five fast, wide strides before he whipped around and paced back. Clyde hunched his shoulders, trying to disappear.

Jesse stood up. In the darkening window, he checked his reflection. Moderately bad, but something was missing . . . oh. The patch. He found it in his pocket and dragged it on, adjusting it over his right eye. There, that was better.

Turley came through the swinging doors of the Rogue just then. He talked; Wylie listened, but never looked at him. He was the emperor of his little kingdom of thugs and crooks and arsonists. Maybe he even used the royal "we." Throwing a dollar on the table, Jesse went out to make his acquaintance.

Clyde saw him first. He whispered it, but in the twilight hush Jesse distinctly heard him say, "He's over there. He's coming." Wylie turned around slowly, pivoting his bulk on surprisingly small feet.

Jesse took as long as he could getting to him. A laughably long time; he hoped he wouldn't laugh in Wylie's face when they finally got together. But they were acting like a couple of elk, or was it moose—which ones locked horns and fought to the death?—and that tickled him. He sobered, though, at the thought that he was probably the only one here doing any acting. Merle Wylie looked like the real thing.

Jesse halted about three feet shy of him. He could imagine a long, yawning, childish silence stretching out while each waited for the other to speak, so he broke it before it could get started. He whispered, "Wylie."

"Mr. Gault." He jutted his chin—a kind of greeting. Turley and Clyde flanked him like bookends.

"You want to talk to me," Jesse said, "you'll have to lose Billy the Kid and his lovable sidekick."

Wylie thought that over while Turley simmered; you could almost see steam coming out of his ears. "All right," he decided. He gave Turley a look, and immediately, like a whip-trained dog, Turley turned and walked away. Clyde followed. They only went as far as the corner, though; at Stark's Saddlery & Shoe Repair they turned around and glared, their thumbs stuck in their gunbelts. Jesse thought of sulky children sent off to bed early.

Now what?

"Walk with me down to my saloon, Mr. Gault. I'll buy you a drink." Wylie had a smooth, almost rich tenor voice at odds with his burly physique. His dark eyes protruded slightly and his forehead bulged; his jaw looked hard enough to split rock. Jesse supposed he was handsome if you were drawn to big, bulky things. Boulders and grindstones, concrete slabs.

"The Rogue's closer." The Rogue was right behind them. Strains of "My Darling Lies Yonder" on Chico's piano, soft and sweet, were coming through the swinging doors.

"I prefer my place."

"I prefer Cady McGill's."

Standoff. They stared at each other, blank-faced, hard-eyed. It went on until Jesse decided to add a little smile, gleeful and kind of nuts, to his expression. That might have been what did it—Wylie snapped, "Fine," and strode, stiff-shouldered, toward the saloon—but he wasn't sure. Wylie wasn't like the others, an instinct told him. He wasn't going to be half so easy to scare.

Things were quiet at the Rogue tonight. A few diehard gamblers played poker at a couple of tables, and a few cowboys were shooting pool in the back, but the roulette and blackjack tables stood empty. Levi was reading a book behind the bar; Chico was only noodling now, not even playing a song. Jesse looked around for Cady, and spotted her at a back table talking to Willagail. She stood up when she saw him—or maybe when she saw Wylie, it was hard to tell. She'd changed out of the blue dress and white apron. Yes, indeed. What she had on now was a shiny, slinky, sort of silvery-green deal that had something in it, some wire miracle that pushed her bosom almost up to her throat. It looked about as comfortable as chain mail, but it sure was an eyeful.

"Evening, Cady," Wylie said in a monotone, barely moving his lips.

She slitted her eyes and nodded once. "What do you want?"

"Nothing I could get here. Comfort. Intelligent clientele. Honest whiskey."

Cady suggested Wylie do something Jesse had always thought was physically impossible. He shivered; the temperature between these two was below zero and falling. The reason for it hit him all of a sudden, like a smack in the face. They used to be lovers. Had to be. Hostility this strong, this obvious—what else could account for it? He'd disliked Wylie before on principle, and now he despised him. Now it was personal.

Cady spun on her heel and moved away. At the bar, she said something to Levi while Jesse and Wylie took seats at an out-of-the-way table, and not long after that the bartender loped over to ask what they wanted.

Wylie let out a short, derisive laugh. "Listen, buck, I wouldn't drink the water in this place."

Levi's limpid, heavy-lidded eyes blinked at him slowly, patiently. "All right, boss," he said in the oddest voice; it sounded almost tender. Was this some Buddhist response to provocation? Jesse had never heard him call a man "boss" before. Wylie made a nervous, impatient gesture and gave him his shoulder.

"I'll have a double shot of that fine, fine bottled in bond you served me last night, Levi," Jesse said, overcompensating. "And a beer chaser," he threw in. What the hell.

They sat without speaking during the time it took Levi to bring the drinks. Jesse slouched in his chair— his *screw you* posture, guaranteed to annoy—while Wylie sat stiff and heavy, his strangely small hands resting on his beefy thighs. Cady, Jesse noticed, stood with her back to them at the bar, pretending to ignore them; but more than once he caught her watching them in the mirror.

"So. Wylie," he said, taking a sip of his whiskey after Levi set it in front of him and went away. "Why don't you tell me what's on your mind."

He waited a whole minute before saying, "Who hired you?" as if Jesse hadn't spoken first. His way of controlling the conversation.

Two could play that game. "Say, I read the other day where your old friend Cherney skipped town. You miss him? Guy like that, must seem like you lost a brother, Merle. A twin."

"What do you know about Cherney?" His bulging, bulbous face was ruddy to begin with; when he got mad, it turned the color of saddle leather.

"Me? Nothing. I told you. I just read the papers." He said it like he was lying, though, just to make the bastard crazy.

He gripped the edge of the table. He had clean, short fingernails, shiny and buffed. "What are you doing in Paradise, Gault? Who hired you?"

Jesse took a sip of whiskey, set the glass down and picked up his beer, took a slug and exhaled with deep, exaggerated satisfaction. He'd take any odds on a bet right now that Wylie wished he'd ordered something, anything. "What makes you think anybody hired me? Nice place, Paradise. I like it here. I might just—"

"Cady, right? Admit it. I know it was her."

Jesse put a cigarette in his mouth and lit a match to it. Blew smoke at the ceiling.

Wylie's grip on the table tightened. Whitened. Suddenly he relaxed it and sat back in his chair, smiling falsely, crossing one heavy leg over the other. The metal glint of a boot gun flashed before his pants leg covered it up. He patted his dark red hair, which was thick as a beaver pelt, and a ruby ring on his middle finger winked in the lantern light. "How much is she paying you?" he asked in the silky tenor. "Well? Come, you might as well tell me."

"Why? Assuming she's paying me anything. Why would I tell you?"

"Because whatever it is, I can better it." He looked around at Cady's clean, comfortable saloon, smiling a little derisive smile, his black eyes contemptuous. "I can double it. Triple it." He leaned forward, massive body stiff and intense. "Name your price, Mr. Gault. Just tell me what you want."

Ah, thought Jesse, *the magic words*. Now that they were out, he felt disappointed. In the end, Wylie had been as easy as all the others.

He started to drop his cigarette on the floor, remembered Ham, and flicked it into a nearby spittoon instead. "My price to do what?"

Wylie lowered his voice. "Burn her out."

Burn her out. A picture flared in Jesse's mind: the

pretty, red-painted Rogue in smoky, stinking ruins, and Cady in the street watching it smolder, hugging herself in her paisley night robe, trying not to cry.

"Burn her out?" he said in shocked, carrying tones.

Wylie jerked back, as startled as if Jesse had thrown his drink in his face. "Shut up!" He hissed it, glancing around, flushing. "Shut up, God damn you. Are you insane?"

Maybe so. He would never burn down Cady's saloon—he would never burn down anything—but he could've lied and said he would. He could've blackmailed Wylie. Or stolen a fortune from him and never had a twinge of conscience because the bastard was a thief and a bully and God knew what else.

But he wasn't going to do any of those things. And if that wasn't insane, Jesse didn't know what was.

"Oh, that's right," he said in the creepy whisper—reverting to Gault. "Arson's your specialty, isn't it? I heard about the old livery stable. Who did that one for you? Turley? Tell me, how many horses got barbecued in the process?" Wylie shoved his chair and started to stand. "Sit down!"

He did, after putting on a careless sneer to show he didn't have to if he didn't want to.

Really, you know, Jesse thought—far from the first time—the majority of grown men were about a boulder's throw, maturity-wise, from scabby little boys. "I got one thing to say to you, Merle. When I finish, you can get up and leave."

Wylie made the same anatomically improbable suggestion Cady had made to him. This thing was going around.

Ignoring it, Jesse said slowly and clearly, "If anything happens to this saloon, if so much as a window gets cracked, I'm going to come after you. You can try to hide behind those two hoodlums outside, but it won't do you any good. In the end it'll boil down to you and me. And then it'll just be me."

"No. No. That's not how it's going to be." White saliva drooled in the corners of his lips. He looked mad enough to spit, and maybe just plain mad, too. As in insane. One ace shy of a deck. "I'll hire a gun of my own, somebody faster, smarter, a killer, you won't stand a chance. You better keep looking over your shoulder, Gault, because you'll never know when it's coming, you'll be—"

"You better keep looking straight ahead, because I don't shoot men in the back. Know why? Because I like to see their eyes when they're dying. I like to see the fear get cloudy and the desperation set in. And then I like to see the emptiness. The coldness. Blank. Dead."

Wylie's chair scraping the floor sounded like fingernails on a chalkboard. He was reduced to cursing, crude, vicious oaths in a hoarse voice, as if he'd been shouting all day. Jesse laughed at him. But when Wylie finally ran down, hurled a last curse and stalked away, he almost groaned with relief. Because he'd just remembered the boot gun.

If Cady had any doubts left about whether or not Jesse worked for Wylie, the names she and everybody else could plainly hear Merle calling him finally set her mind at rest. And if they hadn't, the look on Merle's face would have. She was in his path—he had to cross in front of her to get to the door—and she had to make herself stand still, not shrink against the bar or flinch from the anger in his black, bulging eyes. How could she ever have found him good-looking? And charming, too—imagine that. It hadn't even been that long ago. Either she'd been crazy and blind, or he'd changed. Or both. More likely both.

She watched Jesse take off his hat and scratch his head with both hands, hard. "Play something soft," she told Chico, touching his shoulder as she passed behind him. Jesse saw her coming and sat up straight, quit slouching. The way he looked at her . . . she became aware of the twisting of her hips as she maneuvered through the mostly empty tables. "Hi, Stony. Hey, Bailey, how're you doing," she greeted her few scattered customers, but she never really stopped looking at Jesse. The closer she got, the sweeter he smiled. The gladder she felt.

"Hey," she said, and for a few more seconds they just beamed at each other. He had on black, as usual—black denim trousers and soft leather boots, a faded black shirt of worn linen. He still had traces of dust on his pants, from rolling in the street with Ham—a spectacle she wouldn't have believed if she hadn't seen it with her own eyes. "What'd you say to Merle?" she broke off grinning at him to ask. "He looked like he swallowed a can of fishhooks."

"Told him to deal me out of his business proposition." He leaned over and pulled the chair next to him out from under the table, offering it to her.

"Which was?"

"Big bucks for a little fire."

"A little fire. Where?"

He surveyed the room with a lazy eye. "Up that wall, maybe. Behind the bar, definitely. All that booze would make some real pretty fireworks."

She ought not to be shocked, but she was. Wylie hated her enough to do almost anything—she'd known that for months. She'd known it since the day, in his saloon, when she'd pulled out her gun and told him to keep away from her or she'd plug him. A stupid move, in retrospect, but it was his fault. He'd provoked her.

"Well," she said, feeling a little weak. "I guess I should thank you."

"Sit down, why don't you?" He gestured again at the chair, and this time she came around it and sat. "Want a drink?"

"You've got on your eyepatch again," she observed.

He touched it with his fingertips, as if he'd forgotten it. "I can take it off now." He did so, whipping off his hat first, then the leather strap that tied in a knot in back. Immediately he covered up his exposed right eye with his cupped palm. "Always smarts for a little while at first." After a few seconds he took his hand away, blinking rapidly, squinting. "I still don't see too well. But it's a whole lot better than nothing."

It ought not to make such a difference—his right eye looked just like his left eye; she wasn't seeing anything she hadn't seen before. But she had the same reaction to him now as she'd had on the street this afternoon, when she'd first seen him without the patch. He was gorgeous.

"I thought you'd have a scar," she said inanely.

"I do. Can't you see it?"

"I'm a little nearsighted." But even when she leaned close, even when her head was no more than seven inches from his, she couldn't see any scar. Just a beautiful, slightly slanted gray eye surrounded by long black lashes, and a straight, sleek, very masculine eyebrow cocked over it.

"It's faded a lot over the years. But I can still make it out. It's right here." He ran his finger along the bone of his eye socket.

She still couldn't see anything. "You're more sensitive to it," she guessed, and he said that was probably right.

"Care for a drink?" he asked again, signaling to Levi, who was shaking his head at something Doc Mobius was telling him at the bar.

"Anything wrong?" she asked him when he came over, drying his hands on his apron.

"Yeah, real bad news, Cady. Doc jus' tol' me that Mr. Forrest Sullivan done shot hisself to death."

"No. Oh, no."

"Maybe a accident, but maybe not—Doc ain't sayin'. Happen in Mr. Sullivan's barn; oldes' chile found him there this afternoon."

"Oh, Levi. Oh, my God, all those children." And Mrs. Sullivan, who nodded to Cady in church sometimes. Whatever would they do now?

"Want another drink, Mr. Gault?" Levi asked somberly.

"Yeah. Thanks. Cady, you want something?" The

way he said it, soft and gentle, felt like a light touch on her hand or her shoulder.

"No. Yes." Such indecision. "Levi," she said boldly, "I'll have a beer."

"Make it two."

Levi grunted and turned away.

"Forrest Sullivan," Jesse mused after a minute. "Isn't he the one . . . didn't you tell me the bank foreclosed on his sheep ranch?"

"Yes. Now Merle will get it. It's what he's been wanting. Damn him." She could've said a lot worse. But she already had, and Jesse had heard her. She felt a little embarrassed about that. Merle Wylie had a way of bringing out the worst in her. "I liked Forrest," she said quietly. "He didn't come here often— didn't drink much, and I don't ever remember seeing him gamble. But he didn't care if other people did, you know? Even though he didn't frequent saloons himself, he didn't call them dens of iniquity. He didn't judge." Jesse nodded. "Mrs. Sullivan's like that, too. I wish there was something I could do. But . . . I don't really know her." Louise Sullivan sang in the church choir, taught Sunday school, served on the Town Ladies Committee. She was respectable. She might nod to Cady every once in a while, but that didn't mean she'd welcome her sympathies. Definitely not in a visit. Maybe not even in a note.

She sighed. "If he did shoot himself on purpose, it's Wylie's fault, just as if he'd pulled the trigger."

Jesse said nothing, but his silence seemed sympathetic to her. When Levi brought their drinks, Jesse clinked his glass to hers, making her smile at him. The strong, yeasty beer tasted good and went down easy. Surprisingly easy, considering how long it had been since she'd drunk one. Not since last summer, as she recalled.

"What do you know about Dr. Mobius?" Jesse asked.

"Doc? Not much, I guess. Why?"

"Just curious. He never talks."

"No. He came here about two years ago, I think. Anyway, right after I came. Before that, there wasn't a doctor; if you got sick, you had to go to Jacksonville." She glanced over at the bar, where the doctor stood in his usual spot, hunched over his usual sarsaparilla. "It's true he keeps to himself, but I think he's a nice man. Mr. Shlegel—that's the man who owned this bar before me—he saw him a few times. But he was really sick, and Doc sent him to a specialist in Eugene. I know Glen went to him once for . . . something." Black eyes and a broken wrist. "She said he was kind to her."

"You never went to him?"

"Me? Oh, no. I'm never sick." It was true, and she was proud of it. She gave the wooden table a humorous rap with her knuckles, though. Just in case.

He sipped his beer and she sipped hers, and they watched each other in a companionable silence. A house deck lay on the table. Jesse picked it up and began shuffling the cards. He had strong hands, not a gambler's hands, but long-fingered and smart. She watched him set the cards down in four identical piles, then scoop them up again, over and over.

"High-low?" he offered, smiling at her, and she shrugged. Why not? Reaching, she turned over a ten; he beat her with a queen. "You lose."

"What are we playing for?"

He pulled on the side of his mustache, thinking it over. They were both smiling slight, secret smiles. *We're flirting,* Cady realized. "Let's play," he suggested, "the winner gets to ask the loser a question, and she has to answer it."

"Or he."

"Or he."

"I'm not sure I like this game," she said. "Does the loser have to tell the truth?"

"Absolutely."

"Then I definitely don't like this game."

"Too bad—you already lost. Here's your question." Glancing around first, he leaned toward her, snaring her with a steely, narrow-eyed, intense stare. "What," he said very slowly, very quietly, "is your favorite color?"

She was so surprised, she gave out a loud, unladylike bray of laughter. When he grinned, two deep creases appeared on either side of his mouth—manly dimples. She was growing very fond of them. "My favorite color," she mulled. "It used to be blue, but now it's green."

"Is that right? Mine, too. Except mine's always been green."

She batted her eyes at him. "We have something in common."

He passed the deck over; she cut again, lost again. "How old are you?"

"Now, that's rude, you can't ask a lady that question."

"No? Okay. How much do you weigh?"

She laughed again, giddy and lighthearted. Was it the beer? Everything he said was funny. "I have no idea."

"Well, I get to keep asking till you answer one." He looked up at the ceiling, thinking. "What's the most embarrassing thing you ever did?"

Disarmed again, she dissolved into giggles. She'd been sure he would ask her real questions, hard ones requiring lies or distractions for answers. Of course she was attracted to him, no sense denying that, but now he was making her *like* him, too. For her own good, she hoped he never found out that funny, silly Jesse was a hundred times more dangerous than humorless, flinty-eyed Gault.

"Give me that deck," she said, "I think you're cheating." She reshuffled the cards, and they cut again. "Ha. I knew it—I win."

He shook his head, chuckling at her. "What's your question?"

She had a million. "When and where were you born, and were you happy growing up?"

"That's three."

She lifted her eyebrows in a dare.

He stroked his eyebrow thoughtfully. "Lexington, Kentucky, 1846. Yeah, I was happy. Usually. Till the war came."

She stared at him, chin in her hand. 'Forty-six? That made him thirty-eight years old. He sure didn't look it, not at all. She thought he looked about her

age: twenty-five. Twenty-seven or -eight at the most.
The gray in his hair . . . she'd always thought it was
premature, but maybe it wasn't. She liked it anyway.
Pewter-colored. It was beautiful in the lamplight, that
contrast of dark and light, black and silver.

They cut again, and this time he won. "How do
you like the saloon business? Does it suit you?"

What a nice question. Except for Levi, she didn't
have anybody to talk to about things like that. "Yes.
And no." The interest in his face encouraged her to
explain. "The thing about owning a saloon is, you
have to think like a man. You might like flowers on
the bar or curtains on the windows, different pictures
on the walls." She flicked a glance at the naked lady
oil painting over the bar. "But you can't act on any
of those changes because your customers wouldn't
like them. They'd hate them. So instead you have to
think about spittoons and pool tables, whiskey
brands and poker chips. Ash cans."

"Think like a man."

"Yeah. I like the business side, though. The record-
keeping, the carefulness you have to exercise. And
especially," she confided with a grin, "the way the
profits edge up a little bit every month when you've
been smart and clever and done everything just
right."

"I'll bet."

"It's just the saloon part I get tired of once in a
while. Not that I'm complaining. But it's a man's
business, the day-to-day part, and I'm always . . ."
She didn't know how to say it. She felt as if she was

constantly having to push her femininity aside, bury it, to get the job done.

"You're always a woman."

"Well. Yes." For some dumb reason, she blushed. "Want another beer?"

"Okay. But just one more," she warned, meaning it.

The Rogue had nearly emptied out. The handful of drinkers who were left glanced over at her and Jesse from time to time, interested, speculating. By tomorrow everybody in Paradise would know she'd spent the whole night laughing and drinking beer with the gunfighter.

"Cut the cards," Jesse said. She turned over a five and groaned, then clapped her hands when he drew a four.

"Tell me about your childhood."

He sent her a crooked smile. "How come you're so interested?"

"I just am. Do you have any brothers and sisters?"

"No." He hesitated. Without looking at her he said, "I had a cousin, though."

"Were you close?"

"Yeah." Suddenly he grinned, a little mysteriously, she thought. "Real close."

"Tell me about him. Or her?"

"Him."

"What was his name?"

"Marion. Marion Gault."

"Younger or older?"

"Younger. Nine years younger."

"Are you like him?"

He smiled again. "Nope. Marion and I, we're pretty much opposites. He's . . . never amounted to much, to tell you the truth. When we were little he always looked up to me, tagged along after me. Thought the sun rose on my head—you know how kids are. When we all went off to war—me and my father and his father—he stayed home and tried to keep the farm going. A horse farm; they raised thoroughbreds and racers. But he couldn't do it. His daddy died at Vicksburg, and then his mama took sick and died the year after that. By the time the war ended, one army or the other had taken all the horses, and there wasn't any money to get more."

"What did he do?"

"Headed west. Worked odd jobs. He didn't really know what to do with himself. He was kind of . . . aimless."

His quiet mood puzzled her. "Did you try to help him?" She looked down. "Sorry. This isn't any of my business."

"I had my own life. And I was on the run from the law in Kentucky by then because—well, I expect you read about that in the paper."

That reminded her. "Are they still after you?"

"No, no. It happened fifteen years ago, the statute's run out. Anyway—Marion and I, we've run across each other a time or two since then. Matter of fact, I saw him not that long ago." Again he smiled the mysterious smile. "In Oakland."

"That's where you got shot," she remembered.

He took a sip of beer. "But this was before. My

cousin was working a job busting mustangs for some rich rancher in Sonoma."

"Well," she said uncertainly. "At least he's found work with horses."

Jesse laughed without humor. "He hates it. Breaking horses, he can't stand that. Plus working for somebody else . . ." He shook his head. "It makes him crazy."

A pause.

"Enough," he said abruptly, shuffling the cards, coming out of his mood. "You got a hell of a lot out of me for one piddling four of clubs. Cut."

She lost.

His slow, devilish grin made her stomach flutter. "Miss McGill."

"What."

"How'd you get that tattoo?"

She tried to stare him down. His eyes were twinkling; hers probably were, too. "What tattoo?" What got into her? She wanted him to drop his eyes, look at her *there*.

He did.

"That one," he said softly.

She tore her gaze away to look down innocently. In this dress, she knew it was invisible unless she leaned over. "How do you know I've got a tattoo?"

He blew air through his nose. "I've seen it. You might say I've studied on it. What is it, some kind of bird?"

"An eagle," she answered, taking a slow, deep breath. For his benefit. Good grief, she hadn't flirted like this with a man since—she couldn't remember when. Even with Jamie O'Doole, she'd never been this brazen. "It's a symbol of freedom. I wear it in honor of someone . . . someone I used to know."

"Who?"

"His name was James. James Doulé. He's dead now." She dropped her gaze into the depths of her beer. Contemplated the foam sadly.

"Sorry to hear that."

She lifted her head, tossed it bravely. "He was a mercenary soldier, an American. He fought with Garibaldi in the Red Shirt army. But then . . . he was shot and killed in the struggle to liberate Naples. I wear this"—she brushed her bodice with her fingertips—"in his memory."

She waited a few mournful moments before looking up. Jesse was scowling into his own beer. He looked . . . he looked *annoyed*. She scoffed at the thought that her story had made him jealous—ridiculous; a few days ago he thought she was a prostitute, and that hadn't bothered him one bit. Still. Jealous? Why, what an intriguing idea.

"It's late," she noticed.

"Yeah." He looked up, and when he smiled at her her heart flipped over. "Only time for one more question." He turned the deck over to the ace of spades on the bottom. "Well, will you look at that."

"You did that. You put it there."

"Can't prove it."

She sat back with a show of resignation. "Okay, hit me."

"Tell me why you were so mad at me. You know. That day in your room."

"I wasn't mad," she denied automatically.

"Yes, you were."

"No, I wasn't."

"Yes, you were."

"No, I wasn't."

"Okay." He rested his forearms on the table and leaned in, hunching his shoulders. "I'm sorry for saying what I did, Cady. Thinking what I thought."

"Really, it doesn't matter in the least."

"Matters to me. I got the wrong idea, and I want you to know it wasn't because of anything you did. Or said, or—looked like. It was just me being stupid."

She stared into his gray eyes and felt herself falling, falling. Here they were in a saloon knocking back beers, she in a shameless hussy dress she could barely sit down in because the hips were so tight— and he thought mistaking her for a whore was all *his* fault. She'd've laughed if she hadn't felt a little more like crying.

She didn't do either one, of course. "I told you, you don't need to apologize. It's not the first time somebody's . . . made a mistake about me. Probably won't be the last. But . . . thank you for saying that. It means a lot."

The bar was empty; even Chico had gone home. Levi was blowing out the lanterns.

"I'll walk you around to your back door," Jesse said. "To say good night."

To kiss her good night—that's what he meant. She tried to think, but her mind went blank. She allowed a little pause, so he would at least think she was thinking. "Well . . . all right."

Levi just said good night to them, didn't stare or look knowing or make a crack. That was just one of the things she loved about him—his live-and-let-live attitude.

Outside, the half-moon floated behind cloud wisps, hazing the blue-black sky. Somewhere far off an owl hooted; down at the end of Noble Fir, Stony Dern's dog wouldn't stop barking. Cady and Jesse didn't make small talk as they walked around the corner. Their steps sounded too loud on the board sidewalk; She was glad when they came to the worn grass path through the blueblossom bushes that led around to her back door.

Boo appeared out of nowhere. Ignoring Jesse, he arched his back and rubbed against Cady's skirt. "Who's this?" asked Jesse.

She bent down to stroke Boo's head. "My worthless excuse for a cat." She opened the door, and he scurried inside.

"You ought to keep this locked, Cady."

"I know, I've meant to. I forgot this time."

He poked his head in. The moonlight made it bright enough to see that her small room was empty and undisturbed.

"Well," she said. "Night."

"Night." He smiled knowingly, and she couldn't help smiling back. It was partly nerves, but it was also because being with him made her feel good. Made her feel like laughing. She waited, barely breathing, for the moment, the first movement toward her. She wasn't expecting it when he took off his hat. He dropped it on top of the dahlia stake she'd stuck in the ground yesterday, and she shivered to think it was because he wanted his hands free.

"Cold?"

"No." She was just rubbing her arms for the heck of it.

He covered her hands with his big ones, those handsome, long-fingered hands she'd been looking at all night. She stopped her nervous chafing. Very slowly, so she could pull away if she wanted to, he took her hands and put them on his shoulders. Pressed them there, gave them a little pat, then hooked his fingers at the back of her neck and drew her up close.

It was the first time she'd touched him. He had touched her—that day in front of her mirror—but this was the first time she'd touched him. She was acutely aware of that as she molded her palms over hard muscle and bone, warming skin, soft linen. He slipped his fingers into her hair, cupping the back of her head. Tipping her chin up, he surprised her by kissing it. She smiled, and he kissed one side of her mouth and then the other. His mustache tickled. He was just the right height, tall but not too tall; even this close, she didn't have to crane her neck to see him. Kiss him.

She kissed him. Couldn't stand the wait any longer, nice as these nibbling preliminaries were. She put her hands on either side of his face and brought her mouth to his, brushing lips with him. Someone said,

"Mmmm," she wasn't sure if it was him or her, maybe both, and her thoughts started to scatter.

He said, "Cady," a wisp of a word in his throaty whisper, pressing her back. She liked it, the door frame behind her, Jesse's long, hard body in front, leaning into her, pressing against her. She murmured, "Jessss," and squeezed him tight, feeling so strong and competent, and in the next second a delicious weakness washed over her, sapping all her strength.

She sighed. She let her head fall back. She felt the toe of his boot slide between her shoes—just that—pushing her feet, her legs, a little bit farther apart, and the bottom dropped out of her stomach. She clung to him, twisting her head from one side to the other, loving the feel of his hot mouth on her throat. She hadn't been expecting this. A good-night kiss, she'd thought, not this long, sweet ravishment. How could she stop? "Jesse . . ."

He moved lower, touching her skin with his tongue. She put her hands in his hair, breathing deeply, arching her back. She felt his teeth on the swell of her bosom, a wide, soft horsebite that made her laugh, breathless, and made sparks shoot down, straight down into her vitals. In one smooth move, he slipped his hand inside her gown and held her naked breast, at the same time he lifted his head and kissed her full on the mouth.

She moaned. He murmured something. She couldn't make it out; something sweet, complimentary. Not for a second did she feel maneuvered or manipulated—because she knew he was as aroused, as *surprised* by this as she was.

But she said, "Wait . . . Jesse, wait . . ." when his hand on her waist stroked down to the front of her thigh, twisting in the fabric of her skirt, making a gentle grab for her crotch. Too fast. Men were always too fast.

"Okay," he conceded, "okay," breathing hard against the side of her neck. He took his hand away. And kissed her again, sliding his tongue in her mouth.

Oh, God. But she knew exactly what she was doing. A few more seconds of this, that was all she'd let him have, because then it really had to . . . it really had to . . .

"Stop."

She couldn't believe it when he did. Stopped. Right away—no whining, no pretending he didn't hear or he was too carried away to obey. He stepped back and let her catch her breath, not holding anything but her hand.

"Want to go for a ride with me tomorrow?"

"Umm." A ride? What was tomorrow?

"You ride, don't you? Horses," he specified when she kept frowning at him. "Wake up," he whispered, leaning in to kiss the tip of her nose.

That was how she felt, groggy, as if she'd been sleeping and dreaming the loveliest dream. "I don't ride very well." Oh, and "I don't have a horse."

"You could rent one from Nestor. I have a *great* horse." She smiled—he looked so pleased with himself. "Where would we go, Cady? You could show me the country. I haven't been anywhere but here since I got here."

"Jesse." Now she was waking up. "I'm busy tomorrow."

"All day?"

She nodded.

"What about Saturday?"

"No. Can't."

"How come?"

"Busy."

He kept his smile, but let go of her hand. "Sunday," he said softly, not a question this time.

She looked down.

"Any point in me going through the rest of the week? I'll do it if it'll work."

"Jesse, listen." She was glad when he backed up another step; it gave her room to think. "I just . . . I just don't see any point to it. You and me going for a ride or anything."

"Why not?"

Because you're a hired gunfighter! *How many men have you killed?* That's what she *should've* asked him, not where he was born or if his childhood was happy. *How can you shoot a man down in the street for money?*

"Why not, Cady?"

She shook her head. Should she tell him? What if he got mad at her? What in the world made her think she could trust this man? He was smiling at her, a stiff, sad smile that might've melted her heart if it hadn't tripped a memory. She'd read somewhere that Billy the Kid was always smiling. Billy the Kid was a real friendly fellow. He smiled while he drew on men and shot them dead.

"You know—it's late," she said abruptly. "I think we'd better say good night. Levi will want to lock up." He made a movement toward her. Instinctively, she shrank back, into her open doorway. She watched his face go from surprise to understanding, then cynicism. Her heart sank.

His lips curled. "Oh, now I get it. It's okay to kiss me here in the dark, but not go for a ride with me in broad daylight. Why didn't you just say so?"

She twisted her hands, miserable.

"Fine. That's fine. Believe me, my heart's not broken." He started backing away. "Besides, you've got that solid gold reputation of yours to uphold. Don't forget that. No, sir. Wouldn't want anybody to find out the lady blackjack dealer and saloon owner went out riding horses with *Jesse Gault*."

He spun on his heel, went four steps down the walk, spun back around, and strode toward her. She thought he wanted his hat, which was still dangling on the dahlia stake. "I take that back. Didn't mean that last part. Forget I said it. Okay?" he demanded when she only stared at him.

"Okay."

"Okay. Good night." He jammed his hat on and walked away again. This time he kept going.

Cady dropped down on the stoop. "Boo?" she called plaintively. The cat ignored her, didn't come out to comfort her. She could've used some comforting. She replayed the scene with Jesse in her mind a few times, giving it different endings. They got more and more daring, the endings; more and more injurious to her solid gold reputation.

She stayed outside until the moon went down, brooding and sighing, mulling and sulking. When her rear end got sore, she went in and got undressed for bed. "Oh, forget it," she muttered to herself, settling the covers around her. "Just go to sleep and forget it." She was giving herself the same advice at dawn.

Seven

Jesse came into Jacques' restaurant the next day while Cady was eating her lunch. Unthinkingly, out of nothing but habit, she smiled, even started to reach for her glass and the salt shaker—move them out of the way so he could sit down with her. She stopped herself when he touched his hat and walked on by, heading for an empty table in the corner.

She froze, then went hot all over. Men didn't snub her very often. Women did, but not men. *You deserve it*, an unwelcome little voice informed her—the voice of her conscience. *Do not*, she argued, rattling the newspaper, drawing her conscience's attention to it. If anything justified her decision to stay away from Jesse Gault, installment two of Will Shorter's interview with him did. And Jesse could try all he liked to make himself sound like a cross between Robin Hood and Sir Galahad, but nothing got around the fact that he'd killed so many men he'd lost track of the number. "Ten or twelve," Will quoted him as saying. "Or maybe it's fifteen by now."

Of course, they were all asking for it. They all drew first, every one of them, and they were all rotten hombres or low-down card cheats or thieves or degenerates who deserved what they got. And Gault was an avenging angel, a victim, a reluctant hero, an innocent bystander. A righter of wrongs with two smoking six-guns. Funny how his image kept changing. Interesting how he kept reinventing himself. She remembered when he was a cold-blooded hired killer who'd just as soon shoot you as look at you. When was that, a week ago? Now he rolled in the dirt with children, when he wasn't mugging and preening for photographs with awestruck townsfolk. Or charming the pantaloons off jaded lady saloonkeepers . . .

She snuck a glance at him over her coffee cup. He looked away fast—he'd been staring at *her*. He looked back, nodded to her with a quick smile that didn't reach his eyes, and started to read the menu. Since he ate here every day, and since Jacques' menu hadn't changed since 1878, she knew he was pretending.

Well, this was stupid. Last night they'd kissed, and today they couldn't even talk to each other.

Jacques' daughter came over to take Jesse's order. Michele was a plain, full-hipped, big-bosomed girl with a sweet, shy manner. She leaned toward Jesse. He said something that made her throw her head back and laugh. Cady's mouth dropped open. She hardly ever got so much as a smile out of Michele, the girl was so bashful. Well, it ought not to surprise her. Glendoline got sillier by the day over Gault, and now Willagail was starting. Maggie McGurke, the girl Cady employed to change linens and clean the guest rooms, came down every afternoon with new stories about what he'd said to her, the joke he'd told her, the wonderful way he'd flirted with her. And just this morning Enid Duff, the postmistress, an old maid if there ever was one, had tried to pry information about him out of Cady. "Is he married?" she had actually asked.

But the last straw was Lia Chang, the laundryman's daughter, the girl Levi was trying to court by reading books about Buddha. "He belly handsome man," she'd confided to Cady behind her father's counter, handing over Cady's clean, folded laundry. "Belly kind man."

"Kind? Lia, he's a *killer*."

"Oh, no." She smiled calmly, beatifically. "He not kirrer."

"But he *says* he is. He *admits* it."

Her lovely, moon-shaped face stayed placid and serene. She said no more, and Cady got the distinct feeling she was humoring her.

It was all so ridiculous. How could grown women throw away every bit of their common sense just because a man was good-looking? A little mysterious? And funny. Sexy as hell.

She took the opportunity to stare at him while he spread butter on a piece of cornbread. She liked the way his hair grew. It was too long, but it always looked neat anyway. Shiny black-and-silver hair that flowed through your fingers like . . . the silk tassels on her paisley shawl. She liked the way he carried himself, too; he could slouch and keep his nice broad shoulders straight at the same time. He had one long leg crossed over the other, and she couldn't take her eyes off the tight pull of worn black denim seam down the length of his thigh. "He sleeps buck naked," Maggie McGurke had informed her and Willagail this morning. *How do you know?* Cady had started to ask, but stopped herself. She didn't want to know.

Now he had his elbows on the table, hands steepled, tapping his fingertips together while he stared off into space. He looked—oh, this was silly, and yet—he really did look . . . a little lonely. But pretending not to be. That's what got her. He adjusted his silverware, lined it up just so, picked up his empty glass and studied the manufacturer's mark on the bottom, set it carefully back down. Folded his hands on the edge of the table and frowned into the distance, as if thinking deep thoughts.

She thought about his apology last night. "Didn't mean that last part. Forget I said it, okay?" What he'd said *had* hurt. But he'd regretted it. He hadn't wanted her to be in pain for longer than about thirty seconds.

She stood up. The swiftness with which he looked over told her he'd been aware of her the whole time, not thinking deep thoughts at all. A few heads turned as she made her way to his table. What was she going to say? She didn't know until she said it.

"I didn't explain myself very well last night." He shoved his chair back and stood up—a courtesy she wasn't used to. "In fact," she added nervously, "I didn't explain myself at all."

"It doesn't matter," he said with an airy wave. But his gray eyes pierced her.

She was still holding the newspaper. "I've been reading about you. The life you've led. All the men you've . . ." Saying the word seemed rude, so she let that sentence dangle.

He grinned at her. "Pretty exciting, huh?"

"No, it's barbaric." His face fell. "Even allowing for bragging and exaggeration—"

"Hey, I wasn't bragging," he interrupted, offended. "And I never exaggerate."

"Then that makes it even worse. A woman would have to be out of her mind to want anything to do with Jesse Gault." She laid the folded-up newspaper on the table and tapped on it with her knuckles. *This* Jesse Gault, she meant.

"Wait now, you know you can't believe everything you read in the papers."

"Well, make up your mind! Is this stuff true or isn't it?"

He dipped his head, rubbing the back of his neck while he peered at her through his eyelashes. "Well, yeah. Sure, it's true, I told you. But still."

"Still?"

"Still. Couldn't you get around it? Overlook it?"

"Jesse—" She glanced around, lowered her voice. "Jesse, you *kill* people."

"Well, right, yeah, but . . ." He stuck his fingers in his hair and pulled, frowning, thinking hard. "But, hell, Cady, it's not like I'm going to kill *you*."

Her jaw dropped. He cocked his head, trying a boyish grin on her, trying to get her to smile back. "This," she said seriously, backing up, "is the strangest conversation I have ever had."

"Wait. Maybe I could reform. Hey, Cady? Wait a sec, let's talk about it!"

But she hurried back to her table, put money on it for Michele, and bustled out of Jacques' without turning around or saying good-bye. She needed fresh air, the dusty street under her feet, *reality*.

He was too good-looking—that had to be it. Because for half a second, "It's not like I'm going to kill *you*" had actually sounded reasonable to her. Oh, she had to stay away from Jesse Gault! Compared to him, a loaded gun was as safe as a puppy!

The next day she was still thinking about him. She sat at her desk in her tiny office, gazing into space instead of updating her inventory lists and reconciling her bankbook, two Saturday chores she always got out of the way before lunchtime. But today the columns of numbers danced out of focus every time she tried to stare them down. She'd given up; with Boo purring on her lap, she'd abandoned herself to full-time daydreaming.

"Miz Cady?"

She looked up and smiled at Ham, happy for any diversion. His wide-eyed, clean-scrubbed face was very dear to her; in two years, she'd come to adore Levi's little boy. "What? Come on in. What are you up to?"

"Poppy say come back an' tell you." He sidled up to her, leaning against her shoulder so he could see what she was doing. "You payin' bills?" His enormous brown eyes warmed sympathetically; he knew how she hated this job.

"Nope, not right now. Boy, you smell good. What'd you do, take a bath?" She gave him a squeeze, even stole a kiss on his sweet-smelling neck. He pretended to be embarrassed, but she knew he liked it. "So what are you supposed to tell me?"

"Oh. Joe Redleaf, he come in an' want to see you."

"Joe? He's here? Now?"

"Yep. He wearing a *suit*."

"Goodness." She stood up, brushing eraser crumbs from her skirt, patting her hair into place.

"You like him?" Ham asked interestedly, watching her hurried primping.

"Well, of course. I've always liked Joe." She chucked Ham under the chin and didn't tack on, *Just not as much as he's always liked me.*

"Joe!"

He was standing at the bar, talking to Levi. He turned, and his strong, serious face broke into a rare grin. Rushing over, she gave him an exuberant hug; but when he tried to kiss her on the mouth, she laughed and gave him her cheek.

"Look at you! I haven't seen you since—when, Christmas? Oh, you look *wonderful*." She held him at arm's length, sweeping him with a long, up-and-down appraisal. He looked so much older, like a man instead of a boy. He did have on a suit, but the coat was frayed at the cuffs and a little threadbare around the collar. A secondhand suit, then. Somehow that made him look even more dignified.

"*You* look wonderful," he said with feeling, and she laughed again, basking in Joe's admiration. She was used to it, but she didn't take it for granted. She realized she'd even missed it.

"How long have you been home?" she asked, taking his hand and leading him to an empty table. "Levi," she threw over her shoulder, "bring Joe a beer and me a lemonade."

"Since Wednesday."

"*Wednesday.*"

"And I have to go back on Monday."

"Oh." She made a disappointed face. "How are your parents?"

He rolled his eyes. "The same." Which explained why he'd been in town for three whole days without coming to see her. The Redleafs were dirt-poor and very proud, with sky-high hopes for a son who was so brilliant they were half afraid of him. Cady couldn't really blame them for not being thrilled about the passion he'd developed two years ago, at the age of eighteen, for a saloon girl. True, she owned the saloon now, but that hadn't lifted her up one inch in the Redleafs' estimation. If anything, she'd sunk a notch.

"Do they know you're here?" she asked. Joe shrugged, which meant no.

Levi brought their drinks, and Cady lifted her glass in a toast. "To you, Joe. To old friends."

"Old friends." His dark eyes devoured her; the intense look in them would've unsettled her if she hadn't known him so well. "Tell me what's been happening to you, Cady."

"Oh, my life's dull as dishwater. Tell me about

you. Tell me about school. Are you still making A's in all your subjects?''

He nodded, looking down, pretending it was nothing, but she knew what his grades meant to him. He had to do well, because he was on a scholarship at Berkeley. Someday he'd be a lawyer, and his dream was to work for the cause of justice for poor people, Indians in particular. He only had a fraction of Rogue Indian blood himself, a sixteenth, he'd once admitted to her, but Joe was the most *Indian* Indian Cady had ever known.

''So do you like your courses and your professors? Why do you have to go to school in the summer?''

He started to talk, tell her everything, and while he spoke she watched the veneer of adulthood and student sophistication wear thinner and thinner. In no time at all, he was her old Joe, painfully earnest and endearing. In six months he'd gotten taller, more muscular. He had strong black eyebrows that grew together over his hawkish nose, giving him a fierce look. But his new haircut, short and parted in the middle, cut down on the ferocity; between it and his steel-rimmed spectacles, he looked pretty much like what he was: a serious young man with a purpose.

''So tell me about this Gault,'' he demanded, surprising her with the sudden new topic.

''Oh, Gault.'' She gave an evasive laugh. ''He's the talk of the town, all right.''

''He's a murderer,'' Joe said flatly. ''I hear he's been hanging around you night and day.''

''That's not true.'' She clucked her tongue. ''Night and day. How ridiculous. Who told you that?'' *Mur-*

derer. It was what she'd been insisting to everyone, especially the lovestruck females of Paradise, that Jesse Gault was, so why did the word sound even worse on Joe's lips? Why did she want to talk him out of it?

"Word gets around." His eyes veered toward the bar, though, and Levi, innocently drying glasses behind it. Joe's parents didn't much approve of his association with Levi, either. But he liked to call himself a "red man," and Levi was definitely a black man, and according to Joe that made a bond between them.

She tsked again. "He's staying here, that's all. Sometimes I run into him."

"Why do you let him stay here?"

"Well, it's a free country."

"If Tom Leaver had any guts, he'd run him out of town."

"But, Joe, he hasn't done anything."

"Who hired him? Wylie?"

"No, absolutely not."

"Who, then?"

"Nobody. I don't think."

"If this *town* had any guts, they'd run him out on a rail."

"Oh, that's democratic."

He scowled. "Meaning?"

"Well—doesn't it make any difference that the man hasn't *done* anything?"

"You're defending him?"

"I'm—"

"You don't wait for a snake to bite you before you

kill it." He had that stubborn set to his manly, serious jaw that meant there wasn't going to be any arguing with him. Once he decided he was right, you couldn't budge Joe from a principle with a stick of dynamite.

"Who owns that roan quarterhorse outside?" A low, familiar voice.

Cady jumped. Speak of the devil. Jesse stood in a splash of sunlight, arms hanging over the swinging doors, looking around the half-empty saloon.

Joe said, "Is that him?" in a quiet, wondering tone. She could understand his confusion. Except for the eyepatch, Jesse didn't look very dangerous today. Good, but not dangerous. He wore his six-guns, and he had on black—he always wore black—but he'd pushed his Stetson to the back of his head, and somehow that changed everything. He'd taken off his silver spurs, too—she'd seen grown men shiver when he walked through the hushed saloon, *stamp-jingle, stamp-jingle*, a really eerie noise if you were half-terrified already. But today he looked . . . normal. Like a regular customer. A gambler, or maybe a ranch foreman. Smart, friendly, and fit. Definitely not like a cold-blooded killer. She started to smile at him and say hi, but caught herself in the nick of time. How could she forget? She wasn't having anything to do with him anymore.

"The roan is mine." Joe pushed his chair back slowly and stood up. "What's it to you?"

Jesse let go of the door and sauntered toward them, his smile fading the closer he got. "He's a beauty," he said softly, stopping beside Cady's chair. "Looks like a purebred." He glanced at her, at Joe, at the two glasses on the table between them. He arched one eyebrow and sneered.

Joe said, "How long you figure to stay in Paradise, Gault?" At the same moment Cady said, "Joe, I'd like you to meet J—Mr. Gault," so that she and Joe said the word "Gault" in unison.

Both men ignored her. She didn't like the way they were sizing each other up, like a couple of dogs sniffing around for an opening to go for the throat. "Mr. Gault," she plowed on, "this is my friend, Joseph Redleaf. Joe's a student at the University of California. He's studying—"

"What's it to you?" Jesse said, as if she weren't even there, as if she were still in her room going over the books. She stood up, to show him she existed.

"He's studying—" she repeated, but this time Joe cut her off.

"We don't like your kind around here."

"Yeah? Who's 'we'?"

"Whoa," she exclaimed with a nervous laugh, reaching across to touch Joe's arm. "Hey, let's—"

But he shrugged away from her and planted his feet. The saloon had started to go quiet at the moment he stood up. He said, "Decent people," into a tense, total silence.

Jesse's smile was pure evil. He said, "Is that right," and his whispery voice brought goose bumps to Cady's arms. "You able to back that up with anything but spit, youngster?"

"Wait, wait," she sputtered, trying to get between them.

"If you mean do I own a gun, the answer is yes."

"Joe, for God's sake. Jess—just," she corrected hastily, "just stop this, both of you. Come on, let's sit down. Levi, bring—"

"I don't get in gunfights with children," Jesse whispered.

Joe reddened, clenching his hands into fists. "Maybe you're just a coward," he accused, and Cady wanted to cover his mouth with her hands to shut him up.

Jesse only smiled, which made her hair stand on end. "Think so?"

"No, he doesn't think so, he just said that, it just came out, he's—"

"Could be another way to settle this," Jesse said right over her—she'd disappeared again.

A fistfight. She groaned, but she felt weak with relief. "Okay, but take it outside, will you? I can't afford—"

"You big enough to ride that roan, youngster?"

Joe finally stopped flexing his fingers. "Yeah, on a good day, when my daddy helps me up. What'd you have in mind?"

"A race."

"How far?"

"A mile? Quarter mile? You decide, college boy. But you might want to take a look at my horse before you say yes."

Joe laughed in his face. "I don't think so." Excitement made his dark eyes glitter. "What's the stake?"

"Loser keeps on riding. Rides on out of town, leaving all these decent people alone."

"Oh, now," Cady started to say, not sure what

came next. Joe raced horses for fun—nobody ever beat him. If he won and Jesse kept his word . . . "That's a silly bet," she protested, trying to sound jovial. "I know—why don't we all have a beer and start over. Drinks on the house. Let's—"

"When do you want to race?"

"What's wrong with now?"

"Not a damn thing."

"Let's go."

She blinked rapidly, hand outstretched, mouth open. Neither man so much as glanced at her as they moved away, heading for the door. There was a brief scuffle while they tried to walk out of it simultaneously. Jesse got through first, but Joe was right on his boot heels.

The news spread like a prairie fire. Within ten minutes, close to every man in Paradise was standing on one side or the other of Main Street, along with most of the children and a good portion of the women. Nothing this exciting had happened since the revival meeting last fall. Somehow Nestor Yeakes became Jesse's second, so to speak, coaching him about the pitfalls of the course they were going to run—three miles, beginning and ending at the corner of Main and Noble Fir—and offering anybody who would take it five-to-one odds on Jesse's horse, a gorgeous black stallion called Pegasus. Nestor knew horseflesh; his faith in the black gave people serious pause. But they'd seen Joe Redleaf race his roan gelding a dozen times, and they'd never seen anybody beat him. Anyway, how could they bet on a stranger and against one of their own?

They did, though, some of them; Cady saw at least four men, including Stony Dern and Gunther Dewhurt, slip money to Nestor muttering under their breath and giving quick, surreptitious head jerks toward Pegasus.

"Bareback?" Jesse looked astounded, watching Joe lead his saddleless horse to the starting place, an imaginary line across the street between the Mercantile and Digby's General Store.

"It is a man's way," Joe declared, falling into the formal, disdainful tone he used when that sixteenth of Rogue blood in him took over. Not only had he taken off his horse's saddle, he'd taken off his own shirt and shoes, and tied a red bandana around his high, intelligent forehead. Cady guessed the idea was to look more like an Indian, but since he'd left on his silver-rimmed spectacles, the effect wasn't all it could've been.

"Nestor, take off Peg's saddle," Jesse directed, smiling as if this were all a joke. But it was an act; she could tell he was as excited as Joe. Men could be so childish. They weren't going to gun each other down in the street, though, so she didn't care.

"Ham, come on over here. Hurry up, get out of their way."

He came reluctantly. She set him in front of her, pressing him back against her skirts, and she could feel the excitement quivering through his skinny shoulders. "Who gonna win, Cady? Who you think?"

"Who do you want to win?"

He turned his head and whispered, "Mr. Gault."

She made a surprised face. "I thought you liked Joe," she whispered back.

"I do, I do like 'im! But Mr. Gault, he awful nice to me, an' now I know him better."

"I see." He'd known Joe Redleaf all his life, Jesse Gault for a week and a half. Child's logic and a few quarters.

"Who *you* want to win?"

"Oh, I really don't care. Whoever has the faster—"

"Oh, my God, oh, my God," sighed Willagail, who stood on Cady's right, and at the same moment Glendoline, on her left, said, "Whoo*wee*," on a long, soft, breathy sigh.

Following their eyes, Cady saw what had them enthralled—Jesse Gault taking his shirt off. "Oh, honestly," she clucked. Well, women could be just as foolish as men, only about different things. Jesse threw his black shirt on the sidewalk and started to take off his boots, heel-to-toe, holding on to the hitching post for balance. He was one tall drink of water, she caught herself thinking, a phrase she could vaguely recall her mother using years ago. His skin wasn't as sun-browned as Joe's, and he didn't have Joe's thick, bulging muscles in his arms and shoulders. His physique was leaner, longer. More graceful, if you could say that about a man's body. More . . . beautiful.

Barefooted, he walked over to his shiny-coated stallion and stroked its long neck, telling it something in its twitching ear. She studied his handsome back, his shoulder blades, the bumps in his long spine. He'd taken off his gunbelt. His black trousers hung low; she followed the line of his backbone where it disappeared into his pants. Ham craned his neck and looked up at her, and she realized she was humming to herself. She'd just said "Mm mmm" right out loud.

It was a perfect afternoon, not a cloud in the sky, the blue air sharp and clean and not too hot. People stood two and three deep on either side of Main all the way down to the east end, where it petered out in front of Lisabeth Wayman's boardinghouse. The race route was going to be the big oval wagon trail between Paradise and the Rogue River and back, a distance of about three miles. They would take the same route Cady often took on her Friday afternoons off, along the cliff edge, past River Farm, past her mine and Wylie's mine, down the flat valley floor and then home through the thick, wooded hills in the west. She worried that Jesse didn't know the land at all, and Joe knew it like the back of his hand. If Jesse lost, would he keep his promise? Keep on riding and never come back? Was she seeing him right now for the last time?

"Jesse!"

He turned.

Everybody turned.

She flushed with mortification. She'd said his first name out loud!

He grinned at her, and her heart skipped two consecutive beats. He swept off his hat and made a silly, barefooted bow—and she had the craziest, the most ridiculous desire to weep. "Good luck," she called out tightly. "And Joe—good luck!" she remembered to add.

Then Sam Blankenship yelled, "Mount up!" and the two racers got on their horses. "On your marks! Get set!" Ham started jumping up and down. He landed on her toe at the same moment Sam yelled, "Go!" so Cady missed the takeoff.

She saw the galloping rear ends of the black and the roan disappear in a dust cloud at the end of Main Street, and then it was over. All the excitement, the noise, the shouting—everything stopped, and she wondered if anybody else felt as sheepish as she did. People milled around, aimless-looking. Then all of a sudden something really extraordinary happened: Glendoline had a good idea.

"Let's go up and see if we can see 'em from the balcony."

"Yeah!" Ham began leaping again, and Cady backed out of his way. "Can we, Cady? Can we?"

"Sure, but I doubt if we'll . . ." Nobody was listening to her. Glen, Willagail, Ham, even Levi, they turned their backs on her and hurried back down the street toward the Rogue. "Be able to see much," she finished to herself, picked up her skirts, and ran after them.

She was right. They couldn't see much, but the view was a lot nicer than the dusty street, and this way they'd be able to catch sight of the racers as soon as they broke out of the trees at the extreme western edge of town. "How long will it take?" Ham wanted to know, and Levi said, " 'Bout ten, twelve, fifteen minutes, I 'spec'."

"Ten minutes!" Ham couldn't get over it. "To go *three miles?* I thought it took a—a *hour*, a—"

"Nope. 'Bout twelve, fifteen minutes on that track, them horses. I seen a race once down in Santa Barbara, colt name Equal run a mile in two minutes flat."

Ham, who was sitting on his father's shoulders for a better view, pursed his lips and tried to whistle.

"Course, that be on a real racetrack, with a little puny fella ridin' 'im. 'Bout as big as you is all he was, dressed up in shiny yellow pants made outa silk."

" 'Cause he a jockey, right?"

"Right."

"A jockey," Ham breathed. Levi winked at Cady, thinking the same thing she was: Ham had a new career goal. No more cowboy, no more sea captain. They wouldn't hear the end of this for months.

The minutes crawled by. Now she *was* hot, and there wasn't a speck of shade up here. Plus she had to listen to Glen and Willagail go on about Jesse Gault's chest. It put her in a bad mood. You'd think they'd never seen a man without his shirt before. "How come you call him Jesse?" Ham interrupted her cranky thoughts to ask, and Willagail and Glen shut up to hear the answer. Even Levi turned to look at her.

What could she say? "That's his name. His first name."

"He *told* you?" Glen said, amazed.

"Jesse," Willagail repeated, trying it out. "Jesse Gault. Jesssee." She smiled a slow smile. "Yeah."

"They comin', they comin'!"

Levi made a grab for Ham's calves before he could lean too far over his head. Everybody crowded over to the left edge of the balcony, craning, straining. "Who's ahead? They neck and neck! No, Joe got a nose on 'im—no, Mr. Gault's horse—I can't tell!"

"Jesse's winning!" Cady shrieked it, but her voice was barely audible over all the yelling and screaming down below. She was pounding her fists on the wooden railing, crying, "Go, go, go, go, go!" at the top of her lungs—when she saw the blood.

She clutched at her temples, horrified, dumbstruck. His stallion flew by in a cloud of dust and grit, a full length ahead of the roan, but she didn't wait to see the end. Spinning for the doorway, she sprinted down the dark hall, the stairs, through the empty saloon and down the long, echoing boardwalk, out of breath and racing for the finish line.

A cheering crowd surrounded him. She saw money changing hands, heard men yelling, "Hot damn!" More people had bet on Jesse than she'd thought. She caught a glimpse of him from the back before he slid off his horse—hands everywhere, helping him down—but then he disappeared. "Let me through. Please. Let me by." Her urgency finally cleared a path, and she ran to him. "Jess, Jess, are you hurt?"

"Hell, no. Ran under a limb, didn't duck far enough. I'm fine." Nestor was shaking his hand up and down like a pump handle and smacking him on the shoulder, the back. Jesse threw his arm around his sweating horse's neck. Out of affection, Cady thought, until she saw his knees buckle. She yelped, reaching out, but she couldn't stop his slow slide to the dirt. Looking surprised, he landed hard on his rear end. His horse took two polite steps sideways, and Jesse keeled over the rest of the way, flat on his back.

Doc Mobius appeared out of nowhere. "Stand back," he commanded, "give him some air." Everybody obeyed except Cady, who dropped to her knees and hovered over Jesse with fluttering hands. "It's a scalp wound, that's all," Doc rumbled, feeling around in his hair. "Scalp wounds bleed like the dickens." He used his handkerchief to wipe blood off Jesse's forehead, and she saw with huge, knee-weakening relief that the wound wasn't anywhere near his eye. Her worst fear—she could acknowledge it now—was that he'd reinjured his right eye. That he would be blind in one eye again.

He came to while they were carrying him into the Rogue. He weighed more than he looked; it took three men, one of them Joe, to get him down the street and into the saloon. They were headed for the stairs, fixing to carry him up to his room, when he started to protest that he was fine, perfectly all right, they should set him down right here by the bar, for convenience, because he meant to drink half of it up tonight, and everybody else was welcome to the other half, on him.

Doc Mobius finally agreed, after about two dozen men begged him to, and in no time Jesse was ensconced in the corner table by Chico's piano, hoisting a beer to himself and then one to Joe. Doc Mobius said, "I've got to stitch up that crease in your head, though," and Jesse said, "Fine, do it here." Somebody ran and got the doc's medicine bag, and with about forty men looking on and offering free advice, he sewed up Jesse's head. Willagail made a good nurse. Cady wanted to do it—assist the doc, hold Jesse's hand—but at the first prick of the needle she had to leave the room.

Eight

Chico was playing his version of "The Gypsy's Warning," which meant pounding it out three times faster than normal and racing through the lyrics:

> "Trust him not, O gentle lady,
> Though his voice be low and sweet.
> Heed him not, that dark-eyed stranger,
> Softly pleading at your feet."

Sheer velocity had the oddest people on their feet. Nestor Yeakes, who as far as Cady knew had never danced in his life, was two-stepping with Willagail; and those two old coots, Floyd and Oscar Schmidt, were prancing around the floor with each other. It was a sight to see.

"Dance with me, Cady," Jesse begged with a grin, trailing his hand across her back as she passed behind him, on her way to a side table with a tray of beer glasses. She laughed at him and tossed her head, flirting like a girl. She kept going, but she was tempted. There was such liveliness in the air tonight, some kind of innocent gaiety that was hard to resist. Part of it was the size of the crowd—enormous, she even had Wylie's customers; his saloon must be stone empty, she gloated—and part of it was Jesse.

He had a way about him. And it wasn't only that he was standing round after round of drinks for the house, either. It was *him*. He made people feel good. Even Doc Mobius—she wouldn't have believed this if she hadn't seen it—Doc Mobius, who never even smiled, had actually laughed at Jesse's cracks about not cutting his head off by accident, his jokes about inept doctors and idiot patients. Who'd have thought? Everybody else was as surprised as she was—pleasantly surprised, though. Jesse Gault wasn't only an outlaw gunfighter; it turned out he was also a comedian.

Finding out he had a first name, a regular one like everybody else, not "Diablo" or "Serpent," broke down another barrier. He just wasn't the same man tonight, that was all. Cady couldn't take her eyes off him, and neither could anybody else. Was it the alcohol? No; he made a lot of toasts, but he'd just take a sip afterward, not chug down the whole glass like the others.

But the most amazing thing was the way he treated Joe. No—the *most* amazing thing was the way Joe treated *him*. This was something else she'd have had trouble believing without seeing. They'd become mates, buddies. Great good friends. Right now they were singing "Hell Among the Yearlin's" with their arms around each other. Along with everybody else, she'd heard the story of their horse race a dozen times already—how Jesse had led all the way to the river when Joe's mount caught up with him, how they'd both flown like birds over a huge fallen oak tree lying in the road, how Jesse's stallion had slowly, slowly narrowed the gap between them, how a low-lying maple limb had almost killed him but hadn't slowed him down, and finally, how he'd overtaken Joe on the home straightaway, with blood blinding him and dizziness threatening to unseat him. If he'd told it by himself she wouldn't have believed it; he sounded too heroic. But Joe backed up every valiant detail and even threw in new ones Jesse either forgot or was too modest to mention. The terms of the wager had long ago flown out the window; nobody even mentioned Joe leaving town.

"He don't even look the same anymore, do he?" said Levi as he filled glass after glass from the beer keg and set them on her tray. "Look like a whole different fella."

"Yeah. You ought to hear the stupid things Willa-gail and Glen say about him these days."

"I *do* hear." He made a disgusted face, and they both laughed. "He don't pay them no min', though. Not like he min' *you*."

"Me." She snorted, started to say something smart. But she caught Jesse's eye, and he smiled at her over the heads of twenty men, through the cloudy cigar smoke and the strains of "In the Baggage Coach Ahead." A little tickle in her chest made her forget what she was going to say. Lordy, Lordy, he was a good-looking man. He'd put on his shirt but he hadn't buttoned it, and he never had put his shoes

on. All he had to do was stand there, an unlit cigarette in the side of his mouth, laughing and swapping
yarns with his new pals, and she was a goner. What
made her think she was any better than Glen or Willagail? The only difference between them was that
she knew enough to keep her mouth shut.

She likes me, Jesse gloated. *She's crazy about me tonight.* If he'd known a horse race was what would
turn the trick, he'd have challenged Joe or somebody
else a long time ago.

"C'mon, Cady, have a seat," he invited the next
time she floated by with a tray.

"Can't, no time." She said it with a smile and a
twinkle in her eye, though, and he knew she would've
if she could've. The boys were running her ragged.
She was just a waitress like the other girls tonight,
with no time to talk or flirt or deal blackjack. She
hadn't even changed into one of her slinky saloon
dresses. Not that Jesse minded. He liked her in her
daytime clothes just as much. Maybe better. Right
now she had on a black skirt and a black-and-white-
checked vest over a plain white blouse, and she
looked pretty as a picture. The blouse had a little
black tie around the collar, but she'd untied it because she was hot, and she'd unbuttoned the buttons
down to her bust. Not far enough so you could see
her bird tattoo, but enough to remind you in case
you forgot, fat chance, that it was there. He liked the
way her hair was coming down in thick hanks from
that neat daytime bun on top of her head. Pretty soon,
unless she did some fast repair work, it would all be
down around her shoulders, shiny and dark brown,

sexy as hell. He couldn't wait to see that. Trouble was, he didn't want anybody else to see it. Just him.

When had this happened?

"Paradise used to be called Coquin," Sheriff Leaver was explaining to him. "Which means 'rogue' in French. That's what they named the Indians around here—Rogues. They didn't have much use for 'em back in the olden days."

Joe, who had been deep in conversation with Sam Blankenship, the insurance and real estate man, turned around at that. Any talk of Indians always got his attention. "No," he said, "the French didn't have much use for them. So they stole their lands and trapped the animals that sustained them, and then the English came and finished the job they'd started."

The sheriff groaned and rubbed his face with both hands. Sam Blankenship slid down in his chair. "Christ, Joe, could you let that go for one night? Tom here's trying to tell Jesse the history of our town."

"Go ahead," Joe said with dignity. "But do not forget to tell him of the massacre of my people at Gold Beach."

"Your people," scoffed Stony Dern. "Joe, you're whiter'n I am."

"I am one thirty-second Tu Tu 'Tun, one thirty-second Nez Perce, on the side of my great-great-grandfather."

"Yeah, well, I'm a hun'ert percent Irish," piped up Shrimp Malone, "but you don't see me goin' on about beer and potatoes and singin' 'Katie Me Darlin'.' "

Everybody laughed. Even Joe.

"Anyway," said the sheriff, "as I was saying. They

discovered gold here in 'Coquin' back in 1852. I mean to tell you, this was one thriving little town for about four years."

"What happened?"

"The gold dried up. That emptied the miners out, and a smallpox epidemic drove off everybody else. Place turned into a ghost town."

"Is that right? I didn't know that," Jesse said politely. "I thought it was always here, always called Paradise." Sheriff Leaver's pride in the town surprised him slightly. It was an all right town, nothing wrong with it, but nothing really special as far as he could see. And Leaver wasn't the only one; Stony and Sam, the two coots Floyd and Oscar, Gunther Dewhurt, even dirty old Shrimp, they all seemed genuinely fond of the place, and anxious to tell him about its semicolorful past. "What happened then?" he asked obligingly.

"Well, in—"

"They done found gold again," Shrimp declared gleefully, cutting Tom off. "North o' here no more'n a mile. You done raced by the ol' Well Head Mine, you and Injun Joe—didn't you hear the stamp mill? Course, it ain't the Well Head no more. Now that Wylie owns it, it's the Rainbow." He leaned over and spat on the floor.

"Shrimp, what is that spittoon for?"

The prospector jumped guiltily. "Sorry. Forgot."

Cady kept going, didn't even break stride on her way to the bar with another empty tray. But Jesse caught her eye as she passed, and she sent him a private smile that blinded him. Made him go deaf, too; he missed the next part of the history of Paradise.

". . . big boom's about over now, though," he caught the sheriff wrapping up. "People who came here for gold fifteen years ago and fell in love with the land are finding other things to do now. Farming, cattle. Logging. Sheepherding. Some folks say the railroad's coming to Grant's Pass one of these days, and then you'll *really* see some growth."

"I hope it don't come," Floyd said.

"Now, why would you want to say a fool thing like that?" complained Oscar.

" 'Cause that's what Wylie's countin' on. When the Rainbow dries up, and Clarence Carter's mine, and the Sarena, and the Eagle, and the Pickaxe—which you know they are all gonna peter out sooner or later, just like Shlegel's mine, Cady's now, done two years ago—I'm sayin' when they all go, Wylie'll be the only one left standin', on account o' by then he'll own everything in the whole goddamn district. And everybody."

Silence.

"Shit, Floyd. Talk about a wet blanket."

Halfhearted laughter. Jesse looked around at the suddenly dour faces of his friends—he was starting to think of some of them as friends. Floyd wasn't the wet blanket, Wylie was. Just the mention of his name brought people down, he'd seen it happen a dozen times. He caught himself about to say, "Why don't you do something about him?" That was a sore subject, he'd heard, between the sheriff and the townsfolk. And besides, what if one of his brand-new buddies snapped back, "Why don't *you*?"

He changed the glum mood the only way he could think of. "Hey, Levi! Another round!"

The gay evening wore on. The pendulum clock over the bar chimed ten; some men got up and staggered out, and some men started drinking in earnest. Jesse fell quiet, content to watch Cady at work, cool and efficient, sharp-tongued sometimes, other times sweet as your little sister. But gradually he began to notice things about her—the fatigue in her ready smile, the droop in her shoulders, the hand she pressed to the small of her back while she waited for Levi to fill another batch of glasses. She was flagging. Willagail and Glendoline looked whipped, too, but he didn't care about them.

When she turned from the bar, he stood up, blocking her path to a back table. She smiled, lifting one shoulder to rub against a damp cheek, waiting for him to move. Her mouth fell open when he took the tray out of her hands and stepped around her. "What are you doing?" She followed him back to the bar, laughing. "Jesse? What are you—"

"Listen up!" he called out in a loud voice, and the saloon instantly fell silent. "From now on, any man who wants a drink on me has to get it himself."

"Jesse, that isn't—"

"Got that? Because this lady's through."

She started to protest. He cut her off by dipping suddenly and plucking her up off her feet. She shrieked, and the whole room erupted in laughter and good-natured applause. "You're drunk," she accused, locking her hands behind his neck. Her breath smelled like lemons. Lemonade.

"Not a bit." It was true. He'd drunk enough to make his head stop hurting, not enough to cloud it. In fact, he'd never felt better in his life.

He carried her back to his table. She started to squirm, thinking he was going to sit down with her on his lap. He surprised her by saying, "Get up, Malone," and kicking the prospector's chair leg. Shrimp scrambled up as nimbly as he could with a cast on his leg, and Jesse set Cady gently down in his vacated chair. He pulled his own chair up close and sat. And then he bent and hauled her feet up onto his lap.

"Hey! Now, what—"

"Shhh. Quiet." He tucked her black skirts and white petticoats around her ankles, very modest, before he started pulling on the laces of her high-heeled boots. She gaped at him. Joe, who was, as usual, talking to no one in particular about the Rogue Indian wars, stopped in mid-atrocity to stare. So did everybody else. Ignoring them, Jesse wriggled off one boot and then the other, tossing them to the floor. "Mmm, feet," he said, leaning over, pretending to sniff her stockinged toes. She squealed, trying to yank her feet away, but he held on. "Hold still." He cupped all the toes on her right foot in his hand and began to bend them all the way back, then all the way forward, back, forward, using a strong, firm pressure. Cady let her head fall back and groaned in ecstasy.

The men looked away, or laughed, or shifted with embarrassed amusement. Jesse knew what was in their minds. Same thing that was in his. Funny—he'd seen men get dangerous in situations like this, but nothing like that was going on here. He'd have sensed it if it was. Not a one of them didn't wish he was in Jesse's place right now, but nobody meant him any harm. Or Cady.

And that was all her doing. Touching her like this wasn't allowed—as long as they'd known her, she'd made just this kind of thing off-limits. And yet tonight she'd given permission, and Jesse was the lucky man. They envied him, naturally. But they didn't despise him, and they respected her right to choose. Because they respected *her*.

Conversations started up again gradually. Jesse kept Cady's feet as long as she let him, massaging her insteps, grinding his knuckles into her heels, doing his best to drive her crazy with how good it felt. But eventually she drew away. She didn't get up, though. She said, "Thanks. That was great. You've got good hands," and stayed where she was. Neither of them said much. They sat and listened to the talk, the singing, the jokes, the drunken horseplay. They smiled and nodded at the others, throwing a word or two in occasionally. For cover. So nobody would realize how completely wrapped up they were in each other.

Joe Redleaf stood up, holding onto the table for balance. Staggering but dignified, he approached them and made a wobbly bow. "Good night. Goodbye. Until we meet again, my friends."

Jesse got up to shake hands. "You don't have to go. I mean, you know. Leave town. That was just talk."

"Yes, I know. But I was going anyway."

That cracked them up; they slapped each other on the shoulder, chuckling and laughing.

Cady stood, too. "I'll walk out with you, Joe." They moved away together. At the double doors, she turned her head to look back at Jesse. Her expression calmed him. *Wait*, it said. *I'll come back.* He sat down, feeling peaceful. No jealousy. *You're the one*, she might as well have said out loud. He knew it as well as he knew anything. Tonight was the night. Inevitable. It couldn't have happened sooner or later, only now. Everything that had happened on this long, perfect day had led up to this night.

Cady came back. Moving toward him, she looked calm, too, he thought. Calm and sure. She came straight to him.

He said, "Want to go for a walk?"

She bent and picked up her shoes. "I'll just tell Levi."

Jesse told his friends good night, and went outside to wait for her.

He looked tall and lanky in silhouette, backlit by the moon. Cady paused just outside the swinging doors to look at him. He had his weight on one leg, hip cocked at a loose angle, one long arm braced against the upright porch post. He was watching the moon. Its platinum face had that openmouthed, anguished look it took on at three-quarters full. He slipped his hand in his pants pocket; his shirt opened, and the white of his ribs, his side, flashed for a second. Then he turned his shoulder a fraction of an inch, and he was covered up again.

Cady shivered. Just that quick whiteness, that

gleam of pale bare skin, silver-on-black, Jesse's skin, had her chest tightening, her heart pounding. Anticipation. Such a deep-boned lust, and so *fast:* she could hardly believe it. *I'm not like this.*

He turned. Had she made a sound? When he didn't smile at her or say something funny, the breathlessness inside her grew fuller, harder to bear. She came toward him casually, as if nothing was happening. "Doesn't the air smell good?"

He nodded. "You smell good."

She blew a laugh. "I smell like cigars."

He shook his head. Facing her, he finally did smile. She grinned back, relieved, keeping her eyes away from his naked chest. She'd seen it off and on all night under his open black shirt, but that was different. Now it was just them, standing by themselves in the moonlight. Jesse without his shirt felt as intimate as . . . as her without her blouse.

She said, "Joe told me what you did." He rubbed the bridge of his nose, as if he couldn't recall, didn't quite know what she meant. "You gave him money."

"Ah." He looked slightly annoyed. He must have told Joe not to tell.

"That was awfully nice of you."

"Oh, yeah." He dismissed it, turning back to squint up at the moon.

"He's so poor, you can't imagine. It'll help him so much. And you don't even know him. Jesse, that's just . . . so . . ."

He gave a rough laugh, not wanting her to finish. "Yeah, well, I'm rich, so I won't miss it. Plus I was drunk when I gave it to him."

He was not. But she only lifted an eyebrow at him. If that was the way he wanted to play it, fine with her. He touched her fingertips with his, just a gentle clutch of knuckles, and they stepped off the sidewalk and into the street.

The hard dirt felt cool under her bare feet. She looked down, watching Jesse's white feet flash under his dark trousers, her white toes swish out from under her skirts. How companionable, being barefooted together. Playful. Like two kids, holding hands while they headed for the swimming hole.

But they turned together, without any hesitation, into the path that led through the blueblossom bushes to her back door, and her childhood-playmates image disintegrated. Adult games, that's what they were going to play tonight. The pent-up, breathless feeling returned. She couldn't get enough air.

"I thought you were going to lock this."

"Forgot. I should. I do sometimes." She hadn't even *closed* the door, she saw as they walked up the two steps to her minuscule porch. It had been hot this afternoon; she'd left the door open for air. What a long day this had been. She thought of Ham, coming into her office to tell her Joe was here. Had that really been *today*?

"Want to come in?" She flushed. What a dumb thing to say.

"Thanks." She saw his lips quirk, and felt even stupider. But she was happy, too. In fact, she felt on the verge of laughter. Hysteria? Not exactly. More like . . . euphoria.

"So." She went to the bureau and struck a match

to the oil lamp. "This is where I live." As if he'd never been here before. "But you knew that," she added inanely. Where was all that confidence and calm she'd felt a few minutes ago? It had deserted her the moment she'd seen Jesse in the moonlight. My, but she was a silly girl. "Do you want a drink?" She pivoted away from him, pressing her hands to her hot cheeks. They'd just come out of a saloon, and she was asking him if he wanted a drink. She didn't even have anything in here anyway, no bottle, nothing.

Fortunately he said, "No, I've had enough." He wasn't drunk, though, she could see that. If anything he looked the opposite. Alert, focused. Focused on her.

She turned away again. She thought about stalling, of saying, *Would you like to see my photograph album?* Luckily he caught her hand just then and tugged on it, forcing her to face him. "I like it when you look like this," he told her.

She melted. "I'm a mess."

"Yeah, I know."

They relaxed into smiles. He lifted his hands and slipped them into the hair at the back of her neck, and she unbent a little more, tilting her head back, resting it against his palms. He had a cowlick now, from where Doc Mobius had clipped the hair away from his head wound. A black slash of hair, one-sided, cut across the high white of his forehead; she ran her fingers through it, neatening it. His heavy eyelids dropped, hiding his eyes. He said, "I've been looking at you all night."

"I know. I could feel . . . I could feel it."

"Couldn't take my eyes off you. Kept thinking about this. Kissing you."

"You can kiss me."

But just before their lips met, she said, "Jesse."

"Yes?"

"You know . . . some people think I do. But I don't."

"What?"

"This."

Before he leaned his forehead against hers, she saw understanding flicker in his dark gray eyes. He took her hands and squeezed them. "Then that makes it even better. Makes me even luckier."

She put her arms around him, standing on tiptoe to hold him. "Oh, *Jess*." When he kissed her, she saw white lights pop and shimmer behind her tight-closed eyes, little silent explosions echoing the ones going off in other parts of her body. Why had she waited so long for this? She tilted her head to get closer; she wanted to kiss him deeper, stronger. His hands rubbed under her arms, down her sides to her waist, lower, sliding to the back of her and pulling her up against him. He started backing up and she followed him blind, not letting go. She didn't want to stop kissing him even for a second.

He banged into the back of the bed, though, and they separated, both of them panting and shiny-eyed. They sat on the edge of the mattress, embracing again immediately. But they didn't kiss. They just held each other, and she could feel the faint, subtle shake of his body with each heartbeat. With hers.

"I slept . . . I sl . . . What is that?"

She let go of him to see what he was looking at. "Oh." She smiled, closing her eyes while he pulled a strand of hair back and kissed her temple. "My mother sewed them. Words to live by." On two pillow shams at the head of her bed; she'd taken them with her wherever she went for the last fifteen years. Not because they were pretty, or nice, not because she even liked them. But because they were all she had left of her mother.

"What do they say?"

She hadn't realized how faded and torn the embroidered threads had grown—Jesse couldn't even read the words. " 'I Slept and Dreamed That Life Was Beauty.' And the other one says, 'I Woke and Found That Life Is Duty.' " She laughed softly. "Mama's philosophy."

Jesse looked at her, not the pillows, peering at her in the semidark to see if she was sad. "I don't know anything about you," he said, a wondering note in his voice. "You know more about me than I do about you, Cady."

"Oh, well. I'm not so interesting." Ha ha. She thought she was very interesting. She was getting more interesting by the day.

"Well, I want to know everything about you."

"Okay. I'll tell you my life story. Right now. It's very long."

It broke him up. He fell over backward, chuckling and snorting. She lay beside him, laughing in sympathy, feeling the bed shake under them. Her heart felt huge, too big for her chest. "I've always wanted this," she confessed to him, wiping away a laugh-tear gliding into her hair. He didn't ask what she meant, so she didn't know if he understood or not. She didn't mean just a lover. More than that. Someone she could play with. She hadn't thought it through—in fact it had never occurred to her till now—but it seemed to her you could trust a lover that you could laugh in bed with.

He rolled toward her, propping his head on his hand. He put his other hand on her stomach. Her giant heart, the one too big for her chest, jumped into her throat. Such an intimacy, this hand on her stomach, and it was only just beginning. He kept her gaze while he spread her little checkered vest away from her right breast, spread the other half back from her left. He took hold of one end of her loose black cravat and began to pull it out of her collar. Slowly. She listened to the high swish of taut silk pulling, pulling, felt it making the circuit around the back of her neck.

"I'm stripping you. I'm taking off every stitch of your clothes. You'll be nude in two minutes."

"Yeah." That was all she was capable of saying. He started sliding buttons out of the buttonholes of her shirtwaist, and she followed his dark fingers as they crept lower and lower. He tugged the blouse out of her skirt and folded the sides back, uncovering her chemise. Plain white cotton today. Drat. It wasn't as if she didn't have plenty of smart, sexy underclothes, a drawer full of them that nobody ever saw. Just her luck.

Jesse didn't seem to mind, though. He came up on his elbow and hovered over her, his longish hair falling around his face. "So pretty." He tugged on ribbons, unsnapped snaps. "Aha. And now a corset. Sometime—not now—would you explain to me why women like you wear these things? Women who don't need 'em, I mean."

"So men like you will take them off of us."

Click. Chink. Corset hooks coming unhooked. She felt cool air on her chest, then warm skin—Jesse's hand. *Click, snap.* She was free.

"Ahh," she exhaled on a high, deep sigh. He smoothed his whole hand over her breasts, one and then the other, squeezing softly. Rubbing them around, making them move. His eyes lit on the tattoo under her left nipple. He stroked his thumb over it, frowning, as if he wanted to erase it. She thought he would say something, but he kept quiet, and she couldn't read his expression. What was there to say, anyway?

He dipped his head and took a swipe of her nipple with his tongue, and she squealed, clenching her toes. Then he started in earnest, tonguing and sucking and nibbling on her. She felt her body getting longer and longer as she stretched and strained under him. Electrical shocks. Sparks that wouldn't stop, just kept jolting and zapping through her, lighting a fire deep down. *Should've closed the door*, she thought through some kind of a fog. *I'm making a lot of noise.*

Finally he stopped, which was just as well. It was time to either move on to the next thing or go completely insane.

"Too many clothes," he muttered, wet-lipped, and slid off her. They stood up, Jesse holding her hand

to help her. She needed help: her knees weren't
working at all. He started fumbling with the back of
her skirt, but she distracted him by slipping his shirt
over his shoulders and pulling it down his arms. She
put her flat hands on his rib cage and drew them
up, sliding them over smooth, warming skin and
knotting muscle. His chest had neat, straight hair, all
black, growing down from his pectoral muscles and
meeting in the middle at his breastbone. Cupping his
bare shoulders, she put her face there, pressed her
nose to the center of him, right over his heart. She
drew in a deep breath, inhaling the smell of dust and
horse. Man. Jesse.

"I'm kind of . . . I'm not too clean," he said
ruefully.

"True." She kissed his neck, though. Her tongue
darted out; she took a daring taste. Hm, salty. "Nope,
you aren't too clean," she murmured, hugging him
close. "But you are delicious."

Over his shoulder, she could see his reflection in
her dressing-table mirror. Just him, from the backs
of his knees to his shoulder blades. And her white
hands and arms stroking, holding. She worked her
fingers inside his low-slung pants in back, enjoying
how that looked. It made her hotter, that and the
tight feel of his buttocks, the tops of them, bunching
under her hands. *Oh, man, oh, man.* That's all she
could think of—*oh, man, oh, man.*

He set her away rather abruptly, muttering something that sounded like, "Get serious here," and
started on her skirt again. He wasn't so smooth and
sure-fingered now. In fact, he was clumsy—she had

to help him. She thought of Jamie, how fast he'd been at this, how practiced. Maybe Jesse didn't have a girl in every port, so to speak. Wouldn't that be nice.

She wasn't so sure of herself now, either. Her skirt was gone, blouse gone, chemise and corset and petticoats gone. Except for stockings, she was naked. Jesse just stared at her. A flicker of apprehension crept through her. Men liked everything, they were so undemanding, so unbelievably easy to please. At least the men she knew. But Jesse . . . he wasn't talking. Not saying a word. Did he like the way she looked? She was kind of small. Her breasts were okay, not too little, but the rest of her was small. When she couldn't stand it another second she said, "Well?" with a pretend-laugh—to show she didn't care too much.

He still didn't say anything, but he made a noise in his throat. And he started shaking his head from side to side. Slow, wondering, amazed shakes.

He wasn't disappointed.

That small, freezing sensation she'd had when she wasn't sure began to melt. She could *feel* her body turning sexual, female. She went close and rubbed herself against him. Bold as brass. "Get naked," she whispered in his ear. Leaving him standing there, she climbed into bed.

He quit wasting time. If he'd been a little awkward with her buttons, he was a master with his. All in one smooth move, he undid his fly, bent over and shucked trousers and white flannel drawers off simultaneously, and threw them halfway across the room. So reckless. So exciting. And the look of him. *Oh, my, yes,* Cady thought, going mindless again. *Come right over here.* Thrilled to death, she patted his place on the bed beside her.

Too hot for the covers. Plus she wanted to see him. He wanted to see her, too—"Cady, look at you," he kept saying, putting his hands on every part of her he could reach. They couldn't seem to get close enough.

"Let's hurry," she urged, stroking his back and trying to kiss his mouth, which he had buried in the side of her neck.

He raised his head. "Really? Hurry?"

"I was just thinking maybe we should get it over with. Fast. So then we can start over."

He surrounded her with his arms and covered her with one hairy leg, vibrating with laughter. She laughed, too, although she hadn't been joking. He held her like that, pinned down so she couldn't touch him, and slowly, after a minute or two, her mood changed. She wanted him as much as before, but she didn't feel quite so frantic. He released her, all but his hand on the side of her jaw, two fingers gently coaxing her head around. His eyes . . . she lost herself looking into his eyes. "Jesse, Jess," she sighed. "Oh, Jess."

They kissed. It broke her down, it was so deep, so sweet. Was it more than kissing? Her stricken heart toyed with the idea that it was loving.

He began to touch her, arouse her. It wasn't like anything she'd ever known. Not that she'd known that much. But she'd known some, and this wasn't like it. He had such caring in his hands, he paid such close attention. What he was was riveted. By her.

It made her absolutely crazy for him. She'd learned from him not to say, "Hurry, Jesse, let's do it now, fast, hurry," but oh, God, it was hard to wait. Weren't women the ones who liked to slow things down? Yes. She knew that from her own experience, but even more from things Glendoline told her—unasked; startling, eye-popping things about what men and women, or at least men and Glen, got up to in bed. Yes, and even Jesse had gone too fast that other time. The last time, out there on her back doorstep.

Maybe he'd learned his lesson. Heck. Oh, well.

"Oh, well."

Out loud she said that. She couldn't keep her mouth shut. He had his tongue in her belly button, and she could hardly stand it. Also his arms around her hips, and he was sliding lower. Oh, God. He locked his arms around her thighs and buried his nose, his mouth, in her private hair. *Oh, Jesse, Jess, what are you doing?* As much as it shocked her, she wanted to open her legs. She did. But she couldn't because he was holding them shut tight, and even that was a deep, grinding pleasure, the fact that she couldn't move.

"Oh, oh, wait'll I get you," she threatened emptily, touching the back of his head, stroking through thick, straight, long hair. "I'll get you and you'll . . . you'll be . . ."

All at once he pulled her thighs wide apart and dove over her, landing on his elbows and sinking down on top of her. He said, "Ahh," and she sympathized: a perfect fit. He hooked his hands under her arms and grabbed her shoulders. He smiled into her eyes—he looked so happy, so pleased. *It's not complicated for you,* she thought. *I wish I were like a man.*

She put her legs around his legs, and they kissed, and he came right into her, smooth as silk. He groaned, a really long, loud, heartfelt sound, and then held still inside her. "I couldn't wait any longer, Cady. Sorry."

"I forgive you."

They started to move together, and it was a little ragged at first, both trying so hard to please. But after a while they figured out that they both liked the same thing, at least for now—long, slow, deep strokes, holding tight, and not kissing. Concentrated.

And he liked to talk—that was a revelation. He *said* what they were doing while they were doing it. He named names. That you could do that had never even occurred to her. But she liked it. After the shock wore off, she really loved it. He started to ask her what she wanted—"This? Like this?"—and pretty soon she couldn't talk, couldn't answer. "Nhh," she said, or at the most, "Yah."

She was coming undone. She was coming. They'd barely begun, and she was coming. Oh, good good good, because sometimes she didn't, sometimes—

Brain clicked off. Heat, slick, full, do it, get me, Jesse now, Jesse now—

Yes. Flying out over it, up and over. Just—there. Yes, perfect, ah.

Ah.

He said, "Gotcha," and she said, "Got me," thinking it was over.

He started over. Didn't even change positions, just started up again. "Oh, no," she said, "really. I couldn't." Ha. He knew more than she did. He covered her breast with his mouth, and it was like he'd never been there before. And she was so sensitive now. He'd skinned her or something, made it all new and raw and exquisite. He slid his hands down her back, down to her bottom, and he spread her cheeks a little, opening her up more. She gasped. He widened his legs, and that made her widen hers. He started saying dirty words, and just like that—she was there again, right up to that high place that was so easy, he made it so easy, to leap from and fall, fall, fall. *You come, too,* she thought, or maybe said, and he did. She knew because he drove so deeply and he made the loudest sound, pure joy, just manly ecstasy, she wanted to laugh or cry and press him in, in, *more.*

So greedy. There wasn't any more, this was it. Enough. They collapsed on each other. Cady said, "Well, I never," and that was the God's truth.

She had a little strength left to kiss his mouth and pet the smooth muscle in his forearm. "I love . . . I loved that," she changed it to. She wasn't crazy.

"Cady."

"Hm?"

"Cady." That's all he would say. He kept his eyes closed and said her name some more, smiling. She took it as a good sign.

Nine

Cady sat at the edge of the lamplight, half in and half out, brushing her hair in front of her dressing table mirror. The right side of her head was dark and mysterious, black as midnight, but the left side had fire in it. Red gleams flashing and disappearing, as if they were playing a game with the silver-handled brush she dragged through it in long, lazy strokes, scalp to ends, scalp to ends. Jesse could feel his face going slack, mouth half open, eyelids drooping. She was hypnotizing him.

"You falling asleep?" She caught his eye in the mirror.

"Nope."

"Good." She laid the brush down and stood up. Something red hung on the side of the mirror, a scarf or something, draped over the front and back. She whisked it off and moved toward the bed. He'd seen her in her paisley robe before, that day when Clyde and Turley busted in and tried to scare her, but it hadn't affected him that much. Unlike now. She'd had some clothes on under it then; he hadn't been able to see every naked curve and flare she had, not to mention the soft, springy wobble of her breasts when she walked. He blinked his eyes; he was getting hypnotized again.

She sat on the edge of the mattress, and automatically he reached for the silk belt of her robe. Just to play with. She watched his face, turning her head to different angles, studying him. He smiled, batted his eyes. What was she up to?

"Lean forward," she said. He did, and she snaked the scarf in her hands—it was a scarf—around his neck and started to tie it in a bow. She finished and sat back, giving the bow and his chest a little pat. "Ha," she said. "Just as I thought." She got up and went back to her dressing table, began rooting around in the drawers.

"What are you doing?"

She returned with more scarves. "May I?" She lifted his right arm and tied a blue and green one around his biceps. He started to laugh. "Colors," she explained, beaming. "I wanted to see how you look in something besides black."

"And?"

"Lovely." She tied a third one, pink, purple, and orange, around his left wrist. "My dear, you are quite fetching."

"I'll fetch you if you don't cut it out."

"Oh, I'm so scared." She had a hat hanging on her wall, floppy straw with a bunch of yellow flowers and ribbons. She went and got it, then came toward him grinning, purposeful.

"Oh, no, you don't." He ducked and caught her by both wrists, yanking her on top of him. She

shrieked, and he couldn't resist tickling her. They
had a wrestling match that didn't last long, only until
he rolled over and pinned her. Giggling, snorting,
they panted in each other's face, and it was so good,
so perfect, he started to tell her the truth—that this
was the best day of his life, the *best* day, he could
still hardly believe it. But before he could say it, she
said. "Jesse, why *do* you wear black?" And then she
said, "Jesse. Why do you shoot people?"

It broke the mood.

He closed his eyes rather than examine the urgency, almost a desperation, that flared in her beautiful face for one unguarded second. "I don't shoot
people. I don't just go around shooting people.
Jeez, Cady."

"Oh, that's right. They always deserve it." She
pushed him up and scooted out from under him,
tugging at her robe, going all modest on him.

He could see a fight coming on if he didn't head
it off quick. "Listen to me, because I'll only say this
once." He put Gault in his tone, took out all the
Jesse. She stared at him, arrested. "We can talk about
anything you want, anything under the sun, except
for one thing. My business. Which," he pointed out,
"you knew all about before you invited me in here
tonight."

He reached for her hand. "Cady," he said in his
own voice, working the stiffness out of her fingers.
"Cady girl. Let's not spoil this." He brought her hand
to his mouth, pressed his lips to the inside of her
wrist. "Everything is just right. Isn't it? It's perfect."
She didn't speak, so he kept on nibbling her, wooing

her, teasing her soft, strong, thin-fingered hand with kisses. He lifted his head. Her brown eyes resting on him were melancholy and distrustful and fond. He smiled, trying to make her smile.

"Okay," she said at last. But he hadn't wooed her, he saw, hadn't changed her mind or made her forget anything. She'd made a decision, that was all. For right now, this night anyway, it was in his favor.

"I still think you should wear colors," she said lightly, pulling her hand away, stretching out beside him, and plumping pillows at her back. "You'd still scare the hell out of everybody, if that's what you're worried about."

Not as much, though. He'd given the subject a lot more thought than she had. "Think so?" He sat up, scarves flying, and reached for the straw hat he'd wrestled away from her. He set it on the back of his head. "Listen, sidewinder, one wrong move and I'll plug you."

She doubled up with laughter, leaning against his shoulder, helpless with it. Ah, she was back, his Cady girl, just the way he liked her best—loose and laughing. He put his arms around her, and pretty soon they were kissing. "How's your head?" she asked, carefully avoiding his sewn cut as she stroked her fingers through his hair. "It must hurt. That was quite a whack."

"Nah, it doesn't hurt." Big man. "Feels funny, is all. The stitches." He touched them gingerly with his middle finger, following the thin, jagged, prickly line along his tender scalp.

"Let's see." He bowed his head and she leaned

over him, barely grazing the stitched wound with her fingertips. The warm, mingled scents of sex and Cady's soft rosewater cologne rose from her half-open robe. It made him dizzy. He slipped his hands inside, cupping her luscious breasts. She stopped exploring his head wound and held still, breathing slowly and evenly. The freedom eagle or whatever it was still soared for her nipple, and would still be soaring toward it when she was eighty years old. "I don't like this bird," Jesse revealed, then scowled, surprised at himself. He toyed with the idea that he was jealous of the bird, then discarded it. He was jealous of the big brave Italian freedom fighter she wore it in honor of. The fact that he was dead was only marginally consoling.

"You don't?"

"Oh, it's okay," he said, backtracking. Nothing she could do about it now, so what was the point of bitching.

She sat back, looking down at the vivid blue tattoo on her bare bosom. She fingered it lightly, idly, and his body tightened. He was reaching for her when she said, "I told you a little fib about how I got it." He paused. She took a deep breath and shut her eyes. "Actually, I lied. Is what I did. Do you want to hear the real story?"

"Yeah, sure." He sat up straighter, interested, ready to be relieved. "I never liked that story anyway."

"Ha," she said without smiling. "You probably won't like this one any better."

"Let's hear it. Come over here." She looked so uncomfortable, even a little woebegone, he put his arms around her and made her sit close, tucked up against his side. "Okay. Out with it."

"I told you I wore it in memory of my lover."

"Right. The Red Shirt. He helped liberate Naples."

"And you believed that?" She looked him in the eye, amazed.

"Well, sure. Sort of. Yeah. Why wouldn't I?"

"Because it's . . ." She started to laugh. "It's ridiculous."

He laughed, too, to humor her.

"It's not even an eagle."

"It's not? Let's see." She pulled the lapel of her robe open and twisted around toward the light. Her breast was such a beautiful distraction, he'd never examined the bird closely before. "Hmm." It had wings, an eye, a beak, a tail. "What is it?"

"It's a . . . Can't you tell? It's a . . ." She didn't want to say the word.

"What?"

"Jesse, it's a damn seagull."

"A *seagull*. Ah, so it is. Now I see. There's its—" She shut her robe, ducked her chin, and crossed her arms over her chest. She looked mortified. He felt bewildered. "Okay. Well," he said carefully. "How did you happen to get a seagull tattooed on your bosom?"

"I was young," she said sullenly. "Really young."

"Ten? Twelve?'

"Eighteen."

"Uh-huh."

"I was going out with this—well, first of all, my

father had just . . . no, before that my mother died, and I was . . ."

He slid down in the bed a little, patient. He looked at the ceiling, not at Cady; sometimes, he knew from experience, that made it easier to talk.

She sighed. "I grew up in Portland. My father came and went a lot. He never stayed too long."

"What did he do for a living?"

"Different things. I guess mostly he was a fisherman. But he drank. A lot."

"Your mother?"

"Died when I was fifteen. So then I stopped going to school and started working. In the salmon canning factory. Have you ever canned salmon, Jesse?"

"Can't say as I have."

"Don't ever do it. No matter what happens, how low you sink or how poor you get, don't ever do it."

"I won't," he vowed solemnly. He could feel faint tremors of revulsion shudder through her body where it touched him. "So then what happened?"

"Well, then my father disappeared for good. I'd just turned eighteen. I met this man. Boy, really."

Now they were getting to it. "What was his name?"

"Jamie. Jamie O'Doole."

"Jamie O'Doole." He smiled, making the connection.

She laughed softly. "Not James Doulé. I don't know what made me say that." She picked up his hand and began playing with his fingers. "Oh, I do know. The true story is kind of, well, sordid. Tacky, as my mother used to say."

"But your mother thought life is duty."

"That's true. She sure did. Sometimes I didn't even blame my father for leaving us. I wished *I* could leave." He gave her hand a soft squeeze. "So anyway. Where was I?"

"The man-boy."

"Jamie. He was a sailor. I thought he was so handsome. Shall I tell you what he looked like?"

"Not unless you have to."

She shifted, facing him. "Why not? Because you'd be jealous?"

"I'm afraid I'd have to kill him."

She smiled, but sadly. "Maybe he's already dead. I used to tell myself that's why he didn't come back for me."

"What an idiot. Him, not you."

"Oh, I was an idiot, too. And if I ever forget it, I've always got this to remind me."

Now he could guess, but he asked anyway. "How did you get it?"

"Exactly the way you think I got it. And I don't even remember. I was too drunk."

"Poor Cady," he murmured, smiling.

"Poor Cady." She clucked her tongue scornfully. "It was his last night in port. He asked me to marry him, and of course I said yes. I hadn't—we hadn't . . . done . . . oh, you know. We hadn't had sex yet. So that night we drank a lot. Celebrating our engagement," she said with a combination of amusement and bitterness. "He said I should get a tattoo just like his, and I thought that was absolutely the most romantic thing I'd ever heard. I was *wild* to do it. And I did—obviously—but I don't remember anything about it. Maybe I was unconscious by then. I do remember afterward, though. Vaguely. I lost my virginity to him, and I can't even call it lovemaking. It was definitely not a memorable experience."

He hugged her, gave her a soft kiss on the temple.

"The next thing I remember is waking up in the morning. Very sick. Alone. I had a tattoo and no lover, and I never saw Jamie again."

"And now you don't drink."

"Beer every once in a while. Hard liquor"—she shuddered again—"never."

They lay quietly for a time. "That," Jesse ventured, "is a very sad story."

"No, it's a very stupid story. I've never told it to anyone before."

He thought about that. "Why did you tell me?"

"I guess . . . because I thought you'd understand. I don't know. I just wanted to tell somebody. I've kept it a secret for eight years. It embarrasses me, but it's not so terrible, really. I mean, I didn't kill anybody or . . ." She broke off.

He lay still and didn't say anything.

"So anyway. That's it. The story of Cady's tattoo. And if you tell anybody, I'm afraid I'll have to kill *you.*"

He laughed with relief, grateful to her for turning it into a joke. Serious talk about killing people didn't have any place between them tonight. "You can call this lovemaking," he promised, just before he wrapped her up in his arms and kissed her. Her response, eager and immediate, thrilled him. He'd never had a lover quite like Cady. He slipped her arms out of her robe, got her flat on her back, her head off the pillow. He used his knee to prod her legs open, relishing the sound she made, a kind of gasping hum, when he did it. God, she liked this almost as much as he did. He started telling her what her skin felt like, and it wasn't even a stretch to say words like "warm silk" and "cool water," and when he caressed her between her legs, "hot, slick glass." She began to moan—he loved that sound—and clutch her hands at nothing but the air. Her hair looked black against the sheet, curling and falling and twisting, twining through his fingers. How many lovers had there been between him and her faithless sailor? He wanted to know. Didn't want to know. He tickled the damn bird with his tongue, slowly, followed its flight path to her nipple, making her arch and groan. He felt her small hands on his back, the sharp bite of her nails. He did something then, he wasn't even sure what, that made her climax. Her thighs clamped around his caressing hand and she rolled toward him, face contorted, forcing a low, grinding sound through her clenched teeth. She drew her knees up and hunched her shoulders, and he could feel, actually feel the soft, rhythmic pulsing of feminine flesh around his fingers.

When it subsided, he gently unrolled her, beguiled by the pink flush on her cheeks and her chest, the way her damp hair stuck to her throat. She looked ravished. And when she opened her eyes there wasn't much to see—they were still vacant, still back there in the mindless pleasure. "Your freckles are standing out," he said tenderly. Maybe not the most romantic thing he'd ever told a woman, but it made Cady laugh.

"I wouldn't be surprised." She pressed a soft, dreamy kiss to his shoulder. "My God, Jesse, how did you do that?"

"It's a secret." He didn't have the faintest idea.

She sighed. She smothered a yawn.

He couldn't keep his hands off her. He ought to let her rest, get her second wind, but if he didn't have her soon—no, now—he was going to explode.

Murmuring to her, calling her baby, whispering to her to come on, honey, come on, he nudged her onto her back again. She smiled and opened her legs for him, and he thanked her and told her that's right, that's it, hovering over her and using his hand to push himself into her slowly, slowly, ready to die from the way she felt, so tight and hot around him. Knees bent, feet flat on the bed, she set that deep, rolling rhythm that drove him out of his mind. He lost all finesse. He forgot to be gentle, forgot everything except how it felt to be inside Cady. And she was with him all the way. And then slowly, imperceptibly at first, she began to stiffen under him, arch her back and grit her teeth. She was coming. She was so beautiful, and he wanted to savor her fierce, silent climax, but it was impossible. Gathering her close, he let himself go, pumping, driving into her with strong, powerful thrusts, not silent at all—he heard his own groaning huffs in amazement. In the middle of it he halfway blacked out, it was just so damn intense.

He rolled away, and they fell against each other. She looked as done in as he felt—more so; she didn't even have the strength to return his grateful kisses. He picked her hand up and dropped it, to see what would happen; it fell on his chest in a boneless heap. "Cady?"

"Mmm."

"Cady?"

"What."

"Do you want me to go?"

"Go?" She opened one bleary eye.

"To my room." He gave her a little shake. "Honey, do you want me to leave now?"

"Leave now?" She yawned on his chest, a big, wet, wide-mouthed yawn, graceless and endearing. "Oh, no, I want you to staaaay. Stay all night." She went limp. Almost immediately a soft snore woke her up, and she twisted around, away from him. She stuck her hand up, twitched her fingers. Bemused, he took it, and she pulled his arm around her, tucking his hand inside both of hers. She fell instantly asleep.

Across the room, the oil lamp sputtered and went out. Good timing. The perfect end to a perfect day. Maybe the best day of his life. He buried his face in Cady's dark, wild hair. His Cady girl. He fell asleep like that, trying to remember if he'd felt this happy before.

In the morning, he was coming back from Cady's outhouse—not the one Rogue customers used but her own neat, clean, private one, down the path from her back door, hidden from casual view by the blue-blossom bushes—when he heard voices coming from her room. Hers and somebody else's. He halted, listening. Then he relaxed—the second voice was Ham's. He ambled on up the steps and through the door, catching the tail end of a story Ham was telling.

"They only got till Tuesday mornin' to git shut o' the sto', Poppy say. Don't even got two weeks. Got till Tuesday mornin' on account o' that the first o' the month." He saw Jesse and grinned. "Hey, Mr. Gault."

"Hey, Mr. Washington." As was his habit, he grabbed Ham around the waist and turned him upside down. A lot of hollering and laughing ensued, but Jesse noticed Cady didn't join in. She rested her back against the bedpost and hugged herself, rubbing her arms in the loose sleeves of her paisley robe. A sure sign she was worried about something.

"Anything wrong?" He righted Ham and sat down on the edge of the bed.

"It's Wylie. Who else?" She gave a chilly laugh. "He's called in a note he owns on Luther Digby's general store. Luther can't pay it. It's so *damned* unfair." She kicked the post with her bare foot, wincing.

"They got a baby," Ham said shyly, wary of Cady's anger. "Poppy say what they gonna do with a new baby an' all this trouble."

"Luther saved and saved to buy that store, and then he worked like a dog to make enough so he and Sara could marry. It's cruel, that's what it is. It's just cruel."

"How come Wylie's got the note?" Jesse had been in Digby's store once, to buy black handkerchiefs. He remembered the woman who had waited on him, a pretty, thin-faced girl with wheat-colored hair. She spoke to him softly and pointed, smiling, to a sleeping infant in a basket on the counter.

"He must've bought Luther's mortgage from the bank. That's how he got the Sullivan ranch. Until Lyndon Cherney disappeared—you didn't know him, Jess, but he was one of the vice presidents at the Mercantile—before he disappeared, he and Wylie were thick as thieves." Ham was leaning against her, looking up at her face worriedly. She put her hands over his ears and said a bad word. "Who else's mortgage does he own? Who'll be next? Isn't there some way to stop him?"

"You could fix it, Mr. Gault," Ham said confidently. "You could make him quit."

"How would I do that?"

"Go down there with your guns an' shoot 'im!"

"Ham," Cady said sternly. "Go on out now so I can dress." The boy said, "Aww," inching toward the office door. "Go on, and maybe later we'll go out for a ride."

That brightened him up. "Okay!" he agreed, and slammed the door behind him.

Watching Cady, Jesse could see his plans for a long, lazy morning in bed going up in smoke. She couldn't sit still, and when he reached for her hand, she pulled away, prickly as a thistle. "Well, *couldn't* you do something?" she finally burst out.

He'd been expecting it. "Go down there with my guns and shoot 'im? Sure."

She waved her hand impatiently. "Of course not. Couldn't you talk to him? Jesse, there's nobody else.

Wylie's killing our town, and the sheriff can't stop it. Couldn't you do *something?*''

That was how he found himself slouching down Main Street on Sunday morning, church bells clanging in the distance. He looked as mean as it was possible for a man to look, with his black Stetson pulled low over his eyepatch, spurs jingling, sun glinting on the pearl handles of his six-guns.

Unlike Cady's saloon, Wylie's was open on the Sabbath, and doing a moderate business. The sweet, nauseating stench of stale smoke hung over the place, reminding Jesse of every hangover he'd ever had. Wylie favored a lot of brass and purple plush; there was dark red paper on the walls, and a red carpet, stained with booze and cigarette burns and God knew what else, on the floor. The joint was bigger and fancier than the Rogue. Also darker and uglier, and a whole lot more vulgar.

Cady had told him Wylie had an orchestra for music, not just one lone piano player. No band was in evidence today, though. Which was just as well. The scattered customers looked a little rocky, a little on the edge; loud music might tip them right over.

Jesse headed for the bar. What little conversation there had been stopped, and he listened to the sinister jangle of spurs and clomp of boot heels in that old familiar, frightened hush. He used to enjoy it. He hadn't heard it at the Rogue in quite a while. Funny; he didn't miss it.

Wylie's bartender was the reverse of Levi Washington. He was white, not black; fat, not skinny; ugly, not handsome. Looking at him, Jesse had an idea that he might not be the kind of fellow who read books about Buddha to impress his girlfriend.

"What'll it be?"

"Wylie. Where is he?"

A war waged in the bartender's piggy face. He wanted to say, *Who wants to know*? in the worst way. But he already knew who wanted to know, and he was scared of him. "Upstairs," he finally mumbled through thick lips.

"Get him." The bartender stared at him. Jesse leaned over the bar and said, "Get. Him."

Pig Face sneered and left the room.

Jesse sighed. Time to get nasty. He grabbed a bottle off the bar and carried it to a center table, currently occupied by two silent, morose cowboys nursing beers. "I like this table," he whispered.

They left.

He took a skinny black cigarette out of his pocket and fired it up. Leaning back with the bottle, he stuck his feet up on the table. Took a drag. Took a drink.

Bleck. Gag. Whiskey and cigarettes on an empty stomach. Cady had been so het up about the general store, she hadn't even let him get a cup of coffee first. Jesse wasn't in a good mood.

Luckily, Wylie didn't keep him waiting. He came down a mahogany staircase looking fit and rested, fully dressed in frock coat, striped trousers, and bow tie. Probably on his way to church. It was a good act: he looked prosperous and respectable, a veritable city father. A gentleman. But Jesse knew a disguise when he saw one. Besides, Cady had told him what

Wylie did to women, and what he'd done to Glendo-line in particular. That helped make it personal.

What she hadn't told him was what, if anything, she and Wylie used to be to each other. They hated each other now, that was obvious, but Jesse sus-pected they'd been friends in the past. More than friends. That burned him. And it gave him an even better reason, the best reason, to hate him. Because Cady was his now. Exclusively. Whatever was going to happen between him and Wylie, he wanted it over with fast, so he could get back to her. He missed her. He hadn't seen her in ten minutes.

"Ah, Mr. Gault." Considering the tone of their last meeting, Wylie's face was remarkably pleasant, al-most welcoming. "You've gotten tired of slumming, I see. Have you decided to come and work for me after all? Why don't we go up to my office and dis-cuss it in private."

A little late, it occurred to Jesse that he didn't have a plan, and a smart man didn't play it by ear with Wylie. What was he supposed to say now, "Give Luther Digby his store back or I'll kill you"? The foreclosure was legal, he assumed. Digby wasn't the real issue anyway. Wylie wanted everything, the whole damn town, and somehow Jesse was supposed to stop him. With what? All he had was a bluff. And Wylie was the only man who had never bought it, not completely. Staring at his fleshy face, the thick pelt of dark red hair, the ruby glinting on his finger, Jesse had to admit Wylie scared him. There was a look in his bulging eyes, a combination of intelligence and ruthlessness. No, more than ruthlessness—it was what Cady had said: "It's just *cruel*."

"Where are your two thugs?" he asked, deciding to get it over with quick. If Gault was the only weapon he had, he might as well use both barrels on him and get out.

Wylie paused in the act of sitting down. "What?"

"Turley and Clyde, your bodyguards. They in church?"

Somebody behind him started to snicker, but broke off when Wylie turned his pop-eyes on him. He sat down carefully, folding his small hands on the edge of the table. "What did you come here for?" he inquired. His face wasn't pleasant or welcoming anymore.

"I came to tell you I don't like you."

Chairs scraped. Jesse didn't look, but out of the corner of his eye he saw two, maybe three men scuttle toward the door and duck out.

Wylie pretended to laugh. "And this is supposed to interest me?" His voice shook slightly—but with anger, not fear.

"I don't like how you operate. I don't like it that you burned Logan's livery to the ground."

"That's not true. Who told you that? You weren't even here then. I'll sue you for sl—"

"I don't like it that you turned Forrest Sullivan off his sheep ranch. You ruined him out of greed, and it's nobody's fault but yours that he killed himself."

Wylie jerked back in his chair and stood up. "Get out."

"I don't like it that you're trying to ruin Luther Digby," he went on without moving.

"That's none of your—"

"And if you go through with it, you'll be sorry."

"Are you threatening me?"

"Yeah. Here's another threat, so pay attention. If you or any of your hoodlums go near Rogue's Tavern or Cady McGill, I swear you *won't* be sorry, because you won't live long enough." He tossed his lit cigarette on the stained carpet and got to his feet. "Got that, Merle? Anything unclear to you? Anything you want me to repeat?"

Wylie was quivering, white-lipped, ready to go off. He was livid, literally, but Jesse couldn't tell if he'd scared him or not. "Get out," he repeated. "Go back to your whore." He was spitting again, flecks of foam collecting in the corners of his lips. "Oh, yes. I know about you and Cady. Did she tell you she was old man Shlegel's whore before she was yours? Why do you think he gave her the saloon? She earned it on her back, that's why."

Jesse was a mild-tempered man; he rarely got angry. But when he did, he had a habit of yelling and throwing things—not Gault's style at all. With a superhuman effort of will, he controlled his fury and managed to say in a whisper, Gault-like, "Come outside with me, Merle. Say that to me again. Out in the street at twenty paces. Come on. Bring that gun in your boot."

They stared at each other for a year or two. Every second, Jesse was sure Wylie would do it—call his bluff and agree to a shoot-out.

But he didn't. After eternity and then some, his bullish shoulders slumped; a fake careless look replaced the tension in his face. "I won't fight you. Not that way. Get out of my place and don't come back."

"I'll come back whenever I feel like it. And you won't do a damn thing about it." *Stop now. Go.* But he ignored the voice shouting good advice; he was too riled up to play it safe. "Now apologize."

"What did you say?"

"Say you're sorry for calling Miss McGill a bad name."

Somebody changed a laugh into a cough. Wylie's face turned a ruddy plum color.

"Say it." He went closer, even though it was like walking up to a tiger's cage and putting his head through the bars. "Say it. Say 'I'm sorry.' "

Wylie couldn't make his mouth work. "You bastard," he croaked.

"No, that's not it. I'm sorry. Say it."

"I'm . . . sorry."

"Good. What are you sorry for?"

Jesse could hear the coarse grind of Wylie's back teeth, see the muscles in his jaws strain and flex. "Calling her a whore," he finally gritted out. It sounded like bones scraping.

Jesse stared into his eyes for a long, long time. Then he smiled his maniac smile. "Very good," he whispered.

It took guts to turn his back and walk away. Slowly. He imagined a target between his shoulder blades, bull's-eye in the middle. What would a bullet feel like? Hot and burning, or just a heavy, numbing thud? He reached the double doors and pushed them open casually, not dodging or ducking or making a break. They banged shut behind him, and he controlled a violent jolt. He kept walking, cool and slow, *jingle-stomp, jingle-stomp.* Luckily it was a hot day. Otherwise somebody might think panic was the cause of the sweat running down his cheeks.

Ten

"Why didn't Ham come with us?" Jesse asked, expertly reining the horse around a jagged rut in the road. "Not that I'm complaining."

Cady smiled guiltily. She loved Ham, but she didn't miss him right now, either. "Levi needed him. Levi's got a special day planned, and Ham's vital to it."

Jesse glanced over at her. "How's that?"

She leaned closer on the buggy seat and said in a mock-secretive voice, "Today's the day Levi asks Lia Chang if she'll go for a walk with him. He thinks she'll be more apt to say yes if Ham tags along."

"Ah, very devious. Poor girl doesn't stand a chance."

"I hope not." She had watched Levi's slow, gentle courtship for months, and she was ready for some action. Not being a Buddhist, she was probably even more impatient for it than Levi.

"Know why I'm glad Ham didn't come with us?"

"Why?"

"Because then I couldn't do this." He switched the reins to his other hand, put his arm around her, and gave her a sweet, smacking kiss on the mouth. Cady laughed, delighted, and he kissed her again, softer. She had to reach up to keep her hat on. "Mm, dee-licious," he said against her lips, taking a little taste with his tongue. Just then the buggy hit a hole the size of Crater Lake, and Cady's teeth clacked together. "Ow," said Jesse, rubbing the back of his neck. "Guess I better watch the road." He winked at her.

"Yeah, because I'd hate it if you bit your tongue off." She wriggled her eyebrows. "I mean I'd *really* hate it." She cackled at his expression when he got the meaning of that, and slipped her hand under his arm, leaning against him, tickled at herself. What fun it was to say things like that, wicked jokes and naughty double entendres, to the man you were . . . having an intimate relationship with. That's how she was trying to think of Jesse. The man she was having an intimate relationship with. Glendoline would say he was the man she was having sex with, and maybe that was even better. Blunter; coarser. And it left the emotions out completely, which was certainly safer.

"See that stone post under the oak trees?" she said, pointing. "That's the entrance."

He slowed the horse and made the tight turn. The weedy drive flanked a long, rolling hill, buttercup-covered, that hid the house until the last second. "What is this place?" he asked, glancing around curiously.

A place I like to go to sometimes, she'd told him before they set out, deliberately vague. She'd never told a soul she came here, much less brought anyone with

her. It was private; hers alone. If she built it up, prepared Jesse for something special, and he was disappointed—well, it would hurt. That's all, it would
hurt.

'It's called River Farm," she said offhandedly. "It's
just an old place. Abandoned. I think the house is
pretty. It's coming up—" She pointed again. "There."

She cringed. Had something happened to it? A
storm, vandals—? No. No, nothing had changed. It
was only that she was seeing it through Jesse's eyes,
the clear, unsentimental eyes of a stranger.

What a wreck. The shutters that hadn't blown off
hung at crazy angles, half their wooden slats missing.
The rotting front porch looked dangerous. Only the
attic windows still had unbroken glass; the rest were
either cracked, shattered, or gone. One of the chim-
neys had subsided into a rubble of loose bricks, and
the shingled roof must leak everywhere. Once-white
clapboard sides had almost finished peeling down to
naked gray wood.

"Dilapidated" was too kind a word for a house
that had once been called *Le Coeur au Coquin*.

Jesse stopped the horse at the top of the circular
carriageway, beside the crumbling, overgrown slate
walk. Cady avoided his eyes. "What a dump, huh?"
She patted her knees nervously. "Want to stop here?
We could walk around. The orchard's pretty. I was
thinking we could eat there, if you want. Or not, we
can—"

"Sure, let's get down. I love old houses. Boy, this
place must've really been something."

Her heart did a mad little flip. She couldn't account

for it. What difference did it make what Jesse, the man with whom she was having an intimate relationship, thought about the old Russell place? None at all. None at all. *Get that straight, Cady,* she advised, taking his hand as she jumped down from the buggy.

He did like old houses. He peeked in all the windows, tried all the doors—although with no more success than she'd ever had; Sam Blankenship, who was selling the house for his real estate company, had padlocked every one. Jesse knew what a parapet was, and a pilaster. He admired the sloping dormers, even though they'd lost most of their shingles, and the graceful, three-sided bay window, and the whimsical oculus window at the top of the two-story Victorian tower. He kept saying, "What a *place* this must've been," and Cady kept biting her tongue so she wouldn't say, "It could be a place *again.*" But she must not have been hiding her excitement as cleverly as she thought, because when they finished exploring, Jesse put his arm around her waist and said, "You love it, don't you?"

"It's okay." She shrugged, made a face. "Yeah, I like it. You know. It's just nice. Old."

Why couldn't she tell him? *This is my dream house.* Why couldn't she say that? Well, because once she started, who knew what she might say next? She might turn coy, say something like, "Don't *you* have a dream house?" And he might laugh at her, and she'd hate that. But she'd deserve it.

He unhitched the horse, the same good-tempered gray mare she always rented from Nestor, and let her graze where she would. Back in town, Jesse had said he wished he could ride Pegasus and rent Cady another horse or try her on Bellefleur, and to hell with the buggy. But yesterday's three-mile race had taken a lot out of the stallion; he needed a rest. Cady didn't care. She rode, but not well; the buggy was fine with her. She didn't think she'd ever met a man who loved horses as much as Jesse did.

"The river's over there, behind those trees. Can you hear it?"

He lifted his head, listening. "I thought it was the wind."

"No, the river. Want to go look?"

A path of sorts led from the driveway into a thicket of shaggy, moss-hung live oaks, gnarled and low-canopied, hiding the sun. It used to be a road, she told him; the Russells had cleared it so they could drive to the cliff edge of the river. But now it was only a track, rocky in places, completely blocked by fallen trees in others. He held her hand, helping her past obstacles she'd climbed over unassisted a dozen times before. Being with him, seeing his face, touching him whenever she liked—it was pure pleasure. Too sweet. A lot had happened since the night she told him she wouldn't go riding with him because she didn't care for his profession.

The trees gave out. All at once the river's wild roar hit them, and it was like a blow to the chest, a genuine assault. "Sometimes you can see prospectors down there," Cady almost had to yell to be heard, pointing down the sheer rock face of the cliff. "There's not much left to pan, though. It's all been placered out."

Jesse nodded. His light eyes looked colorless in the blinding glare of water and sky. "It's beautiful," he mouthed. The river's power had all but silenced him, she saw. He would love it, of course—its raw, raging energy would appeal to him. She loved it, too, but sometimes the Rogue was *too* strong, sometimes it battered at her senses and she had to get away, retreat into the sober quiet of the woods.

For a long time they watched the mad race of the blue-green water, the explosions of white where it collided with invisible rock. You could lose yourself in the raucous sight and the thundering, deafening sound. Cady had to pull on Jesse's hand to get him to move, and she had to shout, "Aren't you hungry?" to get him interested in leaving.

Behind the house, a crumbling stone wall separated the backyard from the orchard. Two leggy old apple trees shaded part of the wall from the overhead sun, and they decided to have their picnic there. Jesse made such a fuss over their lunch of salty ham biscuits, fried chicken, and tart cucumber salad that Jacques had packed into a pasteboard box for her this morning, she wished she'd had something to do with making it. Did she even know how to cook anymore? She used to, but that was so long ago, she doubted if she could boil water now. But she certainly wasn't going to say that to Jesse.

Why not?

"You know, I'm starting to like this sour mineral water," he told her, replacing the cap on the bottle and passing it to her.

She nodded. "I know, it takes a while. I hated it

when I first came here, but now city water tastes like dishwater to me. Too hot, and it doesn't quench your thirst." He nodded back. She loved it when they agreed with each other.

Between bites of a radish, she listened to the rising song of a meadowlark somewhere in the orchard. Over their heads, a Douglas squirrel scampered across a branch in the apple tree. A little green lizard sunned itself twenty feet away on the wall. Bees buzzed in the clover, and the sound of crickets was a low, raspy constant. Could Jesse hear it?

"Sometimes I forget you're deaf in one ear," she said softly, idly. He was cutting a slice of vinegar pie and didn't look up. "Jesse?"

"Hm?"

"I said," she said, laughing, "sometimes I forget you're deaf." How funny that he hadn't heard that.

"Oh." He chuckled, getting the joke. "Well, I'm not totally deaf. And I can almost always hear what *you* say."

"Really? Why?"

"I've gotten used to your tone."

"Oh." She'd been fishing for a compliment, something flowery about her voice. "How old are you, again?"

He took a big bite of pie, and eyed her steadily across the laden, blue-and-white-checked cloth while he chewed slowly, thoroughly. He swallowed. "Thirty-eight."

She stared at him. "Wow. I mean—not that that's old or anything." It was *ancient*. "You don't look it,

that's all. You could be . . . why, you could be
twenty-eight."

"Thank you." He smiled, complimented. "It runs
in my family. Both sides. We all look young." Before
she could pursue that, he said, "Look what Joe
gave me."

"What?"

He took something, a little stick, out of his shirt
pocket. "It's a toothpick."

"Oh."

"It's made out of deer bone."

"Nice."

"He made it himself, and he gave it to me." He
looked so pleased, as if getting a gift from a friend
was something he wasn't used to. Well, how could
it be? Who would give a present to a gunfighter?
How could he even *have* friends? You might give him
money so he wouldn't kill you, but not a present.

"Jesse . . ."

"Yeah?"

"Oh . . . nothing."

"What?"

"No, nothing. Never mind." She wasn't going to
spoil this day with questions she knew he didn't
want to answer. "Can I have a piece of pie? Or were
you going to eat it all by yourself?"

After lunch, she took him on a walk through the
old orchard. "Altogether it's three hundred acres, but
only about half of that is fruit trees. The rest is mostly
pastureland. And fir forest on the hillsides. It's right
smack in the middle of the valley. La Vallée aux
Coquins."

Out of the blue, Jesse said, "I'd have horses if I lived here."

She leaned against the smooth trunk of a pear tree and turned down the brim of her hat, shielding her eyes from the sun. "What kind?" she asked carelessly.

"I don't know, but purebreds. Arabians and racers, Tennessee walkers, Cleveland bays. Ponies." He looked down, grinning self-consciously. "Guess I'd have to narrow it down."

"You like them all."

"Yeah."

"Like your cousin Marion."

He frowned. "Marion? Oh—right. Yeah, Marion's crazy for horses. We're both like that." He took her hand and they started to walk again. "What's down there?"

"A meadow. Want to see?"

"Sure."

They matched their steps to each other, and swung their arms between them the way sweethearts did. Cady's heart felt high in her chest, too full or something, some thrumming kind of excitement. "What a *beautiful* day," she cried, turning her face to the sky and inhaling a lungful of the clean, sunny air.

"Glad to be out of the saloon?"

"God, yes!"

"But you like it, don't you? Owning the Rogue?"

"Oh, sure. Yes, I really do. But this is so nice. Away from the smoke and the spittoons and the— oh, you know, all that. And the men," she added, laughing. "Sometimes the men are just a bit too . . .

manly." She decided to tell him something else. "It's nice to get away from the women, too."

"The women?"

"In town. The respectable ones who turn their shoulders to me in the street. Or pull their children away if I say 'Hi' or smile at them. It's good to be away from that for a day. I love the country."

They had walked out into the center of a wild-flower meadow. Thigh-high asters and wild sweet william spread out on every side, nearly as far as they could see. The air smelled so sweet, it almost made her dizzy. "Let's sit," said Jesse, and they dropped down right where they were, surrounded by blue and purple flowers. He put his arm around her, and she didn't realize it was for comfort, not just pleasure, till he said, "To hell with them, Cady. They're not worth two minutes of your time worrying about 'em."

"I know."

"What have they got against you, anyway? You're a businesswoman."

"Right."

"They're jealous, that's all."

His indignation warmed her like sunshine. "Well," she was moved to admit, "they think I'm a little bit more than a businesswoman."

"Do they?" He stuck his deer bone toothpick in his mouth and squinted at her. "How come?"

"Oh. You know."

"You mean because of Shlegel?"

She went stiff. "What do you know about Mr. Shlegel?"

"Nothing."

"Who have you been talking to?"

"Nobody."

She pushed away so she could see his face. He had only been talking to one person who would've put doubts in his mind about her and Mr. Shlegel. "Wylie."

"The hell with him, I don't care what he says. Cady—"

"What did he tell you?"

"*Nothing.* Okay, okay, he said you used to be together. You and Shlegel. That's all."

" 'Be together.' I'm sure that's exactly how he put it. Did you believe him?"

"It's none of my business."

"Thank you very much."

He put his hand on her arm when she started to get up. "Wait, now, wait. What I'm saying is, it wouldn't matter."

"What wouldn't?"

"If you had or you hadn't."

"It *wouldn't matter*?"

"Shit." He needed both hands to keep her from streaking away. "Hell's bells, I'm not saying this right. Cady, don't be mad."

"I'm not mad."

"Yes, you are. No, stay still, don't go leaping up like a damn grasshopper. Hold on and let me explain."

She quit straining away from him and said. "No, let *me* explain. Gus Shlegel was the kindest, best-hearted man I ever knew. He was something Paradise hasn't seen since he died: he was a gentleman."

"Okay."

"I wish we *had* been together."

"Okay."

"I wish he'd *married* me."

"All right."

Why was she so riled? She sat there and fumed for another minute, then let it go. "Sorry." She glanced at Jesse. He smiled at her hopefully, but she saw something else in his eyes. Hurt? "Jess . . ." He put his hand flat on the grass, next to hers. Their fingers touched. "What do you think of me? You must have made some assumptions about me. My past. Men—I'm talking about men."

He looked at her, but didn't answer. She didn't doubt he was thinking thoughts about ten-foot poles.

"I run a saloon, I deal blackjack, I sell liquor to drunks. Sometimes the girls I hire take men home with them. I tell them not to, but they do it anyway. So—most people have an opinion about me. Given those facts. What's yours?"

"Cady." He started shaking his head, laughing. "No way."

"No, it's all right, you can tell me. What do you think of me? How many men do you think I've been with?"

"I don't care."

"Yes, you do."

"Okay, I do, but I'm not asking."

"How many? Ten? Fifty?"

"Cut it out."

"Come on, guess."

"Would you quit?"

She heaved a sigh. "Well, if you're not going to even guess, I'll just tell you."

"You don't have to tell me. I don't even want you to—"

"Two. Before you, I mean. One was Jamie, and the—"

"I don't need to know this."

But she couldn't stop. "And the other was a schoolteacher. He lived in Monterey. That's where I ended up after I left Portland. I met him when I was twenty. He wanted to get married—just like Jamie," she said with a shrill laugh, "but he neglected to mention his wife in Oakland."

Jesse lay back, pulling her down beside him. He didn't look at her, but he brought her hand to his lips and pressed it there, over and over, and he murmured, "Okay, baby. Okay."

She wilted against him, and all the prickliness and the strange, unwarranted hostility drained away to nothing. Tears burned behind her eyes, but she willed them away. "There was a minister, too," she said tiredly, "but we didn't really do anything. I might've, but I made the mistake of telling him about Jamie and the schoolteacher, and that was the end of that."

"Good riddance."

"Yeah. Imagine me a minister's wife."

He kissed her wrist.

"Jesse," she whispered. He turned his head, and she kissed him on the mouth. "Let me tell you. I'm almost finished."

"All right."

"I don't know why I want to tell you."

"It's okay. Go ahead."

She looked up at the high, streaky clouds scoring the blue sky. "After that—after the minister—I decided to go home, back to Portland. I got as far as Paradise, and Mr. Shlegel offered me a job in his saloon. Since I was broke, I took it. I figured I knew what he really wanted, and I figured I could handle it. But I was wrong on both counts. He turned out to be a gentleman, and I ended up . . . halfway falling in love with him. What he knew and I didn't was that he had a bad heart and a year to live."

"Ah, Cady."

"He was a big bear of a man, Jesse. German. He had a heavy accent—at first I could hardly understand him. And such a beard—he looked like Saint Nick. Toward the end, I took care of him, nursed him. And when he died . . ." She swallowed. "I took it hard. I'd made him into my father, I think, after he wouldn't let me be his lover."

"He wouldn't *let* you?"

His incredulity made her smile. "Nope." She could tell him the truth, that Mr. Shlegel's illness had made him impotent, incapable of being anybody's lover—but Jesse didn't need to know that. And Mr. Shlegel had revealed that to her in confidence, with great sorrow and shame and disappointment. Nobody knew it but her, and nobody ever would.

"Of course everybody *assumed* we were lovers. Everybody in the whole damn town. Well, except Levi."

"I like Levi."

"I love Levi."

They rolled their heads together and touched fore-heads, smiling

"Are you through now? Is this the end of your life story?"

"I guess. Mr. Shlegel left me everything he owned, and here I am."

"Here you are."

"You could tell me *your* life story."

"Read the *Reverberator*, it's all there." He rolled onto his side and put his hand on her stomach. She knew him now: when he put his hand on her stom-ach, he wanted to make love.

"Jesse. We're outside. We're in a field."

"So?"

"So—"

"I thought you and Wylie used to have some-thing. Together."

"Wylie! And me? *Wylie?* Are you crazy? I wouldn't—"

"I was wrong," he said calmly. "It's just that you two hate each other so much, I figured somebody must've broken somebody's heart."

"Oh.' She relaxed again. She could see how he might've thought that. Why did she get so mad at him for thinking the exact same thing a hundred other people had thought before about her? With them she shrugged it off; with Jesse she got furious. Why was that?

Why was she asking herself questions with such obvious answers?

"I pulled a gun on him once."

His jaw dropped open. "You what?"

"What made it worse was that I was in his saloon at the time. People saw. If you humiliate Merle in public, you can get yourself into a peck of trouble."

"Yeah," he said feelingly. "Why'd you pull the gun?"

"He tried to— Well, he took me out to dinner once," she said, starting at the beginning. "This is back when I thought he was _nice,_ if you can believe that. I'd heard some stories, but I was giving him the benefit of the doubt."

"Uh-huh."

Even Mr. Shlegel had liked him, she recalled; they had been fairly friendly rivals. "So afterward, we were in his saloon, and he made a suggestion. I declined. Politely. I got up to leave, and he put his hands on me. I couldn't believe it! He really wasn't going to let me go."

"So you pulled out your .22."

"I had no choice."

"I guess not."

"Ever since then, we've been enemies. Oh, Jess, thank _God_ you straightened him out today." She came up on her elbow and hugged him with fierce gratitude. "Wylie's been poisoning the town for months and months. If you hadn't come along when you did, I don't know what he would've tried next." She kissed him soundly. "Thank you."

"I'm tired of talking about Wylie," he said uneasily, and she thought, _Aha,_ an unexpected side to Jesse: modesty. "No more, okay?"

"Fine with me." She sat up. The asters grew two feet high in this fragrant meadow. No one came here, but even if somebody did, she and Jesse would be invisible. Especially if they were lying down.

She smiled a soft, dreamy smile, and began to open her dress for him.

Jesse's eyes warmed. Such sweetness, such—appreciation. In a corner of her mind, Cady wondered if there was anything she wouldn't do for him. Slipping her arms out of the sleeves of her pretty flowered frock—her best, she'd worn it for him—she basked in the heat of the slanting sun on her shoulders, her cheeks. She started to untie the ribbon at the neckline of her shift, but then she stopped. She wanted him to do it. She sat back, braced on her arms, aware of the thrust of her breasts against the thin white cotton. Smiling, she offered herself to him.

He sat up fast, but his cupped hands when he touched her were gentle and patient. Painstaking. Pleasure-taking. To please him, she'd worn no corset. He caressed her through the material of her chemise, stroking and pressing, softly squeezing, rubbing his thumbs and his fingertips over her nipples. She closed her eyes. She sighed. She slipped her hands through his hair, smelling the hot sun in it. He put his mouth on her breast and kissed her, right through her shift. The cool and the wet and the friction of cotton made her nipple tighten and peak, and he drew on it until she couldn't bear it. Then he soothed her with kisses, soft trails of them across her chest, in the hollow of her throat. Her chemise came away in his hands, and she was bare to the waist. "Sorry," she murmured.

"For what?"

242

Patricia Gaffney

"This." She fingered the little blue bird, the mark of her foolishness. "I know you don't like it." She didn't either, but eventually she'd forgiven herself for it.

He put his lips there. "There's nothing about you I don't like."

It wasn't just talk—he said it as if he meant it. Something was happening. As good as it had been last night, this was different, and she thought he knew it, too.

She unbuttoned his shirt quickly and pressed herself to him, needing to be as close as heart-to-heart. "Jesse," she said between kisses, "oh, Jesse." He took her down, laid her on her back, with his hands for a pillow under her head, kissing her and kissing her. Tears kept clogging her throat, and she kept swallowing them down. *Silly*, she thought. As sweet as it was to give Jesse her body it was only a symbol. The real gift she'd already given him, and it was the truth about herself. Did he know it? Could she stand for him to know it?

Probably not. The likelihood of this affair ending in happily-ever-after was so remote, it was a laugh. On her. *Oh, Cady, you've done it this time.* Picking men who were good for her had never been her strong suit, but oh, this was going to be a disaster.

Off came their clothes. They came together, and everything seemed to get brighter. Her skin was flushed, sensitive, and the way he touched her wasn't so gentle now. She loved the sweat on his forehead, the passion and the *helplessness* in his face when they made love. He couldn't stop kissing her; he held her as if he would die without her. "Ah, Cady, ah, Cady," he panted, and she loved the frankness of his desire for her. She'd never been with a man, never even kissed a man who didn't try to hide something of himself, no matter how far the sex carried him away. But Jesse let her know how much he wanted her without an ounce of shame, and she was learning there was nothing more seductive than that.

"Hurry," he advised in a rough mutter, arching over her. She could feel his muscles straining, trembling. He was hanging on for her.

"Such a gentleman," she whispered lightly, although her heart was bursting. She let love take her, just love, not the excitement of skin or heat or friction or even the deep, steady throb of him inside her. And she came gently, silently, like a flower opening, so quietly he didn't know it—she had to tell him, "All right, Jesse. All right."

After, she didn't speak at all for the longest time. Couldn't. Afraid of what she would say if she opened her mouth and started talking. Much better to shut up.

But it made him worry about her. "Honey? You all right?" He probably called every woman he slept with "honey," but when he said it to her it made her melt. Every time. "Was it okay?" He kissed her, coaxing a smile. "Come on, tell me I was great. Hm? How was it, Cady girl?"

She hid her face in his shoulder, afraid he'd see too much if he looked into her shiny eyes right now, and fell back on a standard answer.

"It beats canning salmon."

*   *   *

They drove past Cady's mine on the way home. The sun was setting; pale orange beams seeped through the low, mossy tops of the live oaks verging the road, softening the air, the twilight. Buzzards made slow, stately circles high up in the whitening sky. Cady loved the peaceful silence, but Jesse broke it to ask, "Why does Wylie want your mine if it's finished?" and she roused herself to try to explain it again.

"I've told you—that's just how he is. He's like a rotten little boy. He wants all the toys, and he'll make everybody's life miserable till he gets them."

"But that doesn't make sense. Are you sure the Seven Dollar is worthless?"

"Sure, I'm sure. It has been for years. Look, there's the turnoff to Wylie's. It starts about half a mile back, right up against the cliff from the river. It's called the Rainbow, and naturally it's thriving," she said bitterly. Then she remembered: Jesse had taken care of Wylie. Threatened him, she assumed—he wouldn't say much about it. What a relief. Wylie had been a thorn in her side for so long, it was going to take a while to get used to the idea of him being harmless. She slipped her arm through Jesse's and pressed, leaning against him lightly. Her gratitude embarrassed him, but she couldn't help it. He was her hero. The whole town's hero.

On the outskirts of Paradise, passing by the little schoolhouse and the lot beside it where the children played baseball, she noticed a nasty, foreign odor that grew stronger as they kept driving. "What *is* that?" she said, and Jesse wrinkled his nose and swore wonderingly. By the time they reached the center of town, the smell had become a stench. People in the street stopped and stared when they saw her, but nobody spoke. Uneasiness crept over her.

"Something's wrong. Jesse, what in the world is that smell?" He looked grim and didn't answer. "Wait, you're passing the livery," she told him. "Don't you want to take the buggy . . ." She didn't finish. She knew where they were going—straight to the Rogue. Because something bad had happened.

Eleven

It could've been worse. They could've burned her out. They'd stunk her out, and that was only temporary. But it was bad enough.

Shrimp Malone was the first to identify the smoldering, smoking, reeking pile of black stuff on the bar—Levi's beautiful mahogany bar, his pride and joy; Jesse had seen him late at night sanding and staining cigarette burns, polishing out white glass rings, rubbing beeswax into the wood until it shone like a mirror.

"It's tires," Shrimp claimed. "Them little rubber tires on ore trucks." Ore trucks? "Them carts they wheel around down in the mines. What you got here is ore truck tires, about fifty of 'em, I'd say. On fire, and stinkin' to high heaven."

The fire department—Stony Dern—came and tried to shovel the tires out through the swinging doors, but the smoke was too bad. He couldn't stay in the saloon any longer than he could hold his breath. Next the sheriff organized a group of citizens to take turns dragging the tires out with pitchforks, but Nestor Yeakes, the first man in, promptly fainted, and Oscar

Schmidt, the second, ran back out claiming he was having a heart attack. All this excitement happened before Jesse and Cady rode in. When they pulled up in front of the Rogue, nobody was doing anything except standing in the street and watching black smoke billow out of the windows.

Cady was useless, so Jesse took over. Shrimp knew a man who blasted rock at the Rainbow and had goggles. With wet towels wrapped around his nose and mouth and the goggles over his eyes, Jesse made three runs into the saloon, but all he managed to do was knock half the tires off the bar and onto the floor. Levi came back from his outing with Lia Chang about then, and insisted on taking a turn. He lasted two trips before he had to sit down.

Others began to volunteer. Sheriff Leaver, Stony Dern, and Will Shorter, Jr., all donned the goggles and towels and ran into the saloon as often as they could stand it. Using shovels, rakes, and a wheelbarrow, with five of them working in quick shifts, they finally lugged every bit of the sticky, stinking rubber out into the street, and then the question was how to put it out.

Throwing water on it didn't work; part of it always kept smoldering, and pretty soon the whole thing would flare up again. In the end they buried it. Once it was out and cold they'd move it, but for now it lay in the street in a heap, under a foot-deep cover of dirt from Arthur Dunne's vetch field, gravel from the cemetery, and horse manure from the livery stable.

Rogue's Tavern was uninhabitable. Everything in

the saloon and above it—all four bedrooms on the second floor—was either ruined or stank too bad to go near. Jesse could kiss his clothes, everything but what he had on his back, good-bye. Cady, luckily, was in better shape; smoke went up, not sideways, and three closed doors from the saloon, the hallway, and her office stood between the fire and her bedroom. She still claimed everything in her room stank, but Jesse said they were carrying the reek around in their nostrils, that a flower garden, a *perfume* factory, would smell like burning rubber to them indefinitely.

"How long is indefinitely?"

They were drinking coffee at Jacques', staring dolefully out the window at the saloon and the big mound of smelly dirt in front of it. "Till you get it cleaned up."

"Cleaned up," Cady said wretchedly. "I wouldn't even know where to start." She hadn't cried—he wished she would—but she looked shattered. Like somebody had beaten her up.

"I'd say you start with turpentine. And paint scrapers, like you were going to strip the varnish off a table or something. You get all the rubbery soot off, then you wash everything with strong soap and water."

"But that'll take forever."

"Days. So you hire people to help you. Plus I'll help, and Levi and Ham'll help. That's four of us right there, and then you pay some kids to pitch in."

"Stony might help," she said thoughtfully. "And Gunther. Jim Tannenbaum. Maybe Stan Morrissey."

"I'd forgotten you had all these men in love with you."

"It's not that, they just want their drinking place back."

"Cady, it's going to be all right. You'll have the place spic and span in no time."

She tried a wan smile, but it didn't work. She put her forehead against the glass and closed her eyes tight. Finally he saw a tear, just one, squeeze past her lashes. "Bastard," she gritted out between her teeth. She made the window rattle by butting her head against it. "Damn that *bastard*."

If they weren't in a restaurant, he'd have taken her on his lap. As it was, he scooted his chair closer and wrapped his arm around her. "Don't worry about him, honey. Don't even think about him."

"Damn that bastard." She seemed to be stuck in a rut.

"Shh. Shhh." He tried to soothe her, but she wouldn't soften, wouldn't unwind from the tight ball of fury and loathing. Until he said, "It's all right, Cady. I'll take care of him."

Then she looked at him. She was red-faced but almost dry-eyed. "You will?"

He nodded. "Yeah."

She watched him for another minute, then laid her head on his shoulder, exhausted. "Okay," she sighed. "Okay, then."

He took her home. He tried to make love to her, but she couldn't relax. So he massaged her feet in-stead—he was good at that. That did it. She fell asleep on her stomach with one leg in the air. He kept on rubbing that one skinny foot, softening his touch little by little, before laying it down on the mattress and gently covering her up.

He stretched out beside her. For a long time he lay quiet, listening to her breathing, watching moon shadows crawl across the graceful hills and valleys of her pale, sheet-covered body. Trying to think of a way to "take care" of Wylie without getting himself killed. Finally fatigue swamped him. When he drifted off, he still hadn't come up with a plan.

It took three days to get the saloon clean enough for customers, and three more before you could go upstairs without holding your nose. More people pitched in than Jesse could believe or Cady could imagine, some for pay but most for nothing, and yet it still took forever to wipe down the walls and the ceiling, the floor, every stick of furniture, every glass, every ash can, every spittoon. The naked lady over the bar was ruined, destroyed, fit for nothing but the garbage heap. Or so Jesse thought, until a veritable tidal wave of opposition to trashing her rose up from the regulars—Stony and Sam, Leonard, Jersey Stan, Gunther Dewhurt—and a committee formed spontaneously to try to save her. Research was done; theories were tested; experiment performed. Years ago, Leonard Berg, it turned out, had refurbished houses for a living; he knew something about oil paints. He made a concoction. With a crowd of naked lady fans looking on and offering suggestions, he applied it to her soot- and goop-blackened charms. Presto! Like magic she was re-formed, restored to voluptuous splendor before their admiring eyes.

After that everybody seemed to take heart, even Cady, and the work went faster. Leonard had a brainstorm and tried applying his miracle formula to the bar, and enough gunk came away that it could be sanded down and refinished. This was a major discovery. A new bar would've cost at least a thousand dollars, a good one, anyway, and Cady was already racking her brain and going over her accounts, looking for a way to pay for it. Now she wouldn't have to. Things were starting to look up.

In a way. Jesse had a problem, however. The further along repairs and cleanup proceeded at the Rogue, the more time Cady had to dwell on the man responsible for making them necessary. "Did you talk to him? Did you do anything yet?" she took to asking once or twice a day. "All in good time," Jesse would say, with a hint of sinister mystery in his manner, hoping to imply he had some fiendish plot afoot. But he didn't. For the life of him, he couldn't figure out what to do.

He went to the sheriff's office and acted like an irate citizen, but that backfired. "Of course I know it was Wylie," Tommy Leaver admitted readily, "but what can I do about it? There's no proof. Nobody saw anything, or else they're not saying. Cady left her back door open and somebody, probably Turley and Clyde, snuck in and set those tires on fire. You know it and I know it, but what can I do? Wylie will deny it, and then what? If I tried to arrest him or any of his boys, they'd shoot me down before I could get my mouth open."

"You could deputize some men, get up a whole crowd. With that many—"

"I tried that. Nobody'll do it. People are scared, nobody wants to risk getting killed. Who can blame them?" He straightened his neat string tie, slicked back his perfectly combed hair—he was the *neatest* sheriff Jesse had ever seen—and fixed him with a speculative eye. "You could take him, though," he said earnestly.

"Me?" Jesse laughed with fake heartiness. "That'll be the day." Too late, he saw the trap he'd walked into.

"They're scared of you. I could make you a deputy, Mr. Gault, and you could—or *we* could, I'd go with you—we could take Wylie into custody."

"Yeah? Then what? You just said he'd deny it, so what happens next?"

"Then—then we try to get some of his men to go against him. If they see him locked up in jail for questioning, they might get scared. All we need is one. We could—"

"Hold it, hold it. Sorry to disappoint you, Sheriff, but you got me mixed up with somebody who gives a damn."

"But I thought—you and Cady, I just thought—"

"Yeah, well, what's between me and Cady has nothing to do with the *law*. The *law* is something I don't mess with, ever. Got me? Jesse Gault does not work for sheriffs, see? Jesse Gault never has and never will be a *deputy*." And he stalked out, all snotty and pissed off, definitely on his high horse, before the sheriff could say another word.

That was a close one. Not to mention stupid. And now he was back where he started. What the hell had he gone to Leaver for anyway? How un-Gault-like could you get? Desperation was driving him these days; he couldn't see straight. He'd started avoiding Cady, for Pete's sake, just so she couldn't ask him if he'd taken care of Wylie yet. He missed her like crazy. He had no idea what he was going to do.

No—he did have one idea, one middling bright notion, and as soon as he thought of it he got itchy to do it and get it over with. It had nothing to do with Wylie, not directly, and it would have to stay a deep, dark secret from everybody, even—no, *especially*—Cady. But that was okay. *He'd* know he'd done it, and afterward he wouldn't feel so damn helpless.

His luck at gambling had been up and down, nothing consistent, so his net worth had stayed about the same for a couple of weeks: roughly five thousand dollars. He didn't know how much money the Sullivan widow needed to keep her sheep ranch, and he didn't know how much Luther Digby needed to keep Wylie from foreclosing on the general store. If he asked, it would rouse suspicion. So he would split it in half, he decided, twenty-five hundred to the widow, twenty-five to the Digbys. Now the only question was how to get it to them without anybody knowing.

Except for the dog, Mrs. Sullivan was easy. Under

the guise of finding new trails to run Pegasus on, he found out from Nestor where she lived: two miles outside of town on the road to Jacksonville. Then it was just a matter of waiting for midnight, stuffing money in an envelope, scribbling "From a friend" on it, and sliding the envelope under her front door. He forgot she lived on a sheep farm, though, which meant she had a sheep dog, which meant he wasn't going to get anywhere near her front door. But she had a box for deliveries, at the bottom of the quarter-mile-long driveway to her house. Was that a safe place to stash twenty-five hundred bucks? He decided to take a chance, and by ten o'clock the next morning the news was all over town that a miracle had struck the Sullivan family in the night.

One down. The Digbys should've been even easier, but they weren't. He waited until the next night, and he almost got caught. What the hell was the wife—Sara, her name was—doing up at one in the morning, floating around downstairs in her nightgown, holding a candle? Taking inventory? Making herself a cup of hot milk? Whatever, she spotted him, just as he was straightening up from slipping the envelope under the door. Their eyes locked. He wheeled and sprinted for the blackness of the alley, positive she'd recognized him. A few sober moments of reflection reassured him, though. She had a candle under her chin; naturally he could see her perfectly, down to her blond eyelashes. He'd been in the pitch-dark, through wavy glass, hat pulled low, shirt collar high. She'd seen a man, that's all. He was safe.

Speculation ran wild. Who was the mysterious

"friend" whose generosity had saved two Paradise families from ruin? Who could it be? The *Reverberator* had a field day wondering, guessing, interviewing, opining. The minister, Reverend Cross, was high on the list of suspects, although nobody could figure out where he'd have gotten all that money. An old spinster lady named Miss Sleet reputedly had thousands stashed away in her mattress, but she was so mean and stingy, nobody could feature her as the anonymous benefactor. There were other possibilities—Otis Kerns, the bank president; old Mr. Deaver, who owned the saw and lumber mill. They were cited most frequently, because they were the richest.

Nobody ever mentioned Gault, and Jesse figured he was the second-to-last man anybody would figure for a Good Samaritan. The last being Wylie.

What Wylie made of these secret, last-minute bailouts, Jesse could only imagine. The son of a bitch must be going crazy. Which wasn't much of a punishment for what he'd done to Cady, but it was something. Jesse began to feel a little better. Broke, but better. It helped that in all the excitement about the money, she forgot to ask him what he was going to do with Wylie. It looked like the whole mess might just blow over after all.

He should've known better.

His room was habitable again, but he'd taken to spending the night in Cady's, and it was a hard habit to break. One night, though, after the saloon closed, she went upstairs with him while he got a clean shirt for the next day. They started fooling around, one thing led to another, and they ended up falling asleep in his bed instead of hers.

In the morning, he was glad. He had a high, east-facing window, and the sun beaming in on Cady's skin, mellow gold against the white of the sheets, was as pretty a sight as he'd ever seen. He kissed her half-awake, loving her drowsy-eyed smile and the starting-to-get-interested sounds she made in the back of her throat. These were the times he liked best, when it was just them, nobody else, and they weren't talking. The trouble with talking was that it usually meant lying, and he was getting sick of that. Kissing Cady was much better.

They were doing more than kissing when the first shriek came.

The window was open or they might not have heard it—it came from the back of the building. And since it was Ham's voice, Jesse didn't think much of it, not at first; *He's playing*, he assumed. But Cady knew right away. Critical moment or not, she called everything off by rolling out from under him and scrambling out of bed. She'd have run out of the room bare-ass naked if he hadn't thrown her shift at her while he grabbed for his pants.

By the time they hit the stairs, Ham was screaming in short, panicky, repetitive bursts, horrible, earsplitting; Jesse's heart pounded in his chest as real fear got a grip on him. This wasn't a game: Ham was in some terrible trouble.

They found him writhing on his back behind the blueblossom bushes, and Jesse's first thought was that he was ill, sick to his stomach—he was lying by the open door to the outhouse. Then he saw the snakes.

Three of them—four—five—a sixth slithering out of sight under the floorboards. Rattlers, fat and muscular and brown-blotched, flat, triangular heads swerving, clubbed tails chattering. Cady screamed once. Jesse yelled for her to stop, but she kept moving, white arms flailing, and all except one of the snakes curled and coasted away in fright. The last one bared dripping fangs, reared up, and lunged at Ham's bare foot, striking him on the heel. Instead of screaming, he uttered an awful sound, strangled and despairing, a hopeless croak that made Jesse's blood run cold. He managed to grab Cady's flying hair and yank her back before the snake could coil and strike again. Ham curled onto his side in a tight ball of panic. Barefooted, desperate, Jesse ran at the snake, stomping and shouting curses and waving his arms. Instead of charging again, the reptile cringed away, forked tongue flicking, spitting; with a flash of dusty scales it changed direction and skittered, rattling, off into the long grass.

Cady dropped over Ham, covered him like a blanket with her body, cradling him, crooning to him. Gently, then not so gently, Jesse pried her away. "Move, honey. Come on, Cady. That's it, that's a girl."

Bad, it was bad. The snakes had bitten Ham in two places Jesse could see, his heel and his calf, and there might be other bites under his clothes. "Run for the doctor. Hear me? Go get Doc Mobius. *Cady.*" Her swimming eyes focused on him. She shook her head, reluctance to leave Ham, even let go of him, obvious in every line of her face, her body. Jesse told her again to *go*, repeated it, ended up shaking her by the shoulders. With an angry sob, she finally scrambled up and ran out of the yard.

Jesse scoured his brain for everything he knew about snakebite. Don't let the victim move—moving made the venom spread faster. Scooping Ham up as gently as he could, he carried him into Cady's room and laid him on her bed. He'd begun to shiver and whimper. Tears streaked the dirt on his face; his big dark eyes were glazed. "You're all right, you're going to be okay, hear me? Where else did they get you, can you tell me? Where'd those slimy bastards get you?" While he talked, he undid buttons and pulled the kid's skinny, shaking arms and legs out of his shirt and corduroy knee pants and drawers. Another purpling puncture wound was swelling on his bony kneecap. Jesse shook a pillow out of the case and tied it around Ham's thigh, just above the knee. *Between the wound and the heart*, he remembered; that's where you wanted to cut off circulation. He shook out the other pillow and tied that case—the one that said Life Is Duty—under the boy's other knee, above the calf wound and the bite in his heel. Then he wrapped him in the coverlet and tried to think what else to do.

The room started filling up with people, neighbors and passersby who had heard all the yelling. Some of them he knew, some he didn't. Everybody had advice, and all of it was urgent, had to be done *now*. Jesse sat down next to Ham, who was crying silently, dazedly, and put his arms around him, not just to comfort him but to keep everybody away from him. Where was Levi? Where was the doctor?

Cady found him in his tiny rented house next to the livery, up and dressed, thank God, and heating coffee on the wood stove in his kitchen. Almost all she said was "snake" before he ducked out of the room. Ten seconds later he was back, with his black bag in one hand and a glass bottle of something yellow and liquid in the other. "Put that on," he advised as they hurried out through the door, and she saw a worn gray frock coat hanging by a hook in the wall. For the first time she realized what she had on: her chemise and nothing else, unbuttoned to the navel but staying closed, sort of, out of habit. "Good God," she muttered; and then, "I don't care." But she grabbed Doc Mobius's coat and stuck her arms through it as she trotted after him down the street, and when they burst into her room at the Rogue she was as modest as she had time to get.

Good thing: it was full of people. Jesse's face when he saw her made her heart clench. Doc told everybody to get back, get away, and her neighbors—Jacques, the Schmidts, old Mrs. Sheets, Lisabeth Wayman, Arthur Dunne—started to drift outside, murmuring and shaking their heads, taking last looks back. Jesse didn't get up, but he put his arm out, and Cady went to him and let him embrace her, his hand strong and sure on her hip. "Ham," she said. "Oh, Ham." His eyes were closed, so she let herself cry. Jesse squeezed her, or she might've broken down. He looked so bad! "How is he? He'll be all right, won't he? Won't he be fine?"

Doc Mobius ignored her, and she took some comfort from the sure-handed, impersonal way he touched Ham. But then he stripped the quilt away from his skinny, naked, brown-skinned body, and she saw two ugly black dots, livid and swollen, in his knee. Two more in his other leg. Oh, God—two more in his foot! Jesse caught her as she sank to the mattress edge, weak with dread and revulsion.

Doc did things. She tried to watch. She saw him make two deep, oval slashes in Ham's knee, and she saw him pull the skin away from his calf and snip off skin, flesh, and bloody wound with a pair of scissors. She saw the piece of broken fang he cut out of Ham's foot. Mostly she saw black, from burying her face in Jesse's bare chest, and bright colors from pressing her fingers against her eyelids. Ham was barely conscious; he didn't scream until the doc swabbed the yellow liquid—chloride of lime, he said it was when Jesse asked him, white-lipped—into all three wounds.

Thank God Levi didn't come until it was over. Cady let go of Jesse and stood behind Levi with her hands on his shoulders while he hovered over Ham's limp, sweating body. "He ain't breathing right." She could hear him trying to keep the panic out of his voice. "The poison gettin' to him? Doc?"

Doc Mobius stood up, his bones creaking. His face wasn't reassuring, but then he always looked like death warmed up. "Come outside with me," he said, and Levi got up slowly, stiffly, and followed him out of the room.

Jesse grabbed Cady's hand. She wanted him to hold her tight and tell her everything was going to be fine. Instead they sat down on either side of the bed and looked at Ham, and touched him softly, and murmured things to him.

Levi came back by himself. Jesse gave him his place on the bed. "He gone to get some other kinda medicine. Perma something; he got to make it up special in his office." He reached for Ham's hand and kissed it. "He say you done jus' right," he told Jesse. "The cases you tied, they was the right thing to do." Jesse nodded gratefully. "You, too, Cady— gettin' 'im so fast. He say that was a good thing."

"How is he, Levi?" Cady got up the courage to ask.

His Adam's apple bobbed in his throat. He dipped his bald head and whispered. "He can't tell. Say he young and strong, and that's good. But three of 'em . . . three . . ." His lips pulled apart in anguish and tears started to roll down his cheeks. "But he got this other medicine, and it could help. He give it in a shot, and maybe it get to the heart before the poison. It an anti . . ."

"Antidote."

"Yeah." He wrapped Ham's little hand up in his two big ones, hunching over him, eyes shut tight, and stayed that way until the doctor came back.

Permanganate of potash, five grains to two ounces of water; he put it in a syringe and injected it three times, in three different places. "I'll do it again in a couple of hours. Meanwhile, watch him close and keep him quiet. He'll probably just sleep, and that's the best thing. He's got a *good chance*, I'm telling you," he said with force in his voice. "I think he'll make it. I do, that's the truth. Anyhow, we'll know in a short while. Stay with him, Levi, and try not to worry so much." His tired face creased in a smile; he knew how useless that advice was.

Cady and Levi nursed Ham all day. Jesse disappeared. She didn't realize he'd gone for good until an hour went by and he didn't come back. She knew where he was—she felt it in her bones: Wylie's. *Good*, she thought. *I hope he kills him. I hope he shoots him dead*. Did Levi hope so, too? She looked at him curiously. He sat in a chair pulled close to the bed, his big hands folded, eyes closed. He might've been praying. He must know as well as she did that Wylie was behind this—Glen said that Arthur Dunne said there was a gunny sack in the outhouse. But something told her Levi wasn't sitting there hoping Jesse would shoot Wylie. Even before he'd started reading about Buddha, Levi was a gentle man. A good man. A much better person than Cady was. If she had her hands around Wylie's neck right now, she'd squeeze until his eyes popped out.

In the afternoon, Doc came back for the third time. When he said Ham was going to be okay, Cady broke down.

She tried not to; her blustery tears were making Levi cry, too, not to mention sending Willagail into hysterics. But she couldn't help it. Relief knocked the props out from under her; she just gave way. It was the one and only time in the long, awful day when she was glad Jesse wasn't there with her.

She went to his room and lay down on his bed. Just to wait for him, and rest her eyes. She couldn't remember ever feeling so tired in her life.

When she woke up, it was dark and he was sitting beside her, watching her. "Jess, did you hear?" She rose up, into his arms, and they held each other close for the longest time. She had such a feeling of rightness then, close to contentment, of being exactly where she was supposed to be.

She thought she'd cried out all the tears, but here came more. But they were gentle tears, sweet ones even, all the bitterness gone. And Jesse felt so good, solid and warm and real. Her man. She whispered his name, the only way she could say to him, *I love you*.

He started to kiss her. As lovely as that was, she arched away—she wanted to talk. "What happened, Jess? Where's Wylie?"

"Where is he?"

"I mean—did you kill him?"

He stiffened, let his arms fall. She saw the flash of his teeth in the semidarkness, and heard his airy laugh. It didn't sound real. "No. I let him live."

"Well. That's good. I guess. Tell me what happened. Where was he? What did you do to him?"

"We talked. Cady, let's not get into it now, okay? I'm beat." He started taking off his boots.

She stared at his back. "You talked to him? That's all? Well—what did you say?"

"What difference does it make?"

"I just—"

"Everything's fine. I took care of it."

"That's what you said before."

He kept his back to her and didn't answer.

"Jess? That's what you said before, and look what happened. Ham almost *died*, he—"

"I know that, Cady. I was there."

"So—did you—what did you—"

"I *said* I took care of it."

"How?"

"It doesn't concern you."

She thought about that for a few seconds. She'd covered herself with the blanket; now she threw it back and got off the bed on the other side. "I guess I don't agree. Is there some reason you won't talk to me about this?"

"I told you. I'm—"

"Beat." She moved around until he had no choice, he had to look at her. "You didn't do anything, did you?"

"I talked to him."

"You talked to him." She went to the bedside table and lit the lamp. When she backed away from the light, Jesse got up and moved to the window. To the shadows. "So now he's shaking in his boots, is that right?" she said in a quiet voice. "Did he promise never to do it again?"

"Cady."

"Did he say Ham was the last little boy he'll ever try to murder?"

"He didn't mean to hurt Ham."

Her skin prickled; she felt ill. "Oh, that's right, it

was me he was trying to murder. Then it's okay. No harm done."

"Shit."

She hated this revelation. She couldn't stop shaking her head. "What kind of a man are you?"

"Cady, damn it, it's a job for the law."

"A—" She stared at him in disbelief, almost speechless. "A job for the *law*? Did I hear you right? Did you say it's—"

He cursed again and spun around, smacking his hands on the windowsill. The long, handsome back, the lean hips, the hard arms she'd wanted around her a few minutes ago—they only looked obstinate to her now. Obstinate and mean.

She tried again. "I'm not saying you should kill him." She kept talking over his mirthless bark of laughter. "I don't even *want* you to kill him. If Ham had died, then I might. No," she admitted, "then I *would*. But, Jesse—how can you just do *nothing*? How can you let him get away with it? And what's next? What will he—" He interrupted, said something she couldn't hear. "What?"

"This is not my fight."

She blinked at his dark outline, bent motionless over the brighter square of the window, and tried not to believe he'd said that. Seconds ticked past, until the silence between them grew intolerable. She said, "I see," and for some reason, maybe her hollow tone, that made him turn around and face her.

"Cady, listen."

"Nobody's offered you money. I see. You'll shoot

a man down in cold blood if the price is right. Then it's your fight."

"That's not—"

"Let me tell you something. I wouldn't give you ten cents if Merle Wylie had a razor at my throat. Keep away," she warned when he started toward her. "Oh, God, you make me feel ashamed." If she said why—for loving him, for lying with him—she would start to cry. "Is that it, then? You won't do anything?"

"Cady—"

"Yes or no. Just tell me yes or no."

"I told you. I already—"

"Talked to him." She waited until she could speak clearly, no quavering and no crying. "I want you out of my place tonight." She stuck her arm straight out, warding him off again as she backed toward the door. "Not tomorrow morning. Pack up and get out tonight, you hear me?"

She waited, but he didn't answer. She couldn't see his face clearly. His hands at his sides looked clumsy, helpless, clenching and unclenching. "Get out of my place," she said again. Still he didn't move or speak, so she jerked the door open and left him standing there.

He didn't leave. He'd be damned if he'd leave. What was she going to do, throw him out? He wished she'd try. He felt like getting into a wrestling match with Cady. He felt like pinning her to the ground, rolling around, making her holler. Maybe it didn't make sense, but he was as mad at her as she was at him.

A day of the silent treatment went by, though, and his anger started to break up, lose ground. He could see her side of it too well. Since she couldn't see any of his side of it—that was the whole point; he'd fixed it that way on purpose—how could he blame her for hating him? But oh, it hurt. He went around with a hole in his chest that ached, like heartburn or something. He could hardly stand it. He shouldn't care so much—when had this started?—but he couldn't get over it. He couldn't stop hearing her say, "God, you make me feel ashamed." He knew exactly what she was ashamed of: taking a chance on him in the most personal, the most important way a woman knew. Women were like that about sex; unless they were whores, it meant the world to them. Cady felt like she'd cheapened herself with him, and he could hardly stand it.

He didn't pack up and get out, though, and she didn't do anything about it. At first he thought that was a good sign, that maybe she was relenting. But then he figured it was more likely she just didn't want to talk to him. And she had a pure genius for avoiding him. He could plant himself in front of her and start talking, and she'd put on that poker face she wore when she dealt blackjack, look straight through him, and walk away. It happened twice, and it took so much of the heart out of him, he couldn't do it again. He left her alone.

He paid a visit to Ham. He and Levi lived in a little two-room place behind Wayman's boardinghouse. It used to be a horse barn, but now it was a little house, painted blue and white by Levi, neat as a pin. Jesse had seen Lia Chang, the laundryman's daughter Levi was so crazy about, but he'd never spoken to her. The door to the house was open, so he knocked once and walked in. Before she jumped up, Lia was sitting on the edge of Ham's pallet-bed, spooning some funny-smelling concoction into his mouth. She made a low bow, and the long black pigtail down her back slid over one shoulder. Jesse bowed back. She barely came up to his breastbone; she must hit Levi around the navel. She had a sweet face, and when she smiled, it was like looking at an angel. As soon as he saw that smile, Jesse wanted her for Levi.

"Mr. Gault! Hey!" Ham struggled up on his elbows, trying to lift himself higher on the pillow.

"Oh, sorry. I got the wrong house—I heard there was a sick kid here. Be seeing you."

"Wait, that's me!" Ham said, laughing. "I'm sick!"

"You are?" He peered at him, scratched his head. "Well, if you say so. Is this your nurse?"

"This is Lia," Ham said, and Jesse heard the fondness and affection in his voice.

He said, "Hi," Lia Chang said, "Much honor," and they did the bowing thing again. "You visit," she said in a soft voice, and bowed herself out of the room.

Jesse sat down on the bed. "What's this stuff?" He picked up the bowl she'd left on the table, sniffing it.

"Soup. Lia, she make it herself. She call it a tonic for vital energy. It ease the mind an' soothe the nerves."

"What's it taste like?"

"Horse manure."

They shared a laugh, and it was good to see Ham so lighthearted, because he didn't look too healthy. He looked weak, and his skin, usually a handsome milk-chocolate color, was pasty gray. "So, pardner, how're you feeling?" Jesse asked, giving him a gentle cuff on the cheek.

"Okay. Can't do nothing yet, but Doc say I be stronger in a few days."

"That's good. You had us pretty scared there for a while."

"I know it. I'm sorry."

"Wasn't your fault."

"Poppy say it is," he mumbled, playing with a button on his nightshirt. " 'Cause I snuck in Cady's backhouse 'stead o' the other one."

"Why did you?"

" 'Cause it smell better an' the paper be softer."

He chuckled. "Pretty good reasons."

They talked for a little longer, but Jesse didn't want to tire him out. He got up to go, wishing he'd brought Ham something. He ended up giving him a bullet from his gunbelt, and that turned out to be inspired. Ham loved it—except for one of his six-shooters, Jesse couldn't have picked a better gift.

Levi arrived home just as he was leaving. They said, "Hey," and talked about how Ham was doing, passed the time of day for a few minutes. Covertly, Jesse studied him, but he couldn't detect, now or at any time in the past two days, the slightest hint of hostility in Levi's manner. Not even disappointment.

So. It was only Cady who hated him. Well, that was something. Not much, though. Because Cady was the main one, the main person in the world he didn't want to hate him.

When had this happened?

He decided to get drunk. Where, though? Paradise only had two saloons, and he sure as hell wasn't going to get drunk at Wylie's. He'd barely gotten out alive when he'd gone over there after the snake incident, attempting to bluff Wylie one more time. "Try something like that again and I'll make you pay," he'd threatened creepily. "I'll start with your gun hand, Merle, and then I'll shoot your knees off. Feet next, or maybe elbows. Then your gut, and that's when I'll walk away. Know how long it takes to bleed to death when you're gut-shot?"

But this time it didn't work. Wylie smiled right back at him and said, "I don't think so. I don't think you'll do shit." Jesse had sneered, said something brilliant like, "We'll see," and walked out, pretending he wasn't terrified. But the truth was staring him in the face: Wylie had his number.

So. Where would he get drunk? Cady's face when she looked at him would sober him up, so the Rogue was out. Alone in his room would be too depressing. His balcony? Nah; he might fall off. He might be sad, but he wasn't suicidal. Yet.

"Evening, Mr. Gault." Tom Leaver tipped his white hat and flashed a smile. He was leaning against a post in front of his office, arms crossed, shiny boots crossed, watching the sun go down behind the Mercantile.

"Howdy." Jesse stopped, arrested by something in the sheriff's lonely stance and shy smile. They struck a chord. "Say, Tom."

"Sir?"

"You got anything to drink?"

"How's that?"

"Stashed away in a drawer. A bottle of something."

"Oh. Well, yeah, I have some whiskey. For medicinal purposes, of course," he said with another bashful grin. "And the occasional celebration."

"Hot damn. How're you feeling?"

A hopeful light gleamed in the sheriff's mild blue eyes. "Kinda poorly, now that you mention it."

"Good. Let's celebrate."

"The trouble with women," Jesse pronounced, squirming his shoulders into a more comfortable pocket in the jailhouse pillow, "is they don't know what they want."

"*One* trouble," Sheriff Tom corrected, trying to blow a smoke ring with one of Jesse's little black cigarettes. The effort made him look like a guppy with a goatee.

"One thing," Jesse agreed. "They—"

"Another is, they don't know a good thing when they see it."

"Hear, hear." They saluted each other through the bars from their respective bunks, with their respective whiskey bottles. Half an hour ago they'd polished off the sheriff's half bottle of bourbon; now they were starting on two new ones, easily acquired by sending a passing kid—Ardelle Sheets's boy, Ar-

nold—to the Rogue with four dollars and a twenty-
five-cent tip.

"Take Glendoline Shavers."

"Wouldn't dream of it," Jesse quipped, and they
broke into loud guffaws. The sheriff was a cheap
drunk; just about anything Jesse said cracked him up.

"No, seriously," Tommy wheezed, stretching out
flat on his bare mattress and addressing himself to
the ceiling. "Take Glen. Now, there's somebody the
right man could make a happy woman out of."

"Not to mention honest," Jesse threw in. Since they
were being straight with each other. Tommy didn't
answer for the longest time, though, and he started
to think he'd stepped over the line.

But finally he said, "Yeah, honest," in a melancholy voice. "Wanna know something, Mr. Gault?"

"You gotta start calling me Jesse." He'd told him
that ten times already.

"Wanna know something, Jesse?"

"What."

"I asked Glen to marry me. And she turned me
down flat. Said she likes me well enough, but she'd
rather be friends. Friends." He threw his lit cigarette
at the spittoon. It missed. Jesse knew he was drunk
when he didn't get up and drop it neatly into the
receptacle. This was the tidiest jailhouse he'd ever
been in, and Sheriff Tom was the cleanest man he'd
ever met.

"Well, then she's dumber than she looks and she
doesn't deserve you," he said stoutly.

"Glen's not dumb." He swung off the bunk and
stood up, swaying. "Take that back."

"Okay."

He staggered out of his cell and into Jesse's. "You take that back."

"I said I took it back."

"Oh." He collapsed on the bunk; Jesse had to jerk his legs out of the way fast or he'd have sat on them. "Okay, then. 'Cause Glen's not dumb, she's just young. Doesn't know what she wants."

"Isn't that what I said? Isn't that exactly what I said? Women don't know what the hell they want."

"That is the God's honest truth."

They toasted each other with so much feeling, they almost shattered their whiskey bottles. Jesse slugged down a big shot without choking, but the fire in his stomach afterward burned like a son of a bitch. Too bad he wasn't much of a drinking man. Still, compared to his new best friend, he was a regular Doc Holliday.

He wished he'd realized sooner what a swell fellow Tommy was. Seemed like they could talk about anything. Already they'd been through horses, state politics, dirty jokes, the meaning of life. Now they were starting on women. "Good thing there's no crime tonight," Jesse noted. Otherwise they'd have to give up their beds and drink sitting up.

Tom grunted, took a drink, belched. "Know the real reason she won't have me, Mr. Gault?"

"Jesse."

"She thinks . . ." He leaned back against the cool brick wall and shut his eyes. His pale skin and scrawny chin-beard reminded Jesse of pictures of

Jesus, right after the Crucifixion. "She thinks . . ."
He bared his teeth, fighting back tears.

"Hey now," Jesse started, sitting up.

"She thinks I'm a coward." He whispered it,
scrunching his face up, but by some miracle he didn't
cry. He took another sip of whiskey to clear his head.
"I feel better for getting that out. Funny how I can
admit it to you, of all people. You ever been scared
of anything, Mr. Gault? Jesse?"

"I'm scared of dying." Like Tom, he felt better for
getting it out.

"*You?*"

"Well, hell. What do you think? I go around trying
to commit suicide?"

"No. No, I guess not. But why do you do it, then?
Why'd you pick your line of work?"

"Why did you?" he countered, cagey.

"Because I believe in law 'n' order."

"Hah."

"And I thought I'd be good at it. I didn't know . . .
I wasn't prepared for the danger." He faced Jesse but
didn't look at him. "I know what people call me
behind my back. You think Glen's right? You think
I'm yellow, Mr. Gault?"

"Hell, no. Hell, no. What's brave about getting
yourself killed? Listen here," he said, leaning forward, getting intense. His elbow slipped off his knee;
he caught himself just before hitting his teeth on the
bottle. Hm, drunker than he thought. Good; finally.
"If you face off with Merle or Turley, they'll kill you
where you stand. Where's the sense in that? People'll
say nice things at your funeral, but inside they'll be

thinking, What an idiot that Tommy Leaver was. And a month later, they won't remember your name."

"You're right. Abs'lutely right." He hauled himself up and started for the door.

"Where you going?"

"Gotta piss."

"I'll go with you."

A fog had rolled in sometime; everything looked white and ghostly, not real. In the alley behind Main Street, they relieved themselves against the brick wall of the jailhouse. "Still," said Tom, "I got to do something. This thing with the snakes, thass the last straw. That boy coulda died. And if it hadn't been him it woulda been Cady. That's murder, thass what that is."

"Can't you—"

"I been sending wires and letters to the U.S. Marshal's for a month. They say they'll send somebody, but they don't."

They finished their business and wandered back around to the front. "Quiet tonight," Jesse observed. He could hear soft piano music coming from the Rogue, though, and that big, aching hole opened up in his chest again. God, lonesomeness hurt like hell. If he felt this bad, he wasn't that drunk after all.

Tom was, though. It hit him all of a sudden—must've been the fresh air. He wheeled around to go back in his office and almost fell off the boardwalk. Jesse had to catch him. Their arms got tangled up, and they went crashing against the side of the building. "Shh," the sheriff hissed, missing his lips with his index finger and almost poking his eye out. "Shh—shh! Don't let 'em see me."

"Who?"

"Folks. I'm the sher'ff." He collapsed in hoarse, wheezing gales of laughter.

Jesse got him into his old cell and settled him down on the cot. "You okay? Maybe you had enough."

Tom took a swallow from his bottle, shuddered, and spat it out on the floor. "Aw, no," he mourned, eyeing the mess he'd made. "Now I gotta clean that up."

"I'll do it."

"You will?"

"Sure."

"You're the best, Mr. Gault."

"J—"

"Jesse. Been meaning to tell you," he slurred, stretching out on his back. "That day I asked you to help me? Outa line. Desp'rate. Wit's end. You . . . you're a stranger, could be gone tomorrow. Not your fight," he mumbled, eyes closed. "Gonna do something. Dunno what yet. Something . . ." He passed out with his mouth open.

Jesse found a blanket and covered him up, pulled his boots off for him. Lying there snoring, he looked like an overgrown boy with his wispy beard and pale, freckled cheeks. What could a man who looked like that do against Merle Wylie? Jesse had a powerful urge to save him. The only trouble with that was, Sheriff Lily Leaver was probably a better shot and a faster draw than he was.

"Shit," he mumbled, weaving his way out of

Tom's cell and back into his to get the whiskey. "What the hell am I gonna do?" he asked the bottle. No answer. "Gak." Booze tasted like kerosene to him now, but he slugged some more down anyway.

He wandered outside. The thick, swirling fog reminded him of the inside of his own head. Pretty soon he was weaving down Main Street, pulled by the high, sad notes of Chico's piano. Not many folks out tonight, and the few that were got out of his way fast, he noticed vaguely. Rogue's Tavern came up on him all at once, looming out of the mist like a ship in a gray harbor. Yellow light from the windows looked warm and friendly and inviting. He quickened his stride—which was why he tripped on the step to the sidewalk and smacked his knee on the edge. It didn't hurt, because he was pretty numb by now, but afterward he walked with a limp.

He stopped at the swinging doors and hung on them, peering inside. Hardly anybody here. Chico finished a song, and the sound of Cady's voice, low and sweet, saying, "You're busted, Curly," was another kind of music in the smoky hush. Right about then, it hit Jesse that he loved her. He really loved her.

Welp, no time like the present to tell her. In his eagerness, he shoved the doors open a little too hard. They smashed back against the walls, *crash.* Everybody in the bar jumped, and Levi dropped the glass he was drying. "Miss Cady McGill," Jesse said purposefully, weaving toward the blackjack table. Curly Boggs and a couple of the Witter ranch boys shot out of their chairs like Cady had dealt them all rattlesnakes. The closer he came, the farther they backed up. What the hell? By the time he got to her, stood swaying in front of her, they were all gone. Vanished, disappeared. Maybe he'd imagined them?

"McGill," he repeated hoarsely—too many cigarettes, too much kerosene. But he could still see straight, and she looked good. A sight for sore eyes. For a little thing, she sure had a lot of hair. Piled up all neat and shiny on top of her pretty head. She had a gold dress on tonight, mmmmm, sexy as hell, with long sleeves but no shoulders. How did it do that? He couldn't tell; he was distracted by the hint of a wing, or maybe a beak, in her cleavage.

He scowled. He'd tried to like that bird, God knew he had, but he couldn't. It irritated him. He hoped her sailor boy was feeding the fish at the bottom of some ocean.

"Well, that's just great. Thank you very, very much."

"Don't mention it." He smiled at her, then noticed she wasn't smiling back. "What'd I do?"

"Damn you, Jesse Gault." She came out from behind the blackjack table with her hands on her hips. The term "wet hen" drifted through the haze of his mind. "First you won't lift one selfish little finger to help me, and now you drive away what few customers I've got left. Are you sure you don't work for Wylie? You might as well!" She was steaming, mad as a bull; he'd have let her alone and waited till she cooled off, except for one thing. She kept blinking because she had tears in her eyes. That just did him in.

"Aw, Cady girl. C'mere, honey—"

"Don't call me Cady girl, and don't you touch me." When she pushed him in the chest, he fell over the chair behind him and landed butt-first on a table. Cady's brown eyes went wide. "You're *drunk*."

"No, I'm not." To prove it, he got up and came toward her again. "Got something to tell you."

"What? You're going to go down to Wylie's right now and tell him to stop?"

"No, this is something—"

"Then I don't want to hear it. I want you out of my place. Why won't you go?" The tears started again.

"Aw, Cady, will you just let me talk?"

"No. Out, Jesse. *Out.* Levi, make him go," she pleaded, swishing out of his reach in a whirl of gold skirts and rhinestone jewelry. He started to go after her, but he stumbled over another damn chair. He sat down in it hard and watched her stalk off, high heels clacking, bustle sashaying.

"Shit," he sighed mournfully. Levi appeared out of nowhere, holding out a glass of vanilla soda. Jesse shuddered away from it, his insides quivering. "Say something good, Levi. Gimme some o' that Buddhist wisdom."

The bartender sucked in his cheeks, thinking. "Want nothing. Be nothing. Go nowhere."

Jesse peered at him, bleary-eyed. "That's it?"

Levi shrugged. "What you expect on short notice?"

Twelve

Cady couldn't sleep. Nothing new there: ever since she'd kicked Jesse out of her bed, she'd slept badly. Tonight, though, she couldn't even keep her eyes closed.

Everything was a mess, her whole life, and everything she didn't want to happen had happened. She tossed the covers off, pulled them back up, threw them off again, thinking about her sorry history with men. Was it her fault? Something she was doing? She'd been so proud of herself lately. She hadn't been in love, meaning in trouble, for years. Men: trouble. She gave Glen that brilliant piece of advice all the time, and now look at her. Ha ha. Another one of life's hilarious jokes on her.

Had she suffered like this when Jamie left her? It was getting hard to remember, but she didn't think so. She definitely hadn't when the Monterey schoolteacher's wife turned up. Really, only Mr. Shlegel's death had hurt this bad, and that had been a clean, clear ache, just ordinary grief over losing somebody she'd dearly loved. But this thing with Jesse Gault was worse, and that made no sense at all. How had it happened? He was a hired killer! She'd known him for less than a month!

Oh, she'd gone over it a hundred times, there was no point in telling herself again how completely impossible he was. Anyway, she'd managed to get over the hired killer part pretty easily, hadn't she? That had stopped bothering her, sort of, a long time ago. But this new wrinkle—the fact that he wouldn't do anything about Wylie even after what happened to Ham—would not go away. She couldn't set it aside, let Jesse be her lover again and pretend nothing was wrong. It eliminated him. She'd been stupid in the past about who she gave herself to, but this was a flaw in a man even she couldn't overlook.

Too bad it had to show up in the one man she wanted for her own, for life. She'd really done it this time.

The next morning, red-eyed and exhausted, she paid a visit to Ham. He still looked a little gray around the gills, as Levi put it, but his spirits were high and he was itching to get back to his busy, little-boy life. "I get to get out o' bed today," he chattered, "Doc say so. Hey, Cady, lookit what Mr. Gault give me." He pulled a bullet from a little cloth pouch in his pajama pocket. A bullet! *Let this be a lesson to you,* Cady chided herself. *You're in love with a man who gives out bullets to sick children.*

Lia Chang came in. Cady kissed Ham and gave up her place by the bed so Lia could give him his lunch, a bowl of ginseng and lotus seed soup—to improve circulation and reduce internal heat, Lia claimed.

Ham ate it, which Cady decided must mean he really liked his father's new girlfriend.

And how did she feel about *that*? Jealous? Resentful? Abandoned? Standing beside Lia, watching Ham dutifully open his mouth and swallow the soup she spooned into it, Cady had to admit she felt all three. She'd gotten used to thinking of him as the next best thing to her very own child. She loved him so much; when he'd almost died, she had honestly and truly wanted to trade places—save him with her own life. Now, though, just as much, she wanted him to have his own happy, loving family. A real mother, who could look after him and take care of him all day, every day, not just in her spare time. She sighed, sending him a gentle smile over Lia's shoulder. She guessed she had the best kind of love for Ham. She loved him enough to give him up.

"Lookin' peaked," Levi pronounced as she was leaving. "You feel all right?"

"Fine. I'm not sick, if that's what you mean."

He scrutinized her, squinting his eyes to see her better—Levi needed glasses. With anybody else she'd have taken offense or been embarrassed or tried to cover up. But Levi, her best friend, never judged or criticized, so there was never any point in getting defensive. "Saw Mr. Gault this mornin'," he mentioned. "He look even worse than you."

"I'm not surprised," she said with a sniff, as if she didn't care. "I expect he's lying in some alley right now, holding his head."

"Nope. Saw him walkin' outa town."

"Well, he can keep going for all I care."

Levi smiled sweetly. "You still mad at him."

His placidity needled her. "Why aren't *you* mad at him? That's what I can't figure out. It was your son who almost died," she pointed out, but she felt hopeless and silly even as she said it. "I thought—everybody thought Jesse was becoming a friend, somebody we could trust. And now this." Levi just kept smiling. "Don't you think it puts him in a new light? Don't you think it shows what he really is?"

"Could be. But what if he trying to go straight?"

"What?"

"What if he through with killin'. What if he trying to get shut o' that life."

She blinked at him. "Oh, Levi," she breathed. "Do you think that's it?"

He shrugged his shoulders. "Might be. He never seem like a killer to me much. Some, but not much." He rubbed the side of his nose with his index finger, squinting again. "Maybe he tryin' to change for you."

"For me." She sighed it, thunderstruck.

She left Levi's in a daze. It was Friday; by rote, she walked over to Nestor's and rented her usual buggy and mare. All the way out to River Farm, she thought about Levi's theory. Could it be true? Was Jesse trying to give up gunfighting for her? It scared her, how much she wanted to believe it.

But if it was true, why hadn't he just said so? Because he was too proud? Oh, the things she'd said to him, the names she'd called him! She wanted to shrivel up in a ball when she thought of how mean she'd been to him. And last night he'd gotten drunk on account of her—she saw it clearly now. She had wounded him to the quick. He wasn't even that much of a drinking man, and because of her he'd drunk himself silly. Fool! She could've been helping him, encouraging him to stay on the straight and narrow, and what had she done? Chided him for being selfish. Taunted him. Urged him to take blood-thirsty revenge on an enemy of *hers,* not even *his.*

"Oh, Jess, I'm sorry," she said out loud, "I'm so sorry! If I could see you now, I'd tell you." She thought of turning the buggy around and looking for him in town, but Levi said he'd gone for a walk. To try to get over the hateful things she'd said to him, she didn't doubt. Her skin crawled. She was so ashamed.

She heard a noise, a gunshot, just as she was guiding the gray mare through the worn stone gateposts to River Farm. "Whoa, horse," she said softly, pulling on the reins. They stopped. She listened. More shots.

Somebody hunting? This far from town? It sounded like a pistol, though, not a rifle. That probably meant one thing: somebody was having a high old time shooting out the last few panes of window glass in Le Coeur au Coquin.

"Oh, no, you're not," Cady vowed, smacking the mare's rump with the reins and making her jump. "Not if I have anything to say about it."

She slowed down before the house came into view, though. Guns made her nervous. Jumping down, she tied the reins to a tree branch and crept around the bend in the carriageway on foot.

The house appeared, as ramshackle as ever, and as beautiful to her. The shots were coming from the back, toward the orchard, in intermittent bursts: six

shots, silence; six shots, silence. Not a window
breaker, then. A target shooter.

She still didn't like it. Wasn't this private property?
Anyway, in her heart, River Farm was hers, and she
didn't like the idea of people with guns traipsing
over it. Picking up her skirts, she started down the
stony path around the house.

Jesse had been a tad optimistic. He'd brought a
sack full of beer bottles, seven of them, but one
would've been enough. No, more than enough. What
he should've brought was the broad side of a barn.

"Shit," he cursed for the sixty-sixth time, once after
each bullet that flew above, below, to the right, or to
the left of the goddamn bottle on the fence post. He'd
never been any good at this, but you'd think *one* bullet
would've hit the goddamn target by now, if only accidentally. His hands were steady, so was it something
with his eyesight? Damned if he knew. Some brain
path wasn't working right, that's all he could figure.

The damn gun was heating up again, burning his
fingers. He slid his last six rounds into the chambers
and slapped the cylinder closed. This was it. He
braced his legs and took aim, closing one eye and
sighting down the barrel with the other. *Bam.* Nothing. *Bam.* Nothing. He changed his stance, changed
eyes. *Bam.* Nothing. *Bam.* Nothing. He held the gun
with both hands and didn't close either eye. *Bam.*
Nothing. "Shit." He closed both eyes. *Bam.*

Whap.

"Ow!"

He whipped around, holding the back of his neck.

He got a fast look at Cady's wide-eyed, furious face just before she slugged him again with her string bag, *whap*, right in the mouth. "Ow, damn it—Cady, I can explain—"

Whap. "Okay, start."

He danced away, shielding his face with his arms, and she hit him in the chest as hard as she could. "*Ow.* What's in there, rocks?"

"You're not a gunfighter at all!"

"Okay, I'm not."

"Who the hell are you, then? What's your name? It's not even Gault, is it?"

"No, it's Vaughn."

Whap on the chin. "Liar! You damn lying son of a—"

"I didn't lie about the Jesse part," he pointed out, backing up. *Whap.* "*Ow!* Damn it, Cady, would you cut that out?"

She took one last swing, a real roundhouse that, luckily, missed completely. Her momentum took her around in a full circle, and her purse went sailing off into the weeds. She collapsed on the stone wall, mumbling vicious curses, and dropped her head in her hands.

Jesse's heart rate finally slowed down. He holstered the empty six-gun and, out of habit, checked the beer bottle. Gone—shattered. Wonderful. He was a crack shot with his eyes closed.

Time passed. Cady never moved, except to clench and unclench her fingers in her hair every once in a while. He kept thinking she'd start the conversational ball rolling soon, but she just sat there. Disgusted or defeated, it was hard to tell which. Probably both. He went toward her a step. She'd dropped her weapon, but he still felt wary. "Cady, honey?"

"Don't talk to me."

"That's silly. We have to talk."

More time passed. Finally she lifted her head and clamped her hands on her knees. He thanked God she wasn't crying. "All right, then. Explain yourself," she commanded, dry-eyed and grim.

Uh-oh. Maybe not talking wasn't such a bad idea after all. "What do you want to know?" he hedged.

"Who's Gault?"

"Uh . . ."

"No, I know who he is—a *real* gunfighter. *Where's* Gault?"

"Aha." He clasped his hands under his chin and rocked back on his heels, thinking, thinking. "Where's Gault," he echoed philosophically, rhetorically. "An excellent question. Where could Gault be? Since I'm not Gault, and yet there is a Gault, or there was one at one time, where could the real Gault have gone? That's the question. And an interesting question it is, and very much to the point." Cady's bleak stare held a mix of disbelief and distaste, and never wavered. "The problem with that particular question," he plowed on, "is that I'm not at liberty to answer it."

"You're not at liberty to answer it." She said that slowly, distinctly, so the full idiocy of it wouldn't be lost on anyone. "And why is that?"

"Why is that! Another good question." Levi would be good at this; he'd give some circular Buddhist answer that sounded really good, and Cady wouldn't realize it didn't make a lick of sense until days later. "I gave my word," Jesse said without thinking. It slipped out: the truth. How unusual.

She blew air out of her mouth, a popping sound of utter disgust. "Well, isn't that convenient."

She didn't believe him! Now, that rankled. The first time he'd ever told her the truth, and she didn't believe it. "I did," he insisted, "I swore a solemn oath."

"To Gault?"

Touchy territory. Lamely, he reverted to "I'm not at liberty to say."

More disgusted air-blowing. She stood up. "The newspaper said Gault got wounded in the hand in Oakland. His gun hand. Is that when you decided to use him—be him? Well, is it?"

"Yes, but—"

"And you've been extorting money out of innocent people ever since?"

"Innocent!" No, that was wrong. Too late, he corrected it. "Extorting!"

"What a piece of work you are, Mr. *Vaughn*." Her lips curled with contempt, and Jesse felt cold all over, like she'd ducked him in a tub of ice. "What I can't figure out is why you're still here. You've got everybody's money by now, so what's keeping you in Paradise?"

"You." Oh, and also the fact that he didn't have any money.

Before she turned around, he saw pain and confusion crowd out the anger in her eyes. He reached out, touched her stiff spine, but she shrugged his hand off and sidestepped away.

"Cady, it's true. I stayed for you." He had. Money didn't have a thing to do with it.

"Well, you can go on now, because I don't even like you anymore."

He bowed his head. If that was true . . . "Let me try to tell you what happened," he said earnestly.

"Don't bother."

"I—after Gault—once I was—" He stopped, stymied. If only he hadn't given his promise! "Gault got shot in the hand in Oakland. That's true." Well, no, it wasn't. "I mean, that's what the papers said—you read it, I read it. So about a week later I'm passing through Stockton, minding my own business, and what happens?"

"I really don't care. I told—"

"I'm in a saloon, and this guy comes up to me and says, 'I'll give you six hundred dollars not to shoot me.' I don't say anything; I just sit there trying to figure out if he said what I think he said. The guy looks around, he sees nobody's watching, he pulls out his wallet. Takes out six hundred bucks in cash and slides it across the table. 'Are we square now, Mr. Gault?' Now I can't talk at all, I'm just blinking, trying to keep my chin from hitting the table. He starts to get up, but then he leans over and whispers in my ear, 'She was asking for it; if her old man knew what she's really like, he wouldn't've hired you to kill me—he'd've screwed her himself.' Then he gets up and leaves, and I'm sitting there shaking my head and staring at six hundred bucks. And then it hits me."

Cady had turned around. "What?" she asked, sullen.

"He thinks I'm Gault because of the *guns*." He took one of his pearl-handled revolvers out of the holster and tried to hand it to her. "See the eagle on the grip? Custom-made. Mexican. Very rare."

"Gault had this kind of gun?"

"Yeah. No." He squeezed the bridge of his nose. "This is Gault's gun. I, uh . . . I acquired it."

"How?" When he didn't answer, she sneered again. "Don't tell me. You're not at liberty to say."

"I'm not. Cady, I'd tell you if I could, but I can't."

"Because you're so honorable, such an honest man." That made him blush. "So there was never anything wrong with your eye, nothing wrong with your hand. You're not deaf."

"Nope." He tried a smile. "I'm a whole man. Healthy as a horse."

She didn't smile back. "And proud of yourself, too." She whipped around and started walking away.

He followed, miserable. He didn't know if he was proud of himself or not. He wasn't ashamed exactly, because the people he'd taken money from were all lowlifes, they deserved fleecing. But he could see too clearly what he looked like to Cady: a fake, a cheap opportunist. A coward.

"Honey, wait. Can't you try to see it from my side?"

"I already do."

"No, listen." They'd come to her buggy. She put her foot on the step, but he held her arm so she couldn't spring up. "After I started wearing the eye-patch, people were *throwing* money at me. Honest to God. And they were crooks, thugs, nuts, the worst kind—every one of 'em with a guilty conscience over some sin or other. What was I supposed to do? Hand it back to 'em? Who wouldn't—"

"Cherney," she broke in, figuring it out. "*You* drove him out of town."

"I sure did. Talk about crooks—"

"After you swindled him. How much did you get out of him? Plenty. Oh, God, Jesse." She shook her head almost pityingly. "He was a crook, sure, but what are you?" She flung off his hand and jumped up into the seat, started gathering up the reins.

"No, wait. You're not looking at it right. Cady, don't leave. You're mad, and you have a right to be—I should've told you before."

"Yeah. Why didn't you?"

"Because I knew you'd feel just like this. And . . . also . . ." He frowned at his thumb as he stroked it across the scarred leather of the trace. "I liked being Gault," he admitted, embarrassed. "I liked it that you were a little scared of me at first. And then you weren't." He grinned crookedly, not looking at her. "I mean, you know. Would you have given me a second glance if I hadn't been a dangerous killer?"

"Yes."

He looked up quickly. Any comfort he might've taken from her answer evaporated when he saw how hard and determined her eyes were. "Wait—would you just think it over?" He held the rein still when she would've jerked it out of his hand. "You're angry, that's understandable. But, Cady, don't throw it all away. Please. Just think about it before you do anything rash, okay?"

She pressed her lips together. "It's extremely unlikely that I will change my mind about you, Jesse Vaughn. At least when you were Gault you had some kind of a code. A rotten one, but it was something."

"Hey, I've got a code."

"Of self-interest and cheating."

"Cheating! I never cheat. I—"

"And lying to women."

She had him there. "I was going to tell you," he insisted, mumbling.

"Sure you were."

"Aw, Cady—"

"This is not a little white lie, Jess. You've crossed a line. There's such a thing as trust and—*decency* between two people who—who sleep together," she finished tightly, shiny-eyed, and he wondered if that was what she'd been going to say.

"I know it. I don't have any excuse. Except that I didn't want to lose you." But he was losing her; it was happening right now. "Cady?"

"What."

As bad as things were, he had to know the worst. "Do you think I'm a coward?"

Color bloomed on her cheeks; she put her hand on her throat as if it hurt. In a soft, strangled voice she said, "I don't know, Jesse. I guess—I guess I don't know what else to call it."

He hung his head, ready to cry with her. He'd never felt so miserable in his life.

"Well," she said after an endless minute. "So long, Jess."

"So long." But he didn't move. "Cady?"

"*What.*"

"Can I have a ride back to town?"

She shook her head in disbelief.

"I walked all the way out here." He'd needed to think. "Feet hurt. C'mon, give me a ride back."

"Damn you, Jesse—" Now she was mad because he was ruining her dignified exit. "Oh, hell. Get up, then. Hurry the hell up." She scooted away and he climbed up beside her. "Don't say a word, though. Not one word, or I'll put you out." She turned the mare in a tight, skillful circle—she was good with horses; it was one of the things he loved about her—and they trotted down River Farm's long, curving drive to the road.

He obeyed and kept quiet. What was left to say? A sick feeling in his stomach told him that all the talking he'd done had only dug him a deeper grave anyway. It was a gray, warm, lifeless day, with low clouds bulging in a listless sky. Silent and wretched, he turned his head away from Cady and watched dusty wildflowers and patchy scrub pass by the buggy wheels.

The dreary scene slowed down; Cady said "Whoa," softly and the mare changed gaits to a walk. Jesse looked up to see a man standing in the middle of the road, opposite the turnoff to the Seven Dollar Mine. He saw them at the same time and made as if to turn, run, but then he stopped again. His hunched shoulders relaxed; he stuck one hand in his pocket and tipped his hat back, smiling a nervous greeting. "Howdy," he said as they rolled slowly past.

"Hey, George," Cady greeted him neutrally.

"I was just out taking a walk," George explained, although nobody had asked him. "Stretching my legs, getting some fresh air. Nice day."

"Yeah. Well, see you."

"See you." He poked his hat with his finger and waved.

"Who was that?" Jesse asked when they were out of earshot.

"George Sample. Wylie's mine foreman."

"Wylie's man? Why was he standing around your mine?"

She smiled thinly. "I figure he was either relieving himself or sneaking a drink on the job. Or both. He sure looked guilty."

"How far from the road is the entrance to the Seven Dollar?"

"Quarter of a mile, maybe less. If it weren't for the trees, you could see it."

He thought about that for a second, and then he said, "Stop the buggy."

"Why?"

"Stop." She stopped, and he vaulted to the ground. "You go on, Cady, I'll walk back."

"Why? What are you going to do?"

"I just want to see something. Go on, it's okay. Go." He slapped the mare's side, pivoted, and sprinted back up the road.

The lane was empty, George nowhere in sight. Jesse approached the turnoff to Cady's mine cautiously, staying close to the weeds at the side of the road. Using a tree for a shield, he peered around at the narrow wagon track to the Seven Dollar.

Empty. Silent.

He walked out into the open. Grass and thistles jutted up between the old wheel ruts, overgrown and undisturbed. Okay, nobody used this road, but that didn't necessarily mean anything. Keeping close to the thickety edges again, he crept up the lane, sharp-eyed, ears cocked. At every turn, he half expected somebody to jump out at him. He thought about drawing his guns, but discarded the idea. He'd probably shoot his own hand off if he had to fire. Then he remembered—he was out of bullets anyway.

After the last bend, what was left of Cady's mine came into view. He stopped and stared, his nervousness gradually giving way to depression. There wasn't a much bleaker sight on earth than an abandoned mine, he reflected as he took in the rotting outbuildings, leaning timber scaffolds, and rusting machinery in the dusty clearing. He kicked at a stone in the dirt, disconsolate. He'd had a crazy idea, but the devastation all around mocked him, telling him just how stupid it had been. Now all he would get for his trouble was a long walk back to town.

He went closer anyway, drawn by an illegible sign at the mine entrance. $7, he made out when he got near enough to spit on it. And under that, GUSTAF SHLEGEL, OWNER. Cady hadn't bothered to change the

sign, and small wonder. If ever a place was finished
and done with, it was the Seven Dollar Mine.

A rickety, three-sided timber fence guarded the
black entrance. He folded his arms over the top rail
and squinted down, following the line of a broken
ladder that disappeared in darkness. The smell of
raw earth was overpowering and unpleasant. He
picked up a pebble on the rail beside his elbow, held
it over the hole, dropped it. He heard it hit rock and
slither away into silence. The entrance sloped, then,
didn't drop straight down.

He'd never been in a gold mine before. Unless you
owned it, it looked like a god-awful way to make a
living. Shrimp Malone didn't mine, he prospected,
panned along the river and streambeds. He'd probably never get rich, but at least he wasn't shut up in
the airless dark all day, day after day. Jesse shivered,
trying to imagine a life like that. Nothing was worth
it, no amount of gold. He'd as soon be buried alive.

He turned around—and jumped half a foot in the
air. He let out a yelp that startled Cady so much, she
jumped a *whole* foot. "Damn it!" they yelled in unison. "What the hell do you—" "Don't you ever—"
"You scared the spit out of me!" They stood there
glaring at each other, holding their hearts. Jesse
laughed first. Cady grinned, but caught herself before
she could laugh back. She wasn't speaking to him,
she remembered.

"What are you doing here? I wanted you to go on,
Cady, ride back to town. You shouldn't be here."

"Why not? It's my mine. What are *you* doing
here?"

"I just wanted to check something."

"What?"

"Nothing. I had a hunch, that's all. I was wrong."

She narrowed her eyes. "You think it's funny that Wylie's mine captain was hanging around the Seven Dollar."

He shrugged. "I think it's funny that Wylie keeps trying to buy a mine you tell me is worthless. And just happens to be next to his. What does he want it for?"

She'd always assumed he wanted it because that was the kind of man he was—he wanted everything. But Jesse's idea, if he was thinking the same thing she was thinking, made more sense. She moved closer to the shaft, leaning over the splintery post to listen.

"Nothing to hear," he told her. "I already—"

"Sh." He was right, though; after half a minute of intense listening, she agreed with him; there was nothing to hear. But there was something to smell. "Holy smoke."

"What?"

"Ammonium nitrate. Smell it?"

He leaned over and inhaled deeply. "What's ammonium nitrate?"

"It's dynamite."

Jesse straightened. "You mean I was right?"

"Even if Wylie's blasting, it shouldn't come up from this adit. In fact it couldn't, unless—"

"Unless he's tunneled over from his mine to yours."

She nodded, staring at nothing, thinking hard. "I know a way to find out."

"How?"

"Come on." She might not be speaking to him, but just now she was awfully glad for his company. She led the way through the littered yard, past the long, slant-sided mill building, the rusted-out husks of jiggers, grinders, sluice tables, and steam hoists, to a cinder track that led into the woods behind the mine. She thought of the last time she'd walked along this quiet, shadowy trail—in the company of Mr. Shlegel, who had wanted to show her his mining property. It hadn't been completely paid out then; he'd still had men placering along the riverbed.

"Where are we going?" Jesse asked in a low voice, trying to catch her hand.

She pulled away. "Can't you hear it?"

"What?"

"The river." A few minutes later the trail broke out of the trees, thinning to a path that stopped at the edge of the cliff. "Wait," she cautioned when Jesse started into the open. "In case somebody's there." They went slowly, side by side, glancing in every direction. It wasn't necessary to be quiet; the roar of the Rogue a hundred feet below drowned out everything.

Not everything. A low, chugging sound grew louder with every step they took toward the cliff edge. Cady figured out what it was a second before it came into view. "Steam dredger," she said loud enough for Jesse to hear. "That goddamn—polecat!"

"Is that your property?"

"No, but this is. Look, he's following a vein from the Seven Dollar back into the cliff. See down there?" She pointed down at the wheel tracks and the pile of strewn rubble on the rocky bank directly below. "The dredger's a blind—he's placered out on his side. That—*thief!*"

"Come on, Cady, we'd better get out of here." He had to grab her arm and pull before she would budge. "Let's go before somebody spots us."

He was right. She let him lead her away, glad for the dark cover of the pine woods again. They began to run. The closer they got to the clearing, the stronger a feeling grew that they were being watched, followed. She'd tied the buggy to a section of a rusty trommel in the mine yard. "Hurry," she told Jesse as he unhitched the horse. "Hurry, hurry, let's go." She felt jittery as a cricket. Some of Wylie's men were as ruthless as he was. If she and Jesse got caught here, now—she didn't want to think about what could happen.

Jesse swatted the mare, and they cantered out of the bumpy yard, bouncing in the buggy like dolls in a child's wagon. The road to town was empty in both directions—thank God! They were safe, and nobody had seen them. Still, they'd ridden nearly a mile before she started to relax.

"Polecat," she said again, hammering her knees with her fists. She knew plenty of worse words for Wylie, but she was still watching her language in front of Jesse. Which was pretty stupid.

"I don't get it. What exactly is he doing?"

"He's placering with a dredge along the riverbed—

cleaning bedrock after the gravel's stripped away. But it's a cover, a blind. He's placered out, same as the Seven Dollar. What he's really doing is following ore shoots from *my* riverbed back into *my* mine. I saw it!''

Jesse still looked baffled.

''Before there was a Seven Dollar or a Rainbow, they struck virgin placer gold below the cliffs at the river's edge. People made a fortune, and then it dried up. So they switched to mining for lode gold, hoping to follow the ore bodies back uphill to the source, maybe a big underground lode. Wylie had some luck, but Mr. Shlegel never did, he just found a few stringers that petered out. So he gave up.''

''And you think Wylie's found a lode? A big one? In your mine?''

''I don't know what he's found, but it's sure as hell in my mine. Thieving bastard. Well, he won't get away with it.'' She rubbed her hands together. ''Ha. I've got him this time. If I can get Tommy to do something,'' she amended, half to herself. ''But still. Finally. Got the son of a bitch dead to rights. I don't see how he can slither out of this one. This is against the law, and I've got proof. Go straight to the sheriff's, Jesse, don't stop at the livery. By God, this time I'm going to get him.''

But she wasn't nearly as sure of herself as she sounded. Some kind of superstitious dread was making her hands perspire, and she couldn't shake a weird, nightmarish feeling that something bad was going to happen.

Maybe it already had. Jesse slowed the buggy for

traffic on Main Street, and after half a block Cady figured out what was peculiar. Everybody in the street or on the sidewalk stopped and stared at them, but nobody spoke. Nestor Yeakes was lounging in front of the livery, as usual, but when Jesse waved at him he didn't wave back. He just stared.

"Hey, Sam," Jesse called to Sam Blankenship, who was crossing Noble Fir in front of the real estate office. He stopped in the middle of the street—and stared.

"What's going on?" said Jesse, and Cady shrugged back at him, bewildered. She didn't like it. It was more than peculiar, it was downright scary.

Ham spied them at the same moment Cady saw him, coming out of Chang's laundry. Immediately he made a dash for the buggy. She put her hand on Jesse's arm. "Stop, stop—he shouldn't be running—!" Jesse pulled on the reins, and the mare pranced to a halt.

"Cady—Mr. Gaul—Mr.—" Ham stumbled over his tongue, couldn't get the words out.

"What?" Cady cried, disturbed by his face, his manner. He was excited, but that was nothing new; it was the fear behind his eagerness that alarmed her. "Stand still, Ham. Tell me what's wrong."

"They's a man!"

"A man," she repeated, struggling for calm. "What man."

"He up at the Rogue right now. He say—he say—" The whites of his eyes gleamed as he rolled a frightened glance at Jesse.

"*What?*"

"He say his name's Gault!"

Thirteen

"Jesse? What are you doing? Jess—turn the rig around!" Cady tugged on his arm, trying to read the expression on his face. "Where are you going? You can't go to the Rogue, he'll kill you. Jesse!" She punched his shoulder, and finally he looked at her.

"I have to."

"*Why?*"

"Because a man's got to do what a man's got to do."

She hit him again. "Are you crazy? It's Gault, Jesse—the *real* Gault! What do you think he'll do when he finds out you've been impersonating him?"

"Well, I reckon he'll be mad."

"I reckon he'll shoot you!"

He looked grim and didn't answer, just kept driving the buggy toward Rogue's Tavern.

"Damn it. This is because of what I said, isn't it?" She shook him by the wrist in her agitation. "I take it back—you're not a coward. You're not." That only made him smile bleakly. "You're *not*. I just said it because I was hurt. Please, Jess, turn around and get out of town, ride as fast as you can. Nobody'll—"

"Too late. I'm not running anymore."

Why was he *talking* like that? She started to curse, but it did no good; he wouldn't even look at her. Fear finally shut her up; she watched in speechless dread as he halted the mare in front of the saloon, handed her the reins, and leaped down. "Maybe you better stay out here, Cady. Safer." And with that, he left her and went toward the swinging doors.

She clambered down clumsily, shaky-kneed. "In a pig's eye," she said out loud, and the trembly sound of her own voice scared her even more. Ham trotted up, out of breath, holding his side. She gave him a quick, reassuring hug. "I want you to drive the buggy to Nestor's, and then I want you to stay there. Don't come back to the Rogue. Hear me, Ham?" He nodded, but she wasn't sure of him—he'd disobeyed her before. She said it all again, bending down and looking him in the eye. "Don't you come back to the Rogue, Ham, I mean it. Stay at Nestor's till I come and get you."

"Okay."

"Okay. All right, then. Go."

She watched him hop up on the buggy, turn it, and trot off down Main Street. She waited till he was out of sight, and then she ran into the saloon.

It was packed. It looked like church on Sunday, minus the women. Catching sight of Levi's bald, shiny head above everybody else's, she pushed and elbowed her way through a sweaty press of bodies. "Excuse me—Gunther, move—let me by, Stan—" until finally Levi grabbed her wrist and hauled her behind the bar with him. She stepped up on the foot-high riser she used to serve drinks from when Levi wasn't around—and if he hadn't grabbed her again and held on, she'd have waded back into the crowd. Because from here she could see Jesse. He stood beside a table where Merle Wylie sat with another man.

Gault.

God Almighty. Definitely Gault. Looking at him, Cady felt disoriented, almost light-headed, shoved back in time to the day Jesse had come to Paradise. This man, this real Gault with his black clothes and black leather eyepatch and black cigarette, looked older, craggier, not half as handsome, but his . . . his *aura* was the same. No, it was worse. Jesse had looked like a cocked gun, as if he'd as soon kill you as spit on you. Gault looked like he'd much rather kill you.

Amazingly, they looked alike—almost a family resemblance. Same beaky nose, same steely-gray eyes and silver-streaked hair. No wonder it had been so easy for Jesse to be Gault; no wonder so many people had bought it without question. Even her. Especially her.

She felt a hand clamp down on her forearm and turned as Glendoline stepped up beside her, jostling her on the riser. "Cady, *look*."

"I'm looking."

"Who is it? Which one do you think—"

"Hush." Wylie was saying something, and she wanted to hear. All around her, speculative muttering stopped when he scraped back his chair, grinning up at Jesse.

"Well, well, well," he said gloatingly, dragging the

words out. "What a fascinating conversation I've been having with Mr. Gault here. I always knew there was something phony about you. What's your real name, mister? What do you do for a living, punch cows? Polish spittoons?"

Somebody's nervous laugh cut through the taut silence. Cady's hands shook. Where was her gun? In a cigar box on the far side of the bar—she couldn't get to it from here. What would she have done with it anyway? Jesse had his back to her, she couldn't see his face. She could see Gault's, though. Lord God in heaven. If he wasn't a cold-blooded killer, she'd eat her hat and swallow the feather.

He stood up slowly, lazily, like a snake changing position on a warm rock. Face-to-face, the resemblance between him and Jesse was even more startling. His smile was like death, and when he spoke in his whispery voice, so eerily familiar, it made her shudder. "I don't know who you are," he told Jesse, "and I don't much care. You've got something that belongs to me. Couple of six-guns. You can hand 'em over now, nice and easy, and I won't kill you. I ought to, but I won't. But if you take longer than five seconds to lay 'em down on this table, I'll shoot you where you stand. One."

"Jesse!" Terror made her yell it. The way he held himself, the stubbornness in his shoulders, his stiff arms—she had an awful premonition of what he would do.

She was right.

"Listen, you." His creepy whisper echoed Gault's, sibilant syllable for syllable. "I don't know who *you*

Patricia Gaffney

are, and I don't give a damn. If you're not out of my face before I count to three, I'll put a bullet through the eye you've got that phony patch over. One."

Gault blinked rapidly, and for half a second Cady actually thought she saw consternation blur the resolve in his hard, cruel face. But the moment passed, and his vicious smile uncurled again, making her scalp tingle. "Looks like we got ourselves a stand-off," he whispered menacingly.

Menace was all right, menace was fine. At least he'd stopped counting.

"Uh-oh." Glen dug her fingers harder into Cady's arm. "Oh, no, oh, no."

Cady saw what she saw: Sheriff Leaver coming through the swinging doors and trying to push his way through the crowd. Hatless, tie askew, collar crooked, he looked green and sickly, and Cady remembered what Willagail had told her this morning—he and Jesse had gotten drunk together in the jailhouse last night. "Oh, this is just great," she quavered, wringing her hands. "Now Gault can kill both of them."

Glendoline clapped her hands to her face and burst into tears.

"You see the paper this morning?"

"What?" Cady glanced up at Levi, uncomprehending. "Did I what? See the *paper*?"

"Front page. Sara Digby say she seen who left off all that money at her place."

"Who?"

"Jesse."

"*What?*"

"All right, what's going on here?" The sheriff's

reedy tenor sounded anything but authoritative, but it did grab back Cady's fractured attention. Glen's, too; she stopped bawling to listen. "Break it up. I want everybody to get out and go home. Come on, now. There's not going to be any shooting, so you might as well move on. Arthur, Sam, let's go. Stony, Leonard, you, too, Shrimp. Come on, everybody out."

Nobody moved, not one soul. They milled, shuffled their feet, unfolded their arms, but nobody went out the door. Glen wailed, "Oh, Tommy," and Cady put her arm around her. *What's this?* she thought distractedly. Was Glen sweet on the sheriff after all?

"Which one of you is Gault?"

Maybe someday Cady would look back and laugh, remembering how Will Shorter looked asking that moronic question, glasses perched on the end of his nose, pencil poised over his notebook. As if the real Gault would raise his hand and the fake one would slink away, mystery solved.

"I'm Gault."

"I'm Gault."

"You're a liar."

"You're a liar."

"Fight it out," Wylie suggested gleefully. "Right here and now. That'll settle it."

"Fine with me," whispered Jesse.

"I can hardly wait," whispered Gault.

"Jesse!" It wasn't Cady who yelled it this time, it was Ham. She saw him shoving and fumbling his way through the crush of gawking men. Levi let go of her arm and started to vault over the bar, but just then Ham spurted out of the crowd and made a rush for

Jesse. He threw himself against him, slamming into his hip and almost throwing him against the table.

"Okay, hold it!" No more whispering; Jesse's voice rang out clear and commanding as he pulled Ham close, shielding him with one hand on his head and the other on his shoulder. "There's not going to be any shooting in here."

"Outside." Wylie stood up, his eyes glittering with excitement. "Take your fight outside. Guns at twenty paces. You can—"

"Too dark." Gault jerked his chin toward the window. The sun had set; dusk was creeping in. "I want a nice clear shot when I kill the man who says he's me."

"Likewise," Jesse sneered. Cady watched every man in the room look at him, then at Gault, then him, then Gault.

Gault said, "I can kill you tomorrow as easy as tonight."

Jesse curled his lip. "Ten o'clock suit you?"

What? What? She couldn't believe her ears. Clutching at Levi's hand so hard he winced, she yelled, "No!" but nobody paid any attention to her.

"Ten o'clock. In the street." Gault removed the slim black cigarette stuck in the side of his mouth and flicked it on the floor at Jesse's feet. "You feel like committing suicide any sooner than that, let me know. I'll be at the hotel."

"Same goes. I'll be here."

Openmouthed, Cady watched as Gault, the real Gault, the man who was going to kill her lover at ten o'clock tomorrow morning, waded into the withering, awestruck crowd and sauntered through the swinging doors.

It's hard to argue with somebody you're kissing. Hard to hold up your end of a debate with a man who's trying to get your clothes off. Cady was giving it a try, though, and staying as far from the bed as she could without actually going outside. To get sex off Jesse's mind she *might've* gone outside, except it was raining.

"I'm not doing this," she insisted for the third or fourth time, turning her mouth away to avoid his marauding one. "Not until you say you've come to your senses."

"Rather come to your senses."

"Will you *stop*?"

"Can't." His lips were warm and his mustache tickled. She craned her neck, but that only gave him access to her throat. "Cady, I just gotta have you."

He had her pressed up against her bureau, and she could feel exactly how much he had to have her. "If you're doing this for me, I'm telling you, Jess, you don't have to."

"I was hoping to do it for both of us."

"Not—this. Damn it, you know what I'm talking about."

"Yeah, but I don't want to talk about it."

"Will you just listen? Oh, God." He'd finally gotten her dress undone in back, and he was peeling it off her shoulders and down her arms. "Quit it, now. Quit." Such a half-hearted protest; she didn't blame him for ignoring it. "Jess, we have to talk."

"Later."

"No, now." She put her hands under his chin and forcibly lifted his face from the hollow between her breasts. "Please." She was reduced to pleading. His beautiful face, smiling at her so sweetly, worry-free, animated only by lust and longing, was going to be her undoing. "I don't understand you," she wailed. "If you fight Gault, he'll kill you."

"No, he won't. That's not going to happen. Trust me," he ordered, holding her still and kissing her on the mouth. She tried to talk, but he said, "Shh," and kept on, seducing her with the care he took the single-mindedness and the gentleness.

"Oh, Jesse, don't." But she didn't stop him from unfastening her chemise. Instead she buried her nose in his hair, and Jesse buried his in her bosom, stroking her, painting her bare skin with his tongue. "I'll give you money. Do you want money?"

"Sweetheart," he said tenderly, "shut up."

"I've got a nest egg. It's in the bottom drawer, under my stockings."

"How much?"

"Over two thousand dol—"

He covered her mouth with his, pressing his tongue inside and silencing her with sexy, stirring caresses. She lost track of the conversation. It seemed like forever since she'd touched him like this, made love with him like this. "I was so stupid," she whispered when he let her speak. "Do you forgive me? It's my fault we wasted so much time. Oh, Jess, I love you."

"I love you, Cady."

"Do you? Oh, Jesse, do you?"

"I swear it. Marry me when this is over."

She started to cry. "Stupid," she muttered, smearing at tears with her fingers. But she couldn't help it. A war was going on inside between despair and bliss, and she couldn't control herself.

"Marry me, honey. I'll make you so happy."

"How can I marry you if you're d-dead."

He *laughed*. She had an urge to smack him, and a stronger one to hold him so tight, she took him right into herself.

He had the same urge—the latter one. He slid his knee between her legs, making her shuffle her feet apart, and she lost all her will to resist him. She had just enough strength to return his hot kiss and slip her hands inside his shirt, desperate to touch his skin, feel his body. She loved it that he was covered with straight, soft, dark hair. He tilted her back, back, till her head rested on top of her bureau, and he kissed her through her shift, right through the fabric, nibbling on her and making her moan. "I can't stand up—" She had to brace her pelvis against his to stay upright. He rocked her slowly, deeply, humming throaty encouragement against her breast, and she sucked in a gulp of air through her teeth. "I'm falling," she sighed, wrapping weak arms around his neck.

He picked her up and carried her across the room—so much for her bed-avoiding strategy. A wisp of common sense returned while he undressed her. She didn't resist, but at least she didn't help him, and she recovered enough presence of mind to start the argument over once she was naked.

"Jesse, this is all because of what I said, isn't it?" Beside her on the bed, he was taking his boots off. "I *don't* think you're a coward. How could I?" He ignored her and started on his belt buckle. "You don't have to prove anything to me. I mean it—I love you. Do you think I'll love you more when you're a really brave corpse?"

He chuckled again, stripping off his pants and shrugging out of his shirt. Infuriated, she was really going to slug him this time—but somehow he got hold of her wrists and pressed her down to the mattress on her back. "Cady, would you please stop worrying? Nothing's going to happen to me." She dodged his lips, appalled when the tears started again. "Honey, I'm a much better shot than you think I am."

"Oh, right, you're—"

"I *am*. I had a hangover—you saw me at my worst today. I'm telling you, I'm fast. I'm greased lightning. Gault doesn't stand a chance."

He looked so confident, so cocky, she felt herself wavering, actually coming close to believing him. "But . . ." She shook her head, trying to clear it. "You're not an outlaw, you're not a gunfighter. Lord, Jess, you couldn't hit a window in a greenhouse."

"Wrong." He shook his head right back at her. "You ought to have more faith in me. I'm disappointed in you, Cady."

She started to sputter; he started to bite her earlobe. She squirmed, ready to wrestle in earnest, but he covered her with his naked body and, just as before, the finer points of the argument started to blur.

Oh, how could she lose him? She held him tight, tight, lost in the long, strong feel of him, even though she had to keep swallowing down the lump in her throat. They rolled; she landed on top and wrapped him up in her arms and legs. "It was you, wasn't it?" She couldn't stop kissing him, couldn't keep her mouth off his skin.

"What was me?" He had his hands in her hair, squeezing it, combing it through his fingers. He loved her hair, he told her all the time, and she loved it that he did.

"You gave the Digbys all that money. Sara saw you."

"That woman needs glasses."

"No, it was you. The Sullivans—you gave them money, too."

"You're losing it, McGill. Been hitting the bottle?"

Now she did cry. "Oh, *God*, Jess, how I love you."

He rolled again, coming on top and parting her legs with his. She guided him with her hand, arching up, urgent, eager to take him. And when she had him she sighed, a deep, satisfied sound. But there was sadness, too. "Don't leave me, Jess."

"Never."

"I'm not letting you go."

"You couldn't get rid of me."

So softly, he followed the tear trails on her face with his lips, trying to kiss them away. But it was too much, too sweet—he only made her cry harder. So he began to move inside her, to make her forget, make her lose her mind. "Not letting you go," she whispered again, just before sensation blotted out every thought in her mind. Him and her, sex and love, everything came together and it was all mixed, all one. She took him deep and he took her up, up—too high, too fast, how could she bear this? A long, intense lifetime passed, and then she burst. She flew apart, pieces everywhere, she'd never get herself back together. Anyway, there wasn't time—Jesse's hands, Jesse's mouth, Jesse's body inside her body—it all started over again, and this time she let go without a fight. Just let go, gave in and came so gently, so completely. And held him close while he gave her all of himself. A perfect exchange.

He rolled to his side, not letting her go, and lay like a dead man, motionless except to press his lips to her forehead every few minutes. She had a little more energy; she fluttered her fingers along his backbone, and sometimes she stroked him in that ticklish spot right above his buttocks. His whole body quivered when she did that, which just egged her on. "Quit it," he ordered, and she snickered into his neck, where she had her face pressed. He kissed her again, smiling. Trying to think back to a time when he'd ever felt this happy. Age seven, when his father gave him his first horse; that came the closest. But it was still second. This was it. This. Was it.

"Say it again, Cady."

"What."

"You know. That thing you never said before until tonight."

"Oh, that." She pretended to yawn. "I already said it two times. You only said it once."

He laughed, even though he wasn't quite ready to

make jokes. That could come later. "I'll say it so often, you'll get sick of hearing me."

"Impossible." She sat up. The fierceness in her face took him by surprise. "Impossible. I've never felt this way before, never knew I could. Everything's changed. It's you—you're my life, you've become my life."

"Cady." It felt like she'd punched him in the heart. "I'm the same, exactly the same. I always thought this happened to other people."

"Yeah."

"I'm crazy in love with you, and it's for good."

"Oh, Jess, but if you meet him tomorrow—"

"Hush." He pulled her close and held her. "It'll be all right, you just have to believe me. You think I'd let anything happen to us? Do anything to spoil this? Listen. Let me tell you how it's gonna be." He tucked her up against his body and drew the sheet over her, so she wouldn't get cold. "First thing we do is get married."

She squirmed closer. "In church?"

"Where do you think, in the saloon?" They laughed, but then they both said, "Hmm," in thoughtful tones. Then they laughed again. "Well, wherever we do it, it's going to be a big, happy wedding with all our friends."

"And Ardelle Sheets can't come. Livvie Dunne, either."

"Right. No nasty women allowed. Then we go on a honeymoon. Where do you want to go?"

She burrowed in deeper, muffling a real yawn against her hand. "San Francisco?"

"Okay."

"Or Eugene, maybe?"

"Great. Or Portland."

"Lovely."

He smiled into her hair. She didn't care any more than he did where they went. "Or Dubuque."

"Wonderful." She exhaled a drowsy laugh. "So then what?"

"So then we buy that farm you like so much. Le Coeur au Coquin. However you say it."

She went very still. All she did was open her eyes; he knew, because he could feel the tickle of her lashes on his skin. "Oh, Jesse," she breathed, and he knew he'd said exactly the right thing. "Could you really live there?"

"Sure I could. I'd love to live there. We'll fix the old house up and make it shine. And every night we'll sit out on our big front porch and listen to the river. Tell each other how the day went."

"In two rocking chairs, side by side."

"Yeah."

She sighed with happiness. "Just one question. What do we use for money to buy it?"

"What do you think? Some of that gold Wylie's been stealing from the Seven Dollar."

"Oh, mercy, I forgot all about it! I didn't even tell Tommy yet."

"That's okay, plenty of time to deal with Wylie. Where were we? Oh, yeah, sitting in our rocking chairs. So what are we drinking?"

"I'm drinking lemonade."

"I'm sipping a mint julep."

"I forgot, you're from Kentucky. What are we doing for a living? If I may ask."

"You raise pears. I raise horses."

She heaved another deep, contented sigh. "I want apples and peaches, too."

"Good. I can't stand pears."

She brought his hand to her lips and kissed it. "I do love you, Jess. So much."

"I love you, too."

"Say you won't leave me."

"I swear I won't."

"You really swear?"

"On my honor."

She fell asleep with her head on his shoulder, her hand lying, open and trusting, on his stomach. Jesse watched the slight smile on her lips soften and fade as she fell deeper and deeper asleep.

Outside, a warm, drizzly rain made the gutters gurgle. Apart from that and the gentle sigh of Cady's breathing, the only sound was the low whistle of an owl somewhere close by. Through the open window, the odor of damp earth and soggy leaves floated in, heavy and warm, pleasantly dank. Jesse rubbed his face and pinched his nose, trying to banish a seductive urge to close his eyes and drift off with Cady. It was hard to concentrate on trouble, not now when the world had never looked sweeter or the future more hopeful. Still, he had to come up with a plan. Across the room, the clock struck twelve-thirty. Time was running out.

What was Gault doing right now? Sleeping? Doubtful; he'd always been a night owl. Ten A.M. for a shoot-out must seem ungodly to him. And how the hell had he found Jesse in Paradise? Maybe those stories in the *Reverberator* hadn't been such a hot idea after all. Still, he could've sworn nothing would budge Gault from the cushy life he'd taken to so naturally in Oakland. The last time they'd seen each other, he was living high on the hog in a suite at the Paramount Hotel, smoking cigars and drinking five-dollar whiskey, playing poker and romancing women, getting the most out of his retirement from the gunfighter life. He had his right arm in a sling, and he'd told the whole world his hand was shot up so bad he'd never draw again. In secret, he'd paid Jesse the agreed-upon two hundred dollars for "wounding" him, and thrown in his pearl-handled six-shooters as an afterthought. "Reckon I won't be needing these anymore."

Liar. Indian giver.

Hard to tell if he was really mad or not. Most of the time Gault's face just naturally had that *make a wrong move and I'll set you on fire* look. Which was undoubtedly what had started him, all those years ago, on a life of crime. An exaggerated life—in fifteen years, he'd only killed three men, he swore, and Jesse believed him. But his inflated reputation always preceded him. In the end he'd had to fake his own incapacitation, or sooner or later some punk would surely have killed him.

"Yeah, yeah, I'm getting up," Jesse muttered to Boo, Cady's worthless cat, who had jumped up on the bed and was staring sullenly, kneading Jesse's leg through the sheet with his claws. Damn, but he didn't want to get up. He wanted to make love again and then fall asleep in Cady's arms, and not wake up till noon. He wanted them to start living the rest of their lives together.

He kissed the top of her head. She stirred, turned over, squirmed her bare butt against his hip. He suffered the predictable sexual reaction, and glanced around the room for a distraction. The tasseled lamp shade had a seaside vista handpainted in pastels: VISIT BEAUTIFUL COOS BAY, small print suggested at the bottom. Cady's mail-order spectacles lay on top of an open book. He couldn't read the title, only the last few lines on the near page: *"What raft, Jim?" "Our ole raf'." "You mean to say our old raft warn't smashed all to flinders?"* Some book about boats, he supposed. She'd nailed a picture to the wall on his side of the bed, and he'd fallen asleep many a night gazing at it. "Anybody you know?" he'd asked her once. It was a watercolor painting, or rather a reproduction of one, of a man and a woman sitting opposite each other at a table in a garden. She was writing a letter; he was watching her over his newspaper, smiling slightly. Affectionately. A red brick, ivy-covered cottage looked cozy in the background. Everything was pretty and soft, idealized. Sentimental. "No, I just like it," Cady had answered. Jesse liked it, too. "Home," he whispered to Boo, who flicked an eyelid at him. "Play your cards right and we might take you with us."

The clock chimed again. Twelve forty-five. Jesse put his lips on Cady's shoulder and kissed her softly, listening to her sigh in her sleep. Easing out of bed, he found his clothes on the floor and dressed in silence. The light from the tassel lamp didn't reach across the room to her bureau. In shadowy dimness, he silently pulled open the bottom drawer, and riffled through silk stockings and lingerie until he found Cady's nest egg. In a little velvet pouch, as soft and pretty as she was.

He was right: Gault hadn't gone to bed yet. Lucky his room at the Dobb House was on the first floor, and even luckier it was in back—nobody saw Jesse tossing pebbles from the alley at the lighted window.

"What the hell?" Gault threw up the sash and leaned out, wearing only his pants and his eyepatch. "Who's out there?"

"*Shh.* Who do you think?"

He commenced to curse—softly, so Jesse just stood and waited.

"You finished?"

"You owe me money, you lying, cheating, double-faced thief."

"There's a mouthful. How do you figure?"

"Who said you could be me? That was never part of the deal."

"It wasn't my idea. It was an accident. Besides," he pointed out, "it wasn't *not* part of the deal." Before Gault could start up again, he said, "Put your shirt on and come out. We have to talk."

"Damn right we have to talk. You come up here."

"No, too risky. Somebody might see us together. You know where the sheriff's office is?"

"Yeah, I passed it. Why?"

"Meet me there in about ten minutes."

"*What?*"

"Shh. Ten minutes." He touched his hat and set off down the alley, heading for Doc Mobius's house.

Cady wasn't sure what woke her, the sun in her face or the purring in her ear. Either way, when she opened her eyes and focused on the clock across the way, it said nine thirty-five.

Nine thirty-five. The significance didn't register for a whole minute, while she remembered waking up in the middle of the night just as Jesse crawled into bed beside her. He was naked, but he smelled of the outdoors and his hair was damp. "Have you been out?" she mumbled sleepily, stroking his back to warm him. "Went for a walk," he answered. That brought her wide awake. "Jesse, you're not thinking of—" But that was as far as she got. He kissed her into a hot, sharp arousal, and made love to her until she lay too exhausted to move. She'd drifted to sleep listening to the slow, drowsy sound of his voice, telling her again how happy they were going to be.

Nine thirty-six. And she was alone, Jesse wasn't beside her. She shot up in bed, scaring the life out of the cat. "Sorry," she muttered, throwing the covers off and joining Boo on the floor. He shook himself resentfully while she barged over to the wardrobe and yanked it open. Pulling out the first three things she saw—an old corduroy skirt and vest, a yellow blouse—she started dragging clothes on with clumsy, fumbling fingers, missing buttons in her haste and having to start over. Her hair was such a tangled mess, she wasted precious minutes getting it up on her head and in some kind of order. *Calm down,* she commanded, but to no avail. Jesse was gone, and he should've been here. Where was he? She had more than a hunch; she had a deep, dark certainty, and it was scaring the life out of her.

In the saloon, Levi was rubbing beeswax into the bar, his pride and joy; since the tire fire, he took more pains with it than ever. "You're up early," he greeted her, looking up from the shiny, fragrant surface and smiling at her.

"You, too." Neither of them wandered in to work much before eleven on weekends.

"Ham woke me up early. That boy, he got the loudest—"

"Levi, have you seen Jesse?"

He stopped polishing. His face turned even gentler. "No, I ain't," he said softly. Sympathetically.

She tensed. If Levi thought she needed sympathy—

"Hey, Cady. Hey, Levi. What're y'all doing here so early?" They could've asked Glen the same thing; she rarely showed up before lunchtime, no matter how many times Cady scolded her for tardiness. "I couldn't sleep," she confided, plopping down at Chico's piano and picking out the first five notes of "Beautiful Dreamer." She looked as if she hadn't slept: she had circles under her eyes and a pinched look around her full-lipped mouth. Nerves. *About time,* Cady thought, without much sympathy. Glen had treated Tommy Leaver like dirt for years. If she was worried about him now, it served her right.

But Cady's own anxiety intensified. If even sweet

but dim Glendoline thought danger to her man was imminent on the streets of Paradise, something terrible must be about to happen.

"Have you seen Jesse?" she snapped out, interrupting the one-fingered piano recital.

Glen looked up sharply. She didn't answer, just shook her head, china-blue eyes wide with apprehension.

Maybe he'd left town. She hoped he had. Feared he had. But—without even saying good-bye?

Restless, she wandered to the swinging doors. Directly across the street, a knot of men loitered, slouching, spitting; she recognized Stony and a couple of the others. Pushing through the doors, she came out onto the sidewalk. It was a hot, bright blue morning; not a trace of last night's misty drizzle lingered, not even a puddle. She saw other groups of men and even a few women scattered in nervous threes and fours down the length of Main Street. Across the way, in front of the leather and shoe repair, Gunther Dewhurt detached himself from his friends and crossed the street to meet her.

"Morning."

"Gunther."

"So, Cady. You reckon they're really gonna fight?"

"No," she said reflexively. "They won't fight."

"How do you know? Jesse say he wouldn't fight?"

She didn't answer.

"Who do you think he is, Cady?"

"What do you mean?"

"Well, it's looking like he ain't Gault. That other fella, we think he's the real Gault."

"Oh, what the hell difference does it make?" Frustration made her snap at him, too. She was back to wringing her hands. She saw now what she couldn't see last night, that Jesse was in a winless situation. If he fought Gault, he'd get himself killed. If he didn't, they'd call him a coward the rest of his life. And a fraud.

Where was he?

There! Coming out of Jacques', rolling his deer bone toothpick from one side of his mouth to the other. His face, abstracted before, lit up when he saw her. He stepped off the curb and sauntered toward her, smiling. "Morning, Gunther," he said cheerfully, but all his attention was on Cady.

"Hey, Jesse," said Gunther, eager eyes searching, ears pricked.

Cady moved back, away from Gunther and all the other rapt, covert starers on the street. With his back to them, Jesse grinned at her and stole a kiss on the lips. "Morning, sunshine," he murmured intimately, and she melted. Everything about last night came rushing back, the tenderness, the honesty between them. She rested her hands on his chest. "Jess," she whispered, "what are you going to do? I thought you'd be gone by now. Wouldn't it be better to leave town? Just for a while?"

"Leave town?"

"Just for a few days. Gault won't stick around for long."

"Sweetheart." He put his arm around her—for a hug, she thought, but instead he led her back into the saloon. "Cady, honey, I want you to stay in here.

Don't come out till it's over." He looked up at the clock over the bar, and she automatically glanced at it, too. Eight minutes to ten.

"Wh-what?" The blood in her veins turned to slush. "You're not going to fight him. You can't be thinking of fighting him!"

"It'll be all right. Don't—"

"But you *promised*."

"I what?"

"You swore—you gave me your word. 'On my honor,' you said. Damn you, Jesse, you lied to me!"

"No, I didn't," he denied, honestly puzzled. "I said I wouldn't leave, and I won't. That's what I swore."

She was so agitated she couldn't talk, couldn't even cuss. Levi was behind the bar, Glen across the room, both of them watching and listening to everything, but she was beyond caring. Seizing Jesse by the shoulders, she shook him as hard as she could—but he was too big, he wouldn't budge.

Six minutes to ten.

"Cady girl, you have to relax," he said maddeningly. "You said you trusted me. This is all going to—"

She shoved at him and bolted for the bar, jostling Levi aside. There was the cigar box on the bottom shelf; there was her .22 inside it. She grabbed the gun and raced back, cutting Jesse off just before he got to the door.

"You're not going anywhere." She thought she heard Levi chuckle, but she never took her eyes off Jesse. He looked at her in surprise, but not fear. But at least she had his complete attention. "Move back," she ordered, waving her gun. "Go into my office. Move, or I'll shoot."

He smiled. It wasn't an amused smile, it wasn't tolerant, it wasn't patronizing. It was sad. And painfully sweet. She faced it down and didn't lower the gun, even though a crushing sense of futility was making her eyes sting. Jesse moved toward her slowly, slowly; he didn't stop until his chest touched the end of the short gun barrel. His hand closed over hers. Very gently, he disarmed her.

She crumpled, and he folded her up in a hard, strong embrace.

She wanted to cry and cry. When he tried to ease her back, she held on. "Darling," he called her, pressing his lips to her hair. "Hear me, now. I'm going to be all right. Gault's not going to shoot me. Do you understand?" He looked into her eyes. There was a message in his, something he wanted her to know. But her eyes were blind and she was too distraught, too far gone in love and the fear of loss to read it. He squeezed her arms. "Cady, I'll be *fine*. Got it?"

She nodded. But she didn't have it.

He kissed her, smiling crookedly, trying to make her smile back. She couldn't. One last kiss, and then he turned from her, moving through the double doors and out into the sunlight.

She listened to the stamp of his boot heels and the jingle of his spurs. When he stepped from the sidewalk to the street, everything went quiet. Until the clock struck ten.

Fourteen

Gault was right on time.

Jesse stood still and watched him come, swaggering down the middle of the street in no hurry. A lot of brave bystanders lined the sidewalk, but they made sure to hug the storefronts, well back from the street. In the window of the French restaurant, half a dozen rapt faces steamed up the glass—Shrimp and Nestor, the Schmidt brothers, Jacques himself, his homely daughter. Paradise hadn't seen excitement like this since the second gold strike.

Gault ambled to a halt forty feet away. The bright sun, behind Jesse, shone in his eyes, probably blinding him. Good; that's the advantage Jesse would claim when this was over. In spite of everything he knew, a little chill skittered down his backbone. No doubt about it, Gault was one scary character. No wonder men cowered and lost their nerve facing up to that evil eye, that ruthless, eternally smiling mouth. Everything Jesse knew about intimidation, he'd learned from Gault.

Footsteps broke the tense quiet. The sheriff, Jesse assumed. But no—out of the shadows of the boardwalk strolled three men: Wylie, Clyde, and Warren Turley.

Good. Perfect.

They stopped midway between Jesse and Gault; but like everybody else, they kept their distance, staying back from the street. Wylie called out, "Don't let us disturb you—you gents go right on about your business." Turley laughed appreciatively.

Gault never even glanced their way. When he spoke, he had to raise his voice above a whisper so Jesse could hear him. "You can still get out of this alive."

"What's the matter, mister? Chickening out?"

Gault's expression never changed. "Hand over what belongs to me, and you can ride out of here with no holes in your hide."

"Say, that's mighty generous. Considering you're a liar and a fake. I'll pass."

"If that's the way you want it. Ready to die?"

"Hold it!"

This time it was the sheriff, striding purposefully toward them from the direction of his office. Behind him, Jesse heard a woman cry, "Tommy!" and recognized Glendoline's frightened voice. Ignoring her, Tom walked past Gault, and stopped midway between him and Jesse. "Gunfighting is against the law in this town. I'll ask you two to back off. Otherwise, I'm afraid I'll have to arrest you."

Jesse kept staring straight ahead, didn't look around, but he could feel amazement in the air. Was this their sheriff? everybody was thinking. Their Lily Leaver? "Now, Tom," he cautioned, "you don't want to get in the middle of this. Step aside, and you won't get hurt."

He shook his head once. "I'm wearing a gun, and I'm prepared to use it. You, sir," he said firmly, addressing Gault. "Hand over your weapon."

Everybody stared in disbelief. One second Gault was standing still, legs spread, arms at his sides. The next, he was aiming his silver pistol at the sheriff's throat.

Glen screamed.

"I never killed a lawman before," Gault rasped. "It ain't my preference. But I'll do it if you don't drop your gunbelt, Sheriff, and get out of my way."

Tommy didn't move. He only stood up straighter and responded, "You leave me no choice. I'm placing you under arrest." But he still hadn't drawn his gun.

Gault cocked his. "So long, Sheriff."

"No, Tommy, *don't*!" Jesse looked back to see Levi, Cady, and Willagail holding on to Glendoline, trying to keep her from bolting into the street.

The sheriff looked uncertain. "Stay back, Glen," he commanded. An edgy minute passed. "All right," he said finally, grimly, unbuckling his gunbelt and tossing it aside. "But you won't get away with it. The law will come after you and—"

"Cork that," snapped Gault. "Now, nice and easy, get out of my line of fire."

Again Tommy hesitated, clenching his fists in a manly, indecisive way, but in the end he did what Gault said.

Gault's smile turned, if possible, even uglier. "Ready?"

Jesse whispered, "Set, go." He heard a sound, like the collective breath of every soul in Paradise being sucked in. He and Gault twitched their coats out of the way of their shooting irons at the same moment. Flexed their fingers over their gun butts in exactly the same slow, itchy-fingered way. Jesse waited.

And waited. Even knowing what he knew, he could feel sweat start to prickle under his mustache. Must be the heat. Couldn't be fear. Hurry the hell up. Draw, damn it. *Draw.*

Gault drew.

Jesse went for one of his guns, but Gault fired twice before he could even get his finger on the trigger. He dodged right, ducked left, as if bullets were zinging past his ears. Squaring off, he took dead aim in the instant's pause and squeezed off the fatal shot.

Pow! Gault jerked back on his heels. He tottered a couple of stuttering steps, clutching his chest, staring in dull amazement at his red, dripping fingers. He fired again, wild in the air, and fell to his knees. "You got me," he whispered wonderingly, and pitched facedown in the dirt.

The sheriff got to him first. Buckling his gunbelt back on, he commanded the thickening, avid crowd to "Back off! Give him some room, he's not dead yet. Doc! Somebody go get Doc."

Jesse was holstering his smoking Colt when a noise made him turn around. A split second later Cady launched herself into his arms. He staggered backward, laughing, lifting her off her feet. She held on until he set her down, and then she gaped at him, patting his chest, his shoulders, his sides. "Looking for bullet holes?" he teased.

"Jesse, oh, Jesse. How—how did you—"

"Didn't I tell you to trust me?"

"My God."

"What?"

She went white as a sheet. "You *are* Gault."

"Huh? No, I'm—"

"I don't care, I don't care." She flung herself at him again, squeezing him so hard his back cracked. "Oh, Jess, thank *God*, thank *God* you're not dead! I'm never letting you go, never, never, never."

He patted her weakly.

"Hey, Jess," Will Shorter called out from the crowd. "I think you better come over and hear this."

Yeah, he thought. *And Cady better, too.* He took her hand and led her over to hear the gunfighter's dying words.

"Got something to say," he choked out, trying to sit up on one elbow.

"Easy," the sheriff advised, "the doc's on his way."

"Let him talk." Jesse hunkered down next to Tommy. "Sorry it had to be this way," he said with gruff regret.

"No . . . no hard feelings." Gault grimaced in sudden pain, clutching his bloody chest harder. "I'm done for. Gotta tell you . . ."

"What?"

"Him . . ." Blood dripping from his index finger, he pointed weakly up at Wylie.

"What about him?" the sheriff said interestedly.

Everybody leaned forward, even Wylie, to catch the low, slurring words. "Came to my room last night. Gave me money. Thou . . . thousand dollars."

"I did not," Wylie said wonderingly. "I did no such thing."

"Said after I killed him"—he pointed at Jesse—"to kill . . . her." The bloody finger swiveled to Cady.

She gasped.

"That's a lie," Wylie sputtered, dumbfounded. "That's a goddamn lie."

"Said he's been trying to run her out of her place, but she won't go."

"Well, *that's* true," somebody noted, and somebody else said, "Sure is."

"Said . . . said . . ." Gault coughed pitifully.

"Easy, mister."

"Said what he's really after . . . is her mine. Been stealing—smuggling gold out for months."

Wylie went beet-red. He tried to back up, but the crowd behind him wouldn't give way. "The man's raving," he claimed, reaching for his handkerchief. "He's delirious."

"Bragged about setting fire to the old livery," Gault wheezed. "Got his men to do it. Turley, one of 'em was. The other . . ."

"Clyde?" Shrimp Malone suggested helpfully.

"Clyde. Same two that put rattlers in somebody's outhouse, almost . . . killed some kid." Outraged muttering had begun on all sides, but Gault wasn't finished. "And he . . . paid off a banker, Chaney or . . ."

"Cherney," about ten people supplied in unison.

"Paid him to keep his mouth shut, so nobody'd find out about the—skimming they were doing. He bragged about all the fake . . . uhh."

"Fake what?" Jesse nudged.

"Fake . . . accounts he's got . . . stashed away. Said he's bleeding the town . . . dry." His elbow gave out. He collapsed on his back with a groan.

"Make way for the doc," somebody called, and Doc Mobius elbowed through the fascinated townsfolk to Gault's side.

"I tell you this man's raving! He's making it up. Everything he said is a lie." Wylie mopped his pink, perspiring face, looking around for Turley and Clyde. Jesse spotted them at the edge of the crowd, milling uneasily, trying to back away.

"A dying man doesn't lie," Sam Blankenship said slowly.

On cue, Gault's eyelids fluttered; he drew in a long, rattling breath. His left foot twitched once, and then he went still.

Doc put his hand on the dead man's throat; pressed his ear to his chest. "Gone," he pronounced in grave tones. Out of respect, he placed Gault's natty black Stetson over his slack-jawed face.

A few solemn seconds ticked past while everybody stared down at the corpse. Then the sheriff drew his revolver. Shiny as a dime, it looked brand-new and never used. And funny in Tom's grip, much too deadly, like a machete in a child's hand.

"Merle Wylie, I'm placing you under arrest."

"For what?"

"Suspicion of arson, theft, embezzlement, and attempted murder. And conspiracy to murder. That's all I can think of now, but I might add some more later."

"That's ridiculous." Wylie looked around at his neighbors and tried to laugh. "You all know me. I'm a respectable man, a businessman. This—outlaw, this gunman"—he kicked Gault in the hip—"I'm telling you he lied. It's *obvious*."

"Why would he do that?" wondered Stony.

"Yeah," said Sam. "With his last gasping breath."

"How the hell do I know?" Wylie scanned the edges of the crowd, but Clyde and Turley had vanished. "This is a frame-up. A frame-up," he sputtered, "and you won't get away with it."

"Who won't get away with it?"

He didn't answer; he couldn't—he didn't know who his enemies were. Panic showed in the whites of his eyes when he searched the crowd again for his two thugs.

"Put your hands up, Merle."

"Are you out of your mind? You can't arrest me, Leaver. I'll have your badge for this!"

"No trouble, now. Here we go, nice and peaceful."

With a lot more speed than Jesse would've given him credit for, Wylie ducked and scooped up the six-shooter Gault had thrown in the dirt. "Drop it, Leaver. The rest of you, back off." Shocked bystanders obediently cleared a circle. "You." He pointed the gun at Jesse's heart. "Pull those guns out easy and drop them."

Well, well. What an unexpected development. Jesse and the sheriff exchanged glances.

"Looks like you got the drop on me, Merle," Jesse said ruefully. With a show of deep reluctance, he tossed his guns away.

"Now you. Drop it, Leaver. I mean it."

"Do it, Tommy," Glendoline begged from the sidelines.

But instead of dropping it, the sheriff cocked his weapon and aimed it straight back at Wylie. "I don't think so." The sun glinted on his silver gun, his silver badge. "I don't believe you'll shoot me. That's what you pay other people to do. But now it's just you, Merle. And me."

"I'll shoot you! I'll shoot you!"

"No, you won't." He took a slow step toward him, then another. Wylie stepped back.

"Tommy," Glen cried again. "Oh, Tommy, don't!" Catching Levi by surprise, she shook off his hand and made a run at Wylie, waving her skinny white arms and shouting, "No, no, don't you dare!"

What the hell? Before Jesse could react, Wylie dodged and grabbed her, hauling her in front of him. She screamed when he put the barrel of Gault's gun against her cheek. "Drop it," he ordered again, voice quaking with fear and excitement. "Drop it, or by God I'll kill her."

Cady muttered a frightened curse and tried to move, but Jesse caught her before she went two steps. "Don't," he commanded softly. "Leave it." She struggled for a second, then let him hold her. He could feel her violent trembling. With all his heart, he wished he could comfort her without giving the game away.

"Drop it!" Wylie's eyes glittered like a madman's.

Tommy swore and dropped his gun, but he kept on walking. "You're not shooting anybody. Give it up, Merle."

"Don't come near me." He backed up jerkily, dragging Glen with him. Gray-faced and round-eyed, she was too terrified to do anything but stumble after him. "I'll kill her," Wylie swore. "You think I won't? Then I'll kill you."

Empty-handed, the sheriff kept coming. "Give up the weapon. You're finished."

Jesse had a bad moment when Wylie cocked the gun and jammed it harder into Glen's cheek. Tom was right—he was a coward; he paid other people to do his dirty work—but if panic made Merle pull the trigger, the jig would definitely be up.

But he didn't. Tommy didn't stop, he just kept coming and coming—a fine sight nobody in Paradise had expected to see in this life—until he and Glen were chest to chest and Wylie ran out of backing-up room. He looked like a statue, frozen, numb; he couldn't even talk. In the end, the sheriff plucked the gun from his stiff fingers, and Jesse sagged with relief when Tommy stashed it deep in the pocket of his neatly pressed pants. With luck, Gault's gun would never be seen again. At least not until somebody put real bullets in it.

Cady gave a soft cry and threw herself into his arms. Glen would've thrown herself into Tom's, but the sheriff still had a job to do.

"You remain under arrest," he advised the prisoner, reaching behind his back for his handcuffs.

"And now I'll have to add resisting. Glen, did he hurt you?"

"Huh?" She rubbed her reddening cheekbone dazedly. "He sure did."

"Assault, too, then."

"Why, you—"

"And kidnapping."

"You little prick, I'll—"

"Keep it up, Merle. Come on. One more word, and I'll throw in terroristic threats."

Merle shut up.

"Am I drunk?" Cady asked Levi while she waited for him to refill six glasses of beer.

"Not 'less you been nippin' behin' my back."

"I feel drunk. Maybe it's the fumes." He grinned, and she threw her head back and laughed. Drunk or not, everything was so *funny*. And everybody in Paradise was her best friend. If not for Levi, she'd be giving the booze away. "Drinks on the house," she'd instructed when half the town piled in to Rogue's Tavern to celebrate. "You crazy," he'd told her, "you'll lose yo' shirt." He was right; what was she thinking? "Okay, half price," she compromised, and even though he'd disapproved of that, too, she'd held firm. Because this was a day to give thanks and not be chintzy. "Except women," she threw in. "Women can drink free." Levi laughed at that—the Rogue never got female customers.

She caught sight of her reflection in the mirror over the bar. Such happiness—her flushed face shone with it, and she looked downright pretty in her best dress, the dusty rose silk with pale green embroidery on the low-cut bodice. She'd had a shock, though, changing into the dress. Rooting around in her drawer for new stockings, she'd discovered her nest egg was missing. Two thousand dollars—a *catastrophe*. And yet—what a measure of the state she was in that, except for Levi, she kept forgetting to tell anybody! Not even the sheriff! She could only think it was Turley and Clyde, on their way out of town, but that didn't make sense. How would they know exactly where to look?

Another possibility had tapped at the back of her mind, but only once. Since then she'd banished it, and rightly so; how absurd, and how unworthy of her. It didn't bear thinking about. Literally.

The Rogue was jumping. Chico was banging out "Sugar in the Gourd" as fast as he could, and Floyd and Oscar were trying to dance to it. Cady laughed along with everybody else watching the two old fools. "I never knew what a shadow he cast," she confided to Levi as he plunked down the last overflowing mug on her tray.

He nodded; he knew who she meant. "It's like that fairy tale."

"What fairy tale?"

"Them three little pigs. How they celebrate when the big bad wolf gets what's comin' to him."

"Ha. Yeah." It was like that. Merle Wylie had been like a dark shadow over Paradise for ages, and today the sun had come out. Grown men were cavorting like children. Innocence was back and freedom was in the air, as intoxicating as Cady's best bourbon whiskey.

She served drinks to Curly Boggs and his gang, and took orders for more from Leonard and Jim and Jersey Stan. She had so many customers, she barely had time to flirt, an oversight many of them pointed out to her. But she always knew where Jesse was; it was as if she had antennae hidden in her hair. Right now he was at the head of a bunch of tables the boys had shoved together, like the guest of honor at a rowdy banquet. She sent him a secret smile as she sidled past him en route to the bar—and let out a squeal when he grabbed her and hauled her onto his lap, empty tray and all.

"I can't sit, I've got—" A kiss shut her up. Boy, was he an expert at that. Jesse laughing, Jesse's arms around her, Jesse trying to steal another kiss while his pals whistled and whooped— *This is it*, Cady gloated. *I'm really in paradise.*

Jacques Tournier stood up and offered her his chair, and Jesse said he'd let her up if she'd sit in it and quit flying around like a barmaid. "I *am* a barmaid"—she laughed, but she took the chair—"just for a minute," and even took a swig of Jesse's beer when he gave it to her.

Toasting him was the order of the day. She sat through half a dozen tributes to his bravery, his coolness under pressure, his amazing accuracy, his general wonderfulness—all of which he responded to with modest smiles and deprecating mumbles. "Speech!" somebody yelled. "Speech!" Others took up the chant, and after a while Jesse got up, amid thunderous foot-stomping and table-walloping.

"I don't have much to say," he began in a voice so low-key and quiet, the whole saloon shut up to hear him. "I appreciate everybody's good wishes, and it's nice to know you're glad I didn't get shot today. I'm glad, too, but . . . the truth is, I'm not proud of what I did. Killing's a thing no man in his right mind enjoys."

"Yeah" and "Well, that's right," a few men agreed in hushed voices.

"Sometimes there's no way out, though, and then all you can do is try to face up to it fair and square. That's all I did, and I'm grateful it worked out in my favor. But I swear I got no pleasure from that man's dying, and—I hope to God I'll never have to kill again."

He sat down, not to more cheering but to a thoughtful, nearly sober silence. Cady found herself blinking hard to keep tears out of her eyes. Stunned, grateful tears—Jesse was giving up gunfighting! It was the answer to a prayer she'd never even prayed, never dared to hope for. She had so many questions—why had he lied and told her he wasn't Gault? why had he pretended he couldn't shoot?—but they could wait. All she wanted to do now was look at him. Touch him, listen to him laugh. Be with him.

Luther Digby was no drinking man, so she was surprised to see him zigzagging through the crowd, making his way toward Jesse's table. What surprised her even more was that his wife was right behind him. Respectable women never set foot in Rogue's

Tavern, and Sara Digby was about as respectable as they came. But Cady had an idea why the Digbys were here, and the first words out of Luther's mouth confirmed it.

"Mr. Gault, my wife and I want to thank you for what you did for us."

Jesse scratched his chin and tried to look perplexed. "What might that be?"

Luther looked down, a little embarrassed. Maybe, Cady thought, Jesse's charitable gesture didn't sit too well with his pride. "I'll be paying you back as soon as I can. It may take a while, but you'll get every penny, and that's a promise."

"Luther, I don't have the least idea what you're talking about."

Sara spoke up. "Louise Sullivan wanted to come by and pay her respects, too. One of her kids took sick, though, so she couldn't leave home. She says to tell you you'll be in her prayers for the rest of her life."

"Well, that's mighty kind," Jesse said gruffly, "but you tell her for me she'll be praying for the wrong man."

Sara just smiled. She looked frail, but Cady had seen her lift grain sacks almost as heavy as she was. "If that's how you want it, Mr. Gault, that's your business. But I know who I saw at my door that night. I should've come forward before now, but to tell you the truth, I was scared." Impulsively, she reached for his hands with both of hers. "Thank you," Cady heard her whisper. "Thank you for saving us."

Jesse blushed purple.

Chico started in on "For He's the Jolly Good Fellow." Cady assumed it was for Jesse, but just then he held up his hand and waved at somebody in a white hat coming through the doors—Sheriff Leaver. Everybody in the saloon joined in the song, and it was a treat to watch Tommy's serious face break into a shy, delighted grin. Glen found him and grabbed his arm, pressing against him like she'd never let go. She turned her face up, practically begging him to kiss her. But Tom kept his dignity and only patted her arm. Cady guessed it was only vulgar people like her and Jesse who couldn't keep their hands off each other in public.

Tom came over and sat down at their table. Cady sent Glendoline a meaningful look; it said, *Would you please get back to work?* Either Glen didn't see it or she pretended not to. Resigned, Cady started to get up herself, but Tom said, "Wylie won't talk," and she sat back down, too interested to leave. "He says he wants a lawyer, so I wired for one from Jacksonville. That's his right—I didn't have any choice."

Nestor Yeakes commenced to swear. "Won't that beat all if the son of a bitch gets off?"

"He won't. How could he," Will Shorter, Jr., asked, "when half the town heard that gunman's dying words?"

"Still. Ain't no telling what some slick, smartypants lawyer might pull to get him off."

Tom said, "Oh, I don't think we'll have to worry about Merle getting off."

"How come?"

He cleared his throat and stroked his goatee. Cady had an idea Tommy was enjoying his time in the limelight—and why not? Today he'd shown what he was made of. Nobody in this town was ever going to call him Lily Leaver again. "Warren Turley left town this afternoon. Which isn't as—"

"Damn," Cady interrupted. She finally remembered to tell him—"He's got my money!"

Tom turned to her, frowning. "What's that?"

"Sometime between last night and this afternoon, somebody snuck in my room and stole two thousand dollars." Everybody stared at her. "My life savings." She still couldn't get over how philosophically she was taking this calamity. Reaching over, she squeezed Jesse's thigh under the table. It was a matter of priorities, she guessed, and Jesse, not money, was at the top of hers.

"Well, if it was Turley," the sheriff was saying, "things might not be as bad as you think. Because Turley took off, but Clyde didn't, and we just had a real interesting conversation, Clyde and me. He told me where Turley's probably headed—his brother's place over in Kerbyville—and I've already telegraphed the sheriff there to pick him up."

"Hot damn." Sam Blankenship slapped him on the back. "Nice going, Tom. Now let's hope they get him before he spends all o' Cady's money."

She joined in a fervent chorus of *Yeahs*.

Tom cleared his throat again. "That's not all Clyde had to say. I can't get into it all now, it wouldn't be proper. But I'll tell you this: If Merle Wylie gets out of jail anytime in the next ten or twelve years, it'll have to be for his own funeral."

A spontaneous cheer went up. Cady joined in, hoping not too many beer mugs got broken by men thunking them on the tables.

"And, Cady," the sheriff continued when he could be heard, "if you were ever going to get your life savings stolen, now would be a real good time for it to happen. Because it's looking like you're going to be a very rich lady."

All she could say was, "I am?"

"According to Clyde, Wylie's been stealing gold— nuggets, not just dust—out of the Seven Dollar since February."

"I *knew* it."

"His men found a pay streak and traced it back to your mine, and they've been smuggling high-grade ore out for the last four or five months. It might take a while to get it all straightened out, but when everything settles—according to Clyde, who sure seems to know what he's talking about—you'll be about the richest saloonkeeper in Josephine County."

Cady sat back limply, too shocked to respond to the jokes and toasts and good wishes going on around her. A jubilant Jesse gave her a smacking kiss and a rib-cracking hug. "Can I pick 'em?" he kept saying, laughing like a kid. "Can't I just about pick 'em?"

But when the noise abated a little and everybody's attention wasn't on them, he took her hand and leaned across her to say to Sam Blankenship, "Sam, you're still handling the sale of the old Russell place, aren't you?'' Cady's heart leaped in her chest.

"Yep," said Sam, his eyes lighting up. "You interested?"

"How about if Cady and I come see you about it in the morning?"

"Why, that'll be fine, just fine."

"You wouldn't try to gouge us on the price, would you?"

"Hell, no." Then he laughed, realizing it was a joke. "Then again, Cady's gonna be so damn rich, you probably wouldn't notice if I did."

She was still in a daze. Jesse's friends dragged him away to drink with them, but not before he kissed her and whispered in her ear, "When can we go somewhere alone?"

An hour flew by. Once a flurry of gunshots rang out in the street in front of the saloon. But it was just the Witter ranch boys, drunk and happy. The sheriff unwound Glen's arm from around his neck and stood up. "I'll handle this," he announced, squaring his shoulders. He marched outside, and a minute later the shooting stopped.

"Abraham, does your daddy know you're still up at this hour?"

"Yeah." Ham giggled at Cady's pretend-outrage, and stood patiently still while she gave him a hug. "He say I can stay up if I help out an' don't get underfoot, 'cause this a special occasion."

"It sure is that."

"Cady?"

"What." She was refilling a glass pitcher with beer

from the keg herself, because Levi needed a minute to go to the privy.

"Are you really gonna marry Mr. Gault?"

"I expect I am."

He grinned. "Good."

She smoothed her hand over his wiry head, and gave the back of his spindly neck a squeeze. "Yeah," she agreed. "Good."

Jesse reached out and snagged her as she passed behind him on her way to a table to take more orders. He was slouched against the bar, completely at ease, surrounded by men who liked and trusted and admired him, and in its way that was as astonishing a turn of events as Tommy Leaver's transformation into a hero. Miracles happened—here was proof. As soon as she came back to earth, Cady would have to rearrange her thinking on a whole slew of things.

"Say, Jess," Will Shorter said familiarly, bumping shoulders. Behind his glasses, his mild eyes swam a little, but he wasn't completely drunk, Cady gauged—and she was an expert on these things. "How 'bout an interview? Your perspective on the gunfight. Helluva story, my God. At your convenience, o' course, but if we did it now, we could get it in a special Sunday late edition."

"Figured you'd be asking about that, Will. I've been thinking. Got a favor to ask you."

"Anything. Name it."

"Don't run the story."

"Say what?" Conversations around them tapered off; people leaned in to hear. "Don't run it? You serious? Why the hell not?"

"Well, it's like this." Jesse pushed his hat to the back of his head. "I like this town," he said quietly. "Folks here have been decent to me from the start." He took Cady's hand. "I figure there's worse places for a man like me to hang up his guns and settle down."

Will grinned from ear to ear. Stony and Shrimp, Nestor and Gunther, Sam, Tommy, Leonard, Stan, and Jacques—everybody started patting Jesse on the back and trying to shake his hand. "Welcome to Paradise, Mr. Gault!"

"Well, that's the thing." Jesse's earnestness quieted them down again. "See, if I'm going to make a life here, I can't be squaring off for a shoot-out every time some half-cocked saddle bum with a fast gun and a mean streak comes riding through. Cady and me, we want a little peace and quiet."

"You mean . . ."

"I mean it's time to lay Gault to rest."

The reporter scratched his head. "But—"

"Listen, Will. What if you were to write a story about how Gault and a stranger fought it out on Main Street today, and when the smoke cleared Gault was dead. The stranger got on his horse and rode away, and no one knows what became of him. Nobody even knew his name."

Confounded silence.

Finally Shrimp said, "Yeah, but then—who would *you* be?"

"Nobody. Jesse something." He stroked his jaw, looking thoughtful. "How about Vaughn? Vaughn's a good name."

Men started nodding, humming, stroking their own jaws thoughtfully.

"Course, the trick would be making sure the truth never got out of Paradise."

Sheriff Leaver said, "I reckon that's the least this town could do for you in return for what you did for us."

"Hear, hear."

"Damn right."

"We could start getting the word out right away. I can talk to Reverend Cross," Tom promised, "get him to say something in church tomorrow."

"We'll all spread the word," Sam vowed, and the others seconded him. Sam lifted his glass, and pretty soon every man in the bar lifted his, too. "Welcome to Paradise—Mr. Jesse Vaughn!"

Jesse was moved, and he couldn't hide it. "I'm more grateful than I can say," he told his friends, shaking their hands one by one. Cady was in such a state, she was back to blinking to keep from bawling. If things didn't quit getting better and better, she might drop dead soon from sheer happiness.

"How much longer till I can kiss you without the whole town watching?"

She shivered; his breath in her ear sent a sexy thrill through her whole body. Why *were* they still here? Five minutes wouldn't kill anybody. Neither would ten.

"Levi, I'm going outside for some air," she called casually. "Won't be long."

The bartender nodded calmly, knowingly. "Go

on," he said, flapping his hand at her. Giving her his blessing.

She started weaving through tables with Jesse behind her, but every few feet somebody stopped him to talk. "Howdy, Mr. Vaughn. How's it going, Mr. Vaughn? Buy you a drink, Mr. Vaughn?"

"I'll meet you," Cady said in his ear.

"No, I'm coming," he told her, but a table later somebody else collared him. She sent him a smiling, put-upon look, and slipped outside by herself.

She wasn't the only one who had wanted some air. "Hey, Doc," she called to Doc Mobius, who stood hunched over the railing, smoking. Curly was drinking from a bottle on the step; Leonard and Jim Tannenbaum were arguing on the sidewalk. She wandered out into the street, very casual, and began to drift toward the side street that led to the alley behind the saloon.

Ah, privacy. The moon coming up behind the trees reminded her of the night she and Jesse first made love. It was a three-quarter moon that night, too. A good-luck moon for her.

Music floated on the air, soft and sad. One of Chico's dirges. "The Dying Cowboy" or "The Dying Ranger," or maybe "The Dying Californian," they all sounded the same to her. And they all had a million verses, because the main character's death was always long and lingering.

She heard a spur jingle, and hugged herself, savoring a thrill of anticipation. A tall, lean figure, darker black against the blackness behind him, approached her from the corner. She went toward him, smiling, opening her arms to him. "I can't wait to see you in red," she murmured, moving into his embrace. "Or blue or green. Yellow." They kissed.

"You mean that's all I had to do to get you?" He was backing her up against the wall. "Wear colors? Wish I'd known that sooner. Think of how much time I'd've saved."

"You never had a hard time getting me."

"It felt hard."

The wall was at her back. He pressed against her, and she whispered, "Feels pretty hard right now." He laughed, and Cady's heart flew. How she loved making him laugh. She pressed kisses to his face in a soft frenzy, holding him tight. "Oh, I'm so glad you didn't get killed."

"Me, too."

"But, Jess, why didn't you tell me? That you really are Gault?"

"Gault's dead. You're marrying Jesse Vaughn."

"I know I am." And it didn't really matter why he hadn't told her—that was in the past. The future was all that counted, and theirs was perfect. "Mrs. Jesse Vaughn," she whispered, basking in the love in his eyes. "That's me."

"That's you." He kissed her lips, and she lost herself in a blur of feeling, dizzy from the tender way he touched her. "Oh, I don't want to go back inside."

"Let's not."

"I want . . ."

The crisp clop of a horse's hooves made her stiffen. She swiveled her head, and Jesse's lips trailed a path to her ear. "Sweetheart," he whispered—then he heard it, too.

They turned.

A man. Tall, wearing black. On a black horse. Jesse grabbed her hand and said, "Let's go," in a funny voice, but just then moonlight struck the rider's face. Cady gasped.

"Jesse!"

"Cady, let's—"

"It's him!" Shaking, aghast, she shrank back, tried to merge into the wall; stark terror was all that kept her from screaming. Slowly, surely, the gunfighter drew level, turning his awful, one-eyed glare on them. "Jesse—oh, my God—he'll get away. Do something!"

Wearing the oddest expression, a riveting combination of anxiety and mirth, Jesse pulled out one of his six-guns and pointed it at the outlaw's face. He fired—and missed!

Cady's jaw dropped. "Shoot him again."

Bang.

Missed again. Impossible—he was firing point-blank! The gunfighter didn't even flinch. No—he *grinned* as he shambled by, and at the corner he *tipped his hat*. Then, with a jaunty wave, he spurred his black horse and vanished.

Cady took three steps sideways before bumping up against the building again. Her brain felt sluggish, dazed, but she wasn't stupid and she wasn't blind. The truth was beginning to seep through the fog, the way a photograph gets clearer the longer it sits in a tub of chemicals.

Jesse still had that peculiar expression, halfway between panic and hilarity. She caught his eye, but only for a second. "Huh. Must've jammed," he mumbled, blinking down at his revolver. "Say, Cady, did you see that? That guy wasn't dead at all! Hey, I wonder if Doc Mobius is in cahoots with him. The sheriff, too, maybe. Now, isn't that a hell of a thing? What do you suppose—"

To shut him up, she snatched the gun out of his hand. "You lying, thieving son of a bitch."

But he wasn't through trying to brazen it out. "Wait, now. What do you mean? You saw the blood, we all saw it. That guy was dead. Dead as a doornail. Now, how do you—"

"Ketchup. You *skunk*."

"Cady, honey—"

She was ninety-nine percent sure the gun was full of blanks, and furious enough to take a chance on the other percent. Taking dead aim at Jesse's lying heart, she fired.

Bam.

He didn't keel over, but she screamed anyway, from nerves and anger and last-second terror. She felt too weak to fight when he put his arms around her, but as soon as she got her strength back—a minute or two at the most—she shoved him away.

"*Snake!*" she started up again. With a shaking hand, she pointed up the empty alley. "Who was that man?"

"Now, Cady—"

"Tell me, or I swear I'll get bullets. *Who was he?*"

"Shh—shh. That was my cousin Marion."

"Your—you mean *he's* Gault?"

"*Shh*. Yeah. I told you I wasn't Gault. Can I help it if you didn't believe me?"

Oh, if only she had bullets. "You stole my nest egg! Didn't you!" He tugged on his ear and didn't deny it. "Give it back, you slimy, lying snake in the grass!"

"I can't, I had to give it to Marion so he'd die. He wouldn't do it for nothing."

"Go after him and get it back."

"Can't do that, either. See, he's on his way home, back to Lexington. Says he's going to start a new life."

He reached for her, but she shook him off. "Well, you can go right along with him. Shoot each other all the way from here to Kentucky for all I care." She flounced around and started to walk away, but Jesse caught her arm and made her stop. "Quit. Don't talk to me."

"Aw, Cady, listen. I was going to tell you about the money."

"Sure you were." She twisted away again. "Stop following me," she snapped, twitching his hand off.

"Anyway, I knew you'd be rich as soon as we found out Wylie was stealing from the Seven Dollar."

"Which is probably why you proposed to me in the first place."

He stopped her again. The look on his face almost thawed her. Almost. "You can't believe that. I know you don't."

"Why not? All you ever do is lie to me!"

"Yeah, but not about the main things."

"What main things?"

"Being crazy in love with you."

"Hmpf."

"Wanting to be with you all the time."

"Puh."

"Make babies with you. Get old together while we sit in those rocking chairs on the front porch. Listening to the river."

She sniffed. Thought he could sweet-talk her, did he? For the last time, she jerked out of the soft hold he had on her arm. "Leave me alone and quit bothering me," she huffed, flinging away and stalking up the alley. At the corner, she shot a glance back over her shoulder, but only once. To make sure he was following.

He was.

Fifteen

"Poppy! Hey, Cady!"

Beside her on the wagon, Levi waved to his son, grinning and chuckling deep down in his chest. Cady sympathized. Something about Ham and his huge, toothy grin, the pure joy in his face when he was happy, the gangly, endearing way his arms and legs were outgrowing the rest of him—whenever she saw him, she just felt like laughing.

Levi said, "Whoa, horse," and the little mare trotted to a sedate halt in front of Rogue's Tavern. He jumped down just as Ham launched himself into his arms, staggering both of them back against the hitching rail. "You home," Ham exulted, and Levi hoisted him high up in the air to celebrate. "Oh, Poppy, you been gone *forever*."

"Forever," Levi agreed, hugging him hard before setting him on his feet. Two nights was all, but as far as Cady knew, Levi and Ham had never been separated before.

"Welcome home," said a soft voice behind them, and Levi's face split into a grin as wide and joyful as his son's. Cady watched him walk toward his wife, wondering if they'd kiss or embrace. If so, it would be for the first time—in public, that was. She'd never seen them do anything but touch hands in front of people, not even at their Buddhist wedding last fall. Lia was strict about things like that, which made her new occupation—saloonkeeper's wife—an even more interesting turn of events.

Ham leaped up beside Cady on the wagon, and she barely got her hands up for a shield before he threw his arms around her and squeezed. She winced—but managed to change a pained grimace into a welcoming grin before he noticed. She was still sore, but this was nothing compared to yesterday, and by tomorrow she planned to be good as new.

"What'd you do while we were gone?" she quizzed him. "Did you mind Lia? How's your grandfather?"

Ham called Mr. Chang Zĭ, which was Chinese for "Master," and the old man called him Zĭ, too, because the word also meant "son." The two were thick as thieves. In fact, Cady credited Ham for softening the old man up, because at first he'd been against his only daughter marrying a hēirén—Negro. But no longer. Nowadays, although he never set foot inside the Rogue—it went against his religion—on soft summer nights old Chang liked to sit in a rocking chair on the red balcony with his new family, smoking his long clay pipe.

While Ham told Cady everything he'd been doing for the last two days, Levi unloaded a dozen crates of whiskey from the back of the wagon, careful not to jar Cady's seedling flats and burlap-wrapped saplings. Her trip to Grant's Pass had been for two reasons (well, three as it turned out, but the third one was unplanned): first, to introduce Levi to George Nickerson of Nickerson & Spann Liquor and Spirits Wholesalers, and to personally vouch for him so the fact that he was colored wouldn't prejudice Mr. Nickerson; and second, to pick up her precious hybrid pear specimens from the nursery herself, not trust them to the mail service. She'd done that once, in March, with a dozen dwarf apple saplings, and less than half had arrived alive. Never again.

"Please, come in and have tea with us," Lia invited.

"I'd like to, but I told Jesse I'd be home before sunset for sure. Next time?"

"Yes, next time." Lia smiled and made one of her graceful bows.

Ham jumped down off the wagon. Levi said to him, "Did you get Cady's mail like she ask you?"

"Oh, yeah." He stuck his hand in the back pocket of his dungarees and dug out a letter. "You only got one." He handed it up, and she smiled when she saw the return address: "M.N., Golden Leaf Farm, Lexington, Ky." But all she said was, "Thanks, Ham."

"You welcome."

"Well, I guess I better get on." She said it casually, like she wasn't in much of a hurry. But she and Jesse had never been separated before, either, and two days really *did* seem like forever.

Levi tipped his hat. "Meant what I said," he told her in a low mumble. "Don't forget."

"What? What'd you say?" Ham had to know.

"Well, I didn't say it to you, did I?"

"I won't forget," Cady promised, sending him a soft look. How could she? The sincerity of Levi's gratitude had moved and embarrassed her. And for what? Things she'd never give a second thought to, like making sure he got good terms on the sale of the saloon, or going with him for the first time to meet his liquor and beer and tobacco and glassware suppliers. Shoot, wasn't that what friends were for?

"Oh! Oh!" Ham started jumping up and down. "Did you hear who won? Poppy, did you hear?"

"Who won what?"

"The Kentucky Derby! Came through today on the telegraph!"

"Who won?"

"Horse name Buchanan."

"Uh-huh."

"An' guess who ridin' him. Guess!"

"Ham, how would I—"

"A *Negro* man."

"What? No."

"Yes! He name Isaac Murphy, and he the first colored man ever to win the Derby."

"Well, I'll swan. That is something, now. Yes, *sir*." Cady agreed, but she and Levi and Lia sent each other wry, resigned looks over Ham's head. Just when he'd started switching from jockey to deep-sea fisherman for a life's goal, this had to happen. Now it was back to jockey for sure.

They all waved and said so long, and Cady set the mare to a trot down Main Street toward home. Passing the livery stable, she waved at Logan and he waved back. It had been months now, but it still seemed strange not to see Nestor out front, mending harness or dozing in the shade. Part of the settling of a suit against Wylie gave the livery back to Logan, though, along with a cash payment, the terms of which Cady wasn't privy to. But if it was anywhere near as generous as *her* cash settlement, Logan must be sitting pretty.

Riding by the sheriff's office, she looked for Glendoline, but for once she wasn't there. Too bad. Glen liked to sit outside the jail on nice days and rock the new baby. Cady missed her, but it was probably just as well. She was in a hurry to get home, and if Glen had been there with the baby she'd have had to stop. And talk, and hold that baby. She just wouldn't have been able to help herself.

The houses thinned; the road narrowed. Cady took a deep breath and wondered if it was her imagination that it not only looked prettier down here, it smelled better than it did up there around Grant's Pass. Maybe it was just that she was going home. Yeah. That was probably it.

She passed the Seven Dollar and almost turned in, but at the last second she let the horse trot on by. Business could wait till tomorrow. Anyway, Shrimp would've told Jesse if anything interesting had happened while she was away. She had to smile, remembering her reaction when Jesse suggested Shrimp might make a good mine captain. Shrimp Malone? That smelly old prospector? Well, he was still smelly, but it turned out he wasn't that old. And more to the point, what Shrimp didn't know about gold mining you could write on the head of a pin. Next to the Gettysburg Address. He'd turned out perfect, and it was all Jesse's doing.

Ah, Jesse. Married nine months and three weeks, and she could still get flushed just thinking about him. Maybe she'd never get over that. Maybe she'd live to ninety and still get giddy whenever her ninety-three-year-old husband winked at her. Wouldn't that be something? Well, it wouldn't surprise her. Not one bit.

She sat up straighter, nose high, sniffing the air like a hunting dog. "Ahh," she said out loud to Nell, the sweet-tempered little mare Jesse had given her for Christmas. "Smell that? Apple blossoms. Mmm, smells like money." She cackled at herself; she sounded like Jesse. He'd say a thing like that and not mean it any more than she did. For one thing, her orchard probably wouldn't bring in much of anything this year, its first year. (Although next year, when her hard work started to pay off, all the pruning and grafting and budding she'd been doing since February, plus all the tilling, planting, thinning, and spraying she planned to do this summer—well then, *then* you'd see something.) And for another thing, even if she made a million dollars, money wasn't what that airy apple scent smelled like to Cady. It smelled like . . . oh, so many good things. Freedom and independence (which was odd, seeing as how orchard-keeping was a much riskier business than saloon-keeping). And home—her place, her very own life's work, which she loved and was getting good

at. And Jesse. Yeah, it smelled like Jesse. Her wildest
dream come true.

The old stone gatepost at their turnoff didn't list
anymore; Jesse had straightened it up, and painted
it white while he was at it. Steering the horse around
the corner, Cady admired the brand-new sign he'd
ordered from a fancy sign store up in Eugene. LA
VALLÉE AUX COQUINS, it read in blue letters at the top,
and ROGUE VALLEY FARM in red at the bottom. And in
the middle a beautiful black horse flew, with glossy
wings outstretched, graceful as an eagle's. It was the
spitting image of Pegasus.

The sun had dropped behind the tallest orchard
trees, turning everything in the world mellow-gold
and dreamy. Bees still buzzed in the fruit tree blossoms, and spring peepers were tuning up in the wild-
flower meadow, still boggy from the winter rains.
Across a lawn of buttercups and violets, the house
came into view. After a lot of false starts and nervous
stops, they'd finally painted it crocus-yellow—not
white!—with lavender shutters and white pilasters,
parapets, and porch railings. That had seemed like a
very daring move, even foolhardy, especially when
winter came and everything around their cheerful
pastel mansion died, went to sleep, or turned brown.
But then spring came, vibrant and earthy and bright,
and it absolutely vindicated them—made their choice
look inspired.

And Cady had learned a valuable lesson that for
some reason had been eluding her: that she and Jesse
didn't have to *duplicate* the old Russell place, didn't
have to restore it to *exactly* what it had looked like

thirty years ago. They could fix it up and make it theirs, and sometimes—sometimes the changes they decided on would actually *improve* it. Imagine that. And here she'd always thought it was already perfect. Funny: her idea of perfection—something you strove for but could never achieve—kept getting pushed back, expanded. Redefined. She had to keep changing the definition of it because it seemed to her she kept *achieving* it. Which was impossible. By definition.

A man coming around the house from the stables looked like Jesse for a second. Her heart did a familiar little two-step before she realized it was only Nestor. She waved; he waved. She slowed the wagon and stopped in front of the house.

"Howdy, Cady." He touched his beat-up hat. All Nestor's hats were beat-up. He favored straw, and so did the horses he cared for, who were forever taking bites out of his hats. "Nice trip?"

"Real nice. How's everything?"

"Fine, just fine."

She asked the real question. "Where's Jesse?"

"He's down at the stables. Worrying about where the hell you've been."

She smiled, pleased.

"So you better get down there. He's waitin' on you. Got a surprise."

"Oh, Nestor! Is it what I think it is?"

"I ain't talkin'." But he couldn't help winking, and the tickled look on his whiskery face told her exactly what she wanted to know. "Better get on," he repeated. "Leave Nell out front, I'll unhitch 'er in a bit."

"Hot damn." Jiggling the reins, she got the mare going. "Thank you," she called back, and he tipped his half-eaten hat.

Jesse said the new stable looked like the Taj Mahal. An exaggeration; it was white with rust-red trim—end of similarity. Still, there was something pleasingly jewellike in its clean lines, and on the inside it was definitely roomier and more immaculate than any house Cady had ever lived in. So far it only had three occupants—four, if Jesse's surprise was what she thought it was. But that would soon change, because two weeks ago Wylie's lawyers had finally caved in and settled her lawsuit against their jailbird client. As soon as she signed a few more papers, she'd be rich. *Really* rich—enough to pay for all the fruit trees and all the helpers she wanted to make her orchard flourish; rich enough to finish fencing the paddocks and pastures Jesse's horses needed to graze and train and roam in; and most of all, rich enough to start buying the quality stock he wanted, so he could turn Rogue Valley Farm into the finest equine and stud establishment in the Northwest.

"Whoa, Nell." Cady reined the mare in before the closed stable doors. "Nestor's coming in a sec," she told her, springing down from the wagon, shaking out her skirts and fluffing her hair. "Delicious oats any minute. Promise." She gave her a pat on her velvet nose, then cracked open the stable doors and slipped inside.

Whoever would guess that Miss Cady McGill, former saloon owner and blackjack dealer, would grow to love the smell of a horse stable? She had, though, all of it, the whole musky combination of leather and dust and sweat and straw and wood and—yes, even manure. It was a lusty, manly smell. It reminded her of Jesse, so how could she not love it? In its way, it was as sweet as apple blossoms. At least to her.

She might be a little prejudiced.

And then his voice came to her, the words inaudible, but that low, husky murmur so thrillingly familiar it made her mouth go dry. He only used that tone for two things: to talk to Pegasus when he thought nobody was listening, and to whisper sexy things in Cady's ear when they were making love.

Blushing, grinning like a fool, she followed the seductive sound, drawn irresistibly down the wide corridor to Peg's stall. Neither horse nor man heard her; they were too much in love with each other. She paused to look at Jesse, slouched over the gate, one of his worn, dusty boots braced on the bottom rail. He had on a pink shirt and a blue paisley tie, with his oldest corduroy work pants. It was a joke; he did it on purpose, wore outrageous colors to tease her, and also to make fun of himself—the former Gault.

"Proud of yourself, aren't you?" she heard him croon to the black stallion. "Think you're just about the toughest stud this side of Kentucky, don't you? I swear your chest got bigger since yesterday. Pretty soon you won't fit through the door. Huh? C'mere, Mr. Swelled Head. There's my boy. There's my beauty."

"I *could* be jealous."

He did a slow whirl—she'd surprised him, but he was much too smart to make sudden moves around horses, even Peg. "Cady."

Forget jealousy. The gladness in his voice when he said that one word was better than music. He came toward her with his arms spread wide, smiling at her with so much love and welcome, she forgot herself and hugged him hard.

"Ow. Oh, ow, ow—"

"Cady? What's wrong?" He jerked his hands away in alarm. "Did I hurt you?"

"Ha! No, no, it's nothing." She laughed again, anxious to reassure him. "I'm fine, really, just—stiff, you know, from the long drive. Oh, hurry up and kiss me. Jess, I have such a *surprise* for you."

"Is this it?" He kissed her the way she liked best, gently, soundly. Completely.

They swayed, holding on to each other. "No," she murmured with her eyes closed. "This is just extra."

"I missed you a lot."

"I missed you so much. Let's never be apart again."

"Okay."

The only reason he hadn't come with her and Levi to Grant's Pass was because of Bellefleur. Which reminded her. "Nestor says you've got a surprise, too."

He broke away, grinning. "Guess what it is."

"Belle?"

He nodded, grabbing her hand. "God, Cady, wait'll you see. He's *gorgeous*."

A colt, then. Her own excitement mounted as Jesse

led her down the dim passageway to the loose box stall at the end. "Oh . . . Oh, Jess, *look*."

"Did I tell you?"

Belle's newborn colt was all black, except for a white blaze in the center of his Roman nose. He stopped nursing to swivel his head, surveying them with a brown, liquid eye. "Oh, he can stand and everything," she breathed, enchanted.

"Well, sure. He could run if we let him out. His legs are almost full grown."

"Hey, sweet Belle." The proud mother shifted around and ambled over to them. "You did so *well*," Cady praised her, stroking the soft muzzle, letting Belle push her nose against her chest. "What a *beautiful* baby. Was it hard? Did you have a bad time, sweetheart?"

"No, she was great, she didn't even need me and Nestor. Marion popped out in about forty minutes."

"Marion." She snorted, tickled. "You aren't really going to call that beautiful horse Marion, are you?"

"Marion, son of Pegasus out of Bellefleur. Oh, he's a crackerjack colt, Cady. Look at his eyes—see how bold he is? And look at his chest, look at the shape of his head."

"English and Arabian." That was a good mix of bloodlines, she knew—but that was about all she knew. Thoroughbred horse breeding was about a thousand times more complicated than she'd ever imagined.

"What a sire he'll make. Between him and Peg, they'll breed beauties, Cady, nothing but beauties."

"Won't Belle have something to do with it?"

"Well, sure, but we'll buy other brood mares for our stallions—good, blooded females so Belle doesn't get worn out."

"Oh." Lucky Bellefleur, she thought, scratching between her ears. In a year she'd gone from cruelty and mistreatment to a life of luxury and comfort, with a handsome husband and the prospect of lots more children.

The foal—Marion—had curled up in a corner and gone to sleep. Cady hated to go, but Jesse said they'd come back after dinner and look at him some more. On the way out she congratulated Pegasus, who lifted his proud head and flared his arrogant nostrils, taking her praise as his due.

Nestor was unhitching Nell from the wagon. "Where's *my* surprise," Jesse wanted to know. "In here?" he scanned the wagon bed, but all he could see were wrapped tree saplings and seedling flats and bags of some special fertilizer she claimed she could only get in Grant's Pass.

"Nope." She put her arm around his waist, smiling blandly. They began to walk toward the house. He wanted to kiss her and kiss her and take her clothes off and lie down on the ground with her. "I was going to wait till tonight," she told him, "but I don't think I can stand it."

"I know I can't." And he wasn't talking about the surprise. "What is it? Something good?"

"I think I can safely say you're going to love it."

He stopped short. His heart stopped, too. "You're pregnant."

She gasped. "No! *No*. Oh, no, I'm not. Oh, Jess."

Disappointment clouded her eyes. "Are you sorry? I'm—"

"No! I'm not sorry, I'm just . . ." Jesse laughed, not really sure what he was. Okay—a little disappointed. But a little relieved, too. And interested in himself. *You're going to love it,* she'd said, and his first guess was a baby. Well, well, well.

"We haven't been trying or anything," Cady fretted. "I haven't even been thinking about it. I guess I didn't know how you felt."

He touched her cheek. "Well, I'm for it, but I'm not in any big hurry. That is, if you're not."

"No . . ." But there was a gleam in her eye that hadn't been there before. It fascinated him. He started to kiss her, but just then Michele called down to them from the front porch.

"Dinner in twenty minutes?"

"Yeah," "Great," they yelled back.

"Welcome home," she called to Cady, before disappearing into the house.

Cady slipped her arm through his. "So. Did she take good care of you while I was gone?"

"Too good. If I ate everything she puts on my plate, I'd weigh more than Peg in a week."

"I know, but it's so *good*. But you're right—I'll have a talk with her about portions."

"She's used to cooking for a crowd at Jacques's."

"I still can't believe we've got her."

"I can't believe we've got a housekeeper at all. I mean, *any* housekeeper."

"I know. I know."

They marveled about it all the time—their good

fortune. Having each other was the best, but now they also had *things*. It was a first for both of them. And together they were learning that material prosperity, unlike so many other things you coveted once and then acquired, really *was* all it was cracked up to be.

"Well, look at this."

"Oh, Jess, how sweet. Did you tell her to do it?"

"Yeah. No," he admitted, laughing, when Cady slanted him a dubious look. Michele had put a fresh, cool glass of lemonade on the arm of Cady's rocking chair and a mint julep on the arm of Jesse's. They sat down carefully, took up their glasses, and toasted each other.

"To you."

"To us."

"Welcome home, honey."

"I'm never going away again. Not without you."

They leaned over and kissed. Then they drank, and they both said, "Ahh," afterward, meaning the drink *and* the kiss. "This is it," Jesse gloated. "Definitely. This is the life."

"I've got something for you." She pulled an envelope from her skirt pocket and handed it over.

He was hoping it was the surprise, but it wasn't. " 'M.N.,' " he read, chuckling. Marion thought he was so funny. He couldn't write "Gault" on any of his letters to Paradise, so he'd taken to calling himself "Marion Nogunsatall" when he corresponded with his cousin.

"Ha. Hm."

"What's he say?" She leaned over, trying to see.

"He's gone and bought that tobacco plantation."

"Good."

"I guess."

"Don't you think he'll make a good farmer?"

"I have no idea. A year ago I'd have said no, definitely not. But then, I never thought I'd end up owning a stud farm, either."

"And I never thought I'd really have my own orchard."

He looked at her and smiled. Cady's happiness meant the world to him. "Think it's because we live right? Virtue rewarded?"

"*Hah!*"

Well, that answered that. "Here's to Marion," he offered, clinking glasses.

"To Marion. I hope he's as lucky as we are."

"And as happy."

"Oh, that would be impossible. Nobody could be as happy as I am."

"Except me."

Good thing they were alone; sometimes Nestor overheard the things they said to each other and laughed. Or made retching noises. It cramped their style.

The first star of the night winked on in the paling sky. High, high up, an osprey flashed them its white underside as it floated and dipped over the river, looking for its evening meal. Jesse sighed. Over everything, the land, this house, their lives, the whispery, muted roar of the Rogue was a sturdy constant he dearly loved and rarely noticed anymore. Only when he listened very carefully. But it was inside him, part of him. Deep and steady, like his love for Cady.

He set his glass down. "I want my surprise, and I want it now."

"Oh, all right." Cady put her glass down, too. "Think Michele's in the kitchen?"

"Probably. Why?"

She stood up. "I can't show it to you here. Come over this way." She pulled him out of his rocking chair and made him walk over to the side porch, a secluded spot, empty except for a swing hanging by a couple of chains from the ceiling. She and Boo took catnaps in the swing, and sometimes in the evenings Jesse came out here and smoked a cigar.

"Over here." She went behind the swing and into the corner, the shadowy L between the house and the porch rail. He followed, mystified, and stood in front of her, and she peered over both of his shoulders to make sure they were alone.

"What?" His imagination was running wild.

Smiling a bit tensely, she started to unbutton her dress.

"Aha." He grinned, reaching out to help. He liked this surprise already.

"No, don't, Jess. You have to wait."

"Okay." Fine—he liked watching, too. She had on her traveling dress, as she called it, which was practical and gray, and wouldn't have looked sexy on anybody but her. She got the buttons undone to the waist and peeled herself out of the top, then started on her white chemise.

"Uh, dinner's in about five minutes," he felt obliged to point out.

"That's all right, this won't take long."

"Really? Now you're talking. Let's—"

"*Wait.*"

"Okay, okay." He settled back against the rail again, resigning himself to Cady's timetable. Whatever she had in mind, experience had taught him it would be worth the wait.

She got her shift undone and shrugged it over her shoulders. She bit her bottom lip, looking up at him through her lashes with an interesting combination of worry and amusement.

"*What?*" The suspense was killing him.

She took one last, cautious look around. "Ready?"

"Cady—"

"Okay!" Carefully, gingerly, she slipped the shift over her shoulders and down her arms, uncovering her breasts.

His expectant grin faded. He stared in dismay. "Oh, honey. Sweetheart, what happened? Baby, did you hurt your . . ." He stopped talking and blinked down at her left breast, at the blotchy, too-pink, slightly swollen tattoo under her nipple. Gradually the shape of it came into focus, and he felt a slow smile spread across his face.

"It's still a little sore. I think it'll be nice, though," she said, shy. "Do you like it?"

All he could say was, "Cady."

"A woman did it. In Grant's Pass. All she had to do was add legs and a tail, and make the beak a nose. Oh, and ears. But the wings are the same."

"It's Peg," he said wonderingly.

"Yeah. I think it looks like him, don't you?"

He nodded. It was funny; he ought to laugh. But he found, to his surprise, that he was too moved to speak.

Cady said, "You always hated that seagull. You never said, but I know you did."

It was true. He leaned in and kissed her, whispering against her lips that he loved her, he loved her so much. And then, oh, so gently, he lifted her breasts and placed a soft, soft kiss on her brand-new tattoo. When he looked up, he saw tears in her eyes.

"Jesse. Oh, Jess. This is your brand on me. Because I'm yours."

He made a joke, because otherwise he'd have cried with her. "Peg will be so proud."

She swiped at her eyes, laughing. "Well, I wasn't planning on showing it to him."

"Dinner!"

Jesse called loudly, "We're coming," and a second later the screen door slammed.

"Help me." Cady began to pull at her clothes, her fingers clumsy and urgent. He tried to help, but four hands only made it worse. They started giggling. Their tender moment was over, but he had one more thing to say.

"God, Cady, I'm so in love with you. Do you think we're in paradise?"

She frowned down at all the buttons they'd done up wrong, and hurriedly redid them. "I don't know, Jess," she said distractedly, "but I can tell you one thing."

"What?" He stepped sideways, letting her edge around the swing ahead of him.

She reached back and took his hand. "It beats canning salmon."

Sweet Everlasting

Carrie Wiggins is as shy as she is beautiful. But the devastating secret that shattered her girlhood has left her terrified of the very love she desperately longs for. Only in the wild beauty of the mountains does she feel safe from the feelings she stirs in men and the cruel mockery of the villagers of Wayne's Crossing.

Handsome, aristocratic Tyler Wilkes has turned his back on social privilege and professional honors to set up a medical practice in the rural turn-of-the-century town of Wayne's Crossing, Pennsylvania. There, serving those who need him most, he hopes to forget the bitter memories and weariness that haunt his days.

Chance brings this sophisticated doctor and this fawnlike mountain girl together. But something as strong as fate breaks through the barriers of birth and breeding, pride and fear, which have kept them apart . . . as each seeks to heal the other's wounds with a passion neither can deny and all the odds against them cannot defeat. . . .

"A stunning romance of enormous beauty and emotional power . . . exquisite."
—Kathe Robin, *Romantic Times*

"Breathtaking . . . Beautiful . . . Tender . . . Will renew your faith in unselfish love."   —*Rendezvous*

Crooked Hearts

When Grace Russell meets Reuben Jones, she's dressed as a pious Catholic nun and he's posing as a blind Spanish aristocrat. But he soon gets an eyeful when the pretty sister lifts her skirts to adjust the little silver derringer strapped to her thigh. And so begins this sexy, rollicking ride through the gambling halls and sinful streets of 1880s San Francisco, where two "crooked hearts" discover that love is the most dangerous—and delicious—game of all.

"Heartwarming and delightful . . . the best matched hero and heroine since Hepburn and Tracy . . . a pure pleasure."
—Elaine Coffman, author of *Heaven Knows*

"Absolutely marvelous! Reuben and Grace will tickle your funny bone while they steal your heart. It's been a long time since I read a book this wonderful."
—Joan Johnston, author of *Outlaw's Bride*

"Sexy, funny, and wildly entertaining!"
—Arnette Lamb, author of *Chieftain*

"Fabulous! Unusual and beautiful, warm and witty . . . one of the funniest and most entertaining stories I've read in a long, long while—Gaffney is right on target."
—Rebecca Paisley, author of *Midnight and Magnolias*

To Love & To Cherish

Anne Verlaine's four-year marriage to Geoffrey, Lord D'Aubrey, was a living hell. Her only comfort was her lovely new home—the village of Wyckerley in the heart of Devonshire. And even more irresistible was her attraction to Christian Morrell, "Christy," the vicar of All Saints Church. He looked like an archangel, his strength something palpable, his golden-haired handsomeness a source of light in her dark life.

Anne's husband had once been Christy's closest friend, but war and life had scarred Geoffrey inside and out. Now he was going to leave her behind in Wyckerley, with the shocking truth of their marriage still hidden as deeply as his dangerous plans.

Anne had no right to want Christy to love her, and no choice but to need him, even though she risked his ruin—and her own. But he was everything to her. She would defy this world for him . . . and the next.

"One of the most hauntingly beautiful love stories I've ever read."   —Penelope Williamson

"Destined to become a classic."   —Mary Jo Putney

To Have & To Hold

Sebastian Verlaine, the new Viscount D'Aubrey, was
cynical, sophisticated, and too handsome for his own
good. He was also bored. Why else would he agree
to sitting on the bench with two fellow magistrates
to judge the petty crimes of his tenants and neighbors? It was all a lark—until a beautiful prisoner
came before him, and he realized he held her fate in
his hands.

Rachel Wade knew everything about helplessness
and sexual degradation. Her husband's violent death
had freed her from that nightmare, but ten years in
prison for his murder was only another kind of torture. Now a jaded viscount was offering her freedom—but at a price. "Housekeeper," he termed her
new position at Lynton Hall. "Lord D'Aubrey's
whore," the scandalized villagers called it.

A cynical, unkind bargain. But neither of them
guessed how the tables could be turned. How a game
that began in base desire could lead to a breathtaking
gamble in love.

"An emotional roller coaster, complete with a
dark, tortured hero, a complex heroine, and sex
scenes so charged . . . I was riveted."
—Susan Elizabeth Phillips

"A sumptuous, luscious all-night read. I loved it!"
—Bertrice Small

"Compelling!"
—Virginia Henley

Forever & Ever

Patricia Gaffney enchanted readers with her creation of Wyckerley, the Victorian English village that became the setting for *To Love & To Cherish* and *To Have & To Hold*. Now she returns for one more marvelous visit to a place of old-fashioned warmth and unexpected passion. . . .

Conor Pendarvis has a bitter past and a driving ambition—exposing the harsh working conditions in Miss Sophie Deene's copper mine is only the beginning. Sophie Deene is her father's daughter—proud, fiercely independent . . . and bound by convention. She might hire a handsome, insolent Cornishman to work in the mine, but she wouldn't fall in love with him. Impossible. Unthinkable. What would people say?

But she swallows her pride for love, defying everyone, believing Conor has forgiven her since she improved her mine, never thinking he could betray her. And he risks everything he thought he wanted for a love that he believes is once in a lifetime, a love that will last. . . .

"Patricia Gaffney is in the top echelon of romance writers." —*Rendezvous*

Patricia Gaffney won the hearts of readers around the world with her marvelous Wyckerley trilogy set in rural Victorian England. Now her amazing talent shines even brighter with this completely original, utterly mesmerizing love story that will take your breath away. . . .

Wild at Heart

They called him "the lost man." He was beautiful, wild. Raised by wolves, without speech, without civilization. And when he was captured and locked in a room to be studied by scientists, he was treated more like an animal than a human being.

Only Sydney, daughter of a renowned anthropologist, saw beyond the wildness to the man. Something in his fierce loneliness called to her, imploring her to help him—to save him. Fascinated, drawn by compassion and then desire, Sydney used gentleness to tame him, patience to educate him, kindness to make him her friend. And he would need a friend, for the world was not nearly so understanding, and his new life was still haunted by the mysterious tragedy of his past.

But now he wanted more from her than friendship. He wanted all of her—her love, her heart, and her soul.

"Simply glorious."

—Nora Roberts

🐙 **TOPAZ**

PASSION RIDES THE PAST

☐ **FALCON'S FIRE by Patricia Ryan.** Beautiful and impulsive, French-born Lady Martine vows never to fall in love after her mother dies of a broken heart. A powerful and handsome English lord, Sir Thorne Falconer also vows never to love. By arranging Martine's betrothal to his son, he is assured that a grand manor will be his. But he doesn't count on his overwhelming attraction to Martine—and her fascination with him. "A richly textured pageant of passion. A grand adventure!"—Susan Wiggs (406354—$5.50)

☐ **THE RAVEN'S WISH by Susan King.** Duncan Macrae expected violence and rage when he was sent to seattle the ancient feud between the Frasers and the MacDonalds, but nothing could prepare him for the strangely haunting warnings of a girl who foresaw his death. For in his heart he knew that Elspeth Fraser would be his love, his life, his soul. (405455—$4.99)

☐ **BLACK THORNE'S ROSE by Susan King.** Emlyn de Ashbourne knew that to give herself to the man of mystery known as Black Thorne was to plunge into outlaw love—but Emlyn was swept up in a heedless desire that burned all bridges behind her as she changed from a helpless pawn to a passionate player in a game of daring deception and desperate danger. (405447—$4.99)

☐ **TIMELESS by Jasmine Cresswell.** Robyn Delany is a thoroughly modern woman who doesn't believe in the supernatural and who is also beginning to believe that true love is just as much of a fantasy—until she is thrust into 18th-century England. (404602—$4.99)

☐ **NO BRIGHTER DREAM by Katherine Kingsley.** When Andre de Saint-Simon discovers that Ali, the mysterious young woman whose life he has saved while on his travels, is the long-lost daughter of his mentor, he promptly returns her to England. But Ali knows that Andre is her destiny and arranges his marriage—to herself. (405129—$4.99)

☐ **NO SWEETER HEAVEN by Katherine Kingsley.** Pascal LaMartine and Elizabeth Bowes had nothing in common until the day she accidentally landed at his feet, and looked up into the face of a fallen angel. Drawn in to a dangerous battle of intrigue and wits, each discovered how strong passion was . . . and how perilous it can be. (403665—$4.99)

*Prices slightly higher in Canada

Buy them at your local bookstore or use this convenient coupon for ordering.

PENGUIN USA
P.O. Box 999 — Dept. #17109
Bergenfield, New Jersey 07621

Please send me the books I have checked above.
I am enclosing $_____ (please add $2.00 to cover postage and handling). Send check or money order (no cash or C.O.D.'s) or charge by Mastercard or VISA (with a $15.00 minimum). Prices and numbers are subject to change without notice.

Card #_____ Exp. Date _____
Signature_____
Name_____
Address_____
City _____ State _____ Zip Code _____

For faster service when ordering by credit card call **1-800-253-6476**
Allow a minimum of 4-6 weeks for delivery. This offer is subject to change without notice.